MW00784604

CLAIMED BY EARTH

The Elemental Chronicles

Book 1

GINA MANIS

Printed in the United States of America

First Printing, 2023

ISBN 979-8-88955-477-6

Books by Manis Publishing
2593 Mayo Road
Altoona AL 35952

Author Note:

Hello Reader,

This is the 2nd edition to *Claimed by Earth.* If you have read it before I am thrilled your taking another read of it. I hope you will not be disappointed as I have added three new chapter with an additional twenty thousand words throughout.

This book was my first book ever published and since September 2019, I have grown as a writer with the help of so many other authors and editors. I want to thank them all and they know who they are.

Enjoy the book and at the end, there is a little piece of *Taken by Fire* at the end.

Warm Regards,
Gina Manis

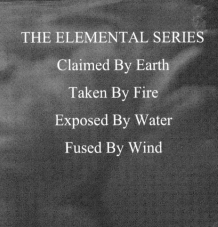

This book is dedicated to my mother. You are the reason I became a writer.

Prologue
CELINE

"It is time, Celine," Alice says to me now that midnight is on us and the moon is highest in the sky. I nod and begin to remove my clothing for the sacrifice. The fire burns in front of me, the only light in the back of the convent gardens. It is the only place I thought the other nuns wouldn't see us if anyone rose from their sleep.

Even as I disrobe, I second guess if this is the best idea. Would the Elementals even acknowledge my calls to them? Is what I offer enough for them to break my curse?

I hear a grunting sound over the wall and look out to see Brown, the largest and most fearsome ogre. His eyes lock with mine as I lift my shirt over my head. Why can't he just leave me alone to do this? I hate him and all the trouble he has caused for the nuns since I arrived.

"He is watching me," I tell Alice, and she looks up, seeing him too.

"Ignore him, Celine," she says. "We must do this now before it is too late."

I nod but turn away from him as I finish removing my clothes. It shouldn't matter that he sees me naked, I tell myself. He is just a monster. Maybe he even sees my hideous form like everyone else.

Well, everyone except for the holy nuns. They are my only comfort from the curse.

Slowly, I lower myself in front of the fire. Alice places a bowl of water in front of me, a bowl of plants from earth to my right, and an empty bowl to my left for wind. Last, she lays down the knife within my reach. Alice then moves to the other side of the fire and, placing the same items around her, she then removes her clothing as well.

A rush of gratitude for Alice overcomes me for a moment. She is my best friend and a Mage who came to the convent almost two years ago. Her magic can open the gates between our world and the Elementals. She is my anchor in this sacrifice and apart of it. Without her, I wouldn't be able to do this. My sister's curse has prevented my own powers from coming forth and keeping me bound in this curse. I love her so much for doing this with me.

Earlier tonight, we bonded as blood sisters. Our destiny will always be tied together. I feel her magic coursing through my blood. It makes me so much more aware of my Water Element. My powers. I have never felt them before, but I do now. They are moving in me in rolls of tidal waves against the hardened walls of the curse, wanting to mix with hers. I hope this sacrifice will knock the walls down.

Alice starts to chant in the Mage tongue as she calls to the Elements to surround us. Yet only to the three of my choosing. Earth. Wind. Water. I join her, letting the unfamiliar words tumble from my mouth. Our eyes meet across the fire as I feel the first stirring of Wind around us, and then suddenly, it begins to rain steadily. The plants around us stretch, and I can see the roots making lines in the soil around us.

Alice nods for me to begin, and I know the Elementals are with us. I pick the knife up, knowing I have to cut deep so they know I am willing to give my all to them. Everything I do will affect Alice too. I cut into the roots and leaves of the bowl to my side and then place the blade under my left breast, cutting straight into my skin.

I cry out and drop the knife into the bowl of earth in front, and my blood coats the leaves and roots. I move the knife over into the water and what blood is left on the blade disappears in the water. I have to do this again and lift it back to my left side, where blood is running down my body. I place the knife under the other wound and hurriedly cut myself again.

The pain is so bad, and I can't help the tears as they stream down my face. I drop the blade back into the water and watch as it turns red. I place the knife in the empty bowl, and the blade spins around its rim. I can barely see it through my tears, but I catch it and, raising it to my side once more, I cut sharp and fast to my side. The blade spins, and I shakenly put in back into the bowl.

Clutching my wounds, I bend forward into a bow from the pain. I know I have to stand up, but all I want to do is curl into a ball. It hurts and there is so much blood running down my body, over my hands, that I can feel it pounding out in pulses.

"Stand up, Celine. We have to do this now," Alice calls to me, and I look up, seeing her arms outstretched and blood running from her side also. Her life lies in the balance, too, if I let us bleed to death.

Forcing my legs under me to move, I stagger as I get to my feet. I can already feel myself growing weak from the blood loss. The wind is blowing with force around us in a circle as the rain pours down. I can see it pooling at my bare feet with the blood as the ground soaks it up.

The roots in the ground break out, starting to crawl up my body, around my legs, to my hips. I lift my arms as it comes around my waist, upward they crawl, over my breasts and down my arms, forming into my body. I surrender to the rain, wind, and roots.

The wounds at my side don't hurt as much now as I let the three Elements take over my body, holding me within their powers as I am lifted into the air.

Different colors flash around me. A humming begins in my ears, and it is Alice's voice, still chanting as she offers me to the Elementals. I close my eyes, feeling them in layers wrapped around me. My skin is alive and tingles with their touch. There is no pain any longer; instead, a sense of pleasure. I feel them invade my body and push against the walls of my curse, trying to touch my own powers, seemingly unable to break through. But they do pump in my veins along with Alice's blood.

A whisper in my ear, a feminine seductive call. *"You want us to break the curse?"*

"Yes," I breathe, hoping they will grant me this.

"You become one with the Mage and use her power to call us?"

I'm not sure if these are questions or if they are stating what I have done, so I ask instead, "Will you break the curse on me?"

"You have our attention by delivering your life into our hands." The wind continues to flow over me, and the rain pours down all the while, the roots of the plants twist around me. "But we want more. Give us a chance to birth our powers again. Allow us to become strong once more in this world."

"What is that you want me to do?" I ask her, willing to do anything to escape this curse.

"We will each send you one Element, strong and powerful. Mixed with your royal bloodlines and that of the now Mage that flows in you, you will give life to the Elemental Mages."

"The Elemental Mages?" I am not sure what she is talking about.

"Our Elements are dying out, as you well know; blood mixes with humans and weakens us. The Mage's magic will never die and will keep our magic safe for the future. Will you agree?"

I know I don't have long to think about this, but I realize she is asking me to bear three children to three different men. "Will you break the curse if I agree?"

"When you have completed the task, we will."

"But I can't have children with men while I look like this," I tell her, knowing that when a man looks at me, he will shun me like the others. I also wanted my powers. "Free me from the curse, and I promise to do this for you all."

"They will desire you. We will make certain of that. The ones we send will not see your curse. Only when you give us the children, will we lift the curse."

"But that can take...so long," I say, not liking the idea of waiting. "With my powers, I can take on Fire that is burning the land as well. I can make the realms safe once more for all."

"Fire can be a pain, and if you want to defeat him, you should use the powers we give you. Our three Elements will be strong enough to do as you desire."

"Please lift the curse," I beg of her. "Please don't let me live like this."

"This is our offer," she tells me, her whispered tone never changing. *"Will you take it?"*

"Yes," I say, knowing that they will not lift my curse now but promise to if I give them a child. "I will…bear the children for this earth, but you have to promise me one thing."

"What now is it you want?"

"I want there to be love with the Elements you chose. Send only the three that I can love and give me love in return."

"Done," she whispers, and I feel the air rush around one more time before it lessens, the rain lightening as the roots lower me back to the ground and slowly retreat from my body. I crumble to the ground as the roots leave me entirely, and everything returns to the way it was, apart from the ground being wet and muddy under me.

"Celine," Alice whispers on the other side of the now-tiny fire. Her eyes are dark and shiny, the leap of the flames reflecting off them. "What did they say?"

I sit up, my eyes never leaving hers. "I promised to give forth each of them a child. They are to send three Elements to me."

"Did they break the curse?" she asks as she sits up too and looks to her side, no longer seeing the cuts I placed on her and me. They are healed now, all except for a small scar for each of them.

"No," I say, shaking my head, sad that they didn't. "I must give birth to the children first."

"But they agreed to lift it, at least," she says, smiling, and I smile back at her and nod. "Soon, Celine. You will be free sooner than you think."

I look over the wall toward Brown and see that he is still there watching us. I fear him more than anything. He is so unlike all the other ogres, stronger, more powerful, and smart. He looks to have a smile on his face, though I didn't think ogres could smile. I can see the wheels turning in his head and know that he is planning something already.

"Let's go get cleaned up," Alice breaks into my thoughts. She is already standing and holds her hand out to me. I stand with her help, to see that mud covers about half of her while I am covered from head to toe.

"She did promise me there would be love between me and the three Elements they send," I tell her, and she smiles. "I will have three husbands, Alice."

"Sounds like a lot of love to me," she says softly.

"Yes, but…it will take me years to give them each a child," I say sadly. "Years before I have my powers."

"But you will feel them," she says, taking both my hands. "One day, you will leave this curse behind you. You must think of that and work to fulfill their request."

"Thank you for doing this for me," I tell her again. "I could never have called them on my own."

"We are sisters now." We hug even though we are both naked and covered in mud. "Wherever each of us goes, we will always have that."

"Yes, we will." I am so thankful to have a sister again. Not just any sister, but one that I can trust with my life as I have tonight. My actual sister, I vow silently, will one day pay for what she did to me.

My actual sister, Elizabeth, took everything from me when she poured this curse on my head years ago. She took my home and the kingdom I was meant to rule. She took what little family I had away from me. What hurts the most is the love I lost. My friend and the one person who meant everything to me. Tate.

Chapter One
QUEEN ELIZABETH
One Year Later

"Come in," I call to the knock at my office door. I know it's them, but I will not get up for the men. I finish the letter to my sister. I hope she will read it because if I fail, her only hope is within.

I seal the letter and watch the three men come into the room. They sit down in the three chairs across from my desk. I appraise them to see if they are up for the job of bringing my sister, Celine, back to me.

All my life, I have done what was best for my kingdom and my people. I rule with kindness and care for all in Clearwater, and they love me for it. I take my pleasures where I want to and reward the ones who see to them. I am the queen, and I do the best I can to rule on my own.

I am a good queen, but I hold dark secrets from them all. The number of people I have tortured, broken, or even killed, would surprise my First Commander, Brier. The madness he must feel from losing his Water Element.

"Thank you all for coming in haste. I have a great mission of utmost importance. And with an urgency I ask that you agree to it," I begin to say. Seeing I have their full attention, I continue. "What I am about to tell you all, I need it to remain secret. Do you all agree?"

"You have my word, Your Highness," High Commander Brier Reef replies as the others agree with their pledge.

"I have tried to be a good queen to my people, but I'm afraid my time is coming to an end. I need a replacement, and I need you to bring her back for me." I look at Tate Forrester, a huntsman who used to be a close friend of my sister's. "My sister, Celine, is alive and lives in a small convent on the borderlands of Earthgate. She has been secreted away for the last five years, and I want you to bring her home."

"Celine?" Tate says in a questionable surprise, and he grips the handles of his chair. "But you said she died. It was what the court had said."

I haven't seen Tate in years, but he has grown into a fine-looking man. Once he worked in the garden here with his family; now he lives in the woods alone and is known as a great hunter.

I guess that is my fault. When Celine disappeared, I told the kingdom she had died, and it had broken him. After some time, he just left, and he has been hard to track down, but I need his expertise and commitment he had for Celine. I know if anyone can bring her back, it is him.

He is the youngest of them, only twenty-one and not as broad as the others yet. His young beard suits him, I think, and I can see he is a severe yet quiet person. Celine would trust him, I know, because he was her friend at one time.

"I know. I made it appear so, but Celine is not dead," I tell him sadly and then turn to the others to explain. "My baby sister, younger than me by ten years, has always been so beautiful and kind. I regret sending her away and for what I did. Now I must make amends, and soon before it is too late."

"What did you do to her?" I can see the unease in him as he moves to the edge of the seat.

"I loved my husband very much as you may remember, Tate. But when his eyes turned to Celine, I was filled with anger. I thought that if she were out of the picture, he would look at me like that again, but he didn't. His death came from my hands when I caught him with another woman. I am not ashamed by that, but I am ashamed of what I did to Celine."

"I can't believe you!" he shouts, standing and coming to my desk. "Celine didn't have eyes for your husband; she had agreed to marry me! I loved her, and you took her from me."

"I'm sorry," I shrink slightly despite my royal position. The intensity from his Element is severe. I don't enjoy being around Earth Elements as strong as he, and for a moment I consider sending him back to the woods. But he is powerful, and that is what Celine needs to get her out of what I put her in. "Celine never told me."

"Why would she?" he spits at me, gripping the edge of my desk. I watch the wood crack slightly under the pressure he holds over it. "Don't think for a minute I never saw the bruises on her. I know you are the one who put them there."

I deserve his words and what misery comes to me in the afterlife for what I did to my sister. My only salvation is the chance I have to lift the curse before I die and give these lands a new ruler. Celine was always meant to rule; I was just the stand-in until she came of age. I had no intentions of giving it to her, but now that I am ill, my life is fading away.

Day by day, I am growing weaker and have just a few months left. Time is of the utmost importance, and I need Celine brought to me so I can set her free from the curse. This will allow me to move on with my new plans and a new life.

"I was cruel to her out of my jealousy. I will admit to that," I say, glaring at him but showing no weakness. I am yet the queen, and he would never dare use his power against me. "I regret what I did, but I cannot change it now. Even still, that is not the worst thing I did to my poor sister."

"What. Did. You. Do?" Tate growls like an animal about to attack its prey. I feel a challenge in it and look away from him. I move to the side of my desk to speak to the others.

"I changed her into a monster. An illusion spell of dark magic so powerful that none can break it. It makes people aggressive toward her and only the nuns at the convent can see her true self. She is safe for now but to break the curse, I need her to come to me," I tell them all.

"How could you do that to her?" Tate slams his fist on my desk. He steps backward and turns around, running his hand through his hair.

"I saw nothing but jealousy for the longest time." I admit to my selfishness only because I need them to agree to this but I am not truly ashamed as I speak to them. Celine should never have angered me as she did, but I will hand my crown to her as she deserves. It will get me away from here once and for all. "Three years passed before I felt sorrow for what I did to Celine. I cannot change the past, but I can change the future, and that is why you are all here."

"Where is she?" Brier asks, crossing his arms over his chest. I have confidence that if anyone can bring her back to me, he can. Brier rose to command at a young age, but he has been my First Commander for many years. Though he is the oldest of the trio at twenty-nine, he has more skills in battle than almost any other in a lifetime. He is a broken Water Element, but the people here respect him highly, and that is why he keeps his place.

"She is at the holy nunnery in Earthgate. She cannot escape because I cursed her with ogres' blood, and they have a thirst for hers. They cannot enter the holy ground of the nunnery, but they wait on the outside. They sense she is there and stay close, waiting for her to leave."

"So, when we take her, they will come after us?" Brier acknowledges. "You want us three to go alone without an army?"

I nod, nonplussed. Their safety is not my concern. "Children and holy people see her as herself," I tell them. "All others see her as a monster and with disdain. I can lift the curse, but only for your eyes. I am not powerful enough to do so for an entire army."

"What does she know of all this?" Lindon speaks up now for the first time. "Does she know you did this to her? And what of her powers? Shouldn't they have come into effect when she turned eighteen?"

Lindon is smart, but he is also cunning. He is known for his trickery among our people, and some consider him a thief. He has a knack for finding things, too, which I feel will come in handy. But the primary reason I want him is because he is a champion fighter among our people. Many of my guards cannot even beat him.

Lindon is twenty-five and is handsome and charming. He can lighten anyone's mood with just a smile. I must admit, I am tempted to try out some of his charms, but I am weary now and could not find the energy from my sickness. At least not for what I would do to him.

"Her powers are still locked inside her. It was another one of my punishments. They will be set free only if she makes it back here to me in time."

"Why break the curse now?" Lindon asks, sitting up in his chair. "It has been, what, five years? What are you looking to gain?"

What I have to gain, they need not know.

"I am dying," I answer him bluntly, saying what I know they want to hear. I am good at that and proud of it, and it is why I am favored as queen. "I have not much longer in this world, and I need to fix what I did to my sister. I would go to her myself, but I need to preserve my energy to break her curse. She must come to me, or she will live as a hag for the rest of her life and will be hunted by ogres."

It is mostly true; I can't leave, anyway. I have much to plan before the time comes with Belinda and Fin, my lover. He is the only other powerful Fire Element here, and I relish having the heat of his powers run through me.

"I will go," Tate says, looking harshly at me. "As long as you pledge to break the curse from her and set her free. She deserves better."

"I'll go, too," Brier says calmly with no emotion, like stone. "But we will all need top armor if we will fight ogres. The best in weapons and a boat. Ogres cannot clear water, and we will need that for our travels."

"Rescuing a damsel in distress is right up my ally," Lindon says with a half-smile as he crosses his arms. Watching him fight on occasion I have wondered if he is looking for death. He fights with no fear and is one of the reasons why I chose him. "Besides, I have nothing better to do, and hell, I may garner some favor with the next queen."

"I will provide you with all you need," I say, handing them each a piece of paper so they can pick what they need from the castle armory and food banks. "Please take today and gather what you need. In the morning, I will lift the curse from your eyes so you can see Celine's authentic form. It wouldn't do for you all to have negative thoughts about her."

They all rise and take their leave. Tate is the last to go, and he gives me a look that could kill if he had power such as mine. I have no time to dwell on it. I must prepare for the strength it will take to remove the curse from their eyes. If anything happens before their return, I am afraid the curse will be sealed.

Having Tate back in Celine's life may be just what she needs. He still seems to have strong feelings for her. If I fail, maybe they could even build a life together. If I had known there was something more between them, perhaps I wouldn't have been so jealous.

I go to the highest points of my castle, to the attic where I keep all my dark magic. Only Belinda and Fin know of this place as I keep the door sealed from sight. Belinda is a powerful sorceress like I was once, and she will help me with my plans in the future. She owes me for saving her life.

My teacher in the black arts was a cruel man, and he wanted Belinda as his. He trapped her with his magic, intending to force her in ways I didn't find acceptable. I may be cruel in my own ways, but seeing what he intended to do to the woman had bothered me. He always felt he had some power over me anyway, and he needed to be taught a lesson. So I replaced myself with Belinda, and she has been true to me ever since.

I had been twenty when I took the crown. Young to be in such power, and, in some ways, lost. Phillip had been there to guide me. He was my childhood friend, and we grew into love. It didn't last, though, as cruelty and hate surfaced between us. He was a Wind Element, and his powers attracted me to him. Being a Fire Element yet queen of the Water Realm surrounded by Waters and Earths was tiring. With no one here to share my powers, a Wind Element gave me the freedom to be myself, and for that, I loved him dearly.

Celine had been most kind to him, always talking and laughing at his jokes. As the years passed, Phillip's eyes became more riveted on her than the day before. When I confronted him about it, he didn't even deny it. He said no man could deny her beauty or her kindness. When he said he had no interest in her, I didn't believe him.

Over time, I watched them together. Phillip had become harsher with me. Celine also changed, becoming more distant. One night after a ball, I saw them dancing together and confronted them. They both denied everything, and it had made me furious. I was not blind, and I saw the love between them.

"You are crazy, Elizabeth!" Celine shouts at me in the hallway. "I am tired of always being blamed for everything. I don't want Phillip like that, and he doesn't want me."

"Every time I turn around, you are with him," I shout at her, grabbing her arm in a bruising hold. "He doesn't smile or laugh with me like that, but he used to. When he wanted me."

"We are the royal family. We must be social with our people," she cries, trying to pull away from my firm grip. "Something you don't like to do."

"You don't have to do it with my husband!" I yell as I slap her hard across her face and let her fall to the floor.

"Elizabeth, stop!" Phillip comes out into the hall and jerks me around to him. "She is just a child. You can't keep abusing her like this. There is already talk."

"If you would keep your hands off her, I wouldn't put mine on her!" I push him away. "How dare you parade her around on your arm!"

"She is fifteen, Elizabeth! She has to have an escort to these things," he yells at me as he helps Celine up. "Who else is going to do it when you won't?"

How dare he touch her! I just told him not to. Rage boiling over in me, I spark my hands at her skirt and light it on fire. Celine screams as she falls back to the ground. Phillip smothers it with her skirt and beats it out with his own hands.

"Celine, are you okay?" he asks her, and she nods even as she shakes in fear. The closeness between them makes me sick, and I am about to do it again when he stands up and slaps me hard across the face. It is the first time he had ever hit me. "You lay one more hand on her, and I am leaving," he says sharply, right in my face. "I will not stand by and watch you abuse her anymore because of me."

"You will not leave me," I challenge him.

"I am already halfway out the door," he snaps. "My bag is already packed."

His confession stuns me. I have no idea he was serious with his threat until just now. I can't lose Phillip. He is everything to me, even if we didn't get along like we once did. "I have stayed this long only because you promised to stop this, but it's only getting worse. I make this promise to you now—touch her again, and I am gone."

I realized then that I needed a Fire Element to help balance my rage and take it from me. So, I sent for one, asking none other than the Fire King for his help. He replied, offering his own son, and I jumped at the chance. The idea of two royal Fire Elements ruling the Water Realm would change these lands and I could allow more of them in. When Prince Damon Firestone came, his eyes, too, strayed to my darling little sister.

That was the last straw. His refusal and Phillip's were enough to send me over the edge. I went to my secret rooms and chanted a spell out of ogres' blood that would give an illusion of a monster.

Knowing that Celine would be dominant when she came into her powers at eighteen, I knew I had to do something about them. Her magic might destroy the curse, but I didn't want that. I had some of her blood and mixed it with her Element of water. I forged it together and locked it into a capsule, then placed it within the blood curse and joined them together.

I pricked my finger and dropped my blood in the potion now, bonding it to myself so that no one could break the curse. Only with my blood could it be altered or broken.

Once it was done, I took the potion to Celine's room by the hidden passage and entered. She was sleeping in her bed as I looked down at her. I hated her beauty, which I didn't have. I hated her for having the love of my husband and the other I so needed. Because of her, I would never get to find the balance I needed. My rage only built inside me, and it spilled out on her.

I didn't realize at the time that by adding my blood, it would cause me to become ill. As the years have gone by, I have become weaker from it, and my only cure is to remove it completely. To do that, I had to have a reason to bring Celine back, and my only thought was giving the kingdom back to her. It isn't something I want but I have made my peace with it. The future is more promising for me if I just leave all together. Besides, the Fire Realm appeals to me as Fin has told me all about it.

In the end, Phillip did leave. He tried to make a new life for himself, but I destroyed him as well, along with that sweet little whore he had been living with. Remembering the way he looked at me in fear as I took his life had pained me greatly, but he should never have left.

"So, did they agree?" Fin asks as he comes into the attic. He stays back, letting me work as I have told him to do before unless I say different.

"Yes. They will leave tomorrow," I tell him as I work on the potion for them now. I motion for him to join me, liking when he is near. I crave the fire and heat of him more now that I am sick and always cold.

"Good. I needed Brier out of the way for a while," he says as he wraps his arms around my waist. "Do you think he will kill the ogre?"

"He will try but I don't know if he can," I tell him as I pour the liquids together. "If he can't, then one of the other can. He must die. If he becomes free, he could spoil our plans."

"I still don't see why we just don't kill your sister," he says in my ear.

"Because I have better use for her alive," I say, annoyed. The truth is I don't want to see Celine dead, but I can't tell Fin that. He is my Fire Element, my balance, and I need him for what I am planning to do. An Element cannot kill their own blood, and I didn't like the idea of it altogether. It is why I cursed her, not killed her, in the first place. "You will see in the end."

"Um, your twisted little plans always seem to work out so well," he says, laughing a little. "I am just happy to know that damn ogre is as good as dead. He is a loose end that need not get out."

"Yes, and it's kind of ironic, don't you think?" I say, finishing up the potion and turning into his arms. "Brier will try to kill his own brother and not even know it."

"Your wickedness turns me on," he says, picking me up. "Do you have the strength?"

"For you, my love," I say as I let him carry me from the room. "I will find it."

Chapter Two
CELINE

"What are you up to this time, Brown?" I call to the two ogres digging holes along the stone walls of the convent. Brown, the larger of the two, is always doing something to get me out of its holy walls. I hate the problems he has caused for the nuns since I have been here. "You know you can't come in these walls. What good is a hole going to do?"

I don't expect him to answer. Ogres don't talk but Brown can say a few words. His differences from the rest are abundantly clear when he works alongside the other ogres.

I gave him the name Brown because he is, yet the other ogres are greener in color. Ogres are big and fat with massive shoulders that have them slump forward, but Brown is not like them. He stands straight, and his bulk is made of muscles, defined and building. He also wears a cloth around his middle to hide any indecent parts, but the other ogres go nude and their big stomachs hide their nether regions.

I sigh and look out over the land surrounding the convent that is my prison. I am trapped here all because of ogres like these who want me to step foot outside so they can drink my blood. This side of the convent is lush and prosperous, the property lines up with the forest in the distance, and the home of Brown and many others like him. The other side of the convent is mostly covered in scorched and burned lands closer to the borders of the Fire Realm.

I had been working in the gardens, my usual chore at this time of day, singing one of the nun's songs when I heard Brown on the other side. Curious, I climbed up to see what he was doing to find him and his friend digging holes along the stone wall.

Raising my voice so he can hear me, I call, "I see your friend has returned as usual," scorning the other beast's return. Once a year, when Brown had something big planned, another ogre would come to help. It looks like they are getting to work on it, but I have no earthly idea what digging in the ground will do. "I don't know why he helps you. I doubt you would share even if you ever caught me."

Brown and his friend ignore me as I talk, and it makes me a little mad that he does that. Even though he makes little sense when he does, it is better to argue with him. It helps me get out some of this aggression I always feel from being locked behind these walls.

"Why don't you just leave me in peace and go find yourself a female ogre and make some little ogre babies with her?" I ask him, and he stops his digging and looks hard at me before bending down and starting to dig again with his enormous hands. I smile to myself, knowing I got his attention with that.

"Come on, Brown!" I exclaim, walking across the top of the wall a distance from him. One time he jumped up and almost pulled me off, so I keep a distance now. "It's been five years now. How long are you going to torment the nuns and me before giving up?"

He stops once more and steps closer to the wall. I prepare for him to try again to grab me. The last time he tried, the protection barrier stung him, but he had hit me too, almost knocking me down.

"Wall fall," he says with a growl. "I...see...you."

So that is his plan? To bring the wall down, not to get in, but so he can see inside? A laugh bursts through me at the thought.

"You already see me," I remind him, pointing to the tall tree he usually climbs to spy on me. Yes, the way he watches me is creepy, but what am I going to do? We have had a twisted relationship for the past five years, and he has tried just about every crazy scheme to get me out of these walls. "Don't think I don't see you climb that big tree over there and watch me."

He shakes his head at me before saying, "Tree dead."

I look over to the tree and see for the first time that the leaves are not blooming on it like all the others. It is dead and the top where he usually perches looks like it is about to fall over. Most likely from him climbing it all the time.

I look back at him, knowing that is exactly what he intends to do. "You would destroy the wall of the convent just to watch me? That's low, Brown, even for you."

He just smiles at me, and I get the feeling that if ogres laughed, he would be guffawing.

"You...mine," he says possessively, and I want to vomit.

"I am not yours!" I shout at him, and he just smiles back. Tired of dealing with him anymore, I jump off the wall and leave him to his plan. I have no plans to become a meal for him now or ever.

I march through the gardens, stopping at the entrance and wash myself off using the barrel of water. I have to do something about

Brown before he brings the wall down. Mother Frances needs to know what he is planning. I find her in the central courtyard with a group of nuns under the old oak tree, making basket weaves. These women are most gracious and giving, and I love them all. They smile at me as I approach, coming up alongside the mother.

"Mother Frances, please, may I speak with you for a moment?"

"Of course," she says, putting her work down and walking a short distance away with me. "What is the problem, my child?"

"It's Brown. He is along the back wall by the garden, digging holes all down it," I tell her as I turn to face her directly. "He is planning to bring it down somehow."

"Oh, goodness." She touches her forehead with concern, and I hate that he does this to them because of me a little more. I don't see why she doesn't just kick me out and be rid of us both. "He should know by now he cannot step foot on these grounds."

"I think he is doing it to watch me," I tell her, throwing my hands in the air. "The old tree on the outside has died, and he is afraid to climb it. I don't know why he just won't go away and leave us in peace."

I am so grateful to have her and all the nuns in my life. Most people see me as nothing more than a monster, but not the nuns. Only the pure of heart can see my true form. I live a simple life but one in peace, even though I am not one of them. My religion or beliefs differ from theirs but Mother Frances lets me stay, protecting me from the outside world.

"Do not fret so, my child," she says, touching my arm softly for comfort. "If it weren't him, then no telling how many would line our walls daily."

"Yes, but look at all the things he has done to us," I say, thinking of all the ways he has tortured us over the years. "Like the fire spears or the boulder toss."

"I will take Sister Marie with me, and we will have a look at what he is doing," she assures me, taking my hand, rubbing the back of it in a calm manner. "I don't see how he thinks digging some holes will make the wall come down."

"Knowing Brown, he will find a way," I say, not sure myself.

"Why don't you rest for what's left of today?" she says, leading me past the main buildings. "There are some new books in the library you can go through. A new donation has been made, and you have always loved searching through them."

"There are?" I am so glad to hear that. I have had nothing new to read in the past several months. Donations always brings an array of books, and the dark part of my mood shifts in anticipation that I could find something to help with my research.

"Go, my child, and don't worry," she breathes with a calming smile. "I will see to Brown with Sister Marie and will find a solution as we always do. God has always protected us, and His power will keep us safe."

I nod to her and go on as she directs me to the library and the new books, smiling. The nuns' faith is strong and has kept us safe from the ogres. Mother Frances is the most caring of them all and in many ways, like a mother to me.

I go to the library to study the Elements, too. I like to learn about them and hope the knowledge of Earth, Wind, and Water will be able to help me. It is easy to find a book on them, but not so easy to find a book explicitly detailing the Fire Element. Fire is a darker power, and the library here doesn't stock books of things the nuns consider evil. But it is more than that — because those in the Fire Realm keep themselves more secret to the rest of the worlds. Only when they raid have others seen them and the powers they hold. Mother Frances inspires me in my thirst for knowledge. She believes that even though I am different, everything has a purpose in this world. My curse included.

I enter the library. I smile to see Sister Alice is at my desk. Though she is a Mage and sees visions of the future, she has come here to live as a nun. Two years ago, she joined the nunnery at the request of her aunt Sara, a powerful Mage, who sent her here to me. We were immediately friends, and though we are the same age, in many ways, she feels like a sister to me.

"Celine, I have been waiting for you," Alice says, closing her bible. "I have something I have wanted to tell you."

"What is it?" I ask as I sit across from her. I let the new books go for now, seeing them in several boxes at the desk over from us. No one is here yet to categorize and stock. Instead, I focus on Alice.

"I had a dream about you," she whispers as she leans over the desk to me. "There were three beams of light and each of them touched you, and your light became brighter. You drew your strength from them, but they gave it freely. I believe it is the sacrifice, and they are coming for you."

"Do you really think it was them?" I asked, raising an eyebrow at her. Alice always has weird visions, but she has always, in part, been right.

"I think so." Her shoulders raise as she holds out her hand. "This is the first vision I have had of you in a long time. The three beams of light have to be the three Elements. You were happy with them, Celine."

"It's a pleasant dream, then," I sigh, wondering what the three men will be like. When I made my sacrifice to the Elementals, I asked only for their most powerful, that they see my true form, and for men I could love. I couldn't see being able to go through with it and give myself to them to conceive their children without it.

Thinking of love, memories of Tate fill my mind. Even after all this time, I miss him so much. I have written to him, but he has never responded. Elizabeth must have intercepted my letters as I couldn't see Tate never coming for me. Most likely, he thought I was dead and moved on. I can see him married now with a wife and child and it hurts to think of it.

"They are coming soon," she says then. "You need to be ready."

I let go of my memories of Tate and nod. I have three strong Elements coming for me, who will not be burdened by my curse and who will hopefully love me. Having three husbands would not be easy but people did marry more than one sometimes. Even a queen could as long as she married a Water Element to stand by her as king. It is what Tate and I had planned as he is an Earth Element. "I am ready. I've been ready for a long time to leave here and start a life. They will make me happy, I am sure of it."

"You are thinking of him, aren't you?" she asks with a sad smile. I look at her but don't answer. "He could be one of them."

"Don't say that and get my hopes up." I get up and walk away from her. I asked for the three strongest, not Tate. I'm sure he is powerful, but what are the chances he could be the one they send? One in a thousand? The odds were not great, and I don't want to be disappointed in my Earth Element because he isn't Tate. "I have moved on, Alice, and I am sure he has too. Tell me about them and don't mention him again."

She looks down at the table and says, "I saw three lights, but one was not so bright, like something dimmed him. They will, however, be able to break the curse and take you away from here. You can finally have a life somewhere else and not fear the ogres so."

"Good thing I always liked odd numbers," I chuckle, a little nervous about meeting them. I knew very little of men but that isn't going to stop me. Alice and I learned that only the most influential bloodlines of the Element could see through the curse and the Elementals would have sent only the best to carry those bloodlines into the future.

The sacrifice was an offering I made to nature, magic, and the Elementals; that if they released me from my curse, I would bond myself to each of their bloodlines. By joining them all together to fight the evil that has taken over the lands and man. With Earth, Water, and Wind, we will all fight back the fires that are claiming the world and I would give them each a child.

I lived with the nuns for almost four years before I came up with the sacrifice. Alice helped me find the information I needed and the magic that would be required. It was only through her magic possible—a sacrifice of myself to the Elements with mine and her blood.

"It's a good thing, though, right?" she half asks and assures me at the same time. "All powers balanced against evil? Surely you will be able to bring Fire to their knees with them by your side."

I exhale as I sit back down and lean back in my chair. "I have faith that they will only send me the best of their kind. With Earth, Wind, and Water, we can fight the Fire, wouldn't you say?"

"Will you warn Mother Frances of their arrival?" she asks.

"No. Mother Frances will wonder how I know they are coming and want to know why," I say sadly. "I don't have the heart to tell her of my offering. I love her, but I don't think she would understand."

"Have you decided what you will do about your sister, then?" Alice has been my best friend and confidant. I have told her everything about my story and she has shared her life with me.

"No," I say with a shiver. "Elizabeth broke my heart with what she did. She should pay, but everything I think of seems so cruel. Despite what she did, my life is good."

"I wish I could go with you," she mumbles. "Be your eyes and make sure you go the right way. But this is something you must do on your own. With your husbands."

"I am to become the mother of earth," I say, still a little shocked at the idea even though I have had over a year to think about it.

"Do you think Fire can truly be stopped from destroying the world?" she asks.

"Man must learn to control Fire. As the other Elements grow stronger, it will weaken," I tell her, hoping it is so. "Only time will tell, but I think we have set it on the right course."

"Just remember this is a haven for you." She reaches across the table and offers her hand. I lean forward and take it, so thankful she is with me. "If things get out of control or something happens, you can find your way back here."

"I know." I smile at her. "Thank you, Alice, for coming to me and guiding me. You have been a loyal friend to me, and I hope to see you again."

"As do I," she says as she rises and comes around the table. I stand, and we embrace, saying our goodbyes now. We both knew this day was coming. Soon I will leave with a mission in hand.

"I should go," she says, pulling back, and we wipe at our tears. "I have kitchen duty tonight. The others will wonder where I am."

"Go, then. I will sit with you at dinner," I say, ushering her along. "Try not to burn anything tonight."

She rolls her eyes at me in good-humored exasperation. "It was only that one time. Not everyone can be as good at cooking as you."

I smile at her as she leaves, and instead of returning to my desk, I go to the boxes of new books. I prefer sorting them alone because if another nun comes over, she will help and then I may not be able to keep the book I want hidden.

Books of ill favor have no business at the convent and are always destroyed. I have only two I keep hidden within my piles of books. Both are slim volumes, one on Fire and another of Mage Magic.

I hurry to flip through the books, taking them all out first and glancing them over. Close to the bottom of the last box, I come across a small red book that doesn't have anything on the outside cover.

Opening it up to the first few pages, I am amazed to see a drawing of flames surrounding two words, "*Elementum Ignis.*" Fire Element.

Chapter Three

I am up early the next morning, dressed, and out the door before the sun comes over the walls. Just a few nuns are around this early, but I am going to the library before the day starts. If I am leaving in a few days, I want to get another look at that Fire Element book.

As I am walking across the central courtyard, the main outside doors at the front entrance open. Someone is coming in, and I rush behind one of the buildings as I usually do when people enter. This time, I am curious as to who is arriving so early and peek around the edge. There is a growing tingle in my blood, and I wonder if it could be my Elements.

Three men enter through the gates, all travel-worn with bags on their backs and swords and bows at their sides. Knives are strapped to their legs, and they even have chest plates of armor. Under them are dark tunics and black leather pants. They are armed with so many weapons I don't even know what some of them are called.

The largest of them is in the lead, and I don't think I have ever seen a man as dangerous looking as he. He has short, dark hair and facial hair along his jaw and looks to be maybe thirty in age. Muscles bulge from his black clothing everywhere. He is so fierce looking with an evil-looking scar running down the side of his face and a few on his arms. I can tell he is a warrior right off and a compelling one at that.

The second is tall, but slenderer in build. He has plenty of muscles, too, but they don't bulge as much. His long, blond hair is tied back, and he is the most handsome man I have ever seen. Maybe he is about twenty-five in age with softer features. I love the lazy smile across his face, and I bet he is the most easy-going one.

The third is shorter than the other two, but his build is in the middle of them. His sandy brown hair and short facial hair make his light eyes stand out. Something about him is different as his gaze wanders over the yard in what looks like excitement.

My eyes feast on him longer than the others, finding him familiar to me. He is about my age and I wonder if I have seen him before. I feel something stirring inside me as I watch him walk toward the main building. His stride is sure and lengthy, and I can see determination and power illuminating from him.

Could he be Tate? It has been so long since I have seen him, and we were so young when I was banished. The Tate in my memory is tall, slender, with boyish good looks, but this is a man, with his face hidden with facial hair, dark, shaggy hair, and a broad muscular build that seems too powerful for my Tate.

These three men are to be my husbands, and I have to admit, I am pleased. I haven't seen many men living here in the last few years, but these have to be some of the most gorgeous men in the realms. Maybe it has something to do with the power they have in them that makes them stand out to me. Whatever it is, they look like gods.

Now, I have my way of breaking the curse. But my motives for breaking the curse aren't for revenge over Elizabeth, rather for protecting the realms. My future husbands are now entering the great hall and will meet with Mother Frances. Soon she will send for me.

An urge comes over me to look my best, and I leave my hiding place, running back to my room. I scramble and almost fall before sliding inside my room. Hurriedly, I close the door, stripping off my clothes as fast as I can.

I had a bath last night, but I still go to the wash station and clean my face and hands once more. Looking at my clothing stack on my table, I slip on the prettiest dress I have—the faded blue one that has little yellow flowers on the top and a solid blue skirt. All my clothes come from donations, and I wish I had something prettier to wear.

I take my hair out of its braid and brush it, letting it fall down my back. I haven't cut it since being here and it is long, reaching past my waist. I keep brushing it even when I feel no tangles, hoping it will make it shine the way my mother used to say when I was a girl.

Quickly, I brush my teeth again, taking more time, and when I look in the small mirror on my wall and smile widely. I am pleased with the white of them. The mirror is only large enough to show my face and is the only one in the whole sanctuary. Mother Frances had brought it to me after I came to live here.

I had cried and hidden away from everyone at first, not wanting them to see the monster I was. I didn't realize that they saw my pure form until she had given it to me. Then she persuaded me to walk outside with her. I remember the first shock of looking in the mirror after my curse. Something about being in the holy lands showed me who I truly was instead of the curse.

A knock and a soft voice calling my name distracts me, and I open my door. A middle-aged nun, Diana, says gently, "Miss Celine. Mother Frances asked me to fetch you to her chamber office urgently. Someone has arrived to speak with you."

I am satisfied with my appearance, knowing they will see me and not the monster I am. Not just now, but after we leave. I will have to stay clear of others until I fulfill my part, which will most likely take me years to do. Still, it is a life of my choosing, and I am ready for it.

The only thing that really frightens me is the ogres waiting on the other side of the walls. The idea of leaving the sanctuary and having them come for me is scary. Yet, they are trapped in this realm. All we have to do is make it to one of the other three realms and we will be safe.

"Thank you, Sister Diana. I will be right there," I say, calmer than I feel as I walk out of my room.

They are most likely still waiting in the great hall. I will have to pass by them to get to Mother Frances's office since it was closest to the nuns' sleeping chambers.

I walk into the courtyard and instantly stop. Seeing all three of them sitting on the benches in front of the doors to the great hall stuns me. Their eyes turn to me, and the shortest of the three stands up. I stare back at him, his intense gaze calling to me. My mind is screaming *Tate*, but I can't really tell if it is him. I hold myself in check, reminding myself not to hope for something that might not be true. I force myself to look away from him, not allowing myself to dream.

The long-haired blond stands next to him and my gaze travels to him instead. He steals my breath away with a charming smile that has me tingling all over. His eyes capture mine with a beautiful sparkling silver I have never seen before. Something is promising in his eyes as they travel down my body, and I feel my breath hitch when our eyes meet again. I only breathe again once I break eye contact with him and look at the last man.

He tilts his head at me with respect and with the manner of a man-in-charge. He is not as attractive as the other two, but older and demurer. The scar running down his face only adds to his strength and power. He doesn't look at me like the others do; his gaze is full of indifference. *What is he thinking?* I find myself wondering as I can't seem to get a handle on him. I can tell that if anyone can get me out of this realm, it is these three men.

As I come closer. I don't speak, but to continue to Mother Frances's office. My pulse races as I walk past them, and I feel each of their eyes on me as I make my way to the main lodge door, reaching for the handle to turn it, but before I go in, I glance back at the first man once again. He is breathing hard, and I can see he is flexing his hands at his sides like he is trying to contain himself. I feel my own hands grow tight on the door handle as we stare at each other.

His eyes are green—flakes of different color greens with a wilderness that lays inside. So familiar my heart stops beating, and there is a sharp pain of significant loss that strikes it up again.

I turn away and walk into the hall, closing the door behind me. I lean against it, taking a deep breath. I shouldn't have looked into his eyes. My hands are shaking as I hold them out in front of me. It even felt like the ground moved when I looked at him.

Getting myself together, I walk to Mother Frances's chamber office and knock on the door. She asks me to enter and tells me to sit down once I am inside.

"Celine, three gentlemen have arrived. They carry a letter from your sister, the queen, asking for you to come home and accept your place as the next queen of Clearwater," she tells me as she looks down at the paper. "The queen has sent the commander of her royal guardsmen, a champion fighter, and an old friend of yours, a huntsman."

I am taken aback that my sister has sent them to me. And she wants me to take the throne? At the moment, though, I am more curious about her mentioning that one man is my friend.

"Who is he?" I ask, starting to breathe hard. Was I not wrong? Could it really be Tate who has finally come for me?

"He says his name is Tate Forrester, and he knew you when you were both children," she tells me.

"Tate," I gasp his name, thinking *how is this possible?* Tate would be an Earth Element like the rest of his family. I had always been jealous of his large family. He had five brothers and four sisters, yet I was stuck with only Elizabeth. He had been the baby and a surprise to his family. With the others all older, we became very close as children, playing in the gardens as they worked.

The color of his hair is darker than I remember, and that is not the only difference. The last time I saw him, he had been sixteen, slender in build, and not yet a man or with facial hair. He has to be twenty-one and definitely a man now. Could five years change someone so much?

"So, you do know him?" She startles me out of all the thoughts running through my head, and I nod. "I am relieved that he is your friend, as he says."

"He was my friend," I confirm to her. Tate and I had grown into more, but before we ever had a chance to explore our new-found love, my sister tore us apart.

"He says that he has come to take you home. Your sister is ill and would like to break the curse and give the kingdom over to you," Mother Frances says, handing me the letter from the small stack of papers she has been reading.

I read it over, not believing it. It can't be! My sister is the one who sent them to me? No, I brought them here; they are mine. I gave myself in the offering. Even Alice had seen it and had been a part of it.

"Celine?" Mother Frances's voice breaks into my thoughts again. "What are you thinking?"

What am I thinking? How can this be my salvation? The very person who had cursed me sent me the very Elements I need to break the curse. No, it can't be right, but Tate... He is an Element and my friend. He is more than that to me, and I don't know how to feel about her sending him.

"I... I don't know," I say, letting out a long-held breath before answering. "I can't believe she sent them to me."

"Would you like to speak with this man, Tate? Maybe he can tell you how things are in your homelands," she says.

"Yes," I say, nodding my head. "May I speak to him alone?"

"Of course," she says politely, rising to her feet. "I will ask him to come here so you can talk in private."

She leaves me alone to wait. I read over the letter again.

My Sister Celine,

Saying I am sorry seems so small for what I did to you, but I am sorry. Whatever happened in the past, you never deserved the unforgivable treatment I made you suffer through. I regret it so much, and I don't ask for your forgiveness because I should not have it. I only want to undo the terrible wrong before it is too late.

Please come home as soon as you can. I am dying, and though I do not expect you to care for me, I hope you will allow me to at least break the curse and give you your life back along with the kingdom. It needs someone like you, and I give it willingly in what I know will be expert hands.

The men I have sent are the very best. They can see you safely home. I have given them potions that keep the curse from touching them. They are good men, Celine, and I need you to trust them.

If for any reason I am gone before you return, I left the spell in our old secret place. I know your power will still be locked away, but maybe you could find someone who could help. It is all I can do as I wait for you. I prepare to use the last of my strength to help you if I can.

Please hurry before it is too late. Your best chance is with me. Allow me to do this for you, my sister.

Elizabeth.

That bitch! How dare she try to take this from me too? I found my own way to break this curse, and now she is offering to save me after all these years?

Some perspective breaks through my anger. My way could take years before it breaks, and Elizabeth could do it now. But to do this would mean I will have to see her. I will have to go home.

And if I do that, I will have to become queen.

Chapter Four

There is a knock at the door, and I stand up as Mother Frances peeks inside. She opens the door wider, allowing Tate to step around her. "I will just be out here if you need me," she says, and then closes the door.

Tate stands beside it, not moving, but his eyes meet mine. I gasp in recognition, knowing that my dreams of seeing him again are finally coming true. The beautiful green eyes of multi-colored hues and specks of brown are the same as the boy I knew so long ago. He is a man now, so different from my dreams of him. I wonder if I have changed that much to him as well.

"Celine." He says my name, a soft, deep sound that makes me tremble. "Do you remember me?"

I let my eyes roam down his body, taking in the masculine aura around him. He is the smallest of the men that came for me, but in no way less manly. He stands almost a head taller than me and could make two of me around. I remember him being much shorter and thinner. What has he been doing to look the way he does now?

His presence fills the small room, and as I breathe in, I can already smell his scent. It is woodsy and of nature, fresh leaves in the rain and sun. Just as his Element, Earth, should be.

"I remember a boy." My eyes come back up to meet his, and I shake my head. "You are not."

He smiles a little at me. "Nor are you just a girl."

My mind is made up. I will not let my sister take this from me. I have my way of breaking the curse; I do not need her. It doesn't matter that she had sent them. Somehow fate had stepped in to make sure they would come. No matter what, they are mine. Tate is finally mine.

"Did you ever get my letters?" I have to ask but am sure he didn't.

"No." He shakes his head. "I was told you were dead. Your sister set your rooms on fire, telling everyone you were dead. She wouldn't even allow anyone to see your body."

"I figured as much," I tell him, looking down. "Do I... look different?"

"You are beautiful," he says without even a pause, and our gazes meet. "I knew you always would be, but seeing you now, I am almost stunned for words."

I feel my face becoming red, yet I can't help but smile, happy that he doesn't see the curse. It is a relief and makes me want to be closer to him now.

"I have been waiting for you," I tell him as I step forward, watching him. I seem to make him a little nervous as he switches his stance. "For you and your friends. I am ready to leave when you are."

He looks surprised by my response. "Don't you have questions for me?"

"Should I?" I ask, stopping just a foot away from him. I look into his eyes and can't help reaching up and touching his jaw with my fingers, remembering our last moments together long ago. "I know why you are here."

He takes my hand from his face and holds it. Stepping a breath closer, he whispers, "If I had known you were alive, I would have come sooner."

"All I care about is now," I say, leaning into him, my other hand coming up to his chest. "I cried myself to sleep thinking of you after coming here. As time went by, my tears dried up, but I always dreamed of you. Hoping that one day, I would see you again."

"I grieved so for you," he whispers, looking at me with love in his eyes. I know he remembers our last time together too. How we had kissed and tasted each other softly but were interrupted by my sister's harsh calls. He runs a finger along my jaw, and I tilt my face up to his, wanting him to kiss me now.

Our lips had barely touched that night in the gardens before it was over. We had never gotten to explore the new wonders of love all those years ago. Now, he is mine, and I know love was always meant to bloom for him and me.

His thumb traces over my lower lip as if he is thinking about it. I flick my tongue out. He seems transfixed, and finally, slowly, he lowers his head to mine, but he stops before our lips meet.

I grasp his tunic in my fist, drawing myself closer to him until our bodies are touching. He still seems hesitant, and I pull a little harder.

"Tate," I whisper his name breathlessly.

"Yes?" he rasps, looking into my eyes with the need I feel inside me.

"Please don't make me wait any longer." I smile gently. "I want that boy, who has become my hero, to kiss me."

He gives me a half-smile as his hand moves around my neck, and he wastes not another second as he gently places his lips over mine.

Instantly, the ground under us shakes. The surrounding wood, the chair, and the desk creak and moan in approval. I whimper as his lips linger on mine. I pull myself closer, wrapping my arms around his neck as he deepens the kiss, locking our lips together and over one another.

I see stars as Tate kisses me, and I can do nothing but melt into his body and lips. This is what our kiss all those years ago would have become. The floods of passion and desire are opening up inside of me, and I feel the connection we had once before forming around us again. The call for us to bond is strong from the sacrifice and the love I have for this man. I feel an even deeper longing to fulfill my promise to the Elements with Tate.

We sway on our feet as a rumble shakes the floor beneath us and sends vibrations into my body. Tate's arms tighten around me, lifting me from the floor as he gently runs his tongue along my lips. He tries to gain his balance as the ground continues to shake, all the while never letting me go. I open my mouth slightly and his tongue darts in, barely touching mine, before the door bursts open. Tate has me back on my feet and at arm's length so fast my head is spinning.

"We are having an earthquake!" Mother Frances shouts at us from the doorway. "Outside, now!"

She turns and moves down the hall quickly, leaving us behind, without question. I don't know if she saw us kissing or not. It all happened so fast.

"We should go." I blush as I take his hand to lead him out. "Mother Frances is scared to death of earthquakes."

As I pull him to the door, he reaches past me and closes it. I turn to face him as he steps closer, pressing me into it and him at the same time.

"Not until we finish our kiss." He smiles down at me and lifts my chin again. "No interruptions like last time."

He doesn't wait for my response as his lips claim mine once more. This time, he's more passionate, his tongue touching my lips and seeking entrance much faster. I open for him and his mingles with mine as the room shakes again. I can feel the tremors in the wood behind me as I reach my arms up to circle his neck and pull him closer.

He tastes fresh and clean to me now, and his smell has changed like sweet fruit from a tree. His scent is intoxicating, and I love how he is making me feel. Like I wasn't alive until this moment, until I am in his arms. My soon to be husband's arms. Kissing him feels natural, like it was always meant to be. I relish every second of him.

It is already clear that I will fall madly in love with Tate. He had filled my childhood fantasies, and now he is mine, and I am his. I belong in his arms, and I am going to do everything in my power to make him happy and spend a lifetime with him.

He pulls back, and the ground calms down again. He looks at me, and I can already see the love in his eyes. It makes me cherish him even more.

"I would love nothing more than to stay in this room with you." His husky voice sends sparks of excitement through me as his hands run up and down my sides. "But I'm afraid there is a minor panic erupting outside, and a search party will come looking for us any minute if we don't show."

"You're probably right." I am breathless, yet playful to him.

"You should meet the others." Reluctantly, he steps back and pulls me with him so he can open the door. My heart skips a beat when he intertwines our fingers together, leading us out the door.

"Yes, I should," I agree as I follow him close as we walk slowly down the hall. Others are passing us in a rush, but they are little thought to me as Tate has my attention so. "Funny how we should get an earthquake just as we kiss."

"Not too surprising," he says with an all-knowing grin. He is the Earth Element. We both know it, but I want to hear him say the words. I want to feel his power too.

"Why do you say that?" I ask lightheartedly as we continue to stroll hand in hand.

"I have dreamed of our kiss for so long, and I thought I would never get the chance again," he breathes with a cheery tone even as he blushes. "It seems only natural I couldn't contain the emotions I was feeling."

"If you kiss me again, will it shake again?" I ask, curious, but desiring the experience once more. The quakes throughout my body while he was kissing me had a sensual feel to them. My first real taste of pleasure had literally been groundbreaking for me.

"More than likely," he says with a devilish smile as he stops and turns to me. His thumb traces along my lower lips. "Which I will make sure is sooner rather than later. No more will I be waiting to taste these lips. It was a mistake I made long ago, but I won't make it again."

A shiver runs through me at the thought of his promise. I am definitely in agreement with him on that. I can't wait to be alone with him again.

"I know a place we can go to later," I say, blushing at him even though I don't want to hide how much I had liked it too. "It is in the gardens."

"I love gardens," he says as we continue to the exit door. I drop his hand, not wanting others to see us holding hands. This is the nun's house, after all.

"Oh, Celine, dear!" Mother Frances calls to me, rushing forward. "What took you so long to get out? I turned my back and thought you were gone, and then I came out here, and you weren't anywhere. I got so concerned…"

"I'm fine, Mother Frances," I interrupt her, trying to calm her frazzled nerves, and look to Tate. "We just needed to finish our conversation before joining you. It was just some slight tremor."

"It felt like the building was coming down!" she exclaims. "Next time, do not be so foolish and take your leave at once. Earthquakes are nothing to take lightly."

"Yes, Mother Frances."

"Mother Frances," Tate speaks up now. "I want Celine to meet my friends. She needs to know who we will be traveling with back home."

"Go, then. But I would like to speak with the commander again before you leave," she states before moving past us.

Tate leads me to the others, not touching me as he seems to understand that he shouldn't. Several nuns had exited the building, but the other buildings around didn't seem to have been disturbed.

Many of the nuns watch us as they slowly go on their separate ways. It has to be weird for them to see me with visitors since I always keep myself hidden away from them, and I have become a bit of a spectacle today.

We are fast approaching the other two men, and my gaze returns intently to them. They move closer and away from the main hall but wait for us to join them.

Their eyes scan over me once more, and I soak them in, too. I am very pleased with their appearances. I, of all people, know beauty is always in the eyes of the beholder. True beauty comes from the inside, yet the outsides of these men are alluring.

"Celine, this is Brier Reef," Tate says, motioning to the biggest of the men. "He is the High Commander of the Royal Guard and is at your service."

"Princess Celine Clearwater, it is an honor." Brier bows slightly to me. "I promise to serve you well, my future queen."

"Yes, and thank you," I say to him with a sweet smile. I can't help but wonder if kissing him would be like kissing Tate. I have to bite my lip at the thought. He seems to like that but shows no resolve in his manners.

"This is Lindon Mountainside," Tate says, pulling my gaze to the other man. "He has his own talents, mostly in the fighting rings."

"Princess Celine," he says, smiling at me and bowing. "I am honored to be here in your hour of need."

"The honor is mine," I tell him, wanting to see what magic he will bring me.

"Tate has informed you why we are here?" Brier speaks up again in a commanding voice.

I look at Tate, and we just smile at each other. There wasn't much talking going on between us in that room, but I can't say that. I will go along with their plans for now. I first want to get a feel for each of them. "I know you have come to take me to my sister."

"Then you agree to go with us?" he asks then, looking pleased that I wasn't going to put up a fight.

"I will go with you." I nod at him as I look at each. "But not because Queen Elizabeth has sent you and promises to break the curse. I go for my own reasons."

"That's fine by me. As long as you're going," Brier says now with a frown. "But I do the queen's bidding, and you are not my queen yet."

Chapter Five

"Mother Frances," I call as I approach her from the other side of the courtyard. She is looking calmer now. "May I offer the men some food this morning? They have traveled such a long way."

"Of course, dear, but first, send them to the guest house so they can clean up before entering the dining hall. You know where to find everything, and so I leave them in your care."

"Thank you, Mother Frances."

"I want what's best for you, Celine, but I do not wish to see you leave us." She grabs my hand before I can leave her. "Ask them to stay the night at least so I can spend a few more precious hours with you before you do."

"I will," I promise her and then add, "Besides, I don't plan to leave these grounds until they do something about Brown."

"Yes, that would be best," she agrees. "It would be much safer, and he has plagued these lands for too long."

"Tonight, I will sing for you if you like," I tell her softly. "It is the only thing I have to offer you before leaving."

"After dinner and for us all," she agrees, hugging me. "I will so miss your sweet voice, but, most of all, you."

"You have been so good to me," I say, hugging her back. "I don't know what would have happened if you hadn't taken me in."

"It was my duty, but you became so much more to all of us," she said, finally pulling back. It pains me to think of leaving her as she has been such a comfort in my life. Elizabeth had been abusive, but here I never had to worry about the next slap or punishment. Mother Frances didn't believe in being cruel. If I ever did anything wrong, she believed in penance to her god and nothing more. Even though we didn't share the beliefs, I respected them and the kind woman who had become more of a mother than a friend. "Now go do your duty to them, and I will see to someone else taking over your chores."

"Thank you," I say kindly to her and return to the men. I am looking forward to spending some time and getting to know them all better. They watch me as I walk back to them and the way they just stand there makes me wonder what they are thinking.

"Mother Frances would like to offer you food and lodging for the night," I say, looking at each of them. "It is not customary to allow men to stay within the walls for such a time, but I think she sees your good intentions toward me."

"Maybe. Or it could be the large purse of coins we bring from the queen," Brier says, and I scowl at his tone. I am offended of him speaking that way of Mother Frances. Before I can reply, he adds, "We should leave today and soon. Time is short, Princess, and it will take at least ten days before we reach your sister."

"Then, this one day shouldn't matter too much." I stand up to him, braver than I feel. "You need to rest, and I cannot just leave without telling my family goodbye."

He sighs but nods at me in agreement. "Then I will allow you today only to say your goodbyes, but we will leave first thing in the morning."

"We should discuss a few things also, and we can do so as we eat. First, Mother Frances would like you all to clean up before entering the dining hall." Having won this minor battle, I choose to push through and tell them. "If you would follow me, I will show you where you can stay."

I turn and start walking, expecting them to follow. Tate comes up beside me.

"I can't imagine having to be stuck in here for years. How did you manage?"

"The nuns are the kindest of souls," I reply. "They have been wonderful to me. I will miss them all very much."

"These walls, they protect you from the curse?" he questions.

"Yes, the land is holy. Evil magic cannot have a head here," I tell him. "When I first came, I hid away from all because of the curse, until Mother Frances told me she didn't see it nor would the nuns. It was hard to believe her at first after spending weeks of being spit upon and abused. The nuns were the first to show me kindness again and spoke with decency to me."

"You say weeks? Where were you before coming here?" Lindon asks now as he comes up on my other side.

I hate even thinking about it, but I tell them. "The people who took me from the kingdom said I was the hag that was stealing their children from the river's edge and had killed them for their youth so I could be beautiful and steal their husbands."

"What?" he asks, incredulous.

"They fed me like a dog with scraps from their plates. They didn't care that people poked me with sticks or threw mud at me. They didn't even let me out of the cage to relieve myself, much less bathe. I lived in filth as we traveled here."

"Why did she send you here?" Lindon asks. His interest spikes my own of him as we haven't gotten to speak to each other yet.

"I guess she didn't have the desire to see me dead, so she paid men to bring me here, trapping me in this place."

"The ogres' curse," Brier speaks up from behind us.

"Oh, yes, the ogres. They make sure I go nowhere," I say, turning to look at him. "Many come and howl in the nights. Some move on, and some stay a while even though they cannot enter. Mother Frances says she had never heard so many until I came."

"We crossed paths with two on our way here," Brier informs me. "We killed them so we would have no trouble once we leave."

"There are many more than two, I can assure you," I tell him. "If you plan to get me to my sister, then you better sharpen your blades."

"Are you not afraid?" Lindon asks me and I can see he is a curious person like me. His questions also show me concern, and I know he must have a good heart.

"Yes, I am afraid," I tell him as we come along the little house close to the entrance of the main gate. "But I am more afraid of never living. I watch people come and go from here, I watch the nuns that leave to visit the villages and do their work. This place is beautiful and safe, but I never leave and when people do come, I hide. I don't want to be trapped any longer. I want to run in the forest, splash in the ocean, meet people and help them. But most of all, I want to use my powers. They are trapped inside, and though I feel them move, I can never reach them. It is the worst of all for me."

We come to the little cottage and I turn to them, but they say nothing to me. I think I have stunned them with my explanation and maybe shared too much. Pushing the door open, I enter, and they follow me in. It is a small guest house with two bedrooms and its own private bath. I open the doors to the rooms, which show two large beds in each and the bathroom going inside.

Towels and soaps are in a cabinet, and I pull them out, setting them on a nearby chair. The men stay in the other room, waiting for my return.

"All you need to clean up is in there," I say, re-entering the room. "Take your time. I will go to the kitchen and have food set aside for when you are ready and then come back for you."

"We will not be long," Brier assures me as he drops his bag. He seems so dangerous and unemotional. He will definitely be a challenge to open up.

I go to the door to leave, and Tate takes my hand, pulling me around to face him. He does not hide his emotions from me. I can see the pain in his eyes as he squeezes my hand gently. He says, "I'm so sorry for what happened to you. I wish I had known. And I promise, you will run in the forest and jump in the ocean. I plan to show you many things in this world."

I smile at him softly and touch his face with my free hand, caressing him. "I know you would have come for me. You were such a good friend. Then and now."

"If your sister wasn't dying, I think I would kill her myself," he says, the spark of fire hitting his eyes.

"Don't worry about my sister," I reply, pulling away to leave. "I will handle her."

He holds onto my hand, not letting me go. I look at him questioningly.

"I have this urge to not let you out of my sight," he admits, looking deep into my eyes. "The animal spirits inside me don't want you to go."

"The animal spirits?"

"My powers are more advanced than other Earth Elements. I can take on many of their forms now, but it also gives me their instincts," he explains to me. I have read of this before, but it wasn't a common gift nowadays in Earth Elements. To know that Tate does have this power shows me how strong he truly is and why they chose him to join with me.

I step closer to him. "I will be back for you soon."

He gently takes hold of my neck, pulling my head closer to his. He rests his forehead against mine, and I close my eyes. Feeling him close to me again, I know, without a doubt, that I belong with him.

As an Earth Element, Tate has control over not just the land but the animals on it. They are a part of him too and I look forward to getting to know that side of him.

Someone clears his throat, letting us know they are still there. I wonder what they think of this show of emotions between Tate and me.

"I have to go," I say, slowly pulling away from him, and he allows it. I look at the other two who are just standing there watching us and smile at them. I wish I could listen to what they say to one another once I leave. Instead, I leave, going straight to the kitchen. On my way, I decide to bring food to them instead of them coming to the hall. We have much to talk about, and I'm not sure if we should do so in front of the nuns. As I enter the kitchen, Alice is there, and I ask her to help me make two trays to carry over to the house.

"So, they have arrived. What are the men like?" she asks me as we work on adding food to the trays.

"I don't know yet," I tell her honestly, adding some strawberries and grapes to a bowl. "Seeing Tate is such a surprise. I am a little overwhelmed at being near him again. I am so grateful it is him who answered my call for the Earth Element and…there is so much love still there. He is different than I remember in some ways, yet the same Tate of my dreams. I can't wait to spend more time with him. He also seems to know what he wants and goes for it."

"What about the dark one, with the scar?" she asks me. "He seems kind of dangerous to me."

I have a feeling Alice is right. "The big one, Brier, is straightforward and serious. He will be a challenge, but there is something about him I want to put all my trust into. He seems to be the most powerful and strongest of them all."

"And the other one? The one with the nice smile. I'm sure he is daring."

I smile when Alice describes Lindon as handsome. I know she is loyal to her god. "He does smile a lot, and it seems he might have a few tricks up his sleeves. I see a playfulness in him I think I will enjoy."

"What do they think of you?" she asks me then, raising a brow.

How do the men see me? Just someone who needs saving? I want to be more than that to them. I have to be. I am pledged to give each of them a child for the rebirth of our world. It isn't about what we want, but what we need. There is only one shot at this for everyone, or everything will eventually die… I just hope I can show them how important this is.

"I will just have to see," I say, still thinking about it.

"Have you figured out which Elements they are yet?"

"Well, Tate, as you know, is Earth; I believe Brier is Water because he shows so much strength and power. Lindon, I believe to be Wind because of his kindness and am attractive to him. It would suit with his powers of seduction."

"So, Tate is the Earth Element then? Is he the cause of the ground quaking earlier?" she asks me with a huge grin, and my face heats.

"Seeing him again reminded me of our last moments together," I say shyly. "It seemed natural at the time to…share a kiss."

"You kissed him!" Alice says in a loud whisper, and I shush her before everyone hears. "Celine!"

"Well, what do you expect? He is to be my husband, after all. We had promised ourselves to each other before I was cursed. I didn't realize he would shake the ground until we kissed."

"Was it that special?" she asks, smiling at me.

"Yes, it was, and you seem a little too curious for a nun," I tease her.

"My calling is strong, but with all the things I see, it is hard not to be curious at times," she confesses. "I know I have a noble purpose and that I must remain pure to do so. But Celine, my visions are not always innocent."

Alice told me once before that she had seen her future and death but never confided in me. She lives with that secret alone. She is an amazing woman, not much older than I, but she has wisdom beyond her years.

"Would you help me take this to them?" I ask her as we finish up. The two large trays are now full of bowls with scrambled eggs, bacon, sausage, pancakes with butter and honey syrup, biscuits with some gravy, and a plate of strawberries and grapes. "I would like for you to meet them."

"I will," Alice answers, and I know she is excited to meet the Elements we called together. "It would be nice to see their faces instead of just their lights."

Alice told me she only saw their Element of power and not the men who carried it. I never really thought much of it until now. To understand how her visions come to her and how she can make sense of them, I will never know.

"Have you had any more visions?" I ask her as we take our leave.

"I had a weird dream last night," she tells me, looking a little upset now. "I saw you cutting your arm and draining blood."

"What?" I ask, surprised. "Why would I do that?"

"I don't know, but…you fed it into an open fire like you were making another sacrifice."

I blanch at the thought of doing that again. The first one had been hard enough, and I could never have done it without Alice. It doesn't make sense that I would make another one when all I need has arrived.

Chapter Six
TATE

"You seemed a little too close with our charge just then, Tate," Lindon says as I face him. I can't believe everything that has happened this morning. When we entered the complex for the convent, I had been excited we had finally made it. Seeing Celine again is a dream come true. Our kiss was the sweetest, most perfect thing to ever happen to me. "What happened between the two of you in that room?"

Kissing her had been like coming home. When she had mentioned our last moments together all those years ago, I knew deep down that she felt the same way. I couldn't wait to know her again and to hold her, claiming her as mine. I wasn't about to spoil that by telling Lindon about our moment together.

"Old friends connecting again," I say, trying to downplay the emotions coursing through me. My Element is reaching out for her, wanting a connection. Every instinct in my body is craving it, and I have to force them under control. I have never had my animal instincts react so strongly before. They are calling to me, *Mate, Mate, Mate.*

"Looks more like old lovers connecting," he says with a wicked smile.

"I told you both about Celine and me." I look at him scornfully. "There was something special between us, and there still is."

"She is more beautiful than what you have said." Lindon smiles as he sits down on the sofa. "My eyes about fell out of my head when she walked into that courtyard."

"She was just fifteen, but now… grown into a woman, she is even more so." I admit it is true. At fifteen, she had been the same height as me and straight in form. Now she has all the curves and mounds of a goddess. Her skin is unblemished to my eyes, and my hands even tremble now to touch her again.

Celine is in no way a simple beauty. I felt weak in the knees seeing her walk across that courtyard. Her long, sun-kissed blonde hair flowed down her back in a luxurious wave as the wind picked it up and caressed her cheek. Large, crystal blue eyes looking at me, capturing my breath and stealing my heart.

Her body is that of an hourglass, I can tell even under that faded dress. Her back straight and breasts out, I let my eyes roam over them once she turned, then move down to a narrow waist and flared hips. I just know those legs underneath her skirt are just as smooth and shaped.

My body responds, just as my mind and my Element do, as I looked back up to her heart-shaped face and those perfectly plump lips. Earlier, I had felt the tremors in my body but had kept them at bay— until we kissed, and I couldn't anymore. The beasts within had reacted too, but I was scared to let them anywhere near her. My animal side isn't tame, and I didn't want to scare her.

"While you two talk, I will take that bath," Brier says to us with a scowl on his face. He enters the bathroom and slams the door behind him.

"What's with him?" Lindon asks, watching him and then turns to me.

I shrug, not knowing. Brier never says too much unless he is giving orders. Still, in the last ten days, at night when he drank too much from the bottle, he had told us some of his life. It hadn't been pretty, just like the scars on his body.

"Just leave him be," I tell Lindon, who likes to rile him at times. "Most likely, what Celine said got to him."

"I can't believe the queen did that to her own sister," Lindon says, standing and moving around the room to check out the small ornaments on the shelves. "How could she do that to her own blood?"

"Elizabeth, as I recall, had been beautiful at one time. Not faded like she is now with her illness." I lean against the door, once more looking for Celine to return even though I know it will be a while. "I don't understand why she was so jealous. She will not get the chance to hurt Celine again."

"Some old feelings of yours seem to be surfacing," Lindon says, coming up beside me. "Tell me something, Tate. Are you going to become jealous when you see me looking at her? Because I have to admit...seeing her now, she quickens my blood."

I feel jealous at Lindon, but it brings back a piece of Celine and my past that could have broken us. That Fire Prince when he came to visit our kingdom just before Celine disappeared. He had been older and seeing Celine notice him had made me so jealous that I made a fool of myself. But it made me realize that if we were ever to be together, I needed to face the facts. Celine was the Water Princess and one day would have to marry a Water Element to rule beside her in her kingdom. I loved her so much. I had finally given in to that fact and agreed so we could be together. The memories of it surface now.

"Celine!" I called to her from across the garden. It was early for me to be here, but I had to see her after last night. "I need to talk to you."

"Tate, I don't want to fight with you anymore," she said, walking over to me. I took her hand and led her through the garden and back to our private area. "Damon is gone, anyway. He just left today."

"I'm sorry I was such an ass last night," I said, stopping and turning to her once we reach our secret place. "I know it was your duty, and I had no right to be so jealous. We have never spoken of feelings between us before, but I must confess to you now. I'm in love with you, Celine."

"Tate," she gasped in shock.

"I have been in love with you for a year now, if not longer." I reached up and touched her soft cheek. "It scared me to say it because I didn't want it to become weird between us, but it is weird, and I need to know... how you feel about me."

"Oh, Tate," she cries, throwing herself into my arms and sobbing. "I love you, too. I have loved you for the longest time."

"I know I'm nobody in this world, and you are the princess, but..."

"I don't care!" she exclaimed, pulling back enough to look at me with a beautiful smile that made me melt. "I need you. I've always needed you!"

I raised my hands into her hair, caressing the back of her neck. "Then will you marry me? I know we will have to wait, but I want to marry you."

"Yes!" Celine shouted, pulling me back into a warm hug with no hesitation or doubts. "But Tate, you know I will eventually have to marry a Water Element, too. My people will expect it."

Being the future queen, Celine would have to marry again and to a Water Element to rule the realm. Even though it was common for other Elements to marry more than one.

"I know, and I'm fine with it," I lied softly. I wasn't really, but I knew I would have to be if I wanted Celine in my life. It wasn't a common practice among Earth Elements to marry more than one other because of their animal spirits and the instinct of having a mate, but I will find a way. I had to have her in my life because she is my mate.

"I know I can only be the second-ranking husband, and I don't care. As long as I have you, I will promise to never let that come between us."

"Are you sure?" she asked me again. "Last night…"

"Last night, after I left you, I started thinking about it hard," I told her. "I don't like the idea of sharing you, but it is your life, and I know if I'm going to be a part of it, I have to learn."

"I don't want to hurt you," she whispered, looking down, and I knew she understood what this meant to me. Even though I didn't have my powers yet, I told her all about my Elements and more. She knew everything about me

"I know," I said, caressing her face and gently making her look at me. "I don't want to hurt you."

I leaned down, brushing my lips across hers for the first time. Something we had both been putting off for way too long, just like our feelings for one another. As it was my first kiss, I was sure it was hers, too. Neither of us were breathing as our lips pressed together. Slowly, they parted...

"Celine!" a shout came up across the garden, and we jumped back from each other in surprise. "Celine, come here right now!"

It was Elizabeth calling for her, and she sounded angry. I looked at Celine, not wanting her to leave but knowing she had to go. She wasn't good to Celine, but there wasn't anything I could do about it. Celine tried to hide it from me because it makes me so angry when I see. To go against the queen could have me banished and then what would I do? I needed to be near Celine, and I hated that I was too young and powerless to help her.

"I have to go," she said, looking down again. "Elizabeth sounds upset with me."

I grabbed her hands, desperate to touch her one last time. "Meet me tonight. Here. At midnight."

"Okay," she said, beaming at me. I could see the excitement in her eyes, knowing mine held it, too. "Midnight. I love you."

"I love you," I whispered as our hands slip out from one another, and she took off running for the back of the castle. I would have never let Celine go if I had known that would have been the last time I saw her.

◊◊◊
LINDON

"Next," Brier says, coming out of the bathroom, and Tate heads for it without another word. He became quiet after I asked him if he would get jealous, as I lost him in memory. I left him to it, thinking it was for the best.

Brier walks over to the door where Tate had been and leans into the door frame.

"What do you think of her, Brier?" I ask him, sitting down on one chair.

"I think her beauty will cause trouble between you two," he tells me, looking out over the courtyard. "I want no fighting among you over who does what with her. Remember, I am in charge and what I say goes."

"So, you're not attracted to her?" I ask, not being able to stop myself. Brier wasn't actually my friend, but he gets me out of trouble more often than not. At the kingdom, I am looked at as the show-off, the fighter with a wild side, and the view isn't wrong. I drink too much, sleep around with the women who crawl in my bed at night, and fight recklessly for the thrill and the coin. I have been this way since I lost my wife in childbirth. Losing Liza and our baby broke me, and I live as though I have nothing to lose but my worthless life. Which is true.

"My attraction to her has nothing to do with the mission in hand," he scolds, looking at me now. "To be honest, I don't care what she looks like. All I care about is her being the next queen and protecting her from harm."

"You would say such things," I say, smirking at him. I saw the way his gaze followed her, and I know Brier enough that he doesn't usually focus on the opposite sex. "I will follow you. Have no worries, my friend. And don't worry about Tate and me. I'm sure we can come to an understanding."

"Good, because we got a heap of trouble coming our way to get her out of this realm and it will take all of us," Brier says, turning back to face outside.

"I know." I agree with him, knowing that it should be where my focus is. Still, I can't deny what she is making me feel inside. It is like I am waking up again for the first time in I don't know how many years. How long has Liza been gone? We had only been married a year, but I knew her my whole life. I was just eighteen, and now I am twenty-four. Six years? Has it really been that long since I have felt alive?

Something is pulling me toward her, and I want to know what it is. My mind keeps bringing up the image of her smiling at me. How she boldly looked at me like she knew something and wanted something from me.

I can even smell her at a distance, something I have never done before. She smells of flowers and rain, and it makes me want to wrap her in my scent and feel hers mixed with mine. It is an overpowering urge intertwined in lust that I am not sure if I can control.

Celine depends on us though, and I need to focus on that. Besides, Tate is already staking a claim to her, I am sure, and she doesn't seem to mind. It isn't like I am about to mess with an Earth Element like him. I have never seen one so powerful before. He has the strength of all his animal spirits too, and I'm sure his bite would kill from any of them. Just like I am sure he had caused the ground tremors. Whatever happened in that room with Celine and Tate has him spinning.

Hell, she has me spinning, and I've barely said a dozen words to her. It is those beautiful bright blue eyes that are singing to me, pulling me in every time they catch mine.

Tate may not be able to hide his feelings because of their past or because of his Element, but I can. At least I'm not an Element and don't have to worry about it giving me away. I'm just not sure if I want to hide these feelings, though. I am a man who always goes for what I want, and I want her.

Chapter Seven
CELINE

Alice and I walk together with our trays to the small house, and I see Brier in the doorway. He watches us as soon as we come out but doesn't move one muscle on his massive body.

"So that is the Water Element?" Alice glances at him and whispers.

"His name is Brier Reef, and he is a commander of the Royal Guard," I tell her, smiling at him. "He has said little to me so far."

"He does look dangerous but I can see him as a leader," she says, curiosity tinging her voice.

"I think I like him. He will be my challenge, and you know how I always like that," I say playfully. "I can't wait to see his powers. I bet he is a powerful force."

"Try not to drown," she says, and we both laugh.

"I swear, Alice, I'm not sure if you make the best nun." Brushing her shoulder with mine, we smile at each other. Not too much since we both had our arms full of food. "Some things that come out of your mouth."

"You're an evil influence," she says, smiling at me as she brushes my shoulder back.

"Come, then, and meet the man I intend to drown in." We laugh together as we make our way to the little house, and I feel a sudden twinge of how much I will miss her when I leave. Alice and I are so close, and there hasn't been a day in the two years she's been here that we haven't been together. Leaving her will be like leaving a piece of myself behind.

Brier is still just watching us. His look doesn't show approval or disapproval at our playfulness with one another, just stoicism. He is hard to read, but I don't mind trying. He stands in different clothing with clean hair; his facial hair is even trimmed. He looks even better than before.

I make a note to gather their dirty things to have them washed before we leave. I always help wherever I can in my free time, and the nuns won't mind doing this for me.

"Hello, Brier," I say as we come closer to him. I look into his eyes warmly, liking the challenge I see there. His dark blue eyes, the color of deep ocean waters, I would imagine, give me a thrill. "Would you mind allowing us to pass?"

He moves away from the door, not saying anything. I walk inside first, followed closely by Alice, and set my tray down.

"This is my best friend, Sister Alice," I tell him and Tate as we set the food down and turn back to them. I look for Lindon but he must still be in the bath. "I thought we could eat here this morning and talk in private."

"Brier Reef." He steps inside the door. "It is nice to meet you, ma'am."

"Nice to meet you, sir," Alice speaks with a gentle smile.

"It's an honor, ma'am, to meet you. I am Tate Forrester," Tate says, stepping closer to us.

"And an honor to meet you," she says kindly. "Celine has told me much about you."

"Alice!" I shove her in the shoulder again, embarrassed.

"What kinds of things?" Tate asks her with a grin growing on his face.

"Umm…just some of the things you did as children," Alice says hesitantly and shoots at glance at me.

"Should we wait for Lindon before sitting?" I think to change the subject and glance at the bathroom door as I turn back to the table, removing the bowls and plates from the trays. The food is still hot, as is the coffee.

"He should be out shortly," Tate says as Brier makes his way to the table and takes a seat without a word.

"Then, please sit." Alice pours some coffee for each man and then sets the coffeepot down. "Prepare a plate for yourselves. We brought a little of everything."

"It looks good," Tate says, smiling as he sits down. I have the urge to run my fingers across the span of his back, but resist. Instead, I sit closer to Brier, wanting to know more of him.

I can tell Brier is hungry as he stares at the food.

"Would you like me to make you a plate?" I ask him as he doesn't reach for the food like Tate is doing.

"No, I am just waiting for your friend to speak her prayer." He looks politely at Sister Alice.

"Please don't wait on my account," Alice speaks up. "I have already given thanks for our food."

Brier nods and fixes himself a large plate that matches his huge body. I sit back and watch him pile his plate high with eggs and sausage and two biscuits hanging off the side. I am sure he will be coming back for seconds once everyone makes their plates. I brought plenty for them to eat, knowing that their travels will have made them voracious.

Tate also makes himself a large plate. He stacks layers of pancakes with strawberries and nuts and pours honey syrup over it all. Alice and I are more modest, but we haven't been traveling. More than likely, it has been a while since their last meal like this. Tate and Brier are already eating as Alice and I make our plates when Lindon comes out to join us.

"Something smells good," he says as his eyes run over me and not the food. He smiles at me, and I can't help but smile back. I am sure he is talking about me with the way he never takes his eyes off me as he sits down and asks, "What should I try first?"

"The eggs are good and full of protein," I tell him, looking away as I feel my face starting to heat. His gaze is making my pulse race and my breathing is coming faster. "You should build your strength."

"Okay, then," he says, taking his plate and loading it with eggs and a biscuit with gravy.

"This is my friend, Sister Alice. Alice, this is Lindon Mountainside," I introduce them before he begins to eat. He looks at me as I speak and then bows to Alice.

"Ma'am," he says politely with a smile and then focuses his attention on his food.

Brier is finishing up his plate and is adding more food.

"Princess Celine…" Brier starts to say, but I interrupt him.

"Please call me Celine," I say to him sweetly.

"Princess Celine, I assume you have read your sister's letter since you have agreed to come with us?" he questions.

"Yes," I say, hoping my curtness annoys him as it annoys me that he keeps calling me princess.

"In that case, we should leave as soon as possible," he says, not seeming to care. "Early morning about two hours before dawn, I am thinking. Ogres should be settling in for sleep, and hopefully it will make our morning easier to travel."

"What about the Mox in the rivers?" I ask him. "I have heard in stories they can eat boats in the night."

"Mox river snakes are dangerous in the night but not in the day. They don't like clear waters," Brier tells me. "With us not being able to stay on the water at night will be a challenge. The ogres want your blood from what I hear, and we saw plenty of tracks on our way in. We will take turns resting in the day as we travel and at night keep watch for them. Hopefully through the day we can move far enough away they won't attack all at once."

"I have personal knowledge of the creatures, Brier," I say his name casually. "I have heard them on the walls for years planning my death. Their crazy roars are just as horrible as their smell."

"Ogres have a craziness about them but are not too smart." Brier is direct now. "They don't hunt together but if they do cooperate to take us out, we will have to run and take our chances on the river. Hopefully, the Mox will not be in the area, but if they are, we might make it to the other shore. Ogres dislike water. This, I know."

"You're right. It's a good plan. But first, we have a problem to deal with before we can go."

"What is that?" he asks me, sitting back in his chair and staring at me.

"There is an ogre nearby." I stare back at him defiantly. "We call him Brown because of his color, and he is also the largest, most cunning, and has sat in wait for years for me to come out. Unlike the others who come and sometimes return, he never leaves."

"Then we will go hunting at dusk and take him down," Brier says like it is nothing. I wish it were that easy. I snort derisively a little and Brier looks at me in wonder.

"Well, you have come just in time because his friend is here, too," I say, lifting my eyebrows at him. "He comes about twice a year and hangs out for a few weeks. They are always planning something to get to me."

"What do you mean?" he asks, his brow coming down low over his eyes.

"Every year, they have tried something to get me out of these walls. The first year, Brown and the other ogres tested the borders. They threw enormous boulders across the wall, destroying parts of the buildings. When that worked, they climbed them. Once they reached the top of the wall, the blessed God keeps them at bay from his holy land. Their hands would catch fire, and they would let go as they cannot enter."

Alice speaks up then. "The second year, they tried to wait us out. For almost an entire year, they would let no one in, trying to run us out of food. But when they realized we grew enough to provide for ourselves, they gave up."

"The third year, they tried to burn us out, setting fires with torches they threw over. Hundreds of them. They would line them up on the ground all around the compound, set them on fire, and just start throwing. It almost worked, but we prevailed."

Alice picks the story up again. "And last year, they knocked a hole in our wall. First, with their fists and, when that didn't work, they rammed an enormous tree in it and succeeded. But they still couldn't get through the holy barrier. We have since resealed the hole."

"Brown tries these plans every year with his friends," I go on. "There are many other things he does alone, though. He has been a constant torment to me and to all of us."

"So, his friend is here now. What have they done so far?" Lindon asks, now joining in.

"Nothing yet, but they are on the east side wall now. Digging," I say. "I do not understand what he is doing."

"Then we will strike first," Brier says. "We will go out at dusk, as I said. You will stay inside, and we will leave early in the morning."

"Okay, but I am telling you, Brown is not like any other. You need a plan and a good one. He has settled in these woods and knows them well. And now, he is not alone," I try to warn him again and don't like that he is dismissing me. I may not be a fighter like him, but I have watched Brown for years, and he is smart.

"Why did you give him a name and not all the other ogres?" Brier asks me, furrowing his brow.

"Because I see him daily. He watches me from an old tree off from the convent," I tell them. "He even speaks unlike the others, and he keeps the others away most of the time. He is why you don't see more ogres around the walls like when I first arrived. It was only after he came that their mumbles and groans ceased."

"He talks?" Brier asks, more surprised by this. "What does he say?"

"He doesn't talk well, and it is hard to understand him at times." I shrug my shoulders. "I can ask him something and he gives a word or two, nothing more. When he first came here, he paced the outside, saying things like, he was hungry, he waits, and...need her."

I look away then, remembering how scared I was of him in the beginning. I would scream at him to go away but he never did.

"He is obsessed with you," Tate says, and I turn to him.

"Why do you think that, Tate?" Brier asks him before I can.

"He is a beast, and I know how they think," Tate tells us. "In his obsession, he has almost, in a sense, provided you protection from the others. By driving them away, he knows that one day you will come out, and he will be the only one waiting."

"But wouldn't it be more than blood he is after?" Lindon says to him. "No way he is waiting around for just a meal."

Tate looks at me, and I see he is concerned. "What else has he said?"

"He mostly mumbles," I tell him, trying to think of the past. "'Come out. You're mine.' I've heard him say curse before."

My last word hangs in the air as we all fall silent. Alice is the first to speak, telling them, "He follows her too. Celine likes to run sometimes around the interior and when she does, you can feel a slight vibration in the ground as he runs beside her on the other side."

Tate growls, and his voice sounds different when he speaks. "He stalks her."

"Brier, what are you thinking?" Lindon asks then.

"It sounds like we will need to kill him before we take the princess out." Brier doesn't look happy, but I am glad he is finally taking me more seriously. His rises from his chair. "I will check the wall and see if I can track him. You two get some rest as you will need it tonight."

"He will have left by now," Alice speaks as Brier moves to leave, and he stops in his tracks. He turns around when she says, "The sun is getting high, and he will leave soon as the sun rises above the wall."

"You mean he comes out in the day?" Brier speaks louder now with his question, not believing it.

"The sun doesn't seem to bother him like the others, but when it is at its highest, he leaves," I explain. "He is sure to show about evening time again."

"If he shows himself then, we will all attack and bring him down," Brier lays out his plans. "If by chance he escapes, we will have to track him through the night, but I want him dead before we leave."

"If you need an extra night, I'm sure Mother Frances will not mind," Alice says. "She would never say it, but Brown is a burden to us all with the damage he has caused."

"Thank you, but we will stay for just one," he tells her kindly. "Princess, pack your bags and make sure they are light. We will be leaving in the morning."

Chapter Eight

Brier was in a hurry to leave but Alice stands up before he makes it to the door. "If you don't mind, Mother Frances might like to know of your findings. Would you mind if I go with you? I can show you where it is?"

Brier looks at her with peaceable, and almost tender, consideration. None of the anger and gruffness he gives me is present in his attitude when he looks at her. I am a little jealous that he agrees and she follows him. I know there is nothing to worry about as Alice would never hurt me and I don't think Brier would either.

It gives me a chance to be alone with Tate and Lindon, and I focus my attention on that pleasurable situation. They are both more agreeable. I start to place the empty bowls and plates on the trays to take them back to the kitchen.

"I guess we should take some time and rest then," Lindon says as he leans back in his chair and watches me. "What are you planning to do today, Princess?"

"Well, umm, I was hoping I could spend some time with each of you," I answer, a little nervous, and look to Tate and blush. "I would love to show you the gardens around back. I have done much of the planting myself, like you taught me when we were young."

"Sure," he says with a huge smile as he looks at Lindon, "Why don't you rest for a while, Lindon. I would like to be alone with Celine." The fire in his eyes when he looks back at me tells me that he has picked up on my hint. "We have some things to get caught up on."

For sure, we have a lot to catch up on, but I also want his help with something also. I force myself to look away as I continue to stack the dishes and say to Lindon, "Lindon, if you like, I would love to show you the library later today. You seem interested in knowledge, and there is a book I would like to show you."

"I would," he says, seemingly surprised by my offer. "Thank you, Celine."

"I look forward to getting to know you better," I say with a smile.

"I will rest, I guess until high noon, and let you two have some time alone." He rises and steps around the table closer to me. A light breeze ruffles my skirts as he comes nearer, and the scent of him fills my senses. He leans toward me and whispers, "Don't have too much fun without me."

"Lindon," Tate growls at him in warning but Lindon doesn't back off as we gaze in each other's eyes. I am already blushing at the idea of being alone with him.

"Don't worry." There is a pull I feel to step closer to him, and I do. Way too close as our bodies brush together and I can't help myself from saying, "The library can be fun also."

Tate takes me by the waist and pulls me back against him, and I snap out of the spell. The sensation Lindon has caused in me is still strong, yet when I lean into Tate, he breathes in my ear, "Don't tempt him, Celine. He is known to seduce many a woman."

"Don't lie to yourself, Tate," Lindon says, stepping away now. "I have no need to seduce any woman."

I take a deep breath, feeling my lungs expand for what feels like the first time when Lindon closes the bedroom door behind him. I chide myself that he is Wind and can easily seduce anyone into doing what he wants. I know it is why I am so attracted to him myself, but it is still more than that. He is one of my Elements, and I am meant to bond with him.

The light effects of air around us, the drop in his tone... does he not realize he is using his powers? The thought makes me wonder more, and I aim to find out later today. For right now I want to focus on Tate.

"You will love the gardens," I tell Tate and lean back into him more, relishing the feeling of his arms around me once again. "I designed them with you in mind."

His embrace tightens around me in a possessive manner, and I smile to myself. I like being in his arms. "It makes me happy to know you have thought of me. I just want to be alone with you so I can taste those sweet lips of yours again."

I shiver at the thought and say, "Then come with me."

"Lead the way," he says and lets me go slowly.

"Will you help me take these to the kitchen first?" I ask him, and he picks up one of the trays, and I do the other. We walk across the courtyard.

"I spend most of my time in the forest instead of the gardens now," he breaks the silence as we come up on the dining hall. "I am a hunter, and I like the time alone in nature."

"I am sure you do." He opens the door to the kitchen for me. "I would love to run in the woods. I like to run around the courtyard but it would be wonderful to be free. To cut through the trees and climb over the mountain and find a spring."

"You will get your chance soon enough."

I place the tray of dirty dishes on a table and start removing the plates and putting them into the sinks. Sister Margarete is doing the dishes. She is a tall, slender woman with a pointy nose and dull brown eyes.

"Morning, Sister Margarete. I hope you are feeling well today," I say, being polite to her. She isn't one of my favorite people, but I always try to be kind.

"I would be better if I wasn't doing all your chores," she says in a huff as she washes the dishes.

"Mother Frances has assigned most of my chores to others since I will leave in the morning," I tell her, which she most likely already knows. I always do my part around here, but Mother Frances told me to enjoy my last day here and not to worry about doing anything.

"Yet you're still here," she says in a sharp tone. "You could still do your part."

Instead of saying anything mean, I turn it on her. "You're right, I could. That is why I am heading to the gardens—to do some work. My friend, Tate, has offered to help me."

She looks at Tate and smiles just a little. "Sir Tate, I am glad you are here to take this…Lady Celine to her home. It is time she leaves since she has no calling to become a nun."

"It is an honor, Sister, to do so," he says with a smile. "Anything to help the future queen."

"Queen?" she says the word in disgust as she looks back at me. "You would make this…I mean, her, your queen?"

"Yes, Sister. It is her birthright," Tate says, surprised by her remark.

"I will pray for your people," she said, turning back to the dishes. "You will all need it."

I pull on Tate's arm before he can say more, and we go out the back door. As we walk through the vegetable gardens, he asks me, "What is her problem?"

"She sees the cursed part of me," I tell him quietly as we pass some nuns. "There are a little over a hundred nuns here inside these walls, and yet only two of them see the curse."

"But I thought the holy land protected you from it?" he asks, surprised.

"It does for holy people," I explain. "I hide from others who come here because they can still see me as cursed. But Margarete and Hildred are not holy nuns. They practice but are not pure like the others, and evil has touched their hearts."

"Are you serious? I have never known a nun to be described as evil."

"Mother Frances knows this, but she will not turn them away. She says they are trying to live a holy life, and to Mother Frances, that is more important."

"Mother Frances seems like a good person," he says. "Allowing you to stay here even though you have never taken a vow."

"She is," I say as I take his hand, and we enter the back gardens. "She has protected me from them and all others. I owe her my life."

"You know, we brought with us offerings of gold to the convent. Enough to see the nuns through many years to come," Tate tells me as his fingers rub against mine. "It came from Queen Elizabeth."

"Do you really think she tells you the truth?" I ask him, moving a little closer. "Do you think she means me no harm?"

"I think she sees her mistake and wants to fix it," he says, looking down at me. "Impending death can have a way of changing people. But it doesn't change what she did."

"She broke my heart," I mumble as I look at him. "She cursed me for everyone to hate and stole me away from everything I loved."

He stops walking and turns toward me, his free hand coming up to caress my cheek. "I never hated you, and as for love…I have held on to it all these years. I never forgot about you."

Smiling shyly at his words, I take his hand and pull back, taking him with me. "Come, I want to show you something."

I lead him to the back of the gardens, to my special place. I hide it from the rest of the gardens by large shrubs. A small section of flowers I had planted myself nestled in this secret spot of mine.

"I come here to be alone, sometimes," I say, pulling him into the small covering of vines. "More when I first came here, but I still do. I like to read here and…think of you."

"It is lovely," he says, looking around and then softly at me. "It reminds me of…"

"Our gardens back home," I finish for him. "Yes, I know."

He looks at me, and I smile up at him, moving a little closer. "Come. Sit with me."

He says nothing as I lead him to a patch of grass by a huge rock. The rock is a remnant of one of Brown's attack, but I had left it here because I thought it added to the charm of my secret place.

I sit down beside it, and he joins me. I brought him here because I wanted to be close to him like we once were when we played in my gardens back home, where I had been falling in love with him.

"Tate, I need to ask you to do something for me," I say with a sweet smile at him.

"What do you need?" he asks me, pulling my chin toward his face.

"Life here has been getting harder each year," I say sadly. "Less food is growing, and before we leave, I was hoping you could use your powers and give it a boost. Would you mind?"

He smiles at me before answering. "You want me to make sure they have enough food and think I would say no?"

"Well, I don't know how it would affect you, and I don't want you to grow weak or anything. You will be fighting ogres this evening," I tell him.

"I can do it. It's no problem." He takes my hands in his. "We can do it together. Place your hands on top of mine."

I entwine my hand through his, and he reaches forward and slides his hand into the dirt in front of us. I feel the cold soil between my fingers, and he goes deeper into the ground with his, then stops and looks at me.

"Close your eyes and just feel," he whispers. I do as he says, and I feel a slight vibration in the ground where my hands are. It slowly moves outward, then all around and under us. I listen, and I hear the surrounding plants respond, but I don't open my eyes. I am lost in the feeling even when I feel Tate retake my hands.

Slowly he raises them, but I can still hear everything growing around us. I don't dare break the spell by opening my eyes.

He places my hands on his shoulders as he reaches down to grasp me by the waist. I gasp at the contact, and I feel him lifting me forward and on top of him. My legs adjust on either side of his as he settles me against his hard, lean body. Still, I don't open my eyes, not wanting the magic around me to be lost.

"There is a power between us even though I know yours are locked away," he breathes a few inches from my face. "That doesn't mean they can't connect inside us."

"How?" I whisper, not knowing if what he says is true. I don't fully understand the powers as he does. Reading about them is one thing but being able to experience and use them is something I have never done.

"If you want to know, kiss me and see," he whispers with a soft dare and a promise.

I open my eyes and look at him. His eyes are on my lips just before he catches my gaze. I feel like that young girl again, who was excited at sharing a kiss with this boy. But he is no longer a boy, nor am I that girl.

I want to kiss him again, and it is one reason I had brought him here. Not just to grow the gardens, but to be close to him. I lower my lips to his and kiss him gently, still new at this intimacy. My dreams had been full of kisses, but now was my chance to feel his lips.

He takes the kiss deeper, kissing me back, showing me how as he did earlier. His hands come around my back, pulling me closer as he probes deeper inside my mouth. I moan at the pleasure of his claiming me. My hands hold his neck, not letting him go as I allow the kiss to consume. I feel the sparks of heartfelt passion taking over my senses as I shiver in his arms.

The ground beneath us begins to groan as the spark starts to burn within us. I move to get closer to Tate, and his hands come down to my hips, bringing me tighter into his lap. I hear a soft growl from him as small tremors shake us.

My body is buzzing with a sense of his power as I feel it building in my stomach and growing warm, alive like I never felt before. It moves down my body and into my core. The small vibrations wake a desire for more. Like he is almost touching me in that sensitive area.

He tries to pull away, but I hold him to our kiss and demand he continues. He does, his hands moving up my back and into my hair, pulling me closer.

The ground rocks stronger as the passion between us grows brighter. Tate tastes so delicious and sweet, like honeysuckles. I don't want him to stop as his tongue dances with mine, and I surrender to it completely.

I feel a trembling start between my legs and gasp at the pleasure. It catches me by surprise, and I pull away from our kiss, needing to breathe. I arch myself into Tate's body, needing to feel him more and press myself down.

His lips fall to my neck as he groans and reaches down, rocking my hips into his. I feel something hard between us there, and I know what it must be, but I have little knowledge of men. I don't look down there.

"Celine, I want you too much." His voice is husky against my throat, and the way he kisses my skin has me melting. It is becoming harder to breathe, but I don't care. He can keep me alive with just his kisses. "We have to stop this."

I know he is right, but he is driving me senseless with his tongue and hands roaming all over me. I don't want us to stop caressing each other; I want to know where it can lead.

"I am yours," I say as I pull his lips back to mine and kiss him deeply. Shock waves of power shoot into the ground, in ripples even more forceful this time. It is like he can't contain his own desires, and they are coming out in a more vigorous burst of quakes. The ground takes the force of them instead of him sending them through me. Like he is protecting me from too much power. His hands come up and cup my breasts, and I shudder at the pleasure of them there. When he squeezes them, I gasp and rock faster against him. The world swirls around us as heat hits my center again, and he pushes upward into me.

I hear a scream in the distance and know that our passion is affecting everything around us. He pulls back from me.

"Celine." He looks at me with blazing green eyes, and I can see the passion within them. He is breathing hard, and I am, too, as we stare at each other. Our need is apparent. "We have to stop."

I can't pull away from him. "It's just a little earth tremor," I say as I bend forward and kiss his neck. Oh, stars, this is even better than when he kisses my neck. His skin tastes and smells so good, like sweet lemongrass.

"It is us making the tremors," he moans, not being able to resist. "But look around."

I pull back and glance around for the first time. All around us, the plants have grown and are in full bloom. Everything is so large and full of fruits and vegetables. I can't believe all I am seeing.

"You did all this?" I ask, looking back at him, surprised he is so powerful.

He smiles at my bewilderment before answering. "*We* did all this."

Chapter Nine

It is several hours later when I finally walk Tate back to the small house where the others are resting. He looks so tired, and I know he needs to rest. I have been selfish in taking up his time today, but I can't seem to pull away from him.

As we reach the house, he takes my hand and pulls me just inside the door.

"I don't want you to leave," he says, pressing me against the wall and running kisses along my neck once more. He feels so good, and I don't want to leave him, but we are in a convent, and it would not be proper for me to stay. I feel I have already crossed that boundary today.

"You need to rest," I say, closing my eyes and arching into him. *Just one more moment.*

"How am I to rest like this?" he asks playfully as he presses his hardness into my stomach. My stomach jumps with a giddiness that I now understand what that means.

"Indeed, how are you?" a voice interrupts us from behind, and we both look to see Lindon standing there watching us. He is propped on the door frame to one bedroom and is smiling at us.

"You have perfect timing, my friend," Tate says and pulls away from me. I have to admit it is a little embarrassing to be caught like this with Tate in front of Lindon. I say nothing, letting them converse for a time.

"Always here to help," he says, smiling and pushing himself from the door. "I even warmed the bed for you, but I was hoping Celine would join me in it, not you."

Tate and Lindon keep talking, but I am watching their body language. They seem to know each other well and get along. It is a comfort to me to see how easy they are together. They will become my life, and I don't want jealousy between any of us. I intend to win their hearts. I can't see having children with each of them if there is no love.

"Celine, are you ready to go?" Lindon asks, breaking my line of thought.

"Sure," I say, looking at Tate one last time to say goodbye. He takes my hand and kisses it gently, saying nothing as his eyes look deep into mine. I can see the happiness there and am thankful that my first taste of love will be with him. Tate is the binder of my past and my future.

"Any day now, Celine," Lindon teases from beside me at the door, leaning closer to me.

Tate pushes him out the door. "Ignore him, love. He is a rake who likes to play with people too much."

"I think I can handle him," I mumble as I slip my hand from Tate and join Lindon. Tate watches for a moment as we walk together toward the library before closing the door.

"You two seem to get along nicely," Lindon says with a knowing grin. "You sure you want to choose him? He is kind of boring, you know."

"Tate is not boring," I correct him. "When we were young, he kept me entertained for hours with our play."

"And I'm sure he can still keep you entertained for hours," he says with a chuckle. "But not as well as I."

"You are very open with your thoughts about others," I say, smiling at him. "Are you the same with yourself?"

"I will let you figure that out on your own." His tone is sweet but mischievous, and there is a glint of wicked fun in his eyes. "I like to bring a little mystery."

"I can see that," I say, leading him down an outside corridor off the central courtyard. On the right side, there are several benches down the wall in between several doors. Most of the rooms hold mission supplies and items for trade or the needy. The library is at the end of the courtyard.

On the left is another courtyard behind the main hall, which we use more for the nuns' personal leisure. A beautiful garden of flowers and trees surrounds it, and another large fountain is in the center. Sometimes on hot days, we splash around in it to cool off.

"So, tell me, what is so special about this library you want me to see?" he asks after a moment of silence between us.

"Just books in this library, but I have some I want to show you," I tell him. I want to understand if he realizes he has powers and that he uses them. "Maybe you can help me figure some things out."

"Why do you think I can help you?" he asks me.

"A fresh pair of eyes can see new things," I tell him. "I have been studying magic for a long time. Only good magic, though. Evil books are not allowed inside, and I don't care to know of dark magic anyway. Alice says it doesn't take much to get you hooked, and I don't care to be anything like my sister."

"I should say not," he states with a bit of disbelief in his tone. "Your sister, of course, being dark magic."

"I don't need dark magic to defeat her," I tell him defensively. "Good magic has to prevail. Otherwise, Fire will consume our world."

He stops and looks at me strangely. "Fire?"

It occurs to me what I say, and I want to kick myself. I didn't mean to mention Fire at this point to any of them. My sacrifice and how they are involved are things I need to lead up to.

"If I become a queen like you all believe, don't you think it will be an issue I will need to address?" I ask him. "I mean, you look over these walls, and on the east side I see a bright and beautiful green forest. Then I look over the west sidewall, and I see smoke and black in the distance. When I first came here, I didn't see it, and now I do."

"You are right," he agrees. "Fire has been getting out of control, and the queen does nothing. I am amazed you are thinking of your duties already. It seems you would be more concerned right now of getting out of here alive."

"I worry about a lot of things," I say, looking away from him. I turn to the open double doors of the library, and Lindon follows me inside.

Large windows run down the left wall with rows of desks and seating areas to relax in. They are open to allow the breeze and light in as a few nuns work at desks in front of them. On the left side are a dozen rows of bookshelves stacked almost to the ceiling.

I lead him to my desk, which has the highest pile of books. "These are my studies."

"Okay, I'm not reading all that," Lindon laughs, looking down at all the books.

"You don't have to," I say, laughing at him as I search through the books in front of us. "I want you to see one book. Please have a seat."

He sits down in the chair, and when I find the book, I sit down beside him. "This is the book on the Elements. It is my favorite book, and I have read it a hundred times."

"What is so special about this book?"

"It tells how the four Elements were born and came together to form the worlds," I tell him. "It is kind of a religion for someone who has one of the powers."

"Kind of small, don't you think?" he says as he flips through the rare book.

I chuckle at him again. "Yes, but it is still powerful. It tells how Fire and Water were the first two Elements and how there was a battle between them at the beginning that caused Earth and Wind to form. The forming of the other two minor Elements balanced the major ones, and with that, life grew."

"How did you come by this little book in a place so large as this?" he asks, holding it up as he looks at me.

"Mother Frances gave it to me when she first brought me here," I say softly. "She knew magic was locked inside me and that I was one of the Elements. To be free one day, Mother Frances said I needed to learn more of them. So, she gave me this book to start my studies. I think she gave it to me because it is more of my bible than hers."

"She must truly be a holy woman to have such compassion for someone who doesn't have her beliefs," he says as I take the book back from him.

"Mother Frances believes in all religions. She says it is the differences in them that shape our worlds," I tell him as I turn the book to the spot where it talks about Wind. "Read this section, and when you're done, we will talk about it."

He exhales, taking the book back. "You know, I kind of had other things on my mind than reading."

"I promise we will do something fun in a while," I say, smiling at him. "But read first."

He leans back in the chair and looks at me one last time before he turns to the book. I watch him, wondering what he will think of Wind when he is done. I hope that by reading about it, it will open him up more to the idea of his own powers.

I can sense his magic and that he doesn't seem aware of it. I wonder how he could be oblivious, though I have read that many Elements did not desire to know their powers. I find that hard to believe. Why would anyone deny the magic they have within them? I want to know what Lindon thinks of it after reading. Then I will try to get him to use his powers if I can.

His magic is powerful, and it has already shown itself to me with a slight breeze here and there but mostly with the seduction he calls forth. *Lindon is the most handsome*, I think as I watch him read my book. Tall and slender, but muscular, too. He is the only one who has his hair long, unlike Brier and Tate. It is the color of sunshine and looks silky smooth, even tied back the way it is now. I wonder how often he brushes it to make it so shiny. I don't think he cares about it like women do.

"You watching me is not allowing me to concentrate." He looks at me as if he knows what I am thinking. Do other women compliment him on his hair often? I'm sure he has gotten some from quite a few.

"I'm sorry," I say, blushing at my thoughts, but can't seem to move away from the thought of his hair and the idea of running my hands through it. Even now, I am thinking of it again. I pull my chair closer to his. "Would you care if I read with you then? Would that help you concentrate?"

I am flirting with him, but I can't seem to help myself even though I know I have to be blushing. He does that to me. Lindon makes me aware physically. His bold personality and flirtatious knack make me want to flirt with him, too.

"I think it would, yes." His gaze roams over me. I like the way he makes me feel like I am sensual and beautiful. The way Wind invokes a passion in his breeze.

I pull my chair closer and lean against the arm of his chair. He slumps down and leans closer, too, and I place my head on his shoulder. His face lingers above mine, taking in my scent. I take him in, too, as our eyes lock on one another. He swallows before speaking. "I'm not sure if I will be able to read this."

"Try," I say, and my mouth stays open for a second. I take a deep breath as I watch his eyes lower to my lips. I close them quickly, biting my lower lip, and I can hear the low rumble in his chest.

"You try," he says, turning his gaze from me and back to the book. I watch him as he closes his eyes, then opens them and focuses on the paper. I tilt my head down, snuggling against him, and read. I already know the book by heart, but rereading it with Lindon, it seems almost new to me.

He reads a little faster than I. I say nothing as he goes ahead and turns the page. I touch only his arm, but somehow, my hand wanders down along his smooth skin. He is warm to my palm, and I can't help playing with a small mole just above his wrist.

"I'm trying to read," he says, not taking his eyes off the book. I don't move, either, but run my hand to the bend in his arm and rest it there.

"I'm sorry," I whisper. "I just like this part of the book."

"Why do you like it?" he asks softly.

"Wind is as soft as a feather and can be hard as a rock. It makes me wonder what seeing this power looks like. How it can pick up a rock and throw it without touching it or…what it can do with a feather and each of its thin strands."

"Oh, I know something it can do with a feather," he says with a chuckle. He turns his face toward mine. "I would be more than willing to show you."

"And would you also show me what you can do with a boulder?" I ask him, tilting my face up to his.

"If it means tickling a beautiful woman with a feather, I'm sure I can take on a boulder," he says, looking at my lips again.

"I tell you what," I say bravely. I have an idea to make a deal. A very seductive agreement at that. "If you can lift a boulder, I will let you show me what the feather can do."

He clears his throat and shuffles in his chair a bit before asking, "Is that a promise?"

I can't believe I am so bold with him. My face has to be red, but something keeps pulling at me to be forward with him. It makes me warm in other places, too.

I lean toward him and lower my voice. "It's a deal if you are willing to take it."

He is breathing a little hard, and I wish I can see some of the thoughts running through his head right now. He flicks his tongue out, moistening his lips, and I can't help but look at them.

"Lindon?" I ask as I lick my lips.

"Deal," he barely whispers to me, and I can feel a slight tremor along his arm, which is pressed against my breast. I pull back from him a bit, realizing we are way too close in this room surrounded by nuns.

"Good. Concentrate on the book," I say, swallowing the lump in my throat as I rest my head back on his shoulder.

"I can see how you will drive me crazy," he says after taking a deep breath and turning back to the book. "But I warn you now…you're bound to go a little mad, too."

I chuckle, and so does he. "Sounds like fun."

"Oh, it will be," he promises.

Chapter Ten

"So, what do you think?" I ask Lindon as we turn the last page and he places it on the table. He looks around the small library for a minute before answering.

"I don't know," he says with a frown. "To be honest, I feel… very close to the Element. Like I know it, but don't quite understand."

"Do you have family, Lindon?" Someone should have talked to him about this before.

"Yes, but both my parents died years ago," he tells me, averting his gaze. "They had been in love with each other their entire lives, and when my mother passed, my father followed soon after."

"I'm sorry," I say, thinking how sad that was, but at the same time, jealous of his loving family. "That must have been hard for you."

"It was, but…I had my wife, Liza," he says, looking at me softly. "She helped me through it, but…she died as well just a year later."

I take a deep breath, holding it as I feel the pain flow from him. *He had been married?*

"She died in childbirth, her and my son," he tells me. "I was eighteen, and I had no one to see me through. It was the hardest year of my life."

Saying I am sorry seems so small and not nearly enough, so I say nothing. I can see that Lindon loved her very much. Apparently, they had both been very young, and most likely, she had been the first love of his life. Just as Tate was mine. I feel tears well up, thinking of all the nights I cried myself to sleep after losing him. It had to have been worse for him, losing a wife and a child.

I can also see why he hasn't gone through the change in accepting his powers. All Elements went through it in their eighteenth year. Grief had a way of canceling them out or locking them up. If Lindon didn't know he was a Wind Element, it would have been easy for him not to have noticed his changes.

"I can see that you loved her very much," I finally whisper. "It must have broken your heart to lose her and the love you had built. Seeing it in your parents and knowing what it looked and felt like, and to have found that for yourself. I can't imagine the pain of losing it."

"It never goes away," he tells me, leaning on his elbows. "It has been years, and I still think of her. In many ways, I don't want to forget."

"Don't," I exclaim, leaning closer to him and touching his arm. "Never forget true love. No matter how short or even tragic, it is worth keeping with us."

A tear slips down my face, but I don't try to hide it. Lindon wipes the tear off my cheek.

"It is sweet of you to cry. I can't anymore." He gives me a small smile instead. "I had to let them go, but I keep her with me…and our son."

"I'm sorry; it is just so overwhelming to hear," I say, wiping the tears away. "I didn't realize my question would be so heartfelt."

"You asked about my family," he breathes. "Painful, I know, but we all feel the loss in our lives sometimes. Mine just came early."

He stands and moves away from me, down an aisle of books. He just told me something personal about himself. I feel the urge to tell him something about myself. I get up and walk to him.

"I lost my parents too when I was young," I confess to him, and he glances over his shoulder at me. "I don't remember my father, but my mother passed when I was seven. I try to keep my memories of her, but they are so few. I always wished I had more."

"My parents were wonderful people, and I have those memories," he tells me with a sweet smile. "But a part of me has always been lost because they weren't my real parents."

"What?" I ask, startled.

He leans on one shelf, looking down at me.

"My actual parents died in a house fire when I was just an infant. My adoptive parents told me that my parents dropped me from the apartment building into their arms just before it collapsed under them. They couldn't have children themselves and felt that it was a sign that they should take care of me, and so they did."

"How tragic," I mumble, placing my hand on the shelf next to him. "How did you find out?"

"They told me this when I was about nine. They didn't know them, that they were just walking by and saw the fire. Everyone was running around trying to put it out, but my father looked up and saw them in a window with me. He said they were screaming for someone to take their child. He stepped forward, shouting back at them it was okay. Then they both kissed me before my real father dropped me into his arms."

He continues only after pushing himself off the shelf and moving farther down the aisle. "They found out later the name of my mother and father. Kate and Lindon Mountainside. There was no record of my name since I was still so young, and so they gave me my father's. I had wondered until that day why I didn't carry their name. They had refused to tell me before, only saying I was adopted and that they wanted me to keep my actual name. It was only until I was old enough to understand that they told me what really happened."

"I think they were right to wait," I say, following behind him. "Tragic as it was, the pain isn't easy for everyone, especially a child. Even for your parents. Both sets of them."

"It was hard for us all. I never spoke with my parents again about it, and the only other person I ever told was Liza."

"Thank you for sharing it with me." I'm not sure what else to say.

"I had a good childhood, and my parents were amazing, all of them."

"Yes, they were," I agree, trying to smile. "We seem to have gotten off the subject. We were talking about the Wind Element."

"Yes, we were." He props himself up on the shelf across from me again. "These powers, air, speed, travel… they seem foreign to me, but others like the smell, breathing, and seduction, I seem to be able to relate to."

I laugh at him. Okay, so he does sense some of them. "So, you think you can smell like the Wind?"

"I smell you." He steals my breath away. A cool breeze flows over my skin, and I look down at my arms, seeing the small hairs rise. He is doing it again. "And it is changing as I speak."

"You want to get out of here?" I ask him, feeling a little hot even after the cold air on my skin. "Grab a bite to eat? There is a nice little fountain where we can picnic."

"Are you on the menu?" he asks, and I almost trip over my feet as I turn to my desk.

"Not today." Still, I don't want to discourage his advances, so I add, "But if you play your cards right, I can see adding myself...soon."

"Smells delicious," he says, his eyes roaming over me. "And getting better every second."

"Do you want to eat or not?" I ask, turning and moving back down the aisle. Whatever he smells from me, I think he should give it a rest for now. I'm not flirting nearly as much as he is.

"Sure," he says, standing now. "Lead the way, Princess."

"Don't call me that," I turn back on him in anger.

"Fine, then I will just call you...Cherry," he says, giving me a devilish smile. "I love eating cherries."

"I'm sure we can find you some, then," I say, mollified. I kind of like the nickname and the way he says it.

He just chuckles at me as we walk to the door. He follows a few steps behind and whispers, "I can see I will have some fun with you. Your innocence is...very refreshing...Cherry."

"And I can see you are not innocent," I retort. "Laying on the charm a little thick, yes?"

"What can I say? I like to flirt with beautiful women," he tells me.

"It is sweet of you to call me that," I say as we walk out of the library.

We fall silent as we walk down the corridor again, busy with many nuns walking by us. I think about all of what he said, and it seems my offering and the things I asked for are being answered. Tate is fantastic and is such a comfort to me. Lindon makes me feel beautiful and desirable, and I enjoy talking to him. I still don't know Brier, but I am sure his closed-off self will eventually open up to me.

"Would you like to help me make us a basket?" I say as we come to the main dining hall. "We can make some extra for the others."

"I would," he says, looking around the hall as we enter. It isn't anything fancy, just several rows of tables with chairs and benches to sit on. There are religious paintings and several crosses on the walls. The floor is made of stone, but the walls and ceiling are all dark timbers.

There is enough room to sit about two hundred people, but there is only a little over one hundred nuns that live here. Mother Frances told me that this convent once had housed many more.

A few nuns are setting out pitchers of water in the center of the tables closer to the back of the hall. The kitchen doors are close by, and several of the nuns look up at us, and I smile.

"Come with me to the kitchen," I tell him as I make my way down the middle. "We cooked some turkeys today, and they will make some great sandwiches."

"Well, I hope you have a big basket," he says playfully. "We men sure like to eat."

I laugh at him. "I'm sure we can find one."

The kitchen is in full working order as about half a dozen nuns are working to prepare platters to set out on the tables.

"Afternoon, Celine," Sister Dawn says to me. She glances at Lindon before she turns back to me. "Mother Frances has told us you will leave us tomorrow. We are all going to miss you so much."

"I will miss you all, too," I say, hugging her. She has been one of the kindest of sisters. "This is Lindon Mountainside from Clearwater. Lindon, this is Sister Dawn."

"A pleasure," Lindon says kindly with a bow. "This place smells amazing."

It does with platters of fresh cooked meats and bread. I always loved working in the kitchen myself.

"Thank you," she replies.

"Lindon and I were going to see about making up a basket of food for ourselves and the others," I tell Sister Dawn. "Do you mind?"

"Of course not," she says, taking a platter from one workstation. "Why don't you take this and go over there and prepare it? Everything you need is right here."

"Thank you, Sister Dawn." I reach to take the platter, but Lindon takes it instead.

"Allow me," he says, smiling down at me. We walk over to a clear area, and he sets it down while I gather some food cloths to wrap our sandwiches in and a basket. I watch as he sneaks a bite of the turkey and smiles, closing his eyes in pleasure. "This is so good. Are you sure you want to leave?"

I laugh at him as he hands me some meat. "I will miss the food."

"In Clearwater, turkey is something we usually get around Winters Giving," he says, taking another bite. "I love turkey."

"Save some for the others," I say, slapping at his hand as he reaches for another piece.

"Okay, then, but we make ours first," Lindon states as I hand him two large slices of bread. "They can have what I leave."

"Deal," I agree, taking up a spoonful of the sandwich spread and place it on my bread. I then hand him the spoon, and he does the same.

I pile on several slices of turkey and cheese on mine, along with some fresh-cut tomatoes and lettuce. Lindon piles his high with turkey, onions, tomatoes, and some pickles and lettuce.

"The sisters make some of the best cheeses," I tell him when I see he left it off.

"I'm not a big cheese person," he says. "But I am definitely a meat person."

"Oh, I can tell," I say playfully. "If you put any more on that sandwich, you cannot put it in your mouth."

"Don't you worry about that," he says with a chuckle. "I will get it in."

I offer him a cloth to wrap it in. I am afraid I cannot pick up the giant thing without breaking it to pieces. He takes it, and we wrap our sandwiches and set them to the side.

We finish making two more huge sandwiches with everything on them and then add some cherries and several slices of pound cake in the basket. Lindon picks it up, and we go out to the fountain.

Talking with Lindon is so easy. He had so much painful stuff happen to him, but he survived. He moved past it, and I was so glad he had. I have a feeling he will be a wonderful husband.

"Thank you for thinking of the cherries," he says, smiling at me as he munches on one. "They are so sweet, just the way I like them."

"I'm glad we had some," I say, taking one myself and biting it off its stem. "We try to grow a variety of fruits and vegetables here."

"I heard the nuns talking in the kitchen," he says, looking at me with laughter in his eyes. "About how well the gardens are looking. As if they bloomed overnight."

"Tate may have had a hand in that," I confess to him, not being able to stop the blush creeping up my cheeks at the memory.

"He did, did he?" he asks, his smile getting even more prominent. "Has he been able to sample any of this fruit yet?"

"No, but I am sure he will like them," I say to him. "If you don't eat them all."

"Oh, don't worry," he says with a laugh, though I'm not sure why. "I will let him have his cherry."

"Why are you laughing?" I ask, not being able to stop my smile.

"I'm sorry," he says, looking away with a slight blush now. "Your innocence is so…"

"What?" I ask when he doesn't finish.

He leans closer to me and whispers, "Just know that you are my cherry, and I have every intention of tasting you."

Chapter Eleven

Today has been the most exciting day of my life. I spent the morning with Tate and then the afternoon with Lindon and both are simply amazing. There is spark of new life being around them today, both making my blood stir and… I don't know. It is just special and new, and I can't wait to get to know more of Brier now.

Lindon and I return to the cottage where Tate and Brier are still sleeping. Tate wakes from the couch in the living area as we come in, and Lindon goes to the door of the bedroom, knocking to awaken Brier. "Time to rise, old man. We have brought you a late lunch."

I sit beside Tate as he rubs the sleep from his eyes as he leans back. "Did you show Lindon the library?"

"Yes, and we read some before going to the kitchen and preparing a lunch and had a picnic by the fountains in the garden," I tell him with a smile. I can't help but put my hand on his leg, wanting to touch him again so badly in some small way. "Did you get enough rest? We took our time so you could."

"Yes, I am fine," he says, his hand grazing my back as he rubs it.

"Come and eat, Tate," Lindon calls from the table as he is pulling out the lunch. "Celine and I made some of the best turkey sandwiches."

Brier opens the bedroom door, still looking tired himself and doesn't say anything as he sits down at the table. Lindon joins him, and Tate and I rise also. I pour them some water to drink with their food before taking a seat.

Lindon is telling them about the massive library we have here and how the nuns were writing their bible out by hand. He tells them also of the kitchen and the wonderful smells inside. He mentions about the nuns being of buzz of how the gardens seem to have grown overnight and their excitement. I glance at Tate, and he just grins at me. But my main focus is on Brier.

He doesn't pay me any mind as Lindon and Tate do, and it concerns me. I feel an attraction to him, and I know it is returned. I can't help but wonder why he is closing himself off from it.

Out of the three of them, I feel that I should have connected the most with him. He is a Water Element, and so am I. Sure, I have never had the chance to communicate with another before, but shouldn't it come more naturally for the same Elements?

I am attracted to him. He has scars—a nasty one on the side of his face—but I pay little attention to it. His eyes hold me spellbound with their deep ocean blue in such contrast to his dark skin and hair. His beard is short and covers only his jaw. *It hides much of his scar*, I think. I wonder if it will be as soft as Tate's if I touch his.

"I don't like people watching me eat," Brier says, startling me out of my thoughts.

"I wasn't watching. I was… thinking."

"Then think and don't look at me," he says, waiting for me to look away before taking another bite.

I look at Lindon, who is sitting beside me, and he just shrugs his shoulders, and then at Tate, who is on the other side of the table. Both are watching to see my reaction to Brier's command, and I can tell they don't like it too much either. I think now is a good time to speak up and see what he may be thinking.

"Do you not like it when a woman admires you?" I ask boldly, putting my elbows on the table and looking at him again. "You do like women, right?"

He looks angry as he drops his sandwich and wipes his mouth with a cloth. I hear Lindon snicker beside me.

"Few like the way I look," he says, turning his face so I can see the scar. "When they look, they stare at my flaws. So no, I don't like it when I am being watched."

"I wasn't looking at your flaws," I tell him. "I was looking at everything else."

"You wouldn't like what was under these clothes any more than they do," he says crudely. "Trust me, honey, you don't want to see."

I do want to see, but he apparently will not give me a chance. He feels that he is a monster, and deep down, I know I will have to show him he isn't. I think of how Mother Frances taught this to me, and I am confident I can do the same with Brier.

"I guess we will have to see, then," I say, sitting back in my chair.

He seems a little taken back by my comment, and I like that. I am getting to him.

"You're strange."

"Maybe you should see that as a good thing." I smile at him as I stand up and move toward the door.

"I don't," he says sternly and then changes the subject. "You said earlier that Brown will be back around sunset. I would like to set a trap for him along that back wall where he has been digging. Do you think you could distract him for a little while so we can draw closer to him?"

"I guess so," I answer. "As I said before, he doesn't talk to me like he used to, but I can talk to him and try to distract him."

"Good. Lindon will stay with you on this side of the wall," Brier tells us as he looks to him. "Tate and I will sneak out and around, blocking him in. When I give the signal, you come over the wall and join us. With the three of us, we should be able to bring him down with little problem."

"What am I supposed to do?" I ask him.

"You stay back and within the walls," he says, looking directly at me. "Once we take care of him, we will sweep the area clean of any other ogres and come back for you around midnight to head for the river. We should arrive around dawn and that will give us a full day of travel and hopefully, we'll leave many of the other ogres behind."

Tate and Lindon seem both to agree but I still have questions. "But once I step outside these walls, every ogre around will come for me."

"We will deal with them as need be as we move," he informs me. "Don't worry, Princess. We will get you to your kingdom safely."

It's not just me I am worried about but them, also. I feel I should warn them again about Brown. "I don't think you realize still of how strong and smart Brown is."

"The three of us will deal with him," Brier says, shrugging off my concerns. It irritates me that he keeps doing this.

"But…"

"Just let us deal with him. No matter his strength, between the three of us we should be able to bring him down," Brier interrupts me now.

"I will say my goodbyes now. Let you all plan without me in the way."

Tate moves to me before I reach the door and takes me by the arm. "We will be back for you," he says, touching my forehead to his, and he whispers, "Thank you for today. It was…"

"It was," I say, agreeing with him without saying what we are both thinking. That this morning, connecting with the others had been so beautiful and sweet. "Be careful."

Lindon pulls me out of Tate's arms and spins me around before setting me back on my feet. "Meet me in the garden tonight?" he asks, sliding his hands up and down my arms. "Before we distract your ogre, maybe we can make some memories in them, too."

I blush at his boldness in front of the others once again. "Thank you for coming for me too, Lindon. I hope you may have learned something today."

"Was I supposed to?" he asks, still smiling at me.

"Yes, you were." I smile at him. "We will talk more later. Goodbye, Lindon."

He lets me go, and I turn, once again, glancing to Tate before looking at Brier once more. He doesn't move from his chair but is looking at me like the others are.

"Goodbye, Brier," I breathe, not sure what else to say. "Be safe this evening and please heed my warnings."

"We will," he says, making it about all of them rather than just him.

I move to the door, hating to go with just that. What if something happens, and I never see them again? I want to be away before I start to cry and make a fool of myself. They won't know what to do with me, I am sure.

"Celine," Brier calls to me just before I walk out. I stop and look at him. He seems unsure and glances at the others, who are watching him, before turning back to me. "I'm sorry. You're not strange… I am."

It isn't much, but it is enough. I smile warmly at Brier, glad that he seems to try at least.

"I like strange," I assure him before leaving. It is hard, but this is what they were sent for. I shouldn't panic, but I have an urge to protect them, too.

Brier wants me to keep Brown's attention, and I need to make sure I do that. A thought occurs to me, and it just might work. I will say nothing to them as I am sure they will stop me.

Before I can start to put it into motion, I need to see Mother Frances. I think it is time I spoke to her about these three men and what I have done for them to arrive. I just hope she isn't disappointed in me.

I move toward the corridor of Mother Frances's chambers. She is usually there at this hour, recording the day's events. I know because I would give her crop reports at least once a week.

Someone else most likely is giving her reports now, but I will check and wait if necessary. I want to give my own crop report to Mother Frances one last time.

I knock on the door and hear Mother Frances call to enter.

"Celine, you're just in time," Mother Frances says, looking up and smiling at me. "Sister Margareta was just telling me that the crops were looking good today. She says our meals will be some of our best yet this season."

"Yes, they have been doing well," I say, taking the seat by Sister Margarete. Mother Frances had included me in the conversation and motioned me forward. "I came so I could tell you before leaving in the morning."

"I wanted to see you as well. I have much to say before you go," she says, smiling. "Sister Margarete, I hope you don't mind us cutting this short today. With Celine leaving, I feel the urge to let things go for the rest of the day."

"Of course, Mother Frances," Sister Margarete says to her. "I understand how close you are with her. Miss Celine, I hope your travels are safe and well."

"Thank you, Sister Margarete," I say, delighted to hear such kind words coming from her. "It means a lot you say such pleasant things."

"I will take my leave," she says, smiling once more at us both and leaving the room.

"I never thought I would hear a kind word out of that woman toward me," I say, turning back to Mother Frances. "It must please her that I am leaving."

"I know it has been difficult with her, but you have handled the situation well these years." Mother Frances smiles at me. "I am proud of you for everything."

"I have been nothing but a burden," I say with a chuckle. "Conflict with some of the nuns, having to hide from all traders and people who come inside, an ogre tormenting us for years…"

"All things that have been more of a burden to you than to us," she interrupts me. "I have enjoyed having you, and I know there are many others who feel the same way."

"How do you know that?" I ask her.

"Because they wouldn't be in the dining hall right now getting ready to throw you a surprise party if they didn't," she says with a pleasant smile. "Make sure you act surprised, you hear."

"What about Sister Margarete?" I ask with a sly smile.

"She made the ice cream you like so much," she says, nodding her head.

"Wow," I say, letting out a laugh on an exhale. "That sure is a surprise."

"I need to ask you about the gentlemen who have come for you, Celine," she says, turning now to a more serious note. "I know you are of an age to make your own decisions, and I will not tell you what to do, but I am concerned. They plan to take you to your sister. The very one who had you brought here and imprisoned in the first place."

"Well, I wouldn't call this place a prison," I say, trying to lighten the mood a bit. "But yes, they intend to take me to Elizabeth. I think I need to face her. Not to break the curse, but because of what she did."

"She could still mean to do you harm," she warns. "Maybe she is not sick at all. If she is, that still doesn't mean she couldn't hurt you."

"I have them to protect me," I tell her. "They are Elements, too."

"How do you know they will protect you from her?" she asks me. "She paid them to bring you to her."

"Yes, but I kind of... well, I called them to me," I say, hesitant to tell her what I did. "I don't know how she was the one to send them, but I asked for them."

"You asked who for them?" she asks, looking more concerned.

"I called out to the Elements to send me three men that would help me break the curse," I tell her. "Earth, Wind, and Water. They all showed up."

"You mean they are Elements of magic just like you?" she asks, not having a doubt. I nod my head, and she asks, "And they just somehow got your sister to send them to you?"

"Well, yes, but as I said, I had already requested them," I tell her again. "In time, they will break the curse for me even without my sister's help."

"Celine, how will they break the curse?" she asks, knowing I am hiding something. I hadn't wanted to tell her all the details.

"I offered myself to the Elements," I finally say. "I will bear each of them a child to help balance the world. Through our children, the land will grow again, seeds will spread, and water will calm the fires."

"You are to have children with them," she says, gaping at me. "Are you sure that is what you want?"

"Yes," I say, not meeting her eyes. "They will do a good thing for me, and I will do something good for all the realms."

"Celine, that doesn't sound like you," she says, frowning. This was why I didn't want to tell her. "You used to tell me how one day your prince would come and save you. Not three of them."

"I know, but things change," I say, needing for her to understand. "I've been here five years, Mother Frances. I am twenty years old. Most women my age are married with children. I want those things, but I lost that little girl's dream long ago. I need to break the curse so I can have a life. A real one and with my powers. I feel them inside, and it pains me so much that I can't let them out."

"So, you offered yourself?" she says, shaking her head as she touches her temple with her fingers. "Don't you realize you just traded one prison for another?"

"They don't feel like that to me, nor does being here with you," I told her. "Tate and I had already promised ourselves to each other before I even came here. That life was taken from me, but now I have a chance at it again. Lindon, I am enjoying learning more about, and as for Brier… I think he needs someone to love him. I feel so much pain in him, and I just want to help."

"You care for them? You have barely known them for a day, Celine."

"I'm sorry, Mother Frances, if I'm disappointing you," I tell her. "But I have faith in my Elements, and I know I can be happy with them. It's strange, I know, and I don't know how it's all going to work, but it will. It has to, or Fire will destroy our worlds for any hope of future generations."

"I'm not disappointed. I'm just… worried," she says, covering her mouth with her hand as she looks at me.

"Please, don't be," I beg her as I reach my hand across her desk. She takes it in hers. "Have faith. I know what I did, and I didn't just do it for myself. I saw a chance to make things better for everyone. My children will bring life back to this world. With all the Elements connecting in such a way, it will restore the balance of nature."

"I don't understand it as you do, but I have faith in you," she finally says, squeezing my hand. "If what you say is true, then yes, it would be the greatest of blessings to mankind."

"It will be," I tell her. "I promise you. It will work."

She smiles at me, approaching me and holding her arms out. I rise into them. "There is an old nursery rhyme I remember as a child. It was about a woman called Mother Earth."

"Really?" I say as we let go of each other. "What was it about?"

"It was about how God created the earth, and then the mother gave life," she says. "Maybe you are that now. Mother Earth."

"In my belief, it is called Mother Nature," I tell her, familiar with the story now. "Only the Fire God is known as the father, and the Water Goddess is known as the mother. Between them, they both created the earth and life."

"Maybe they are the same," she says, smiling at me as she brushes my hair back. "If what you say is true, then go with my blessing. I will keep my faith and pray for you every day to be successful in your endeavor."

"I love you so much, Mother Frances," I say, never speaking those words to her before. "I will miss you."

"I will miss you just as much, my child," she says, hugging me again. We both are weeping when she speaks again. "And I love you, too."

Chapter Twelve

Brown has been nagging me all day. Tate had said that Brown was stalking me not for a chance to feed off of me, but for something else. It had never crossed my mind that he might have wanted me for something before. I just always assumed he was like all the rest of his kind, but that was silly because I knew he wasn't like the others. Tate must be right, so what is his true purpose?

Brier wants me to distract him so they can go on the attack. There isn't much time left before I am to meet Lindon, and we will go to the back wall. I want to see if I can ask Brown a few things and get some answers. I am frightened for my Elements because I don't think they know what they are about to walk into. I feel my only option is to give it my all and distract Brown enough to provide them with the most significant advantage.

In the process, I want to know why Brown is here. The problem is, Brown rarely talks to me anymore, and so I plan to give him a gift. My blood. Hopefully, it will not only distract him but give me some answers, too.

I go to my room so I can be alone for a while and take with me all I need. This will not be easy, but I had done so before when I made my sacrifice. Taking a deep breath, I hold the sharp blade to my wrist and cut deeply; my blood pours out and drops into the bowl below.

I fight the scream of pain, not wanting anyone to come in here. It takes a grueling long time for my blood to fill the bowl, and as I start to feel lightheaded, I know I need to stop. Taking the clean cloth, I bind my wrist tightly. I take the two waterskins I brought with me and divide the blood between them both. Once that is done, I lie back for a minute and let the dizziness pass.

This has to work. I have never given my blood to him before, but I know ogres crave it. They like blood and feed off off it, but whatever was so special about me that they would risk their lives for it had to be strong. I fight through my wooziness and rise to meet Lindon.

"There you are! I have been looking everywhere for you," Alice says as I come out into the back gardens. She comes over to me, and I reach for her, needing her support as I shake the dizziness from my head. "Celine, are you okay?"

"I need your help," I say, clutching the two bags in my hand. "Come with me to the far garden where Brown usually is. I need to speak to him."

"Celine, what have you done?" she asks, seeing the bandage around my wrist and the small amount of blood that has seeped through.

I smile at her, weakly. "You were right, Alice, as always. I did find a need to cut myself again."

"Oh, Celine!" Alice exclaims as she helps me to sit down on a bench. It is good, at least, as I need to tell her my plans. "Why didn't you call me?"

"I didn't want you to stop me," I tell her. "It is exactly a sacrifice like you said. I cut myself for my blood so I can offer it to Brown."

"Why?"

"Because of what Tate said earlier," I tell her. "Brown wants me for something, and I am hoping I can get him to tell me what for."

"By offering him your blood?"

"He doesn't speak as he did before. Maybe this will give him a reason to."

"Celine, this is insane," she scolds me. "You are supposed to be leaving in the morning; you should be keeping your strength up, not wasting it on some ogre."

"I have to know, Alice." I am desperate for her to understand. "He used to speak of the curse. I just always thought he complained about it because he couldn't get to me. But what if, somehow, he knows something about me that I don't?"

"He couldn't," she mumbles. "He is just a beast."

"Have you ever seen an ogre like him before?" I ask her. "You have been here long enough to have seen plenty. And he talks. Why is he so different? I don't know why I have never asked myself these things before."

"I don't know," she says, unsure.

"Elizabeth used ogre blood in my curse. What if she used Brown's, and somehow, I am linked to him? I have to know, Alice."

She sighs deeply as I hold my breath. "That does make sense," she finally admits. "Okay, I will help you, but I am not leaving you alone with him."

"Thank you," I say with a warm smile. "I am feeling better now. Please come with me to the back wall."

She helps me stand, but I walk on my own, not wanting to cause alarm with the other nuns around.

Lindon is already waiting when we arrive. When he sees me, I watch his smile turn into worry, and he steps in front of us and pulls me into his arms. "What is wrong with you? You look pale."

"She bled herself to give Brown an offering," Alice answers for me. "She hopes to gain some answers as to why he is here."

Lindon hisses as he looks me over. "I'm sorry, Lindon. I need to know why he is here. It never occurred to me before that he might be different for a reason." His gaze is unwavering. I sigh deeply and implore him to understand. "My sister might have done something to him."

His eyes soften and he breathes deeply. "If Brier finds out about this, he is going to be mad. Look at you—you're weak. How are you even going to have the strength to leave tonight?"

"I am feeling better, and I will eat plenty tonight to gain my strength. The nuns are throwing me a party."

"Celine!" Alice exclaims. "You're not supposed to know about that."

"I will act surprised," I assure her.

Lindon interrupts us. "Right now, we need to get you perched on the wall so you can call him. Brier and Tate have already left."

I nod at him and point to a small shed. "There is a ladder over there."

He goes for it and props it against the wall. "Alice, do you mind sitting with her up there? I would do it, but I need to stay hidden."

Alice nods, stepping to the ladder and climbing up it. Once she is at the top, I step up to climb as well.

"I'm staying with you until you're settled on top, and I know you're not going to fall over," he says, pressing into me from behind. I shiver at the contact of him. This feels intimate for sure.

I say nothing as I climb, but as I do, my body shifts against his. He groans close to my ear, and my heart beats faster, making me feel dizzy again, and I have to stop for a minute.

Lindon presses into me, holding me in place as he whispers in my ear, "You feel a little too good to me like this, my Cherry. If you knew what I was thinking, you might push me off this ladder."

His breath on my skin is playing havoc on me, and I am sure I would push him off. But I need to focus on what I am doing and say, "Lindon, please don't breathe on me so."

"Get your sweet ass up this ladder before I do more than breathe on you." He presses into me where he speaks with his body, and I begin to climb, knowing our passions are becoming more potent by the second. I needed some distance from him.

He helps me over the side and makes sure I am seated well beside Alice before he moves down. I take a few minutes to breathe in a few times and shake the dizziness and the pleasures of Lindon from my head. Alice tears the hem of my skirt and ties a tighter bandage around my wrist.

The sun is getting low in the west in front of us. I can already see the stars coming out over the tree lines. A breeze is blowing in from the south, making me think our days are about to turn hot. Already it is warm enough to bring the bugs out in record numbers. The lightning bugs are always lovely to watch.

"Brown, I know you're out there," I shout across the forest. "I have something for you. Come to me, Brown, or I will take my gifts and go."

I hear him roar in the distance and know he hears me. I shiver at the loud sound and the power in it. It is a sign that he is coming to me.

I don't call again and wait, keeping my eyes open for him. I don't want him to get too close. A few minutes pass, and I see him moving fast in the woods toward me. Alice and I scurry back from the edge as he gets closer.

Summoning my courage, I watch Brown walking tall and proud, unlike most other ogres. Even though his large muscles push on his shoulders and neck, where others of his kind hunch over from them, he stands erect. His stomach is also toned, whereas most of his kind have enormous bellies. He slows as he walks up to the side of the wall, his head reaching over half its height.

"I hunting," he says in a growl. Once he is standing below me and looking up, he says, "Need kill."

"Oh, I'm sorry I disturbed your breakfast," I say, smiling awkwardly at him. It is early evening time, but I know he had to have come from sleep. He always seems up before nightfall and, unlike the others, doesn't mind the day or the sun. "I felt it only fitting that I saw you today."

He growls at me again. Ogres don't talk, but Brown can even though it is not much. I am prepared for his brief answers. I will have to be on my guard with them because they are often spoken in riddles as well.

"It came to me today that I have been here five years now," I tell him, not sure if it has been that long, but close to it. "I brought you a nutritious breakfast which I think you will enjoy."

I throw down one of the pouches, and he catches it. He shakes his head, though, and says, "No. Longer."

"No, it has been five years," I tell him again. He seems confused for a moment. Maybe time is different for him.

"No," he says gruffly, staring hard at me. I can tell my words anger him.

"Just drink it! I have another for you if you are a good ogre and answer a few questions for me." It may be his last meal, but I can't tell him that.

He huffs at me, turning his nose up. "What you want?"

"Are you not going to try my gift?" I ask him. He looks down at the pouch in his hands and raises it to his mouth, where his sharp saber teeth stand out and rip the top of it off. I see his surprise as he tastes my blood and watch as he closes his eyes and drinks it down.

When it is gone, he throws the canister away and turns back to look up at me. "Good."

"So, you enjoyed it, then?" I say, sighing. "I am not so pleased to know that."

"Yes, but want…" he says with a pained look. "… you come."

"I will consider it if you answer a question or two for me. I have more of my blood if you do."

"Yes." He nods, stepping closer to the wall. I inch back. He sees my movements and stops.

"Were you cursed to be here?" I ask him, trying to speak simply.

"No. Yes," he tells me. Okay, this isn't going so well. He looks like he thinks he is helping at least.

"Were you cursed?" I ask, shortening it more for him.

"Yes," he says, looking annoyed to be asked twice.

"Because of me?" I ask him then.

"Yes," he says, reshuffling his feet.

So, it is true. He is trapped, just like me. It had to have been my sister. Why would she curse such a creature?

"If I escape, will you follow me?"

"Yes. Always," he says, and his answer assures me I am doomed as long as he is alive.

"How were you cursed?" I ask him, not sure if he can tell me that.

"Your blood," he says, like I should have already known that. Maybe I should have. I know little about curses. Nothing was like that here in such a holy place.

"My blood," he says out of nowhere. "Both."

"How were you cursed with my blood?" I ask, confused.

"You come," he says, smiling at me now. "Show you."

"I can't," I tell him, but I am curious about what he is thinking. "Why?"

"You free," he growls at me. "I free. You come!"

"I am afraid," I admit to him. I am unsure why he wants me to come. I have always thought it was so he could eat me, but now I'm not so sure. "Where?"

"To him," he says. "Curse keeps him."

"You mean you want to take me to someone?" I ask, thinking I am starting to understand this ogre for the first time. He doesn't want to eat me; he has been here trying to collect me. "Who is this man?"

He is silent for a long time. "Lee."

"His name is Lee?" I ask. He shakes his head, looking down.

"Want you."

"Why does he want me?" I have no idea who this Lee is. It is a common name, but I know no one by it personally.

He doesn't answer. Instead, he just stands there, waiting for my next question. I have a hundred questions, but I know he can't answer them. It is hard for him to explain just simple ones.

"Why doesn't he come for me?" I ask him then. "He is a man, right? He could just walk in here."

"Yes, but can't," he tells me. "Curse."

"What does he need me for?" I ask, trying to understand.

He tries to speak but can't seem to form the words. Instead, he makes a sign with his hands, raising them and down opposite of each other before leveling them off. I get the impression he is trying to say, "a balance."

"He needs a balance?" I need to make sure. When Brown nods his head, I know I hit the mark. "From what?"

"Fire," he tells me with a grunt.

"He is a Fire Element?" I ask, thinking that is what he is trying to say.

"Yes…more," he tells me.

So, he must be a compelling Fire Element, but I still understand very little of what Brown is telling me.

"Why did he send you and not others?" I ask him. "You can't even reach me trapped in here as I am."

He growls at me and doesn't answer the question. I have a feeling he isn't going to, even if he could.

"Thank you, Brown," I say, smiling at him as he stares at me again. I toss the other canister down to him. "I will consider going with you."

"Yes," he says, his eyes widening and something of a smile playing around his grotesque lips. "Please…come."

"I will consider, but you must promise me one thing." I pause to give weight to this last request. "Do not attack this place again."

"You come, I won't," he promises me with another growl.

"I'm sorry you were cursed because of me," I say sadly. "Was it Elizabeth?"

He doesn't have time to answer as Brier and Tate come charging in. Brier with his sword held high and Tate, not as a man, but as a big grizzly bear.

Chapter Thirteen
BRIER

What the hell is she giving him? I am too far away to hear what they are saying to each other, and I don't understand why the little nun is sitting beside her, either. Earlier, when Alice was showing me this place, and I was making plans on how to attack, she was full of questions, which usually annoys me, but it didn't so much from her. At least they were questions concerning the princess, and she was giving me more information than actually asking.

The princess and this nun did seem close as I had watched them earlier laughing. There is something about the princess that sends some spark through my broken powers. I don't like it, knowing that if I use them, only bad things happen. But I haven't had this pulling in my Element for so long, and to have it suddenly makes me concerned.

I just need to get the princess to Clearwater, and then I can go back to my duties. Sure, I will have to see her sometimes, but I am sure I can overcome whatever this feeling I am having right now. I will just push it down and bury it under all the others.

Right now, I need to focus on this ogre in front of me. The princess was right when she said he was different from the others. His color is browner but it is the way he stands and the muscles that are all over his body that cause me concern. Most ogres slump forward, and though they are all large, none stand straight or have bodies that are outlined in muscles. No, most are just fat beasts who grunt and use their arms to help support their upper bodies as they walk. This beast is something else, and the princess is even now talking to him. Something else ogres do not do.

I move closer behind some bushes as I look to Tate, moving in on the other side of the compound. He is black and stays close to the wall and blends in with the dark gray stones. A grizzly maybe half the size of the ogre, I hope he will be powerful enough to keep him distracted for me. All I need to do is land one blow down between the shoulder blades of the beast's back, and then I will have stunned him long enough to plunge my blade into his heart. With the look of those muscles on his back, I am sure I will need to use all the force I can give. No telling how tough his skin is.

One more bush and I am in place. I can hear the princess speaking with him now, and I can listen to him telling her to come with him. I motion for Tate to make his move, and he starts running toward the beast now. The ogre turns to him, and as he steps back, I come out from behind him and also charge. He does not see me as he is focusing on Tate's grizzly form.

The ogre roars and takes off, charging Tate also, and I am just behind him as the ground trembles from the two of them running toward each other. I see Lindon from the corner of my eye running along the top of the wall with his sword raised.

The ogre swings his mighty arms back and forth, and I know he is going to hit Tate with his massive fist, but Tate doesn't turn as he still picks up speed as he charges.

I run faster, knowing I am losing ground behind the gigantic beasts and I need the element of surprise. The ogre swings at Tate, and the huge grizzly goes flying in the air out into the field. The ogre turns to watch Tate in case he attacks again, and Lindon goes flying in the air onto his massive shoulders. Brown steps forward in surprise as he reaches behind him and pulls Lindon up with one massive fist and slings Lindon over his shoulder on the ground in front of him. The ogre roars down at him as he brings up his leg, intending to smash Lindon into the ground.

I leap onto his back then, and the ogre spins us around as he reaches for me. Just then, Tate rams him into his side, and we all go flying into the wall as Tate latches onto his meaty arm with his teeth. The ogre slings his arm around, slamming Tate into the wall then, and the force of it makes him let go.

Lindon goes on the attack, swinging his sword at the beast, barely cutting into his arms. As I get back to my feet, I leap into the air and kick off the wall, coming up high over the ogre and bringing my blade down into his back. It propels into his back on target but only goes in about halfway. My sword is now stuck in his back, but it at least stuns him and brings the ogre to his knees as I try to pull it out so I can ram it into his heart.

"Do it, Lindon!" I shout, knowing we don't have much time, and he has the advantage standing in front. Lindon pushes his blade toward the beast but the ogre blocks it in the last second. Suddenly, the ogre rolls with me still on his back, and I fall to the ground under him, and his weight stuns me. I watch as he stands up and pulls the blade out of his back and holds my sword in his massive hands. Something I have never seen an ogre do before and realize he is now armed and seems to know how to use the damn thing.

Lindon leaps over Tate and kicks the ogre in the head, but the ogre is fast and plucks Lindon from the air and tosses him outward.

Tate leaps onto him from behind, and they both tumble on the ground. With pure luck, the beast loses his grip on the sword as he blocks Tate, who is going for his throat with his teeth. I pick the blade up, watching the two as they fight and roll together, knowing I have to get the advantage. The ogre is so much more powerful than Tate, even in his grizzly form. He punches Tate in the side, and I hear Tate's grizzly whine in pain.

I see the chance as the ogre pins Tate under him and leap onto his back again. I plunge the sword into his back again in the same place before, and it goes deeper this time, stunning the ogre once more. He falls off Tate onto his back, and without a second thought, I leap over him and plunge my blade into his heart.

A burst of light flashes in my eyes, and I feel myself being propelled backward. I am standing behind the ogre once more as he knocks Tate viciously into the open field. Time has seemed to rewind, and the beast turns to me before I can leap onto his back this time. He looks at me, touching his chest, and then glances down at it like he is looking for my blade to be there.

"What the hell?" I hiss, not sure what just happened. Why in the Gods are we back to this point?

The ogre turns to me instead of charging Tate this time and roars as he steps back, and I don't advance on him. Something just happened, and he seems to know it too. I killed him, but time seems to have reset.

Tate is charging him again, and Lindon is climbing over the wall, about to jump off on the ogre. The ogre turns to him, seeing Lindon, who has stopped and is watching us, but Tate is still barreling down on us at full speed. I hold up my hand and shout, "No, Tate!"

Tate stops only a few feet away and blasts his own roar at the ogre. The ogre looks at me and speaks, "No, die."

Is it possible we can't kill him? What makes him so unique that he is not like his counterparts, and that I have just killed him once, and he is right back where we started before? "I will kill you."

He shakes his head at me and backs away from the wall. "Go."

I step back as he does, but Tate isn't having any of it. He roars and rears up, swinging his massive paws at the ogre almost the same height as him now. He slashes at the ogre's chest, cutting deeply before the ogre swings his giant fist and sends Tate into the wall. Lindon jumps down beside him as the princess and nuns call out at the top of the wall still.

The ogre looks at me one more time before he takes off at a run for the woods. Tate gets up, ready to follow, and I step in front of him. "No, Tate. We can't kill him."

Tate growls at me and looks over me at the ogre running into the woods before light comes around him, and he changes into human form.

"What the hell, Brier?" he shouts at me as he grabs his middle and hunches over. I can see that he is hurt as he wenches from the pain. Blood seeps from his lips.

"He won't die," I tell him, not sure if he knows what just happened. "Don't you recall what happened before?"

"Before what?" he asks me, looking at me, pissed off. "You were supposed to attack him from behind. Why didn't you?"

"Yea, Brier." Lindon joins him, looking for answers. "Why didn't we follow the plan?"

"We did the first time," I tell them, looking from one to the other. "Didn't time reset for either of you?"

"What the hell are you talking about?" Tate steps toward me, still holding his middle.

"I killed him." I try to make my voice sound commanding, though I'm still not sure what happened myself. "We all fought, and I killed him as we had planned, but then…a light flashed, and time reset to right before. Even the ogre seemed to know what happened."

"What are you saying?" Lindon asks, not believing me.

"I'm saying I don't think we can kill him."

Tate breathes deeply and winces in pain again. "Then what are we to do? How are we going to get Celine out of here if we can't kill him?"

I don't know. We just bested the beast and yet somehow, I seem to be the only one to recall it. The ogre did too from what I could tell but nothing explains why time restarted from the beginning.

"Tate. Are you okay?" Celine calls down from the wall, and I look up, seeing her worried look over Tate being hurt.

"I'm fine, Celine," Tate calls up to her as he tries to stand up straight. He walks closer to me and says, "I think he cracked one of my ribs. I will be fine; I heal fast enough from small injuries. I'm lucky it isn't more, or else I would need an anchor to help me."

At least that is good. I know I couldn't be an anchor for Tate, and Lindon was a Wind Element, so he couldn't, either. He denies his powers anyway. Only another Water Element who has healing powers or another Earth Element could be an anchor for him to heal.

"Let us get inside and bandage you up," I tell him as I offer a hand to help him, but he refuses. "Lindon and I will do some tracking tonight while you heal. If the coast is clear, you think you will be ready to leave tonight?"

"I will be fine," Tate assures me as we walk. "A few hours to rest, and a tight bandage should get me through."

I count us all lucky in the second round it was only one of us hurt. The battle we just fought with that ogre almost took us all down. If I had killed him, most likely, it would have still been days before we are were well enough to travel.

Chapter Fourteen
CELINE

"Oh, Tate!" I exclaim as they come back into the front gate and run to him. I saw Brown toss him like he was nothing even as a massive grizzly into the wall and felt the vibrations in my heart. "You're hurt."

"I will be fine," he says, giving me a soft smile even though I know he is in pain. I feel a little faint still myself, but my concern is directed at him now.

"Don't sugar coat it, Tate. I saw you get hit." I scold him more as we all walked to the little hut off to the side where the men are staying. "Alice went for a medical bag. She will join us shortly. I want to see your side."

"I just need a tight bandage is all as I am a little bruised." He is still holding his side even as he says this, putting on a strong front, but I can see him wince as he walks. Most likely, he has a broken rib. If anything happens to him, I don't know what I would do.

Inside, I make him sit in one chair and reach for the buttons on his shirt. Lindon eases into one of the other chairs, and Brier unloads his weapons on a table and crashes on the long chair.

I push the shirt off Tate's shoulders, and he winces, helping me. Seeing him suddenly bare-chested in front of me sends a thrill down my spine. Gods, look at all these muscles. What appeal lays under his shirt. I can't help but touch his shoulder, letting my hand run across it and down his chest. He sucks in a breath with my touch, and I think it is a pain and glance up into his eyes. It isn't pain I see as my hands slide down his chest.

"I brought the medical kit!" Alice says as she bursts inside and looks around. I step back and to Alice, taking the bag and setting it on the table in front of Tate, looking for a large bandage to bound his ribs. I can see the outline of a bruise appearing on his right side. I know Earth Elements can heal quickly unless it is serious. Hopefully, this isn't, and he will be okay, maybe by tomorrow.

"I hope we are still not planning on leaving tonight," I say, looking over my shoulder at Brier, who is the bossy one of the bunch. "Tate surely can't be fighting ogres now."

"Lindon and I will do some tracking tonight while Tate heals. If everything looks good, we will be leaving sometime after midnight," Brier says, and I turn to him.

"How can you even think of us leaving while Tate is hurt!"

"Celine, it's okay," Tate says, taking me by the waist and turning me to him. "I heal fast, and in a few hours, I will be fine."

"But…"

"No buts," he says, looking up at me.

"Um, I hate to butt in, but Cherry here is not at full strength, either," Lindon says, and Tate turns and looks at him.

"What do you mean?"

"She gave the ogre her blood," Lindon says, making eye contact with me.

"What?" Brier and Tate shout at the same time. I could kill Lindon for bringing this up even though I knew he would.

"I was trying to get some answers from him and also to distract him while you made your move," I say in my defense. "And I did find out Brown was cursed, and I am sure by my sister."

"Dammit, woman," Brier shouts and stamps over to me. He towers over me and I find myself leaning into the table for support. "Your blood could have made him stronger, and maybe that is why I couldn't kill him."

"Brier, back off," Tate growls as he stands up and pushes Brier away from me.

"Calm your animal spirit, Tate. I'm not going to hurt her," Brier says, stepping back from us, all the while staring at me like I did something wrong.

I have no idea what he is talking about, killing Brown. They didn't fight him; only Tate is the one who attacked him and ended up smashed against the wall. "He mentioned a man to me, someone by the name of Lee. He said I needed to go to him, and he wanted to take me."

"I don't give a damn what he said," Brier shouts. "My mission is to get you to the kingdom and to kill any ogre that stands in my way."

"But he was cursed like me!" I shout back. "What if he isn't as bad as I thought he was? What if this person, Lee, is important?"

"It is not our concern!" Brier yells. "You weaken yourself, and now Tate has been injured. We don't have time to be waiting around. Every day counts in getting you back to the kingdom if your sister is going to do as she says and break the curse on your head. Now both of you rest while Lindon and I try to clear the area as best we can of ogres because we will be leaving before dawn!"

Brier moves to the table and puts his weapons back on, and I turn to Lindon, who is now doing the same. Brier says nothing as he moves out the door, expecting Lindon to follow him. Lindon comes around the table and touches my cheek.

"Don't pay too much mind to Brier," he says softly. "He is not used to talking with ladies."

"Lindon, please be careful," I beg of him. "Brown is…still out there."

He just smiles at me and then looks to Tate. "We should be back sometime after midnight. Make sure you are both ready."

"I will," Tate tells him, and Lindon leaves us behind.

"I guess I should go too," Alice says from behind me, and I had forgotten that she was still there. "Dinner is within the hour, and don't forget about the party we are planning, Celine."

"Oh, the party." I cover my face, forgetting all about it. I am not feeling up to it, but how can I refuse after the nuns have been working all day to make it special for me? I love them so much, and it is the only chance I am going to have to tell them all goodbye. "I will be there soon, Alice. Let me get Tate bandaged up, and we will come."

"Take your time." She leans over and kisses my cheek before leaving us alone.

"You shouldn't have given him your blood," Tate says, and I can see he is angry at me for doing so.

"Please, let's not fight about it, Tate. What is done is done," I tell him and look up into his eyes. "I have to go in a while and tell my family goodbye and…"

"Hey, now. It's okay," he says, pulling me in his arms as I start to cry.

"I'm sorry. I don't know why I am crying." I wrap my arms around him, not holding him too tightly, thinking I will hurt him.

"It has been a long day for you, I am sure," Tate says, rubbing my back. "I have seen Brier make grown men cry, and you handled him remarkably well."

I pull back and wipe the tears from my eyes. I had more important things to do and didn't have time for any of that. "Let me bandage you up. Will you go with me to my going away party?"

"I will if there will be cake," he says, giving me a slight smile, and I laugh.

"I'm sure there will be." I reach for the bandage still on the table and look at Tate's chest once more. It is already a dark purple on his upper right rib cage. "Are you in much pain? There is something in the bag if you like."

"No, I don't need to take anything." He shakes his head. "I need to keep my senses sharp for tonight."

I nod my head and begin to wrap the bandage around his middle. "Is this too tight?"

"A little tighter," he tells me as he stands there and lets me wrap him up.

"Your bear was…magnificent," I say after a few.

"My wolf is my favorite creature." He winces as I tie off the bandage. I smooth my hands over it once I am done, looking at it instead of at him.

"When I saw you hit the wall…I almost tumbled off it wanting to get to you," I tell him shyly. "If Alice wasn't holding me back, I think I would have."

His hand comes up and caresses my cheek, but I still don't look up and into his face. "I don't know what I will do if something happens to you. I didn't realize how much…I still love you."

"Oh, Celine." He wraps an arm around me and pulls me close, and I let my arms go around his shoulders and hold him tightly. "I feel the same way. I tried for so long to let you go, thinking you were dead. I think my animal spirits always knew you were alive and wouldn't let me forget."

My heart is overflowing with emotions, being with him again. The things we did in our passionate embrace earlier, and the sensual feeling coursing through and pumping in my veins to my heart, is earth-shattering and new. I don't recall this overload on my senses when we were younger, and it is frightening.

Some of these emotions must be coming from the sacrifice. The connection I felt with Lindon earlier also had been startling, but he is seductive by nature. Brier, on the other hand, seems to have some resistance, but I feel oddly safe knowing he is in command.

The attraction with Tate is so much stronger, though. He has been my heart's desire all these years, and now he is standing in front of me. The Elementals have granted me my request. That there will be love among us.

"I was coming to that night. I was going to ask you to run away with me." I look up into his face.

"I waited for you." His hand runs down my neck. "I would have taken you anywhere. I know what she was doing to you, and I couldn't stand it any longer."

"No one could," I tell him, shaking my head. "Even Phillip, her own husband, couldn't make her stop."

"You said yes to me then," he says, cupping my face, and the sparks of life are in his eyes as I look into them. He swallows hard, and I shudder, knowing what he is going to ask me. "Will you say yes to me now?"

"Yes," I breathe with a sob. "You know my answer is yes."

His lips gently take mine, and I press into him as he pulls me close. As kids, this moment had been sweet and enduring, so innocent. Now we are older and have both tasted real passion for the first time with one another. The splendor and joy are exciting and new. Sharing them with Tate makes it that much more beautiful and soul connecting.

When his tongue slips inside my mouth, and I wrap mine around his, I moan as he sucks it gently. His fingers press into my hips as he steps into me, making me step back until I feel my backside press into the table. His hands slide up my side, and he lifts me slowly until I am sitting on the edge. Instincts tell me to open for him, and he presses in between my thighs.

I gasp at feeling him like this again. His kiss turns firmer as I run my hands down his chest and remember his wound. "Tate, your injury."

"What injury?" he asks close to my lips and steals a kiss. I don't feel the ground quake with this kiss, but it does bring a glow to his eyes, and the pupils no longer look human or Element but more animal.

"Your eyes," I say between kisses, trembles running through me, recognizing the change in him. He pulls away from my lips and buries his face in my neck, and I feel his teeth scrape against my shoulder.

"My other half." His voice is more like a growl as he speaks so huskily, it makes me shiver in delight.

The animal sides. I have read much on Tate's powers and know he can change into just about any kind of animal. Today, I saw the bear, but he mentions he is closest to the wolf. How much power do they have over him?

He backs away from me, pulling me off the table and back on my feet. "Why don't you bind me, and we will head to that party? Being alone with you, I'm afraid it is a little difficult to keep my hands to myself."

He is blushing as he pulls away, and I find it adorable. I can't help but feel a little flush myself at the idea of his animal. In the books, I have read that Earth Elements mate with partners for life because their animals unite. I wonder if it will be that way for us since I am not like him.

"Be prepared." I take his hand, knowing that when the time comes for us to be together, I will answer his call. Instead, I change the subject. "The nuns are big huggers."

And we walk out the door.

Chapter Fifteen
CELINE

It is well past midnight, and they haven't returned yet. Tate left me, going to look for them several hours ago. I watched as he changed into a wolf, saying he could track them better and move faster. He promised me he was healed and would be fine, but I still didn't want to let him go.

Dinner had been wonderful with the nuns, and I sang songs with them after eating as others cleaned up. Mother Frances told me I was always welcome to return anytime I liked, and they all prayed for me and safe passage home.

The moon is starting to lower in the sky as dawn will be coming in a few more hours. It shines down its luminous light on the dark earth, helped by millions of stars now starting to fade. Only a few torches are still burning in the courtyard for us, but nothing else is moving.

I have been waiting by the gatehouse almost all night to make sure it is opened when they return. The hours tick by, and still, they are not here. *What is keeping them? Are they okay? Is Brown dead?* I have heard nothing from him, and he would have roared if he had killed something or someone.

Alice brought me a blanket a little while ago, along with some hot chocolate. She sat quietly on the bench with me for the last hour as I paced in front of the gate.

"What is taking them so long?" I exclaim, breaking the silence in my frustration. "They should be back by now!"

Alice says nothing, and that makes me even more nervous.

"You could say something, Alice. Tell me I am overreacting, that this was their plan, that everything will be okay. Something!"

"You need to relax," she says finally, jumping up and giving me a shake. "They have done this plenty of times. They know what they are doing."

"I know." She leads me back to the bench to sit down. "It's just… they said they would be back and rest, and then we would leave first thing in the morning. Well, daylight is just a few hours away now!"

"Why don't you lie down and try to rest?" she suggests, patting the bench beside her.

"I can't," I tell her. Brown is strong and smart. What if something happens to one of them? I have to know they are all okay.

She takes my hand and grips it. "Just breathe, Celine. You need to calm down."

I take several breaths and try to relax, but it isn't easy. Alice hums, and I lay my head down in her lap. My mind wanders over the day with the men once again. Each moment plays over in my head. It is calming me, and, after a while, I do rest.

Kissing Tate, laughing with Lindon, and even fighting with Brier is filling me with light dreams. Lying in Tate's arms after dinner had felt so natural, and this calming sense of peace came over me, like I was where I belonged. I tried to bring up the others and my connection with them, but Tate fell asleep. When we were young, and he asked me to marry him, he knew that one day, I would have to marry a Water Element for the kingdom's crown. He had been upset about it but came around, knowing he had to accept it if we were ever to be together. I needed to know how he felt about it still, and that I would be taking a Wind Element now also.

I wouldn't be able to take the crown with this curse still on me. Tate says Elizabeth wants to lift it, but it makes me mad that she does now after all these years. After I have given myself to the Elementals to break it myself. I wonder why she wants to end it now, and if she really is sincere with it. She has caused me so much pain, and I can't see why she would want to do anything nice for me now.

Alice shifts under me just before she says, "Celine, I see them."

Instantly, I am up and looking over the wall as she pulls the wheel to open the gate. I look over the clearing and see two figures break from the woods. Not wasting a second, I jump down as the door opens just wide enough for them to come in.

Both are short of breath, but I give no time for them to recover as I leap into Tate's arms.

"Never stay gone from me like that again," I demand from him as I hold him close.

"I won't," he says, burying his face in my hair. He doesn't linger as he pulls back and looks down at me. "Celine, it is time for us to go. Are you ready?"

"Yes, I am ready," I say, a little breathless. I look to Lindon, scanning him to be sure he is safe and whole. Then I realize Brier is missing. "Where is Brier? Oh my God, did something happen to him?"

"Brier is fine," Lindon says, stepping up beside us. "He is tracking Brown. The ogre has been leading us on a wild goose chase most of the night. Brier is staying on Brown so we can make a run for it with you."

Tate tells me, "I need you to go for your things right now. Brier is to meet us down by the river. We have to get there as fast as we can."

I don't know what to think about this turn of events. Brier is alone, tracking Brown, and we are leaving hours earlier than expected. As soon as I step foot outside these walls, he will know and come for me, along with countless other ogres. It is still night, giving them the advantage.

I need to have faith that they know what is best. Whatever they had planned before, for some reason, they gave up on it. Something must have changed their plans like this. I don't think Brier is the kind of person who would be careless with his goals. This has to be dangerous.

I grab my two small bags on the bench and turn to Alice, hugging her. "I will not say goodbye because I know, somehow, we will meet again. You are my true sister, and I will always love you."

"I love you, too. And yes, we will meet again," she says, pulling back from me. "Be brave, my sister, and go. You must hurry."

I nod and kiss her cheek before taking Tate's hand. He leads me toward the gate. Just before passing through the door, I stop. I am finally leaving after all these years. Stepping over this threshold will be the beginning of a new life. Everything is about to change.

"Celine?" Tate calls to me, urging me on.

I look at him, a sharp concern hitting my heart suddenly. Will he still see me, or will I become a monster before him? I think I am more scared of this moment than the ogres that are sure to come for me.

"Celine, we have to go," he says, pulling my hand gently.

I look into his eyes and step forward and out from behind the wall. I hold my breath as I look at him in question. I feel no different from before, but am I?

"Tate?" Loud roars come from the distance, and I jump. *How many are out there in the woods?*

"It will be fine, Celine. None are too close," he assures me. "We will protect you."

"Am I different?" My voice is small, even to my own ears, but I need to know.

"No, you're just as beautiful as ever," he says softly, touching my face. "Now, come. We have to get to the river soon."

I take his hand, and all three of us sprint across the small clearing and into the woods. Lindon takes the lead, me following him as Tate takes the flank. I try to keep up with Lindon's pace. I'm doing good except for a few stumbles here and there. Tate helps me up each time, and we hasten.

I don't know how long they intend to keep this pace, but I know I can run a while longer. I have prepared for this in case I ever had to escape. At the convent, I often ran for hours, a habit I had started not long after arriving. I ran around the nunnery repeatedly, always planning my escape. But I had never tried once since Brown had arrived.

It was during that first year that I discovered Brown sometimes ran with me on the other side. Those were when I heard his rants. He had always been so strange, doing things like that. Every time I got close to the walls, he was always there.

An ear-splitting roar breaks the silence and some quieter ones respond. I wonder if one of those roars is his. *Is Brier okay? Will we be okay?*

We are running for some time still when Lindon comes to a stop ahead and is waiting for us. I stop a few feet away from him and Tate does, too.

"How are you... Cherry?" Lindon asks, breathing a little hard but still looking around at our surroundings. Tate is skimming the area, too.

"I'm... fine," I say, taking in the brief break to breathe in what air I can.

A roar sounds out in the distance again, only one this time. It is close. I don't know how close, but closer than when we left. I can tell.

"Tate, over the rise," Lindon says, pointing.

"I know," Tate says, unsheathing his sword. "Keep the lead."

"Stay behind us, Cherry," Lindon says and then takes off in the direction he pointed.

Tate gestures me forward. Lindon is far ahead of us now, and I can see he has been running slower for me all this time. I am holding them up.

Lindon goes over the top of the rise, and I follow a few seconds later. The roar is so loud from the other side that I stumble. Lindon has just attacked it.

Tate pulls me up in his arms and to the top where he pushes me against a tree.

"Stay here!" he says and dashes forward past the trees. I look around and see Lindon duck from a massive blow.

Tate is a few yards away, his sword raised for the attack, leaping into the middle of it. His blade pierces the beast's giant arm just as the creature swings around. Tate's body flies through the air. I gasp at the brutality as Tate crashes to the ground. He kicks his legs up and in a flash is on his feet again, charging back into the fray.

Lindon is dodging punches left and right, his sword striking the beast's middle several times, a few blows landing their marks. He moves so fast, keeping the ogre constantly turning and looking for him.

Tate waits a second before jumping back in, and I see he is going for the back of the beast's neck. Lindon must be working to distract him while Tate lands the kill.

His aim is excellent as he sends the sword right through the thick muscles of the beast's neck. He falls forward, and Lindon leaps out of the way, sliding on his knees. He thrusts his blade into the beast's chest and pulls it out. The creature slams into the ground and doesn't move again.

They killed him in just a few minutes, much faster than I thought it would take to kill an ogre. I come around the tree and run the short distance to them.

"That was amazing," I say, standing close to Tate. "You both made it almost look easy. I don't remember it being that way for the other warriors who brought me here."

"I'm a hunter, love," Tate says, smiling at me. "Brier is the commanding warrior."

"But Lindon isn't," I say, moving to him now.

"I am the master of distraction and the champion fighter," he says with a swagger. "But we don't have time for chit chat, Cherry. One is easy, two not so much, and there are plenty in the area."

"He's right. We must move," Tate agrees. "I'm going to shift, and I want you to climb on, Celine. We need to pick up our speed."

I nod, and he steps back, turning into the bear he was before. Lindon picks me up and sits me on top of him before taking off and Tate follows behind. We are moving much faster now as the trees become a blur and the cool wind rushes over me.

Several roars surround us in all directions and I know they are about to battle again, and this time with more than one.

Chapter Sixteen

The strength I see coming from Tate as he battles with the ogres throughout the night is unbelievable. He is just as strong as the ogres, stunning them with the force of his jabs and kicks. He slams them down on the ground, and Lindon jumps in as fast as lightning and impales them with his blade.

But four ogres are on us now. Tate had just taken down the first and two others are charging both of them. Tate leaves Lindon with the one down and charges full force at them.

He reaches out a hand, and one ogre goes down before he even reaches Tate. I see the ogre struggle with vines around his legs while Tate collides into the second beast.

I turn my head to the left and see Lindon with the fourth, dodging his blows and taking aim, slicing through the ogre's thick skin. It is hard to do any actual damage unless he can plunge his sword through the beast.

One thing Lindon has on his side is speed. I see that part of his Element in him even if he doesn't. He dodges a huge flying fist, slipping under it and moving behind the ogre. He leaps into the air and kicks off a tree, turning in midair. With a battle cry, he slams his sword into the ogre's neck.

Knowing that he is safe, I search for Tate and see two of the mighty ogres slam their meaty fists into Tate's ribs, sending him flying twenty feet. Tate struggles to stand just as they both leap in the air toward him. As one ogre pulls his fist back, about to punch Tate, I step from behind a tree and scream as loudly as I can.

Both ogres stop and look at me. I glance toward Lindon, who is pulling his sword from the heart of the third ogre before I take off in a run through the thick woods.

The two ogres roar and follow me. I can hear the pounding of their enormous feet on the ground. I leap over a fallen log, still running as fast as I can, hoping the others will save me before the ogres catch up.

Suddenly, the ground shakes with a painful roar. I turn to see both ogres on the ground, one on top of the other. Lindon leaps over the top of the massive pile and thrusts his sword into the back of the top ogre. The other ogre gains his position and swipes at Lindon, knocking him off several feet away.

The ogre pushes the other off of him and moves toward Lindon. Lindon stands, holding his sword ready for him.

"Ready to die, beast?" Lindon snarls, a wicked grin on his face that makes me shiver.

The ogre roars, charging Lindon as he stands his ground, waiting for the ogre to get closer. He leaps to the side, slashing his blade out and into the ogre's stomach. The ogre falls forward, and Lindon jumps on his back. Just as the beast tries to get up, Lindon plunges his sword into its neck.

When the beast falls, he turns the ogre over, thrusting the sword into his heart. Then he walks over to the other and does the same. Lindon seems to almost glow from the glory of his two kills as he looks at me and offers his hand. I am stunned by his masculine beauty.

"Come, Cherry." He grins at me like we are just out for a stroll in the woods. I take his hand, and we go back the way we came.

"What was it that you fought to become a champion?" I ask him as we hurry back to Tate.

"Just about anything they put in the ring with me, but mostly men," he says, leading me through the bush. "I went through a rough patch and had nothing to lose."

There is so much I don't know about him yet. It is thrilling and electrifying that I am discovering him all fresh and new. With Tate, I feel I already know him, and things feel natural. Lindon is sparking a new light inside me, and like a moth, I am drawn to him.

It is nearing sunrise now; the sky is becoming lighter. Rays of light are beginning to break through the trees, and it is easier to see in the distance. We meet back up with Tate just a mile away. He is holding his side and takes to his knees when he sees us. I run to him, but I am careful not to touch or cause him more pain.

"Tate, are you hurt badly?" I ask him as I run my hand down his arm.

"That last hit, I think busted up my bruised ribs." He looks at me. "Undo this binding and wrap it as tightly as you can."

I hurriedly unbind him, and he groans as I start to wrap him again.

"We need to keep moving," Lindon says, walking around us and looking all around. "I can smell the fowl creatures close to us."

"How much farther?" I ask him as Tate winces in pain. He can't go on much more; nor can I.

"Twenty minutes," Lindon says, looking at him with concern. "Tate?"

"Take her on," Tate tells Lindon, grimacing in pain. "Get to the boat before the others reach you."

Lindon looks uncertain, and then he surveys our surroundings. It has only been a few minutes since we last heard a roar. The damn things just keep coming.

"No," I say, shaking my head at Tate. "I will not go without you."

"They follow you, not me," he reminds me, looking at us both. "It will be safer for all of us the sooner you get to the boat and in the water."

"He's right," Lindon says. "The ogres will leave him alone to track us."

"But he's hurt," I say, looking at Lindon. "We can't just leave him out here."

"I will catch up," Tate says, taking my hand and looking at me. "Just go, love. I promise it won't be long. I will be right behind you and will always come for you."

We had left Brier behind and now Tate. I'm not so sure how well this plan is going for us. Still, I put my faith in them and agree. I have to believe the ogres will come for me anyway and leave him alone.

Tate looks back at Lindon. "Get to the water and get off the bank. I will catch you down by the river if need be."

"If Brier is there, one of us will come back for you," Lindon promises him.

"Only if Brier is there. Do you understand?" Tate stresses to him. He turns to me again. "Just a little farther, my love, and you will be safe."

I lean over and kiss him softly on the lips. He caresses my cheek as he kisses me back with more urgency.

"Sorry to be the one to say this, but we don't have time for kisses," Lindon says, drawing our attention.

I pull back from the kiss and look at Tate once more. "Stay safe."

I hear another roar in the distance; I no longer jump at the sound. I know what it means; they are getting closer.

"You need to go," he says, urging me to my feet. "I'm right behind you."

Lindon takes my hand, though I still stare down at Tate, unsure of what I should do. "Come, Cherry."

I follow him as he tugs me, and we run together as another roar sounds in the opposite direction. There are at least two more of them. It spurs me a little faster, not wanting Lindon to face no telling how many alone. I would be no help to him. I don't even have a weapon.

Ten minutes pass before there is another roar, much closer to our right. It sets off another cry nearby.

"The river is close," Lindon urges me. "Keep moving, Cherry."

I am moving as fast as I can, but I know it isn't going to be fast enough. The ogres are too close, and Lindon seems to realize it.

Suddenly, an ogre comes over the rise in front of us. Lindon doesn't slow us down but keeps us running toward it.

"Run sharp right when I say," he shouts at me as he draws his sword once more. I have no idea what he is planning but wait for his call. I see the ogre in my peripheral vision as it jumps down the hill and moves closer to us. He runs straight for me, but I stay on course even as my pace quickens. I run faster than I ever have out of fear because I can tell he is heading straight for me.

"Now!" he shouts behind me, and I turn, cutting sharply to the right, running as fast as I can.

The ogre sees me change direction and moves toward me. I lose sight of Lindon and don't know what he is doing, but I keep running just as he told me. The ogre is getting closer, and my panic forces me to run faster.

The ogre is so close that I can feel the air move as he sweeps his arm out from behind to grab me. When I think all is lost, Lindon explodes out of the trees and jumps on the beast, plunging his sword into the back of the monster.

I stop running as he falls. Lindon steps over him, plunging his sword once more into his heart. He then turns to me and holds his hand out.

I take it, drawing strength from his determined look. I had thought it would take them all to bring down just one ogre. I was so wrong. Each of them is as powerful as the others and can handle themselves as well as they can handle me.

"Come, Cherry," Lindon breathes. He is as tired as I am, and still, I feel him full of power. The nickname he has given me gives me a sense of calm, even though I am panting.

We are running again, but the battle is not over yet. I hear yet two more roars close by and not a river in sight. There is a rustling behind us.

"Lindon?" I call to him.

"The river is over the next rise," he says, pulling me forward. "Keep running. Get to the boat."

He lets go of my hand and turns back. I don't want to be alone, but I do as he says.

I am almost at the top of the rise when I hear him taking up the battle against the ogre. I can't help but look back to see Lindon flying in the air and ogres bearing down on his position.

Before I can decide to go to him, another roar behind me directs my attention. The river and the boat are just a few paces away. But another colossal ogre stands between me and it.

I stop in my tracks as he slams the ground with his massive hands and shakes the ground with his roar before charging me. I take off to the right, away from all of them. I don't want to run to Lindon and have him fighting two of the massive and dangerous beasts.

I feel the earth tremble again as he comes closer. I had thought ogres were supposed to be slow, but they are not. Their legs are long, and they leap forward more than run. He is making quick work of the distance between us, but I keep running.

I am running along the top of a small hillside that is getting thinner by the second. I can see the river has a bend in front of me, and I am getting closer to it if I could just make it into the water.

There is a vast slope coming up, and the drop off is huge. But I have nowhere to go, and I can't stop.

I feel the ogre's hand slide through my hair. I am preparing myself to leap in the air over the side, hoping I can make it. In the next instant, his massive fist hits me, and my feet leave the ground. I hit the ground hard and roll down the hill and onto the small riverbank below.

I land in two inches of water, and the pain of being hit stuns me for a moment. Pounding footprints close by shake me out of my haze as the beast is about to be on me. I trip over my skirt trying to get up and hear splashing in the water behind me as I launch myself into deeper waters.

When the beast roars again, I wait for my doom, but it does not come. When I don't feel his beefy hands surrounding me, I turn to see where he is and find Brier standing between me and the ogre on the edge of the water. He is here!

I stop chest-deep in the water and watch as the ogre dodges Brier's sword but Brier comes back, swiping his blade at the ogre's feet, making him crash into the water. The ogre lashes out again, and the sword goes flying on the shore but he pulls a long knife and jumps on the ogre's body as the ogre wraps his arms around Brier, squeezing. A knife appears from Brier's belt, and he plunges it repeatedly into the beast's chest multiple times. The ogre becomes still under him, and Brier climbs off and stumbles into the water as he turns to me.

I move to him, so thankful to see him. He comes to me, and I reach for him, throwing my arms around his neck. He picks me up and carries me from the water.

"Oh, Brier," I say with relief. "I'm so happy you're here."

"Just in time, I see," he says, still carrying me even though we are out of the water now. "Where are the others?"

"Lindon is close to the boat. We left Tate several miles back. He is hurt, Brier."

"I will get him," he assures me. "First, let's get you to the boat."

I relax against him, somehow knowing everything will be all right. Brier will take care of everything.

He moves swiftly with me in his arms, almost running as he carries me to the boat. There are more roars in the distance, but they are still far from us.

Lindon is visible, running through the woods. Brier calls to him, and he joins us.

"I thought I lost you there, Cherry," he says, brushing my hair back as Brier still moves us forward.

"I'm okay," I tell him, smiling a little.

"Where is Tate?" Brier asks Lindon.

"About two leagues back," Lindon tells him. "He got hit again in the same place, and I think it has broken several of his ribs."

"Get her to the boat and in the water," he directs Lindon as he offers me to him. "There are too many in the area."

"I will," Lindon assures him, but Lindon doesn't seem to have the strength to hold me and stumbles. Brier catches me before I fall.

"You're hurt, too?" he asks, looking at Lindon over my head, and I gasp. Two of my warriors wounded because of me and I didn't even realize Lindon had been hurt.

"Just my arm," he says. "You can pop it back into place later."

"I'm going for Tate," he says, helping me stand so I can walk instead. "We should be back within the hour."

Lindon agrees, and Brier leaves us several yards from the boat. He only acknowledges me with a look before taking off at a sprint.

Before I can overthink it, Lindon takes me by the arm and directs me to the boat.

"Come, Cherry. Our battle for the night is over," he tells me as he helps me into what is more like a ship than a small boat.

"But the ogres?" I ask him. I still hear them in the distance.

"The sun is rising," he tells me. "They will give up the chase and look for a place to hide from its light for the day."

"Are you sure?" I ask him again. Brown had never hidden from the light. He preferred the dark, but I saw him plenty in the daytime. I wonder what had happened with him and Brier—if he is dead now.

"I'm sure. Besides, you're on the water now, and they can't sense your presence," he says, jumping into the boat as he pushes it off the bank with a grunt. We float out from the land into the middle of the river. He throws an anchor over the side. "Let's get cleaned up before the others arrive."

Chapter Seventeen

It was a riverboat, and a lovely one at that. I have been on one before, but it has been so long. The boat itself is about fifteen feet long and ten feet wide. There are benches in the front with a friendly openness in the middle. The back has a covering over the top. Under it is a steering column with two seats. A set of stairs in the middle of the floor leads down to a living space below. At the back of the boat, I can see the tops of the massive paddle oars that will turn over when they are in power.

"Let's find something dry to put on," Lindon says, turning to me and removing his weapons. "There is some clothing below for you."

I look back to shore for the others but see nothing. "How long before Brier and Tate come?"

"They should be back within the hour." He removes his belted knives from around his waist awkwardly with one arm. "Go and find something to wear. I will give you some time."

I am tired but move down the hatch and into a small room. There is a kitchen on one side and a bed on the other. I see a little closet over one side of the bed and open it up to see several vibrantly colored dresses.

I reach for a light blue one and pull it close to my face, smelling it. I haven't worn something so pretty in such a long time. The color had faded out of everything I had long ago. All my clothing came from donations and always had to be mended or repaired. I had another dress in my bag, but I think to put this dress on instead. It is so pretty, and I want to look nice for them. It has been so long since I have been in anyone's presence besides the nuns.

I go to the small kitchen, looking to wash up first. There is a small sink, and I stifle a groan when I try the knob and fresh, clean water comes out. The convent didn't have any running water except for the kitchen sinks. Water always had to be lifted from the wells for anything else.

I pull at my wet clothing, stripping down to just my underthings and use a small cloth to wash away the grime. My hair is a mess, and I bend over the sink and wash it out as best I can.

Before putting on the dress, I look in several drawers and find some clean underwear, too. They are smaller than what I usually wear. The soft black silk is refined, and they look like they have never been worn. I bet they are Elizabeth's—if this is the royal boat. The opulence of the small living area and the beauty of the clothing makes me suspect it is.

I dress quickly and sit down on the bed. I find a brush in a small drawer next to the bed, and I luxuriate in brushing my hair.

"If you don't mind, Cherry, I would like to clean up a bit too," Lindon calls from above.

"You can come down," I call to him as I continue to brush my hair.

Lindon walks down and looks pleased with me. "You clean up well with not much to work with."

"I am so tired, Lindon." I yawn, the warmth of the cabin and the comfort of being clean again relaxes me. I slept poorly last night, and after spending the better part of dawn running for my life, I don't think I can go on much longer. "Do you mind if I just lie down here?"

"Go ahead, Cherry," he says sweetly. "I'll be quiet."

"Thank you." I crawl up on the bed and lay my head on the pillow. I close my eyes, glad for the bed and the small comfort it gives. I hear the water running in the sink and Lindon moving around, but rest with my eyes closed. That is until I hear him hiss. I open them to see him trying to pull his shirt off.

I had forgotten he was injured. Sitting up, I crawl out of bed and go to him.

"Let me help you," I say, touching his arm. He turns to me and looks down as I raise my hands to his shoulders and push the damp shirt from his body, letting it fall to the floor.

"I never thought you would undress me so soon," he says with a mischievous smile.

"You're covered in bruises," I say, ignoring his remark and focusing on his injuries. "Are you in much pain?"

"Some," he admits. "Mostly my shoulder, though. It's still out of place. Brier will put it back in soon."

I reach for the cloth in the water and lather it up with some soft soap. "Sit down in the chair, will you?"

He reaches behind him and pulls the chair closer, sitting down. I step in front of him, and he opens his legs, allowing me closer.

I run the wet cloth and soap through his hair first. It is tied back still, and I leave it that way, just getting the grime off the top, which is the dirtiest part.

He closes his eyes as some water runs over his face and down his neck. I rinse the cloth and wash that part of him next. He doesn't have a beard like Brier and Tate, and I like that. His face is smooth, which I find interesting.

I rinse the cloth once more and move behind him to wash his back. He is muscular yet lean. I run the cloth over his skin, wanting to touch it with my bare hands. I don't, knowing it is too soon to be romantic like that with him. The passion and fire are there, but not my heart just yet.

He groans as I run the cloth over a large bruise under his right shoulder blade, and I see some blood under the skin.

"You fought so bravely," I say softly as I rinse the cloth out again and move to wash his arms and hands. He opens his eyes and looks at me. "I didn't realize how strong you all are."

"I am not as strong as the others," he says with a chuckle. "But I am fast and flexible, which makes me a good fighter. I can think fast while in motion."

"Yes, you are," I say as I move to his chest. It is awkward to clean him while he sits in the chair, and he seems to realize it. He stands up in front of me. He is close, maybe a little too close, but the space inside this cabin isn't that large to begin with. I rinse the cloth again and bring it back up, running it across him there. He closes his eyes again, enjoying what I am doing, and so am I.

My eyes take him in, bruises and all, as I move to his stomach, and his breath hitches.

"Does that hurt?" I ask, trying to be gentler.

"No," he rasps and places his hand over mine on his stomach. "I think I should finish from here on. Why don't you lie down?"

"Are you sure?" I ask him, not really wanting to stop now. I swallow as I look up at him.

"I might kick myself later, but yes," he says, smiling as he takes the cloth from me. "Go rest."

I go over to the bed and crawl back in, turning away from him for privacy. I listen for a few minutes as I hear him remove the rest of his wet clothing and finish washing.

I drift off, thinking about what he must look like behind me. Did he remove all his clothing? What does a man look like unclothed? If it is anything compared to his upper body, he had to be toned with ridges of muscles down his legs. Other parts are hard to imagine as I never have been able to talk about such things with the nuns. I've seen some of their statues in books of a male form but to comment on them to nuns would have been embarrassing.

I am starting to doze off when I feel Lindon climb into the bed behind me and take me into his arms. I am wide awake again as he snuggles up to my back. I am so curious of him, I allow it and lean into his warmth, liking the feel of him surrounding me.

His arm slides under my head, bringing us flush with one another. His hurt arm rests over my middle, and I can tell from the way he lays it that he is in pain. I can smell luxurious soap all around us as we have both bathed in it. A rich rose with some kind of citrus scent mixed in.

"I love the way you smell," he whispers close to my neck. His breath on my ear makes me shiver as I feel a pulling of his seduction.

"I smell as you do," I say, stretching a little against him in a sleepy haze as I respond to his whisper and touch.

"That's what I like." His face rubs against my hair. "You smelling like me."

I can see how that may appeal to him since he has such powers over the air. It is his instinct, even if he doesn't know it yet. I'm not sure how to bring up his powers to him, but I needed to soon. I am curious if he knows of them or if he just ignores that they are there.

"We should rest," I remind him, even though I am feeling very sensual lying next to him. "The others will return soon."

"You will not allow me this moment of pleasure to have you all to myself?" he says playfully. "Or do you wish I were Tate instead?"

I turn my head, reaching back and running my fingers through his hair.

"I like that it is you well enough," I say, playing with him now. "I like your hair."

He chuckles as he presses his lower half more into me. "Only for my hair?"

"Much more than your hair," I whisper, letting my hand drop to his laying on my hip. "But I need to rest, and so do you."

"Okay, but tell me something first," he agrees, and I nod my head. "Are you interested in Tate or me?"

"Both," I say, cuddling up to him. "That's not true... I'm into you all."

"Even Brier?" he asks, his voice hitching a little. It doesn't seem to bother him that I am into him and Tate, but Brier is the surprise.

"I will tell you later," I promise him. "Then, I will show you."

"Show me what?" he asks as he rests.

"How much you mean to the realms," I say as I feel sleep wanting to take me. "Rest, Lindon."

"Yes, my Cherry," he says, and we fall asleep together. I feel him moving around later, sliding away from me, but I am so tired, I just roll where he leads. I hear voices, but I am too far gone in sleep now that I can't wake. It soon quiets down, and I rest easy.

When I awaken later, my eyes wander to the port, and I am surprised to see that there is still light outside.

Tate lies before me on his back. He is clean now, but his shirt is off, and a bandage is around his middle. I look down at him and see he has pants on, but his feet are bare. He seems to sleep soundly.

His breathing is steady and calm, and he doesn't snore. His head tilts toward me, and I take in his face. He has changed so much through the years.

At fifteen, Tate had been short, just barely taller than me, but his stature had been broad. He had no facial hair then, and I remember a dimple he had in his cheek. I always loved to watch him smile when the dimple would pop in. I like the facial hair and how he wears it. Short and neat, but thick and manly.

In many ways, he is the same. He cares about what I think and feel. I notice he can still read my moods. My needs always seem more important to him than his own. Tate has always been giving of himself in every way.

Maybe that is part of his Element. How the earth gives life. It would take someone who is a giver to be such an Element as Earth. That part of him has strengthened his Element when he calls on it. But there is the other side of his Element, too. The animal spirit side, which I know can be more dominant. I haven't seen that much of the animal side of him, and I am curious of it as I saw it in his eyes the other day.

I can't lie here all day and moon over him. I need to get up, but to do so, I will have to crawl over him. He is hurt, and I don't want to disturb him, knowing he needs the rest.

Slowly, I rise, pulling my skirt up over my knees and behind me as I scoot closer and lift a leg over his upper thighs. He is lying at the bed's edge, and I feel my body come in contact with his just as my foot hits the floor.

Tate feels it, too. His hands come down on my bare leg and rubs it against his body.

"Celine." He almost hisses my name as I look at him, but his eyes remain closed. I watch him lick his lips as his hands slide up my hips, adjusting me onto him. My center rests on his semi-hard body, and I gasp at the contact of him, but his eyes remain closed. I realize he is not awake as he doesn't move anymore, content with me just sitting on him.

Maybe he is dreaming or remembering us in the gardens. I place my hands on his, moving them away from me and back onto his stomach. He is out, and I am glad he is sleeping so well.

I sit there on top of him, and I feel a pulling force inside me. My waters are stirring, and I do not understand why. Maybe it is because I think we are bonding again, but it feels like something else. Something that wants to come out of me, to do something.

I pull myself over him and stand up by the bed, dropping my skirts around me. Before leaving, I lean over and kiss him on the forehead.

"Sleep well, my love. I will be back later to check on you," I whisper and move to the hatch, open it, and go outside to the others.

Chapter Eighteen
LINDON

"Ow!" I can't help but call out after the damn arm has been out of place for so long. It has grown numb, but now all the feeling rushes into it again as Brier pops it into place. I growl at Brier as he moves away from me and mutter, "Thanks."

"You should have let me do that when I got back," Brier says as he goes back to the steering wheel.

"Tate needed your help more," I tell him, grinding my teeth as I move the arm around. "That last one he fought was a veritable monster."

"You both did well," he says, praising us. It is a tremendous honor coming from him. "You got her here, and you're both alive."

"What happened with you and the one called Brown?" I ask him, hoping he brought him down.

Brown hadn't been easy to keep track of last night. He seemed to appear and disappear in the blink of an eye. I've never known an ogre to move so fast or be so quiet. We had lost him more than kept up, but we had felt we at least had become familiar with the area.

We even tried set a trap for him, but instead of walking into it, he ambushed us within the first half-hour, but then backed off. We tracked him and landed in several traps he had laid out for us. The night went in that pattern until Tate showed up, and we all realized he was playing with us. He had attacked several times, but it was like he wasn't trying to kill us. He was leading us farther out, and when we realized this, Brier stayed to keep him engaged while Tate and I got Celine out.

"I thought when he realized it was just me, he would turn back. But instead, he led me even farther away from the nunnery," Brier says, punching the steering wheel. "He isn't like the others, and I know you and Tate don't recall our first battle with him, but I do. I killed him, Lindon, but time started over, and he knew it too. There has to be a reason for that."

"If you say it happened, I believe you, but I don't think I can help you figure it out." I am concerned because he is still out there, and if we can't kill him, where does that leave us in this mission? "He is out there, and he will come for her."

"We need to be ready for him this time," Brier says, and I can see his mind starting to turn. "He is stronger than the others, and we don't even know if we can bring him down. One of us needs to be with her at all times. She can't be left alone."

"Should we tell her?" I ask him. It is moments like this that I am happy he is in charge. I feel like Cherry is scared to death of Brown, and I don't want her to worry, but she might need to know.

"Not yet," Brier says, turning the boat paddle on and steering the boat into the middle of the river.

"You know she can help us." Devil's advocate has always been my favorite game, and I lie back and rest on the large, cushioned bench. "I think if we listened to her earlier, we would have been more prepared for Brown."

"She told us enough. Let's leave it for now," he tells me. "I'd rather not have a panicked woman on our hands."

"Come on, Brier. Don't you think you're a little harsh?" I ask him, staring up at the clouds as they move across the sky. I always have liked watching them and the calming effect they give me. "She is sweet and kind, and she handled herself well last night. She is someone who I think would do you good."

"I'm not getting attached to her like you and Tate both seem to be," Brier says in a warning voice. "She is to be the future queen. What will she want from any of us?"

"I don't know." I won't say it aloud, but he is right. I am nothing more than a fighter myself. I have no place for someone like her. But even so, I can't help the desire I am feeling for her, and I can feel it rolling off her as well when we are near. She said she was interested in us all, and my heart leaped at the thought. I don't mind sharing her if that is what she wants.

"Besides, out of us, Tate is the one who knows her. It is clear he has been in love with her since they were children. He would be her choice, not you or me." Brier is doing an excellent job of bringing me down. Sure, Tate and she had deeper feelings for one another than what I was feeling, but I don't want to fall in love. I had love once and when I lost her, I swore never to love like that again.

Liza may have died years ago, but the pain is still real. I let my desires with other women fill the lonely void, but it never lasts for long. Cherry already is filling that void in me, and I haven't even touched her with real desire yet. She seems different to me, and I want to get to know that more.

Brier, on the other hand, might not be so good for her. He is so hard, and I'm afraid he might hurt her. I don't tell him what she said earlier because I don't think anything will come of them being together. I wasn't about to tell her that, though. If anything, it would have to be something she sees on her own.

She makes her appearance, coming out on top deck, and is looking breathtaking in that soft blue dress, her hair blowing in the breeze. Her scent travels to me even now across the boat, the same scent that still clings to me. My body responds to her presence and the pull to go to her. My skin is tingly every time she is around, and I resist the urge to touch her.

I sit up and watch as she walks to the front of the boat and looks ahead, my eyes naturally falling to the curves of her body. The sun is low with about another hour of daylight left and as we are heading into the sunset, her dress is sheer in the light, allowing me the perfect view of her lush silhouette. Brier has to see it, too, but I'm not about to take my eyes off her to look and see if he notices.

"How do you feel, Cherry?" I ask her as I watch her skirt sway with the wind. I just want to pull her to me; she looks so fucking delicious, and my mouth waters.

"My legs are sore," she says, turning and smiling at me as she leans back on the rail. She rubs one of her legs up the other, and my seated position gets a little uncomfortable. "I don't think I have ever run so hard in my life."

The boat is turning, and the sun is leaving the side of her, and I can no longer see her outline. Brier must have seen her too and turned us so

I couldn't. I silently thank him because I can't carry on a conversation with her like that.

"You actually did very well," I say, trying to calm my nerves and think of something else besides her soft curves. "You listened to us; hell, you even saved us once or twice, screaming out at the beast. You were a big distraction to them, and we got to use that to our advantage."

"Yeah, screaming sounds like a skillful weapon," she says with a chuckle.

"Have you ever had any weapons training?" Brier says from behind the wheel.

"No," she tells him. "The convent didn't have any weapons, and Mother Frances would not have approved. Elizabeth never saw to it before. She... never mind."

"What?" Brier probes her again. I watch Celine take a moment, her gaze hard before finally answering.

"Elizabeth didn't want me to learn," she says coldly. "If I could fight as she could, I don't think she would have been so quick to... hit me."

"She abused you?" I ask. The surprise in my tone is not genuine. After all, the bitch had already cursed the poor girl; it's not surprising she abused her in the past.

"It wasn't known around the castle," she says, looking down. "Tate knew some, but I recall giving him excuses for my bruises. Most he didn't seem to believe, but he never pushed. She was the queen, after all."

"So, you told no one?" Brier asks before I could.

"Who should I have told?" she asks, throwing her hands up. "Phillip tried to protect me; he pulled her off me several times. He was the only one who ever really could do anything."

"And she was jealous of that, wasn't she?" Brier says then. "How he protected you, and it is why she always accused you two of having an affair."

"How did you know?" she asks, surprised.

"She told us before sending us here," I answer when he doesn't. "She also told us… that she murdered him."

She slides down to sit on the bench, covering her mouth with her hand. I can see this is the first time she has ever heard of it.

"He didn't deserve that," she says as her tears fall. I move over and sit beside her, pulling her gently into my arms, and she comes to me willingly. "I always looked at him as a brother. He was so kind and protective like one should be. I loved him, but Elizabeth always twisted it around. She made me feel bad for it, and it drove us apart. He always stood up for me."

She cries as I hold her to my chest. She seems to need to cry for the man named Phillip. I feel bad that he came to his death only by trying to protect a child.

"Why didn't she just have me killed too?" she asks after a while. "If she hated us so much, why kill him and leave me cursed?"

"Don't think like that," I say, pulling her chin up to look at me. "She killed him years later after catching him in bed with another woman. You didn't have any part in it. I swear."

"But she still killed him out of jealousy," she says, looking down. "And cursed me for it."

"She couldn't kill you," Brier said, speaking up just then, and we look at him. "Blood is a powerful bond even if we don't care for it. My brother tried to kill me once but failed. He hurt me badly, but he couldn't kill me. That is just the way it is with Elements."

"And she hurt me," she whispers, laying her head back onto my shoulder. It throbs from her touch, but I say nothing. The pain is more tolerable than hers.

"You should learn to fight. At least enough to protect yourself from the queen," Brier interrupts our tender moment. "In the coming days, while on the boat, I will show you how to use a knife. I have a spare you can have."

"Really?" she asks, excitement lighting up her face. "You will train me?"

"We all will," he tells her. "Lindon is good at catching people off guard, something you could use. Tate is a hunter and knows exactly where to cut to leave the most damage."

"And you?" she asks when he doesn't continue.

"I know how to kill," he says, looking straight forward. "And strategy."

"Will you show me your powers?" she asks him then, and I inhale, knowing his response.

"No. I have no powers," he says, looking sternly at her.

"Yes, you do," she says, standing and moving toward him. "I can feel them... something..."

"I have no powers!" he growls at her, and she stops. "They were torn from me, damaged to the point where I cannot use them."

"But...you were sent to me," she says, not talking to him but herself now. "You must have them."

"I'm done talking about this!" he shouts at her, and I stand, pulling her behind me.

"That's enough, Brier." I say to him, giving him warning he is pushing this too far. "It's not her fault you don't have them. She just asked."

"Then she should have taken 'no' for an answer the first time I told her," he grits out between clenched teeth, and I know this is a touchy subject for him. . "I will not speak of it again."

"No, wait!" Celine calls from behind me, trying to push forward, but I hold her back. Brier is a real bear when it comes to the loss of his powers.

"Celine, stop!" I say, grabbing her by the arms and whispering to her, "He doesn't handle this very well. Leave him be."

She looks at me, confused, but doesn't attempt to engage with Brier again.

"But the Elementals sent me three powers," she whispers back.

"What?" I ask, just as confused by her statement.

"I sacrificed myself to the three Elementals," she whispers, looking into my eyes. "Three came to save me. Earth, who is Tate. Water, who is Brier. And Wind...who is you."

Chapter Nineteen
LINDON

"What are you talking about?" I ask, staring down at her. "I'm not a Wind Element and what sacrifice?"

I'm not the only one lost in what she said. Brier comes around to stand beside me.

"What sacrifice, Princess?" Brier says, crossing his arms in front of him.

"Um, maybe we could talk about that once Tate is awake," she says, backing up a step and looking at me. "Lindon, you *are* the Wind Element."

"No," I say, shaking my head. "Elements change at eighteen. I did no such thing."

"Yes, but… tragedy can delay it," she breathes, looking at me with such a sad expression that my breath catches. "As time passes, it can become dormant, which is what I think happened to you."

She is talking about the death of my wife and child. Liza and I had married young, so the timing would have matched her theory. Could she be right?

"Brier, can that happen?" I ask him, still looking at Celine.

"Yes, and she is right." Brier looks at me and uncrosses his arms. "You do have powers. I feel them, too."

"What?" I shout as I look him square in the eyes. "Why have you said nothing to me?"

"Because some people deny them. I thought you did, too." Brier holds his hands up and backs up to the back of the boat again. "I've only known you a few years, and it's not like we have shared much of our past."

"I can't believe this." I turn away, looking at my hands. Did I really have powers locked inside me? "All this time..."

"You do use them some, but it's not overpowering," Celine says, stepping closer to me and placing her hand on my arm. "Just small steps, bursts that come out at moments. I don't think you realize it."

I look down at her. How can she see it, and what have I done? "How?"

"That day, in the little house, when I was panicking, you took over my breathing," she tells me. "You just... looked at me so intensely and breathed normally yourself, but you were controlling my breathing."

"I was breathing for you?" I wish someone would breathe for me now. I had been using Elemental powers without knowing it; I feel winded. "That stuff you had me reading about Wind. You wanted me to know what I could do."

"Yes. I didn't know if you knew anything about it," Celine says softly. "And I didn't understand why you weren't expressing your powers more fully. When you breathed for me, it was like you didn't know you were, and I wanted to show you it was okay."

"This is... a little much," I say, walking away from her and sitting down. "Have I done anything else?"

"When I watched you fight the ogres, you were so fast at times. The way you move and jump around them like you just float on air," she says, moving to sit beside me. "And in the library, you kind of brushed Wind against me. You… touched me with it."

"What did it feel like?" I whisper as I look at her, wanting to know if she liked it.

"It tickled me," she says with a smile, looking down. "It felt real… it tingled."

"The power of seduction," I say, remembering what I had read from that book. The Wind Element can have allure and temptation as part of its powers and could manifest in the wind, breath, and vocally. How many times could I have used this and never realized it?

"Yes," she says, blushing as she looks away. "It is one of your powers."

"I'm sure Tate will be thrilled to hear that," Brier says with a chuckle behind the wheel once more. I glare at him, mad that he never mentioned that he felt Elemental powers from me.

"You just have to open yourself up to them, Lindon." Celine takes my hand, and I look at her. "You are capable of so many things. Flying, shifting, wind, air, even the ability to see in time."

"I have seen things in my dreams that have happened," I say, thinking of it now. I always felt like it was intuition when it happened.

"Maybe your powers are not as dormant as you think. Maybe you should just try something. Focus on a power."

"Like what?" I ask her.

"I don't know…" she says, moving her hand in a circle in front of us. "Try moving the air." She says it like it should be simple, but I'm not so sure it will be. How do you move the air?

I look down at my hands, stretching out my fingers, wondering if power lies within them. I try to relax, breathing in and out, pushing my hands in front of me, but nothing happens.

"Try inhaling and blow out the air to move it," she tells me, sitting beside me.

I close my eyes and breathe deeply before releasing it, but still, nothing happens. "It's not working."

"Then let's try something else," she says and pulls me around to face her once again. "How about you try breathing for me? Relax and focus on my own breathing and yours."

"All right." I nod in agreement as I watch her close her eyes and wait. I focus on her and watch as she breathes in and out calmly, matching her breathing to mine. It isn't working, and I feel I need to connect with her if this will work. Reaching up, I place my thumb at the base of her throat, feeling her pulse.

She gasps in surprise at my touch, and I feel something stir inside me for the first time. A current inside me sparks to life, and I hold on to it, not letting it go.

I rub my thumb along her throat, her pulse quickening. So does her breathing, and with that, I latch onto it.

She leans closer to me with her eyes closed, and I inhale her scent, taking it in. As my breath hitches, so does hers. I feel like she is anchoring me somehow, letting my powers come out, and, for the first time, I am seeing them in action.

Softly, I breathe in and out as I let my hand travel down to rest on her upper chest, and she leans into it as her hand settles on my leg. My other hand takes hers, and I feel the power surging through my body, waking up and coming to life.

It is like a light coming on as I gasp for air, and so does she. An electric charge builds inside me now, and it feels so good and real. My senses become sharper with each breath we take together, and I want more.

Opening her eyes, Celine looks at me, and I know she feels it, too. Something is calling to me to touch her. Reaching up, I kiss her shoulder, my hand traveling up her neck and caressing it. My breathing becomes a little faster, and so does hers. The wind around us picks up its current, and I pull it in around us.

Her hand rests on my chest now as she feels me breathing in and out. I see heat in her eyes as she looks up into mine. She resists my breathing then, but I won't let her go from it.

Pulling her closer, I push my hand into her hair as it blows in the wind. She looks so beautiful with it surrounding us as she moans on our next exhale. Letting her head fall back into my hand, her resistance fades, and we are lost in each other.

Suddenly, I feel a rush of intense electrical current pushing through my body, and I gasp at the force of it as it flows into my hands and in hers. I pull her flush with my body, needing to feel her in my arms, and she doesn't resist. My hand trails down her back, and I can feel my fingers tingling with electric currents, knowing that somehow, I am sending them into her body as she melts into my arms. We both moan together as our bodies slide against one another.

I stop breathing for her and ask, "What... is happening?"

"I feel you..." She is breathless and moans as her hands come up and around my shoulders, pulling me closer. "You're calling me."

I can't help myself as I lift her, and she straddles my hips. I need to be closer to her, to feel all of her. She presses closer to me, and our bodies both arch into one another.

The wind is picking up around us even more, and I know it is me. I feel the force pushing out and give it the ability to tie itself around us. As it holds her to me, I let it touch her through her clothing as I take in the scent of her.

"Um, I think you guys need to stop," Brier says from a far-off distance, but I am beyond that.

Reaching forward, I take her face in my hands and pull her lips to mine. I feel the air caress us, putting us in a bubble of air, drawing us closer as I take her in a passionate kiss driven by the electrical currents, the wind, my powers, my demand.

She is intoxicating, and I moan as I push my tongue into her mouth, needing to taste all of her. I kiss her hard, and she matches me stroke for stroke as our tongues dance with one another. I press her into me harder, wanting us closer, and feel her soft hands caress my neck. I forget everything then as I surrender to the powers completely, letting them take me and her within their grasp.

I have to touch her and make her a part of me. I feel a pulling inside to bond with her powers, but I can't reach them. I push my newfound power harder into her, and she groans and shakes in my arms as I cup one breast, sending sparks through it. I push my hips forward, rocking into her as the heat builds in my cock, and I am so hard to have her, here and now.

Suddenly, someone yanks Celine back and pulls her from me. The sudden loss of her closeness is almost painful. I am on my feet in an instant, reaching for her, but Brier pushes me back down as he holds her against him.

"You two need to stop before you destroy the boat!" he yells as he supports her. She looks unsteady. "Get a hold of yourselves. That's an order."

I snap out of it, and suddenly, I lose the emotions that have been spinning inside me. Looking at Celine, I see that she is right and I have powers. I controlled the air and electrical current that had set us both on fire.

"What the hell, Lindon?" Brier shouts at me. "I see you kiss her, and suddenly, you two seem to be wrapped in some little bubble while out here, hell is breaking loose."

"What are you talking about?" I look around and see that we are no longer in the water but on the soft bank by the river. Had I just beached the boat?

"I'm talking about the tornado that seemed to happen in the middle of this boat!" he shouts at us, placing Celine in the seat across from me. "Look around you. Everything is everywhere, and we are no longer in the damn water!"

I see as I look around, that hell, half of the top of the boat cover is missing. Celine and I were so engrossed in each other we hadn't seen what was happening around us.

"Cherry?" I whisper as I look at her, still sitting on the bench where Brier had pushed me down. I think of all those currents I had let go into her body. "Are you okay?"

"I think so," she says, looking away from me. "I didn't realize that would happen."

"I'm sorry. I didn't mean to take advantage of you," I say in a rush, sitting up on the edge of the cushion. "I…"

"No, it's okay," she says, glancing up at me and then around to the mess of our boat. "I wanted you to find your powers, and I think you did."

"Are you two okay now?" Brier asks, looking back and forth between us.

"Yes," we both say, even though I am still shaken by it.

"I feel it now. The powers have come alive inside me," I tell them. "The wind. The current of electricity."

"I'm glad," she says with a smile. She is blushing, and I can tell I had an influence on her actions. Would she have kissed me like that if I hadn't? I don't think she would have. What just happened was unexpected for both of us.

"I overwhelmed you, didn't I?" I ask her softly, and she nods her head. "I'm sorry I didn't realize it until now. I promise not to do that to you again."

"I trust you," she tells me, but I can see that she is a little thrown off by what happened. She isn't ready for me in that way yet. I need to get control over the power of seduction and persuasion. All my powers, for that matter.

I won't touch her like that again until I know she is ready. Until I know I can handle it.

Chapter Twenty
CELINE

Brier pushes some stuff out of his way and moves to the side of the boat. He is angry, but there is a tiredness there too.

"Celine," he says to me over his shoulder, "why don't you check on Tate while Lindon and I get this boat back in the water?"

"How are we going to get it back in the water?" Lindon asks Brier, but still, his gaze locks on mine. Confusion still muddles my thoughts over what just happened. I didn't seem to have control over myself. I felt myself latch onto his powers, guiding them out, but he had been in control of them the whole time. Lindon had opened himself up to me, and I lost myself in his rush of power and lust.

"You have your powers now, right?" Brier scoffs at Lindon. "You figure it out."

Without waiting for a response, Brier jumps off the boat. Lindon stares blankly at me for a moment before shaking his head and following Brier into the water. Shaking myself from my stupor, I move down the little stairway to do as Brier says. Stepping inside, I look over at Tate and he asks, "What happened? I felt the boat spinning and then a hard knock, and we stopped."

I couldn't tell him that Lindon just kissed me, and his powers went off the rails. Lindon and I hadn't planned it; it just sort of happened in the moment. The last thing I wanted right now was to upset Tate while he was hurt and in pain, and I can see in his glazed-over look that he is.

"Lindon has discovered his powers," I tell him instead. "He may need to practice them a little more and on solid land."

Tate sighs and grits his teeth. He doesn't comment on Lindon, and I let it drop. "It hurts."

"I thought you were a quick healer," I say to him. "Shouldn't you be getting better?"

"I am not bruised but broken," he hisses. "I need an anchor of a Water or another Earth Element to help me this time."

"Can I help?" Isn't that what I just did with Lindon? I am sure of it. I had given myself as an anchor for his powers to move forward. It was like a magnetic draw from one to another, and I absorbed the energy from his powers. But I didn't have control with Lindon, and it is why I couldn't pull away from him. Could I anchor his powers also so that he could heal himself?

"I can be your anchor," I tell him, touching his face.

"I don't know if you can. Brier can't, and Lindon doesn't have healing power."

"My powers are locked inside, but they are there," I tell him. "We can try."

" I don't know what it would do to you," he says, shaking his head. "It will take a lot of my power, and there's no telling how you will respond to it. I don't want you to hurt like this."

"But physical doesn't have to be a pain," I tell him after a minute. I remember reading something once before about how you could control the physical contact he was talking about. But to do so, it would have to be the opposite of pain, which was pleasure. "I don't know how, but you can flip it. You should be able to make it pleasurable instead."

"I don't know if I can do that," he tells me. "I've never tried it or been injured like this."

In the past few days, I have had my first kiss with Tate and a tornado of passion with Lindon. I felt passion and lust for the first time, and I learned that I like the feelings. The passion has been so all-consuming that I have been afraid of how I seem to lose control in Tate's or Lindon's arms.

Offering to heal Tate and flipping the physical to pleasure is exciting and scary. I'm not sure if I will be able to pull away from the consuming lust inside me. There is a need inside me calling for a bonding from each of them to fulfill. I have a feeling it is the sacrifice wanting to be fulfilled and have its children.

"Tate, I have something important to tell you." I want to tell him of my sacrifice, but I change my mind. "But right now, I need you to get better. We have to try."

Not giving him a chance to say no, I settle myself gently astride his body, and his hands connect with my legs holding me still. I reach forward and rub my hands just barely over the bandages around his ribs.

"I am your anchor," I say, looking down in his eyes. "Let your power flow through me."

"How do I flip it? I don't want you to feel pain," he asks, looking up into my eyes.

"Don't think of the pain. Bring pleasure to your mind," I whisper, hoping this will work.

He exhales, but he nods his head as he focuses and opens his powers to me. I can feel them surround me. They are so powerful, but they slowly build around my body. His powers seem to absorb right into me, much faster and easier than Lindon's had. I push down on his chest and a sharp pain racks through me. I gasp.

"This isn't working," he says as I feel him pulling his powers back.

"Focus," I say as my hands graze over his chest. I caress his face and lean over, kissing his lips. "It's okay. We can do this."

I feel his power surge into me again, and I search within it for the healing elements. It isn't connecting with my locked powers, but I feel it flowing inside me. I have never felt power like this before, and it is intense. Where Lindon's felt almost freeing, Tate's powers are holding onto me firmly. I wonder if it is the way his Element feels or if it is because he has full use of them, unlike Lindon. Whatever it is, Tate is so much stronger inside me.

He moans, and I feel him invading my senses as sharp tingles run in my chest. They connect with his pain and turn slowly into vibrations, but it isn't pleasure they are translating into. The waves of pain become stronger, but I am not going to stop this now. I tell myself it will be over soon enough, and he will be better.

I gasp when I feel the healing powers and hold onto them now, pressing into his ribs with my fingers as the powers run over him. He moans again, and his hand tightens on my hips, his fingers digging into my soft flesh.

"Celine," he whispers. "The pleasure hurts."

"I know, my love," I gasp out, feeling the pain run through me more. It hurts, but I need to help him take it away. "Open to me."

He looks at me with fire in his eyes. "No, it's too much. I'm hurting you."

"Just a little," I say, smiling down at him despite the pain. "Now, Tate."

He seems to want to fight me, but my command sets off a trigger inside him, opening his power for me to take it in thoroughly. My breath is knocked away as it hits my chest once more and moves down into my stomach. I run my hands over Tate's injuries, pushing into him hard, seeking it, and Tate moans into the pain as he pulls me tightly to his body.

He arches his body up into me suddenly, almost throwing me off. If not for his grip, I would surely have fallen to the floor, but I stay on, and we both groan as another burst of pain hits us and then releases from our bodies. The waves flowing around his powers slide away and settle back deep down into my core.

Slowly, the pain lessens, but my body is tingling and sensitive to his touch. I have taken his pain within me, but I don't know how to release it as it racks through my body. I am feeling tired also and can't fight the urge to rest on his chest even hurting the way I am.

"Thank you, my love," he whispers to me as we relax together and just breathe. "The pain is gone, and I am better now."

"I am glad," I say, breathlessly, not sure how to tell him that I am hurting still.

He slides his hands up my back and the soft touch is painful, sending sharp shards down my spine.

"Don't do that," I moan to him. "I… I am too sensitive."

He stops and asks softly, "Can I at least kiss you?"

"Please do," I say, raising my head from his chest and looking at him.

Suddenly, he bolts up to a sitting position with me on top of him. I hiss as sharp pain runs through me at the sudden movement. His hand grazes up my arms, and I pull them away, surprised that it hurts for him to touch me so softly. It is like I have a current of pain flowing in me, and every touch is pulling it to the surface.

"Turning pain into pleasure didn't seem to work as well as you thought," he rasps at me. He runs his hand through my hair, not touching my skin. I am shuddering and quaking with longing and pain. He looks at me for the longest time, and I wonder if he will kiss me. "You are hurting, aren't you?"

"Do you feel any pain now?" I ask him. He doesn't seem to have these sensations.

"No, I don't. I released the pain once I was healed, and now all I feel is pleasure." His creased brow and tone exude concern. "But you didn't, did you? You still feel the pain. It's trapped in you because you don't know how to have your powers release it."

I nod. Even though it isn't intense pain like before, it is still there, and his touch hurts me. "How do I release it?"

He seems to think about this for a moment. "I have an idea of how, but you have to trust me."

"You know I trust you." I smile at him. "How?"

"It has to be through pain or pleasure," he says softly. "And there is no way I am about to cause you pain."

"What… what are you thinking to do?" I ask, sliding back from him, a little nervous now.

"Love, I know you're innocent, but you have felt pleasure in my arms," he says, running a single finger down my arm. I flinch slightly at the caress slash tingles of pain. He moves his hand away from me, placing it on the bed behind him, and just looks at me. "Have you ever felt the release from pleasure before?"

"What do you mean?"

"A little embarrassing, I know, but honestly, have you ever…touched yourself before?" he asks, and I can see he is blushing. My own face becomes heated, knowing now what he means.

"You mean in pleasuring myself?" I ask as he nods his head, still holding that blushing smile. He was waiting for my answer, and I can't help but hide my face behind my hands. "I…I did once, but…I stopped."

"Why?" he asks me with a smile. "Did you not like it?"

"I did, but…it was a little overwhelming and…I was afraid someone would hear me," I tell him. "The walls are thin in a convent, you know."

"So, you never found a release in it?" he asks again.

"There is a release?" I ask. "I thought it was just about pleasure."

"The pleasure of release." His eyes shift away for a moment, and then he says, "I can do it for you if you'd like."

"Oh. You mean to…touch me…" I am curious of the ideas of pleasure but am I ready for such an intimate act?

"You will be my wife, won't you?" he asks me playfully now.

"Yes," I say, not even hesitating in my answer. I know coupling has to do with this, but I still know little about… it. No one had ever spoken to me about it, and who was I going to ask? "I know how it works, and that there is pleasure involved, but I know little more than that."

"There are lots of pleasure," he tells me, moving closer but not touching me. "And there is a release. It is called an orgasm. I want to give you one."

His face is so close to mine, and with just an inch separating our lips, I can feel his warm breath.

"Don't be frightened, Love," he says, "I will not...couple with you, as you put it. Just to show you how to experience a release."

I am breathing hard at the thought of him touching me there. Am I ready for something like this yet? Before I can overthink it, he leans forward and kisses me gently. My lips tingle, but he is so soft, it mixes the pain with a sense of pleasure. He senses my sweet torture and doesn't touch me anywhere else but my lips with his.

After a little while, I feel his fingers grazing over the tops of my legs, causing them to tingle. They travel up and around my legs in the inner area of my thighs. I gasp as he comes close to touching my center.

"I won't touch you anywhere else this time," he rasps as he pulls back from our kiss. "I long to run my hands all over you, but I feel that isn't the right move for this."

"I'm tingling where you touch," I tell him as his fingers hook inside my underwear. I exhale as my nerves get the better of me, and I brace myself with my hands on his shoulders as I lift myself up and away from him a bit. He takes that to his advantage as I feel the soft material rip as he pulls it in two.

I gasp and look at him, surprised. He is waiting for my reaction. "Tate?"

"You're so sensitive, and I don't want to hurt you any more by making you move," he rasps as he looks at me. "But I must touch you here."

His fingers slide within the folds between my legs, and I can't help the moan that escapes me as his sweet torturous touch, so new and foreign to me, feels so good, even with the slight pain that follows.

"Oh, gods!" I quake in his arms. His fingers gently slide farther down over every part of me there, slowly letting me become accustomed to the feel. "Tate?"

"Do you like that?" he asks, watching me, and I feel myself blushing into his intense gaze.

"I… yes… I don't know," I moan, digging my nails into his shoulders for support. This feels way better than when I had touched myself. Maybe I wasn't doing it right, or I just forgot — it has been so long.

The slight discomfort of pain is nothing compared to the pleasure I get from it. I moan as he flicks a part of me, and I ask him to do that again.

"This is your bud or clit," he says as he flicks it again, and I groan in sweet agony. "It is the most sensitive part of a woman and here is where you will find your release. Do you like me touching you here?"

"Yes," I gasp as he makes a circle around… What the hell did he call it again?

His fingers leave it, sliding down the folds once more, and they slowly make their way down and inside me. I arch into his hand as he pulls his fingers out and then slides them back inside me. The feeling of him filling me is almost overwhelming.

"This is where I will mate with you and make you my wife," he whispers as he slips another finger inside me. "You feel so good here. I can't wait to make you mine."

I groan as he slides in and out of me, and my body moves over his hand.

"I will fill you with my children here," he says, pushing inside me a little hard and deep, and I gasp at how full I feel. "But for now, you need your release."

His fingers slip out of me and back up to that susceptible area once more, and I let out a loud moan as he touches it again. I seem to have grown more sensitive suddenly at his touch. His fingers are working faster with more pressure now, but the tingling of pain is still there.

I groan and shake in his arms as he moves his hand again. I am getting dizzy and can't focus my vision, and my breathing is ragged; I am holding my breath more than breathing.

"You're almost there, Love," he rasps, urging me on. "You're starting to quake. Let it go when you're ready."

"How? It's too much."

"You will know," he groans.

I let out a soft whine when his fingers slide back down and inside me again as waves of pleasure rush over me. His thumb rubs my bud, and my entire body tenses with urges I don't quite understand. I am on the verge of something but not sure what.

He grabs me by the waist, and suddenly I am lying on the bed as I feel his fingers deep inside me—his thumb circles in large motions around my bud as my legs spread wide, seeking more.

"Come for me," he rasps as his rhythmic motions pick up pace. "Now."

His words send me into tidal waves of pleasure, and his demand seems all I need to find the release he is talking about. My body spasms and rocks as every nerve in my body releases a pent-up pressure deep inside me.

I hear an explosion behind us, and suddenly cold water is falling on us in droplets.

My legs come up, cradling his hand between them as his movements slow into an even and gentle touch once more. My body moves with him, riding out the rest of the release of pain, and all I can feel now is a pleasure.

"How do you feel, my love?" he asks as he kisses my neck gently. Little raindrops fall all around us.

"Good," I sigh, relaxing into his kisses and bringing my arms around his neck. "But why is it raining in the boat?"

He chuckles as he looks behind him and I do, too, seeing the faucet sink on the bar lying to the side and water shooting out.

"It seems the boat is coming apart," he says, looking back at me, and we ignore it for the moment as our eyes connect. He brushes my hair behind my ear, asking, "Can I kiss you now?"

"You can do whatever you like to me," I say, smiling up at him.

And he can. I am primed and ready for his mating now.

Chapter Twenty-One

Tate is healed entirely now as we move out of the small cabin of the boat, we find that we are in the water again, heading down the river.

Lindon smiles at me and I can't help but blush as I take a seat with Tate on the opposite bench. He holds my hand and it makes me feel warm inside with the small gesture.

Brier is driving the boat, and when I look at him, he is not smiling. I don't understand what bothers him so much about me.

"Glad to see you weren't killing her, Tate," Lindon goads, leaning back on the opposite cushion.

Oh no! Did they hear us? I hide my face behind Tate's arm, embarrassed for them to know what Tate did to me. I haven't had a chance to wrap my head fully around what did happen and how wonderful it had felt.

"Shut it, Lindon," Tate says, scowling at him.

"How are you feeling?" Brier asks Tate, ignoring Lindon. "You were hurt pretty bad."

"Celine helped me," Tate says, and I lift my head to look at him. He is so handsome with that beautiful smile on his face. "She could not use her powers, but she could anchor me enough so I could heal. Thank you. For doing that for me."

"It was my pleasure," I say, blushing at him. I can't stop blushing each time he looks at me. I keep thinking of where his hand had been and the way his fingers slipped into my…

"I bet," Lindon says with a chuckles, interrupting my intimate thoughts.

"Glad you're up and about again, Tate," Brier says, taking my attention. "We most likely will need you tonight."

"Why? What will happen tonight?" I ask alarmed.

"I don't expect the ogres to be as bad, but am sure a few will show," he says as he continues to drive. "You will be bait tonight."

I shiver at his words, thinking of how it had been last night. All the running and fighting. "Will it be like last night?"

"I don't think so, but we will know more of a number and how far away they are once you step foot on land again," he tells me like he doesn't care. He pulls to the bank, and, after securing it, they all jump from the boat.

Tate is there, waiting to help me down. He always stays close, and I like how secure he makes me feel. He will always be there for me, and I will treat him the same.

Brier has moved ahead and into a clearing now and is looking around. The other men are outwardly caring for me, and his dismissal is upsetting. But I know there is something at the root of his icy reserve. I just have to find my way through to it.

Lindon is also waiting, but he lets Tate be my support. He is backing away from our bond allowing Tate to reach for me, giving us space to feel our emotions for one another first. He is right to do so, even after what happened with us today, I hadn't meant to be physical with him yet, and I didn't think Lindon did, either.

"Come, love," Tate says, motioning for me to come into his arms. "Nothing will happen with all of us here."

I step on the edge of the boat and Tate helps me down. We all wait quietly for the calls of any ogres in the area. A quiet sound comes up from somewhere far away, but nothing as close as last night.

"The ogres hide from the light during the day while we travel," Lindon speaks up from beside me. "Your call to them last night left them miles behind."

"That's good to know," I say, smiling at him.

"I will do some hunting while you all set up camp," Tate says, and I turn to him. "Stay close to Brier while I am gone."

"I will," I promise him. "I must admit I am famished."

"We all are," he says, taking my hand and leading me up and into the clearing where Brier is. Brier has dropped several bags and swept the area clean except for a small space in the middle where I figure he will build a fire. "Lindon, come with me."

"You're not going, too?" The thought of being alone with Brier is both exciting and nerve-wracking. I don't know just yet how to connect with him.

"Just around for some wood," Lindon says, smiling. "I will be back shortly."

"Stay with Brier," Tate says. "See if he needs any help."

"Yeah, Cherry, I think it would be good for you two to have some time alone," Lindon says, the twinkle in his eye sparkling.

"Stop delaying and go do your jobs," Brier calls to them as he makes a makeshift cover between two trees. He doesn't even look at us and is just listens.

Tate and Lindon leave and move into the woods. I look to Brier, who is working but ignores me. I don't know what to do, so I just sit down on the ground and wait.

Brier is intimidating, even though I know he won't harm me. Still, he is the coldest man I have ever met and always seems angry. He is a huge question for me, but I have to connect with him and apparently, find a way to fix his element. How did it get messed up in the first place? It is almost unheard of to have so much trauma that elemental powers are broken. I was cursed and didn't have my powers and that is at least something we have in common.

"All right, get up," he tells me, standing a few feet away. He is undoing a strap around a case knife.

I stand up, and he walks over to me. "This will be your knife. I will show you how to use it over the next week until we reach the castle. There you must invest in some real training with a sword as soon as possible. You may be royal blood, but you still need to know how to protect yourself."

He hands it to me for a minute so I can look over it. I pull it from the case and hold it up.

"It is very sharp, so be careful," he tells me. "Tie the leather and case around your waist. There are two straps, as you can see; one is to be ties around the waist, but they design it for a man and will be too big for you. Just tie it a little lower around your hips."

I follow his directions, but soon I noticed the belt is too big. He sees this, also, and takes it back from me, pulling the knife out and digging a hole out up above the notches. Then he gives it back to me.

I put the belt in the cut loop and tie the smaller strap lower, seeing that it anchors the knife to my leg more tightly. Brier reaches down and tugs it, making sure it is tight enough. His face comes close to mine, but he doesn't look at me.

"Good. Now keep it on and get a feel for wearing it," he says steps back looking at how it fits me. "There are smaller knives for women that you can wear under your dress that you may like more, but I have nothing like that."

"You're giving me your knife?" Though I may not know him well yet, I can see that this is a kind gesture coming from him.

"Yes, but if you are going just to give it away later when you have your own, I prefer to have it back." He points his finger at me, and it reminds me of my old nursemaid when I did something she didn't like.

"I won't give it away," I swear to him. I haven't had many gifts in the last few years. Nuns were not known to give gifts, even though they celebrated the changing seasons. "I like it. Thank you."

He nods, shifting on his feet and then speaks again. "Pull it out."

I pull it from the case and hold it in front of me.

"When holding a knife, you want to grasp it, but not too tightly," he tells me as he steps forward and adjusts my grip on the knife. "Hold it here, closer to the blade. It gives you more control. Good. Now, when you're using it to kill, always go for the neck, whether animal or human. It's where an animal will go if it attacks you, so remember that and protect yours above everything else."

"Neck. Got it," I say, focusing on what he is telling me.

"If you attack and can't go for the neck, anywhere else is good to slow it down and cause damage but as soon as you can, stab and slice the neck for the kill and to end the fight," he says as he makes a stabbing motion with his hands. "Don't go frontal in the stab. Come in from the side. That way, you can use your other hand to block or protect yourself."

"Go for the neck attack to the side," I say. "Will this work on ogres?"

"No. Their skin is too thick. It takes genuine force to penetrate their skin," he tells me. "The best place to bring them down in the back of the neck, then stab them through the heart. To kill an ogre, you must kill the heart. Getting them in the neck stuns them for a minute. Only then do you run your sword through the heart, and it does take a lot of strength."

"Maybe I will surprise you one day by killing an ogre," I say, smiling at him.

"Don't even attempt it," he says, looking at me sternly. "My job is to protect you, not save you from yourself. I show you this to protect you from man and animal attacks. We are out here in the woods and though I doubt they will attack you, it is good to know your surroundings," he tells me. "But men will always come after you at some time or another. Once you become queen, someone will always want you dead."

"Thanks for the warning," I sigh knowing it is true. I remember once my mother being attacked when I was little. We had been playing in the gardens from out of nowhere a man came at us. I don't remember much because I had been so little, but I remember seeing him on the ground dead and had started to cry. Mother had come over and picked me up, carrying me into the castle. "Just show me how to use it, please."

For the next thirty minutes, Brier shows me how to thrust and shove the knife around his body and places to aim for maximum damage. Lindon comes back but doesn't interrupt us; instead, he starts a fire and sits back to watch.

"That's enough for today," Brier says, wiping the sweat from his brow. "Tomorrow on the boat, I will show you where to hit with just your fist."

"Thank you, Brier," I say, touching his arm. "No one has ever taken the time to show me how to protect myself before."

He pulls away from my hand and backs up. "I will go lay some traps. Stay with Lindon."

I watch him walk away from me, a little disheartened that he pulls away from my touch. With nothing left to do, I sit down beside Lindon.

"It's not you," Lindon says to me. "Brier doesn't like to be touched."

"Why?" I ask him.

"I don't know." He shrugs and looks away for a moment. "I've known Brier for several years. He is head guard at the palace, and I always have to deal with him when I get into trouble. We have formed a unique bond over time. We play cards together and drink sometimes. He is serious, and I'm not, but we have always liked each other. That doesn't mean that he's open with me about his past."

"What about Tate? You seem close to him."

"Tate has always been more of a loner." He pokes at the fire. "I've seen him around the city off and on throughout the years, but we never spent much time together. Not until this. But over the last few weeks, we have grown to be good friends, I think."

I fall silent, thinking about how they all seem to know each other. Kind of like strangers coming together to form a family. That is how it is to be with all of us. I am determine that we will one day all be a family.

"Tell me about you and Tate," Lindon says out of the blue. "You grew up together, yes?"

"I've known Tate since I was seven," I remember him as a boy and smile. "When my mother passed, I just wanted to run away. But I was a princess and couldn't escape. Tate was there in the gardens where I liked to hide. When people used to come looking for me, he would tell them I wasn't there. Eventually, we became friends and played in those gardens all the time after that."

"It grew into love, didn't it?" he asks me. "I can see you both care very much for each other."

"Yes, it did," I say, not wanting to hide my feelings from Lindon. There is something about him that makes me feel like I can tell him anything. "We promised ourselves to each other just before my sister cursed me. I cried myself to sleep for almost a year, thinking of the life we could have had. I thought it was lost a long time ago but now…"

"Now, you are together again," he says, softly and bumps my shoulder. "So, I just have one more question for you."

"What's that?" I ask, smiling at him, too.

"Where does that leave you and me?" he whispers leaning closer to me.

I should have known the question was coming. There was too much heat to deny after that kiss. It is about time I tell the men my intentions and the sacrificed I made for them. I had hoped Brier and I would have found some common bond before I went about claiming I want to have their children for the Elementals.

"I don't know yet," I whisper. "But you are critical to me, Lindon, and I need you in my life.

Chapter Twenty-Two

We are all sitting around the fire eating later in the night when the conversation starts. So far, no ogres have shown up or set off any alarms that Brier has set, so we have relaxed and enjoyed our meal of some bread I had brought with me and some boar that Tate had killed. Some of it was hanging over the fire, drying so we could have it tomorrow when we needed it.

It is good. A little plain with just some salt on it, but I'm not about to complain. There is a small kitchen on the boat and they stock it with some dry goods. Tomorrow, I will find something to cook for us all while we go downriver.

Tate and I are sitting beside each other. He has his arm loosely wrapped around me, and we laugh as we feed each other pieces of the meat. Lindon and Brier are talking more to each other, leaving us alone. But then Lindon raises his voice.

"So, Cherry, you said earlier that you had something to tell us all," he says, looking at me. "How about now?"

Yes, I do," I say, pulling away from Tate and drinking some water. It is now or never. Now is as good of a time as any. "It's kind of a long story, so please bear with me."

I look at each of them, and they nod in agreement. So, I take a deep breath and begin.

"I was happy in the convent, for the most part, but I could never leave or go outside the walls. I could never travel to the river and take a swim with the other nuns or go and pick wild berries with them in the forest. Not even to the fields to pick fresh flowers for the tables. When people did come, I always hid away never wanting them to see the monster I was. I was trapped there and each day, the walls seem to become smaller and smaller."

"That must have been so hard for you," Tate says softly as he rubs my back.

"It was." I had come from a life of a princess where people always surrounded me and there was always someone new to meet. "About three years in, I realized I couldn't live like that for the rest of my life. I needed to find a way out, so I started some research. There was some information on Mages that said they could see the future. I thought if I could get a Mage to come to me, maybe they could help guide me and I could find a way out of the curse. I found a summoning spell and cast it. I didn't even know if it worked because I didn't have any magic but a few months later, Alice came to the convent."

"Sister Alice?" Brier asked me. "She is a Mage?"

"Yes," I say, looking at him. His interest in Alice sparks something akin to jealousy in me again.

"That is why I felt magic on her," he says as he throws a small bone he has picked cleaned with his teeth into the fire. "I knew she wasn't an element and thought she might have been a witch. But it made little sense to me why she would be in a convent as a nun."

"She came to me soon after her arrival, telling me that her aunt Sara, the King's Mage, had sent her. That she was there to help guide me in my endeavor to find the next Water King. She told me things, and we grew into great friends. Try as she might, she couldn't find an answer for me to escape."

"The queen's curse sounded like it was solid when she told us," Brier says, reaching for another piece of meat. "It would take more than magic from a Mage to break the curse."

Brier is right; it did take much more than just Mage magic.

"Some new books were donated, and we were putting them away in the library when she touched one book and had a vision. It was a book on the old ways, old magic—mostly good, but some parts were not. It wasn't until I read it a second time that I realized it might just work for me."

"You found a way out of the curse?" Lindon asks with a small smile in my direction.

This is coming to the hard part. They are all looking at me, waiting for me to go on, but I pause for a minute to take a deep breath.

"The book told me I could make a sacrifice to end my curse, but I would have to give my life to do so. I had no magic to call to the Elementals and so Alice offered to do it for me. We had to become blood sisters and in the sacrifice, She would call to them, while I took our joined lives."

"You would have just given yourself over like that?" Tate asks me, touching my arm, and I look at him. "Just to be free?"

I need him to understand. "You don't know how I felt being trapped there. I can't explain how useless I felt in this world. Every day, I looked over the walls and could see the fires moving closer. I couldn't help but think one day they would reach the convent and then what would happen? Would the holy lands be saved but be surrounded by fire? Would the nuns leave and I would be all alone? If I left, would I just become a meal to the ogres? I couldn't just wait around and find out. I needed to act while there was still time. I had to ask the Elementals for help, and I felt so blessed that Alice was with me. That she would be so willing to risk her own life for mine. I couldn't let her do that in vain and promised her I would find a way to save the realms from burning. To save the convent she so loved. It was the only thing I could offer her and I will see that it is done."

"Okay, we get it," Brier says. "What happen with the sacrifice?"

He can be such an ass, but I suppress the urge to roll my eyes and explain what we did next. "We did the sacrifice and called on the three elements, leaving fire out. We felt that if I offered to fight the fire, they would break my curse, but they didn't want just that. They wanted more."

I stop for a moment not sure how to tell them the next part. The part that involved each of them.

"What did they want?" Brier probs sitting up straighter on the other side of the fire. His gaze is so intense that I have to look away. I can't look at any of them, so I looked into the fire.

"They would each send their strongest elements to me and in return, I would bear them each a child."

"What?" they all shout almost in unison.

"Are you serious?" Brier asks, and I shudder at the anger in his voice.

"Wait a minute," Lindon breaks in, not sounding angry but confused. "You want to claim all of us as mates and bear our children?"

"That will not happen," Brier shouts, standing and running his hands through his hair. "I want no part of this. I'm not even a proper element anymore."

I stand up because I can't handle him shouting at me while I am still sitting on the ground. His rejection is hurtful, but I will not cower in front of him. "Then why did they send you?"

"They didn't! Your sister did," he spits at me.

"I believe that the Elementals work in strange ways," I step closer to him. "Somehow, the curse is tied into this still, and somehow, they had Elizabeth doing their bidding for my sacrifice."

"Bullshit!" he shouts, stepping closer to me and giving me a hard look. "I tell you, I'm not an element any longer. I may have some traits, but I have no powers they offer."

"And maybe they are just trapped in you like Lindon's were," I spit back at him. "Unknown as it may be, you're still a water element, and they sent you to me."

"She could be right, Brier," Lindon says, still sitting by the fire.

"Stay out of this!" Brier says, pointing at him. "I know you're hot to get in her underthings and would say just about anything to do so."

"Now who's crossing the line?" Lindon shoots back at him. "At least I don't hide my feelings. You're the one who is in denial. I see how you watch her with Tate. You want her just as much as I do."

The mention of Tate's name, I can't help but turn away from Brier and look at him. He has said nothing so far, and that concerns me. Out of all of them, he is the one I need to make this right with.

He is just sitting there. I'm not sure if he is even listening anymore. I walk over and kneel in front of him. "Tate?"

He looks up at me. His face stunned by what I have said. I don't know what to say to him. I need to know what he thinks.

"Celine... I don't... know what to say."

"I'm sorry," I tell him, frightened of his reaction. I have to be firm on this. I can't change it now. I have made the sacrifice in blood and am bound to fulfill it. "I didn't know who would come for me, but I asked the Elementals for a suitable match, for love to bear their children. Seeing you, it was such a relief to me because I knew that they had fulfilled it."

"Celine, I love you, but..." He can't seem to find the words. "You know how I am."

"I do, but you had agreed before. When you asked me to marry you, you knew I would one day have to take a Water element as a husband," I remind him of our past. I need him to feel that way still.

"I lost you after that day. I grieved for you, thinking you were dead," he says, standing up, and I do, too. He is silent for a minute as he paces around, and I don't move. He finally turns to me. "Seeing you again, knowing that we have a second chance... it feels like a miracle to me."

"It is!" I say, reaching for his arm, but he pulls away. "Tate, please. I need you. Please understand, I can't break the blood oath."

"I'm not that boy anymore, Celine," Tate says, stepping right back up to me again but not touching. "I know I agreed to it years ago, but things change. I've changed."

"I'm not the same person, either." I feel like I am about to burst into tears at his rejection. Brier may have already done that, but this is Tate. He is the most crucial person in the world to me. "I tried everything to get out of there. I could have done some horrible things, and I even considered them. But then I thought of what my sister did to me, and I knew I couldn't do something so evil. I gave a blessing to this world instead."

"By offering yourself to men you didn't even know?" he sneers at me, and I flinch. "You didn't know I would be among them, did you?"

I just stand there, and he grabs me by the arms. "Did you?"

"No!" I shout, finally letting the tears fall. "I didn't know the love of my life would be among them!"

There is a brief silence between us as we stare at each other. I don't wipe at my face or hide my shame. I love Tate. I need him to understand and accept me and what I have done.

"Others may have been more willing to share you, but I'm not," he tells me so fiercely that he scares me. "I never wanted to share you in the first place. I could have accepted it then, but not now."

He drops my arms, stepping back from me. Slowly he turns away from me, his hands on his hips. "Knowing you like this, sharing my magic, being with you, loving you. Dammit, Celine!"

I jump as he curses at me. It is slamming into my heart. I am breaking at his painful refusal, and I don't fight the fresh tears from falling. I hate what this is doing to us, tearing us apart. I had hoped that Tate would accept, but he isn't.

I should have told him that first day. If I had, then maybe he could have accepted it, but I waited, and now I will lose him. I can't change what I did and won't because the end goal is too important.

"I'm not sorry for what I did, but I am sorry it hurts you. I saw that I could do something good with my life and with this stupid curse," I finally say to his back. I am glad he isn't looking at me. "You want to break my heart, then you go right ahead, Tate Forrester. But I can't stop this. It's written in blood. If you don't accept it, the power of the Elementals will just send another."

I turn to leave because I can't take the pain of his rejection of any longer, but Lindon is right there, grabbing me before I can run away.

"No, Cherry, you can't go out there," he says as I fight to get free of him, desperate to get away.

"Let me go!" I shout at him as he holds me close to him, taking every punch and slap I throw at him.

"I can't do that," he tells me, taking my hands and trapping them against his chest. "They are getting closer."

"Tate," I hear Brier say. "Step away from camp, please."

I stop struggling and turn to look at Tate, and he looks back at me. He holds my eyes in his, and the pain is written all over his face. Suddenly, he kicks at the log on the ground at his feet, and it goes flying out into the woods, hitting a tree and breaking in half. He turns away from me then and picks up his sword, running into the woods.

I break down then, crying hard as I cling to Lindon. He holds me up in his arms as I crumble and lose all my strength.

He left me. My heart is breaking into a thousand little pieces. How am I ever going to move on? How am I ever going to do what I must do? I knew it would be hard for any of them to accept, but for him just to leave…

"Shh, Cherry," Lindon whispers in my hair. "He just needs some time."

"No, he doesn't," I sob. "He meant it. I know him… I've… I've lost him."

"Shh," he says, finally picking me up and sitting down on the ground with me. "He can't fight you. He loves you too much, Cherry. I know it. He will be back, and he will accept it."

It is at that moment that a roar sounds from somewhere close by and a second one responds.

"Shit," Brier says as he moves around the camp. "Lindon, stay with her. Tate and I will handle them. Be on the alert for another."

"Go," Lindon says, taking the sword Brier offers him, still holding me.

I don't even care that I hear the stupid ogres. I welcome them to come and end my suffering.

Chapter Twenty-Three
BRIER

I feel sorry for Celine, but there is nothing I can do. I can understand her story and what she did, but she has it wrong if she thinks I can help. Still, she isn't heartbroken over me but for her real love, Tate. His refusal had been harsh for even me to hear. I know he loves her; hell, anyone can see the love they have for each other is something few people find in life. I have a feeling he will come around. Until then, I have a lovesick girl on my hands and trying to keep her from becoming an ogre meal.

This is complicating things. Celine sat by the fire, not looking or caring what went on around her, last night. Several times Lindon had sat down to talk, but she just pulled away from him.

When morning finally arrived, I pulled her up to her feet and walked her to the riverboat. There, she went below to lie down on the bed. Lindon checked on her after we had been on the boat for a few hours, only to come back up and say she was still upset.

Then he walked right over to Tate and punched him in the face. A fight almost broke out between them, but I jumped in the middle. It upset Lindon that Tate was breaking the girl's heart. I was too, but I wasn't about to get involved.

We left her alone for the day, giving her some space, none of us talking. As soon as we pull into shore for the night, things don't go any better.

Lindon jumps out of the boat, heading for the shore before it is pulled into shore all the way.

"Where are you going?" I call to him.

"Hunting. I'll catch dinner tonight," he says as he keeps walking.

"But I need you to get Celine," I shout at him.

"I can't do it." Lindon stops and turns to look at me. "I can't go down there and see her tears over that…" he points to Tate. "… any longer. You deal with it."

I sigh and massage my temple as I watch him walk away. This will be a long fucking night.

"I'll deal with her," Tate says as he stands up. "This is all my fault, anyway."

"No, I'll do it," I shout at him, running out of patience with him and Lindon. "Go set up camp, and I'll bring Celine."

After a minute, he nods and jumps off the boat. Dammit, how did I get myself in the middle of this? I have no experience with women and how sensitive they are. I am a hardened warrior, not a nursemaid.

Heading down the small steps, I step inside the tiny room, feeling constricted. I hate this feeling and rarely step foot down in the inner part of it. I hate being confined in any small space.

I sit down on the bed. Celine is sleeping; she doesn't stir. I need to be gentle with her, but that isn't my way.

"Celine, wake up," I say, shaking her arm lightly, and she moves away from me. "It's getting dark now and the mox will soon be coming out. Staying on the boat is not an option you know this. Any movement they will swarm the boat and take it over."

She sits up and turns to me, pushing her messy hair out of her face. Her eyes are puffy from crying, and I feel for her.

Getting up, I go over to the sink, wet a small towel, and move back to her. "Here, wash your face off."

She takes the cloth from me and wipes her face, and I'm thankful I don't have to do it for her. Reaching over, I take the brush and hand it to her next. "Do something with that hair while you're at it."

I step back, leaning on the bar and watch her as she finishes wiping her face and brush her hair. I like her hair. It is so long and pretty down like it is now; I have the urge to touch it myself.

"You know, you can't keep doing this to yourself," I tell her, looking away. "You need to eat, clean yourself up, and get out of this bed."

"Why do you care?" she asks me, dropping her hands to her lap. "You don't want to have anything to do with me, either."

"I know your heart is breaking for Tate, but you're breaking Lindon's heart, you know," I tell her. "He can't stand seeing you this way."

"I never thought he would say no," she says, tears coming to her eyes again. "I love him so much, and I can't go out there and see him."

"This isn't easy for him either. He is torn and stubborn. He has every right not to want to share something as special as you with another."

"But he knew with me returning to take the crown that I could never be just his," she says, wiping her tears away. "He has always known that."

"You're right. He knew that," I say, pushing off the bar and sitting beside her. "You did nothing wrong, Celine. You need to stop this and stand up tall. Be the queen you know you have to become. Own up to what you have to do, and if he doesn't come around, then it's not him refusing you, it will have to be you refuse him."

"I don't want the crown," she says sullenly. "I would be happy to go off somewhere and never go back to that place. But I can't deny what I have to do for the Elementals. If I break the oath, even they could turn destruction on the worlds."

"Most likely, they would." I don't know if that is true, but I need her to believe what she is doing is right. To give her some faith to walk out that door and be active again. "The Water element turned its back on me when I needed it most. I'm sure it would turn on you as well if you didn't do what you have vowed."

"He is such an ass," she claims now, crossing her arms.

Good, she is getting angry. That should help. Maybe I can spread this around a little to get her motivated and light a fire under Tate's ass.

"Yes, and you know what? I think you should go out there and show him what he would be missing."

"What?" she asks, looking at me.

"I mean, you have Lindon, who is head over heels falling for you," I tell her. "He and Tate have already been fighting over you today. Seeing you like this is hurting him and he could use some encouragement. At least he is willing to share you. I say go out there and make Tate feel a little of that jealousy firsthand. He wants to deny you. Well, you have other options and Lindon is just waiting for you to smile at him again."

"Are you serious?" she asks, facing me.

"Hell, yes, I'm serious!" I say, throwing my hand in the air. I can't believe I am saying this to her after telling both Lindon and Tate not to fight over her. But it looks like that is what she needs to see. "Go out there and give your attention to Lindon. Ignore Tate… if that is what he wants, then he needs to get used to it. We have almost a week before getting back to Clearwater. Do you want to be like this the whole time?"

"But don't you think that would be cruel?" There is interest in her voice and a hint of malice, but she is still a sweet person and doesn't want to hurt anyone.

"To the man who has broken your heart? Fuck that!" I tell her. "He has no right to be jealous anymore. He gave up that right when he denied you."

She looks down and seems to think about it. If she takes my advice, I might have to break Lindon and Tate up again, but fuck, I'm not about to have to do this anymore. I will allow myself this moment to speak freely with her. I don't want to become attached to her and give her any real encouragement that I am willing. But I don't want her to give up on them.

"You're right," she says, nodding at me. "But I can't go out there like this. Can I have just a minute?"

"Five minutes," I tell her as I get up and walk to the small door. "And wear a pair of those pants over there. Show off that pretty little ass of yours while you're at it."

"My… ass?" she asks me.

"Men like a delightful piece of ass," I say, smiling at her. "Show off those curves of yours. Make him want it. Flaunt what the gods have given you."

"Okay," she says not so sure of what I am saying but at least she smiles and gets up. I like seeing her smile. Hell, I won't admit it out loud, but I wouldn't mind seeing her ass myself. But I am definitely keeping my distance from it.

"Get ready. I will wait above for you."

"Thank you, Brier," she says from the edge of the bed. She looks like she is about to reach out and touch me, and I back away before she breathes, "for making me feel better about what I am doing."

I say nothing but go on up to wait for her.

"Well, that wasn't as hard as I thought it would be," I say to myself aloud. "Tate will hate me, but fuck it. At least she is up and responsive now."

I have a feeling that if she touches Lindon in front of Tate, he will go off the rails in jealousy. Hopefully, it will open his eyes to see that he needs her just as much as she needs him.

I wait for her as the sun goes down, and we have to get off the boat and out of the water. Those fucking Mox are fucking devils in the early hours just waiting to come out of their holes and find their prey. In no time, dozens of them could surround us, and I'd rather deal with ogres.

"Come on, Celine, we need to go," I call down to her. She pops up the steps just then, and I take in her appearance in awe for a second.

She is wearing brown pants, just as I recommended, and they fit her like a glove. The brown vest she found pulls tight over the white blouse, emphasizing all the right areas. *Damn, she looks good enough to eat.* I can see why the ogres want to have a bite of her. I wouldn't mind it myself.

"What do you think?" she asks me, turning around and giving me an unrestricted view of her backside. It is ripe and plump, standing in those damn pants.

I can't resist reaching out and squeezing one of those cheeks.

She jumps and turns on me. "Brier!"

"Just testing it out," I say, chuckling at her. *Well, so much for keeping my distance.* "Your ass is fine, and that vest is a pleasant touch. Just unbutton that blouse some."

She looked down at her chest and unbuttons two of the buttons.

"One more."

"But that will show my breasts," she says, looking up at me, blushing.

"Are you a nun?" I ask her. I want to see them, and I want her to unbutton it for me. I am pushing my limits but at least I know it will push Tate's also. "Women in the city would do it."

She sighs and then does it. *Fuck, she is a hot little cherry.* Lindon sure has that nickname right as her plump small breasts peek out at me.

"Okay, you're good now. Let's go," I say, turning around before I try to squeeze those plump little grapefruits. Celine is too damn tempting for me to touch, and I have vowed to keep her as far away from me since the first day I saw her. I'm not suitable for any woman in my life, and certainly not one as gentle as she. Besides, she needs a real Water element, not a broken one.

Helping her down, I am quick to release her as we make our way on the shore. As we are walking up to the camp, I hear some roaring in the distance once more. Last night we had killed eight of them, and I figure we will face off with that many again tonight.

We continue up to the camp, and I walk a little behind her, watching the sway of her hips. They are provocative but she walks like a nun in a habit. "Put a little more sway in those hips of yours."

"Are you looking at my ass?" she asks, half turning, her lips quirking a bit. She is teasing me but also blushing and it is so damn cute.

"Yes. Now, do as I say," I demand of her. "You want Tate, don't you?"

"Yes," she admits as she stops and looks down, the smile dropping from her mouth.

Against my better judgment, I lift her chin to look at me. "Then stand tall, be sexy, and he will come to you."

"I don't know to…be sexy."

Gods, the girl knows nothing from living in the convent! "It doesn't take much to catch a man's eyes. Put your feet more in front of each other as you walk and let your hips move back and forth."

She takes a deep breath and does as I say. At least she knows how to follow directions. Those plump little cheeks sway in front of me and I have to adjust my cock in my pants. Tate needs an ass whooping for torturing me like this.

"Perfect. Keep doing that," I tell her as we move forward again. I am fucking tempted to touch that ass again but keep my hands to myself. Instead, I walk up beside her and smile encouragingly. "Stick with me, little princess, and I'll make you a temptress yet."

"I think you're enjoying this too much," she says, smiling at me. I am glad to see her smiling again.

"Oh, I will be," I promise her. Once those two fools get a look at her this evening, they will be drooling. Lindon better thank me later for setting the little hellcat on him.

Chapter Twenty-Four
CELINE

"What the hell are you wearing?" Tate shouts at me as soon as I walk into camp with Brier.

"Pants," I say as I walk past him. His eyes are about to pop out of his head, and I am thankful to Brier for talking me into this.

He grabs my arm, stopping me. "That's not proper for a princess." He glares at me, and I can see his anger at my apparel.

"Then why were they in the royal boat?" I ask, pulling my arm from his hand. I have to admit, seeing his reaction is a little exhilarating mainly since we haven't spoken since last night when he hurt me so.

"Change," he growls at me and I shiver at his demand. Some part of me wants to do as he says but I push it away.

"Can't. Don't have any other clothing on me, and I wouldn't even if I did," I tell him bravely. I spin away from him, letting he see me at every angle and hear him growl again. "I've always wanted to try out pants. They feel a little snugger than I thought, but I kind of like it."

"Dammit, Celine," he roars at me. "Untuck your blouse and cover yourself."

"Why? Women wear pants," I say, rubbing my hands over my hips. I watch as his eyes follow my hands and can't help a small smile. It feels like he is touching me, just like he had a few days ago.

"Because I don't want Lindon looking at your ass when he returns," he says as his eyes raise to mine, and he clenches his jaw. *Good, he is mad and jealous just as Brier said he would be.*

"Oh, but I do," I tell him, walking past and putting some of that sway in my walk like Brier told me to. As I draw closer to the center of camp, I turn back to him and place my hands on my hips. I can see Brier standing behind Tate, smiling and shaking his head. "Lindon will be my husband. I think he has every right to look at me as much as he likes. I will even let him touch it if he wants."

"He touches you, I will kill him," he threatens as he steps forward. "You're just trying to make me jealous."

"You have no right to be jealous." I drop my arms and shout at him. Who does Tate think he is that he can refuse me and then deny the one man here who doesn't? "I intend to make a happy and loving marriage between Lindon and me. He knows what I want and has accepted me, so he gets all rights. I will give Brier a chance if he would like one, too."

"Brier will not touch you. His dick doesn't rule his pants."

"Really?" I ask him. *Oh, he is asking for it.* I look behind Tate to Brier and see him shaking his head at me in warning as he drops the smile. "Well, he sure enjoyed touching my ass earlier."

"What?" He turns to Brier, who just shuffles his feet.

"Well, those pants do look good on her," Brier says with a gesture to me. "I got fucking eyes, Tate, and I am a man."

"I have to admit Brier caught me a little by surprise at first, but… I enjoyed it," I say from behind Tate as Brier glares at me. I enjoy watching him squirm a little too. Afterall, he has refused me also.

"He…llo, Cherry." Lindon whistles, coming into camp and dropping some dead rabbits. I turn to him, and his eyes skim up and down my body. A bolt of electrical current shoots up my legs and right into the center of me.

"Do you like them?" I ask, blushing at him as I take a step closer. I feel a sudden pull towards Lindon like he is calling me to him. His seduction is so powerful and my attraction to him plays a key role also. He takes a step closer. "I thought I would try pants out and see how they fit."

"Definitely like," he says, stepping up to me. "Looks like the little nun is coming out of the cloth."

"You know I never wore the cloth, right?" I say to him, leaning toward him.

"Figure of speech," he says, just a few inches in front of me now. He bites his lip as his gaze falls to my breasts.

"Lindon, I'm sorry if I stressed you out last night and today," I mumble as I slide my hands up his chest. I feel his warm hands touch my hips, as he stares down at me. "Thank you for being there for me. I know what I need and…"

Tate forces us apart and steps in front of Lindon. "Don't you dare touch her."

"What the hell, Tate?" Lindon says to him, stepping back a few paces. "You don't want her, but no one else can have her?"

"That's right," Tate growls as he turns around and grabs me again, pulling me along with him. He is forcing me away from the others and into the woods.

"What are you doing?" I look over my shoulder and see Lindon moving closer, but Brier holds him back. "Let me go, Tate!"

He doesn't listen; he just keeps walking us farther into the woods. *What the hell is he doing?* Finally, he stops and pushes me against a tree, pressing himself hard against me. His lips come crashing down on mine and I whimper from the force of his kiss, pushing at him but he doesn't relent. His tongue is teasing against my own and I soon give in, wrapping my arms around his neck and accept him. As I do, he finally pulls back and stares down at me.

"Okay, you've made your point," he growls at me. "I'm a jealous fool who can't live without you. You happy?"

I am happy that he admitted to it, but I'm not about to say it. He hurt me deeply, and for that, he has to pay.

"I am taking Lindon as my husband," I say as I glare at him. "You, I'm not so sure about anymore."

"Oh, yes, you are!" he growls as he presses his lower body into mine and lifts me against the tree and I feel his leg and other things pressing into soft areas of mine. I can feel way too much with these pants on. "I am and will always be your first husband, or you will not have any husbands at all."

"You don't get to decide that anymore," I yell back at him ignoring the heat of him between my legs and try to squirm away from him. "I do, and I'm saying no!"

"Dammit, Celine! I'm sorry about last night," he shouts at me. "You caught me completely off guard and seeing the light in Lindon's eyes tripped me out. You know I am a jealous ass. I always have been with you."

"You hurt me." I assert needing him to understand how deeply he did. "You know how much I love you without having even to say it. You knew we could never be together if I took the crown unless you were willing to share me, and still, you denied me knowing full well what was to come."

"I do know, but that doesn't mean it doesn't hurt me." His voice is quiet, and his eyes soften just before he closes them, hiding the pain I already saw. He looks back at me now. "I just thought we had some time alone. I know what the future holds being with you, but I'm selfish. I just thought we could work up to it, but instead, you drop this news and it hits like a brick. Claiming you're not taking just one more husband but two...*and* they are here! Standing right in front of us, watching us. Wanting you, and I can't stand it."

He rests his forehead against mine, the anger dripping off him and converting to sorrow. The leaves from the tree above us starts to fall in colors around us, like it too feels his pain. He is upset about this, and so am I, and to be honest, I could live a happy belonging to just one man, to him for the rest of my life. But that isn't my life.

I want to give him the time he needs, but I'm not sure if I can promise him that. The power of the Elementals want me to take them all. I don't know how long I can deny the power as I am already feeling a pull to each of them.

Tate doesn't even know about my kiss with Lindon. It wouldn't have happened if it wasn't for the power of his element calling to me. But I had kissed him, I had hungered for him, and I still do. I wanted to wait with Lindon and give Tate the time he needs, but what if I couldn't?

Even Brier had set me off today. He says he doesn't have his power, but something is calling out to me from him. I have this strong urge to try and heal him so we can be together. Maybe it isn't as strong as the pull with Tate and Lindon, but it is still there.

With Tate, it is more potent than any one of them. After he touched me yesterday, how his power flowed inside of me, I am literally on fire for him. That is why it hurt so badly when he rejected me. Because the need for him is so overpowering, I just want to reach out and hold on to him forever.

I finally speak. "I understand that feeling you have inside of you. Every moment that goes by my hunger for you is building. I felt it the moment I first laid eyes on all of you, and it keeps getting stronger. Because I love you so much already, its ten times worse with you. I can't control it. It's driving me crazy, and I think it is driving you crazy, too."

He lifts his head, saying nothing as he leans in and kisses me fiercely, letting the hunger inside of us consume us. I cling to him as he puts his hands under my ass, lifting me and bringing my legs around him. This position is even more intimate and I gasp as I feel the hardness of him press into my core.

We are wild and hungry for one another, and he squeezes my ass hard in his hands as he pulls me roughly against his body.

"I'll give you whatever you want," he says, pulling back just enough to speak before he claims my mouth again. "Just promise never to leave me."

"I won't," I rasp, kissing him hard, clinging to him. Being in his arms again feels so good and right, I want to be as close as I can with Tate. The urge to seal our bond is so strong and I can't help the need inside me any longer. "Make love to me."

He growls deep in his throat as his lips fall to my neck, and he pulls at my clothing. I grasp his shirt, raising it up, and he pulls back, keeping me pressed where I am with his lower half and rips the shirt over his head. He goes for the buttons on my vest, ripping them in his haste as I try to help him.

Something catches my eyes behind him, and I scream in warning just as Brown pulls his arm back.

Tate reacts instantly, pulling me to the side of the tree, and we hit the ground together as Brown slams into the top of it, cutting it in half with the force of his hit. The tree falls, and Tate rolls us over on the ground as the severed half of it comes right at us. We miss the tree limbs just barely, and Tate jumps to his feet swiftly and draws his sword.

Brown is standing about fifteen feet away from us, as they both growl at each other.

"No touch," he forces out and lets out a roar so loud I have to cover my ears.

"Come on, beast," Tate growls at him, sidestepping closer. Tate is substantial, but I have to wonder if he is strong enough for Brown.

I hear the pounding of footsteps and look to see Lindon and Brier not far away. I sigh in relief that Tate doesn't have to face him alone.

"Mine!" Brown says again, then he takes off into the woods, leaving us alone.

Brier and Lindon are on us then, and Tate helps me up.

"Why did he take off?" Lindon asks, pointing toward Brown.

"What happened?" Brier asks instead.

"He just attacked us out of nowhere," Tate tells him as he pulls me into his arms. He looks so tenderly at me, smoothing my hair back from my face. "Are you okay?"

"Yes," I assure him, wrapping my arms around his middle. I am shaking so badly I need something substantial to hold on to. Seeing Brown running toward us scared me more than I have ever been scared before.

"I didn't even know he was there until Celine screamed. I dropped us to the ground instantly, feeling him coming up fast, and he took the whole tree down in half."

"He gave no warning?" Brier asks him now.

"No. No growl, no roar, not anything, just a full out charge attack," Tate tells him. "He was pissed, too. When he roared, I thought he would attack, but… he just said, 'no-touch' and 'mine'. He was claiming her."

I hear Lindon shout then. "What the fuck for?"

"He didn't like me touching her," Tate says, and I look up at him. "He didn't attack to hurt you. Brown attacked to warn me off."

"Why… why would he do that?" I ask him, still shaking in his arms.

"That doesn't make much sense," Brier says before Tate can answer me. "Ogres don't like humans."

"No, they don't, but he is different, we know that," Tate says, and his words are starting to scare me. "For some reason, he wants her for a purpose. He just showed that to me."

"What are you thinking?" Lindon asks him.

"He has a plan to steal her away from us," Tate says, looking from me to them. "He has been playing us all along, and we seem to playing right into it."

Chapter Twenty-Five

"I've done told you everything I know about Brown," I exclaim for the dozenth time this morning. Last night, we had all been on high alert looking for him to attack at any time, but he never did. I thought if he did, they wouldn't be so on edge now.

As soon as we hit the riverboat this morning, Brier starts the round of questions. Apparently, they didn't want to talk last night because they thought Brown was watching us, so all of their questions bombard me now.

Every time an ogre or two attacks, one of the men stayed right with me the entire time, which endangered the men, but they insisted it kept me safer. Mostly it was Tate but, as the night wore on, he would step up and leave me with the others.

Their concerns had quickly become mine. Brown got under their skin. It makes me shiver to think of Brown's true motives. I've always thought he just wanted my blood like all the others but if that was so, he could have taken me from them long ago.

"There has to be something we are missing," Brier reproaches.

I go through the details as I know them again. "Brown arrived at the convent a few weeks after I did. He never left the area, just as I haven't. He fought off all the ogres in the area, and they all left. For years, he paced the compound, calling for me. Wherever I went, Brown was always on the other side of the wall. He did horrible things to get me to come out."

"What about this man he mentioned before we left?" Tate asks. I can tell he seems more interested in him than Brown. "Are you sure he never talked about him before?"

"No. Brown mentioned no one in all the years he's been around," I say again. "In fact, I don't think he was inclined to answer even then. I don't know why he brought him up the last time we spoke."

"Ogres are not known to be thinkers," Brier speaks up, throwing his hands in the air. "His form and abilities are off, too. And the way he fights… We would have brought him down by now if he was normal."

"Maybe it is time we look at it a different way," Lindon finally says. "What if he is cursed? We don't know why or how, and if he is, he most likely was cursed by the queen who didn't bother to tell us about him. I think this Lee character has to be tied in with the queen somehow. Maybe not on the same side as her, since Cherry doesn't seem to know him."

Tate speaks, "What about us?" No one answers, not following Tate's thoughts. "The queen sent us, but Celine says that she called and asked for us. What if one of us might know of this man, Lee?"

They all seem to think about that for a moment.

Brier speaks up. "I had a brother who had the name, but he is dead. Maybe it's not his first name? Lee is common for a middle name, but we rarely use them."

"I don't know anyone," Lindon says shaking his head.

"It is a common name," Tate sighs, seeming to realize that would not help.

"Elizabeth cursed me because of her jealousy," I say, thinking about my curse. "What if she cursed him for the same reason?"

"Jealous over an ogre?" Lindon asks.

"No," I tell him. "What if he is a man? What if he is Lee?"

"But you said you don't know him," Tate says.

"Yes, but as Brier said, it could be a middle name which we rarely use. Maybe I know him, but just not by the name he gave us." The gears turning, I feel like we are close to something. "Phillip."

"What?"

"You all told me Phillip was dead, but what if Elizabeth cursed him?" I say then. "He always protected me before, and, Tate, you said yourself that you didn't think he wanted to harm me."

"Phillip is dead," he reminds me.

"But you thought I was dead," I remind him, taking his hand.

"Do you know if he carried the middle name?" Brier asks.

"No, I don't, but—"

"It sounds like it could be him. If he was a man, cursed. Tate, how long between when Phillip died to when Celine disappeared?"

"I don't know," Tate says. "I was too much into my own grief to have realized. Besides, I left soon after I thought she was dead. I couldn't be there anymore."

Tate hadn't taken my death well to have just up and left his family. I remember they had all been close and I had always envied that about him.

"So, it could be him," Brier says, thinking still. "If it was, though, why would she send him to you?"

"Torture, maybe?" I suggest. "He couldn't get to me, not speak to me. He was always my protector, but he became my fear. Maybe she would have known he would become that."

"Still, that doesn't sound right," Brier says.

"But he is following us," Lindon says. "He is heading straight for Clearwater and is on our heels the whole way. Maybe he knows Celine fears him and is letting her stay with us. We already know he has avoided attacks with us, and after yesterday, he didn't even try to take her."

"I think you are on to something," Tate says then. "If it is Phillip, he most likely wants out of this curse just as badly as Celine does. If the queen is looking to break the curse on Celine, maybe he thinks she will break the curse on him too?"

"It has to be him!" I say. It makes perfect sense to me. I feel terrible if it is Phillip, but my fears of him aren't as strong now. "What if there is a way I could ask him?"

"No!" they all shouted at me.

"You're not getting near him!" Tate adds. "We don't know for certain he means you no harm."

"But…"

"No, Celine!" Brier cuts me off again. He is good at that, and it is annoying. "He might not want to hurt you, but I have no doubt he would take you if he has the chance."

"But…"

"And he could lie and say he is Phillip so you will go with him," Lindon adds.

"Okay, I get the point!" I shout at them. *Why are we going through all this if we aren't trying to solve the issu*e? "So, what is your plan to deal with him, then?"

"We stay on course and continue," Brier says getting up and moving behind the wheel. "If he wants to follow, then let him, but if he tries to take you, we put him down."

"But what if it is Phillip?" I ask, not liking that idea. He had always been kind to me.

"No exceptions. Our priority is you, not Phillip," Brier says, as he pulls a lever, the paddle starts up, and we are moving again.

"But if it is Phillip, I don't want him harmed," I stand and walk to him. "He always fought my sister to protect me. I can't just let you kill him."

"Then he'd better stay out of our way," Brier says, staring straight ahead now. "End of discussion."

"No!" I say, standing up and grabbing his arm. "You're not to hurt him!"

He stares hard at me. I will not give on this. I need to know if he is Phillip, and, if he is, I have to help him. Even if he isn't and is actually a human who was cursed, he doesn't deserve what my sister has done.

"I don't think you understand how dangerous this is," Brier says, steering the boat to the middle of the river. "He may have played nice with us so far, but he is a powerful beast. We haven't been able to take him down yet, and that is saying a lot. And let's not forget what happened yesterday. If we hadn't come up when we did, he most likely would have killed Tate and taken you."

"You... you don't know that," I say, wavering at the thought of losing Tate.

"Go get some rest, little princess," he growls at me. "And don't even think about finding a way of talking with him. You are not to leave our side."

"Come on, Celine," Tate says, standing up and pulling me to the stairs. "You're tired and should rest."

I go with him only because I know Brier will not listen to me. None of them really will, but I have to see if Brown is Phillip. I have to know and I don't care if I make them angry. I can't just let Phillip die at their hands. He is like a brother to me.

Tate guides me down the stairs and into the small room. He pulls me up against him, my back to his chest, and he slides my hair to one side and kisses my neck. I forget about the rest for the time, enjoying his sweet caress.

His arms come around me. Slowly, he slides the vest off my shoulders.

"What are you doing?" I ask him, letting it fall to the floor.

"I have been dying to get you out of these clothes," his arms circle me as his hands go for the buttons on the pants now. "You are never to wear these again."

"But I like them," I say playfully as he finishes with the row of buttons and pushes them down my hips.

"They drive me crazy," he says as he pushes them farther down my legs. "Step out of them."

I do as he says, leaving me only in the shirt and underthings. I am a little excited about having him undress me, but he doesn't remove my shirt. Instead, he turns me, kissing passionately and pushes me back toward the bed. I feel my backside press against it. Tate picks me up and places me on the edge, my legs falling to each side of him.

His hands are all over me now, skimming over my back and shoulders and down my chest. His hands run over my legs, lifting them around him more as his hands slide down to caress my backside. He breaks our kiss, his lips inching slowly down my neck. His hands come back up and start undoing my shirt.

"Are you going to make love to me now?" I rasp with excitement at the thought as he is undressing me. My nerves are kicking in, but I push them down, ready for this.

He growls at me as he stops unbuttoning my shirt halfway down and nibbles my shoulder. "No, I'm not. I have half a mind to claim you now, but there are a few things we need to get straight first."

"Like what?"

He looks up at me in question. "For now, you are mine and only mine." He presses his forehead against mine. "Whatever you have or need with the others, they are just going to have to wait."

I like the idea of belonging just to Tate for a while but I still have a pull to the others, and he needs to know that.

"I will agree, but only if you realize that I am drawn to them," I tell him. "I don't think I am in complete control of my feelings when they are near me."

He sighs deeply but relents. "Fine, but at least try to resist for now. I can't bear the thought of them touching you right now."

"But why?" I ask needing to know why this is so important to him.

"It is the animals inside me, Celine," he says looking deep into my eyes. "They are becoming wild inside me right now, wanting you and…they can be beastly and forceful. I am trying to keep them down but, when I see you with one of the others, they are harder to control."

I nod, sure I can resist for a while. Tate is too extraordinary and essential for me not to try. The idea of the animals inside him thrill me but I don't want him to hurt the others. With Tate's strength, I don't want to test his control.

"No erotic clothing can be worn in front of them either," he says then. "I have seen some things in this room, so don't go getting any ideas."

"But, I like pants." I pout as I pull my head back to look at him. "Honestly, do you really find them that bad?"

"No, the pants are fine," he sighs, not looking too pleased about them. "Just don't go bending over in front of them and if they touch your ass again, you tell them it is off-limits."

"Okay," I say, smiling at him. "What if you grab my ass?"

"I'm the only one allowed," he says. His hand reaches down and squeezes it to make his point. "No flirting with Lindon, either."

"I don't know if I can stop that," I tell him honestly. "He is such a flirt, and I can't seem to keep myself from responding."

"Then not around me, at least," he hisses through clenched teeth.

"What about Brier?" I ask him since he hasn't mentioned him yet.

"That goes for him too," Tate says seriously. "He may deny his attraction to you, but I know he is. My animals can sense the competition of another alpha."

"You really think he is attracted to me?" I honestly want to know his thoughts. Brier seems to want to stay as far away from me as possible.

"He grabbed your ass, didn't he? Or were you just saying that to rile me up?"

"No, he did," I confess. "But I don't think he was earnest about it. I think he did it just to surprise me and maybe make me feel better."

"Oh, I'm sure he did it because he wanted to," Tate says. "You better watch out for any more of those surprises."

"Is that all?" I ask him then, wanting to get back to what we were doing.

"Do you have any requests for me?" My breath catches for a moment and my heart swells. This is a relationship, and he knows that he is asking a lot from me, yet he is kind enough to reciprocate.

I think about it for a minute. "No more fighting with Lindon or Brier. We have to all get along in this."

"I promise not to hit them without good reason," he nods in agreement.

"If the urge strikes to allow one of them in, you have to take it."

"What do you mean?" he asks pulling his head back from mine.

"Well you say your animals want to take over. If at any time you feel you can control them and will allow for them to join us, you have to allow it." I say hoping he gets my meaning.

He thinks about it for a moment, "If I can be in control of the moment, I might be able to allow them in. But, it is only a theory, I am afraid we will have to test it and see."

"As long as we can try, I am happy with that." I smile at him as I run my hands into his hair. "We have to find a way to move past just us together."

"I reluctantly agree but do so willingly," he says with a smile. "Anything else?"

"You have to make love to me," I say, blushing at my boldness. I am so hot to experience that with him. It will drive me crazy if I don't bond with one of them soon. "I want you to be the first, Tate. I want to share myself with you."

He moans as he buries his face in my neck once more. "I will make love to you repeatedly until you beg me to rest. But not right now."

"Why not?" I ask, hoping we could get right to it. I don't feel any urge to wait. I have been dreaming about him for years. Sure I am a little nervous about it but only because I know there will be some pain the first time.

"Because you are tired, and I know you didn't rest yesterday," he says, pulling back and looking at me. "But soon. Very soon, my love."

"Will you at least rest with me?" I ask, excited that he has agreed and that he promised we would. "I want to feel you next to me."

"I will, for now," he says. "Slide over."

I do, giving him room to join me. He lies on his side, and I lean down to join him, but he stops me. "No. Turn around and face the other way."

"Why?" I ask, wanting to be next to him so I can touch him.

"Because I know what you will do, and I can't stand the thought of your hands touching me." I can't help the laugh that escapes at how well he knows me. "Face the wall, and I will hold you until you go to sleep."

"You are very demanding, Tate Forrester," I declare as I turn over. "I don't remember you being this way when we were younger."

"Oh, yes, I was," he says, wrapping his arms around me and kisses my ear before he says, "You forget all those fights I got into so easy. I was always a jealous ass and beat up all the boys, making them stay away from you."

"You didn't!"

"Yes, I did," he says with a chuckle. "The only ones I didn't dare touch were those from the royal courts. They would have made me leave then, and I couldn't bear the thought of never seeing you again."

"I don't know if it should upset me or if it makes me love you even more," I tell him as I settle down in his arms. Our hands locked together in front of me.

"It was always out of love," he whispers as we settle into the bed. "I love you so much, Celine."

"I love you," I say, and we fall asleep together.

Chapter Twenty-Six
TATE

She looks so beautiful and peaceful in my arms as she sleeps. I had almost crushed her the other day in rejecting sharing her. I knew it was something we would one day have to face, but it was just put out there so suddenly, I wasn't prepared to accept it.

I know I was too demanding and selfish with Celine. It has always been a problem of mine even when we were younger. We were still so close, but any time another boy had come around, threatening us together, I had always run him off.

The sacrifice Celine made was my punishment for being an ass like I am. She is serious about it and has faith; she is doing a good thing for the realms, and I will not take that away from her. I'm just going to have to learn to live with it and hopefully it will all work out for the best.

Despite my protests, I am pleased that it will be Lindon and Brier. I have grown to like them both over the last few weeks. Lindon is more carefree and fun to be around, but Brier is a man who I can tell will always have our backs. In our world, it is good to find two such men I can see sharing someone as special as Celine with. I know they will protect her no matter what.

I ease away from her, needing to talk with the others. I had set the ground rules with her, and now it is time I do so with them. I don't mean to be bossy but until my animals calm down, I need them to give Celine and I a little space. I promised her if the urge takes to allow one of them in. I will do it, but they need to be warned to watch me also.

When she showed up in those pants, showing every curve of her gorgeous body, I snapped. She is going to drive me crazy with Lindon because I denied her in the first place. I couldn't do it. She belongs with me no matter what, and I will never let her go.

I open the door and go up. Brier is resting on one bench, and Lindon is at the wheel. I go to sit beside him so we can talk. Brier, I'm not as concern, and I will let him rest for now.

"I need to talk to you about Celine," I say, looking over at Lindon. He is a major flirt with her and it is something we need to work out.

"For someone who loves her, you did a number on her the other day." The anger in his voice is not hidden, and he refuses to look at me. This is not the friendly banter we are used to.

"I was in shock."

"Fuck that," Lindon says, turning and giving me a hard glare. "If I were her, I wouldn't have forgiven you so fast."

He is right, but I'm not about to tell him that. I am serious about my demand that Celine is only with me for now. I do need some time to adjust to sharing her. I need to take baby steps with the process, or I am afraid of not only being hurt, but hurting her as well. That is the last thing I want to do.

"Look, Celine and I have talked about it, and we have agreed on a few things."

"And you didn't see fit to have Brier and me in on that discussion?" he asks sarcastically.

"No. Look, this sacrifice Celine made to the Elementals threw me for a loop. I didn't handle it well. I wasn't fair to her, and I haven't been fair to you or Brier either."

"At least you can see that now," he says, his voice not so harsh now.

"But that doesn't mean I am okay with this," I tell him. "I have to come to grips with what Celine means to you and him as well and that she is not mine alone. This isn't easy for my animals to accept. To them, Celine can only be mine."

"Will you two please leave me out of this?" Brier says now, sitting up on the bench. "I am not one of her elements, and you all will have to accept that."

"Then why are you here, Brier?" Lindon asks as he motions his hand to him.

"I don't know, but I know it is not for that."

"Bullshit. I see the way you look at her," Lindon confronts him, pointing in his direction.

"Yes, she is a pretty little thing, but that doesn't change the fact," Brier warns. "I am no longer a Water element. If that is what she needs, then it is not me."

I speak up. "If that is true, then we will have to deal with it. But that can be worked out once we get Celine away from here and to a safe place."

"Yes. We need to deal with the ogre tracking us," Brier says, standing up and stretching his back. He has been sleeping in the day on these benches, and though they are comfortable, they aren't much for a good rest.

"I think we should camp on the other side of the river tonight," I suggest to him. "Brown is a serious threat, and he wouldn't dare cross the water."

"We have cleared too many of the ogres out on this side," Brier speaks up, shaking his head. "We could become overwhelmed on the other side by them. If we have to cross in the night, we chance to lose the boat to the Mox even if we make it. It is too risky."

"But Brown is planning something, and we are making it easy for him," I remind him. "I say he is our biggest threat."

"No, I don't think he is," Brier says, sitting back down and leaning forward on his knees. "He doesn't want to kill her or else he would have already tried. If he takes her, we have a better chance of getting her back alive than risking her life with hoards of other ogres."

"I agree," Lindon says then. "We should stay on this side."

Brier is the kind of man you want to have your back. He is reliable and smart with defense and on the attack, and his command is valid. "Fine," I finally agree. "We have several days in this realm. Tomorrow morning, I will leave you both to protect her and go to track Brown. See if I can find out more of what he is planning."

Brown is keen but so am I. If anyone could best his strength, it would be me.

"That could be dangerous if he catches you," Brier tells me. "None of us should try to face him on our own. I've seen what he can do against the three of us even if you haven't and I know you are wanting to engage him again. You shouldn't."

"I am a hunter, and my element is the Earth. I can hide better than any and cover my scent. He will not know I am there," I assure him. I will take Brier's warning but if the chance arises where I think I can best him, I will take it.

"I like that idea," Lindon says, smiling. "Plus, it will give me some time with Celine so I can get to know her better."

"Which brings me back to my point. There are some rules I need to set with you," I tell him, knowing he will not like this.

"Rules?" he looks at me, confused. "What do you mean by rules?"

"I mean, this is mine and Celine's time to reconnect. You will have your time with her, but for now, she is only mine."

"What the hell?" he shouts, not hiding his disappointment. He turns to face me. "She is mine too, Tate. Maybe not Brier's, but I am staking my claim as her element. She wants me and I want her."

"Look, I didn't say that I need a lot of time with her," I try to explain to him. "Celine has already told me she feels a pull to your elements. I know she will not be able to resist it for long, but she has agreed to this. For me."

"Then what am I supposed to do?" Lindon says, and I can see from his resistance that he feels a pull to her as well.

"Get to know her but in a platonic manner for now," I tell him, not being able to resist a smile.

"Platonic? I don't do platonic and definitely not with a woman I want," he tells me, looking forward again. "Asshole."

"Stop thinking with your dick, Lindon," Brier adds in his opinion, then leans back on the cushions. "She's innocent and shouldn't be rushed. You out of all of us should be able to see that."

"I don't intend to seduce her, and I don't mind taking things slowly," Lindon says to him and then turns to me. "But I don't care to stay away from her completely and keep it strictly platonic."

"Look, if you can't stop flirting with her, do it when I'm not around," I tell him. "I will be her first in all things passionate. You are not to touch her unless I allow it."

"You're an overbearing ass," Lindon finally says after a minute. "Look, I know what first love feels like. You two obviously have that, but I am a part of this too, and you need to get used to it."

"I will, but just give me a few days," I plead. "I won't stand in your way, I promise. I just need to wrap my head around this a little better."

I can see Lindon is in turmoil in agreeing to this, but I give him some time. I know I am asking a lot from him.

"I feel… I am just learning my powers, and somehow, she brings them out in me more," he says, looking at me. "I am drawn to her because of them, and I don't have control. They are going to come out again."

I nod. It feels the same to me too. "I have always been drawn to Celine even before we had our powers. I asked her to try, and I'll do the same with you. If I feel I can handle seeing you with her at any time, I will let you know. I don't want to keep you apart, but I have to get a handle on my animals, Lindon."

"You're a beast for doing this to me. I might be able to do a few days if I keep my distance and don't touch her," he finally says, looking away from me. "But you better not rip my head off if I can't. This is difficult for me."

"Thank you, Lindon." My animals are already feeling calmer because he agrees.

"Yeah, Yeah. You just better make it special for her," he demands of me. "And I have no intention of not flirting with her when you are around. You will just have to get over that sooner rather than later."

"Wrap this up," Brier says, looking off in the distance. "We have company down river."

Lindon and I look past Brier and see a warship coming down the river toward us. It is far away, but I can make out the symbols of the royal flag at the top of the vessel.

"Looks like it's from Clearwater," I tell them, knowing they could not see it as I did. My eagle-eye vision allows me the ability to see so far.

"Good," Brier says, standing up. "At least they will not give us any trouble."

They won't since Brier is the commander-in-chief to them, but he will be concerned why they are coming down. Some time goes by before they pull up beside us and tie up to our boat.

"Lindon, make sure Celine stays down below," Brier directs him. "Tate stays with me. If you're leaving tomorrow, you need to know what's going on in the area."

We climb up on the ship by the ladder they throw down. Once on top, we were greeted by his second in command, Edwin.

"Commander Brier." The man stands at attention with several others. "I was hoping we would cross paths. Queen Elizabeth said we might and wanted me to give you a message."

"Second Commander Edwin, it is good to see you," Brier replies. "Why are you in this area?"

"The Fire elements have been hitting the borders of ours through the earth realm for the last week," Second Commander Edwin informs Brier. "We have covered the entrance of the river for your safe passage through, but it seems they are looking for something. I have been directed to warn you and leave a few extra men with you."

"I will take two. Seth and John," Brier says, motioning to the two men behind Commander Edwin and then speaks directly to them. "Bring some extra food with you. We are running low."

The two men nod in approval and turn to take up their supplies.

"I am taking a small party down to the Earth Realm borders to see if anything is going on there," Commander Edwin tells Brier. "I have left Hans in charge at the river's head and Fin is in charge at the castle."

"Good. You say it looks like they are looking for something?" Brier asks.

"Yes. The Fire elements have sensors all along the border and by the river. I am sure they have a party somewhere in the area, and I have sent some men to see if they could find it and report back to Hans, but I don't know. It looks like they are waiting for something. Possibly for you."

"Do you think they know about her?" I ask Brier quietly. It makes little sense why they would want Celine, but with the Fire elements, it is hard to tell what they plan.

Seth and John come back then. Brier looks at them, thinking for a minute and then turns back to Commander Edwin.

"We have had some problems with a very uncommon ogre. He is not like the others. He's stronger, bigger, and smarter," Brier tells them.

"He has been tracking us, and I want him tracked now. Take Seth and John down the riverways and drop them off. You both track the beast and see what you can find out about him but do not engage. If you see anything funny, come ahead to me so we can all deal with him."

"Yes, sir," they say to his command.

"I was going to do that," I remind Brier. To be honest, I want to take care of him and the threat he is to Celine. The thought he feels some claim to her is unsettling to me, and my instincts demand I put an end to him.

"If he sees you gone, he might become suspicious," Brier tells me. "He will not expect being tracked by them. It may give us an element of surprise."

Though I don't like it, Brier is right, always thinking ahead. It is one of the reasons why he is such a good commander. Brier turns back to Edwin then. "Go to the convent on the border and make sure they are well protected. Stay in the area but send someone back to inform us as to what is going on."

"Yes, sir," Edwin agrees with him. "Keep on alert to the Fire elements. We don't know what they are planning yet."

"We will be on guard, and if we see anything, I will have them dealt with once we cross the border," Brier assures him. "We take our leave now."

"Yes, sir," Edwin tells him. "Be careful, sir."

"You be careful," Brier tells him, and we climb back over into our boat. It isn't long before they are moving away from us.

"Do you think they are looking for her?" I ask Brier as he has dealt with them more.

"If they are, we have a traitor high up enough in ranks who has given the word to the Fire King," he says. "I don't know why they would want her, but it appears they do."

"I don't think she will know anything about this," I tell him. "She has mentioned nothing about the fire realm, only about taking on the Fire element with that sacrifice she has made."

"I'm sure she doesn't know anything," he tells me. "And we will not mention it to her. Tonight, I will scout out farther in the woods for these elements, but I think they will be closer to the border. We need to keep an eye out for them in the next few days."

"Do that," I agree with him. "Lindon and I can protect Celine for the night."

"Stay close to her," he tells me.

"You know, I will. And if Brown comes at us again, he will not be walking away this time." I am more than ready to face him, and this time, I will not let his threat go unaddressed.

Chapter Twenty-Seven
CELINE

Something doesn't seem right about the men tonight. Brier isn't even here. He had eaten a bite and then just went off into the woods without a word. He has been gone for several hours now, and Lindon and Tate have taken down three ogres in that time. He is doing something, and they seem to know what it is but aren't telling me anything.

A sinking feeling in my gut tells me it has to do with Brown. Is Brier trying to track him or take him on? He said they wouldn't do that, but with Brier, it is hard to tell what he will or will not do. He isn't too keen on telling me much of anything.

I asked the others earlier, but they had said nothing. I will not get any answers from them, so I'm not going to bother asking again.

Fewer ogres are attacking camp every night now, making it a little easier to rest at times. It is hard to sleep after watching my men take on one of the beasts, but they are insistent that I try. Tate even lies down with me to help me relax. Surprisingly, he also allows Lindon to stay with me when it is his turn to watch.

I will not complain. Being around Lindon makes me feel all warm and sensual. When he touches me, I feel this charge run through my body. He doesn't lay with me like he has before but sits alongside. I think Tate must have said something to him. I do hope Tate can work out what he needs to and be quick about it. The urge to be in Lindon's arms his hard to resist.

Lindon's scent is different from Tate's, and both of them are pleasant but in different ways. Tate is more earthy, like lemongrass and wood most of the time. His scent changes when he is around me and becomes sweeter and fruitful. Lindon is more refreshing, like lemonade and sunshine. To be honest, his scent doesn't make me think of sleeping at all. I feel more energetic and electrified around him than with the others. It has to be a part of his element.

I don't know what Brier smells like. He never lets me get close to him long enough. It is frustrating that he is not accepting the truth, that he is my element, but I will work on him. There is time for us in the future, and I will learn his smell then.

I watch him return a few hours before dawn. He speaks with Tate for a few minutes, but I can't hear anything. He turns to the fire, coming toward me. I close my eyes, not wanting him to see me watching him. I listen to him close by, moving around, and then nothing. After some time, I open my eyes and see he is across the fire watching me.

His gaze isn't as hard as it usually is but softer and... wanting. I inhale, staring back into his dark blues, not being able to look away even if I want to. He doesn't look away, doesn't change his glare, and doesn't show any anger at me for looking at him as well.

He is so strong and such a force that connecting with him has been so hard. At this moment, I feel closer to him than ever before. For the first time, I can see that he wants me, that I am important to him, and it makes me feel all warm inside. It is a comfort and a sign of hope that one day, he will open up to me.

He finally closes his eyes to rest. I hardly ever see him sleep, and I take the time to watch him now. Brier has a dark past, I know. Something awful happened to him. I have the feeling that not many people know anything, much less all of it.

I fall back asleep, watching him, only to be woken up not long after by Tate, who says we need to head back to the boat.

I cook some potatoes and eggs for breakfast on the little stove inside the cabin and take it up on top for us to all sit down and enjoy. I asked Tate where the food came from, and he said Brier brought it back with him last night. The men are quiet mostly, and I don't ask them what is on their minds.

Instead, I look down at the clear water of the river off the edge of the boat. The fish swimming deep below the surface lulls me into meditation. The water is so pretty when the sun is high above and I can see to the bottom surface.

It is like another world within this one. Rocks large and small fill the bed with plants growing up in sections. I can see all kinds of fish, some as small as my hand. Closer to the bottom, I see larger fish as long as one of my legs.

I wish I could touch the water, but it is too far for me to run my hands through. It has been so long since I have been swimming. I wonder…if I jumped in, could I even manage it anymore.

Lindon sits by me, looking down in the water as well. Soon he is pointing out several of the fish and plants, telling me what they are.

"That big one down at the bottom is the great catfish, and it can grow ten feet in length," he says, looking over the edge.

"That makes them bigger than us," I say as we look at each other.

Tate joins us, coming up behind me and sliding his hand around my middle. I lean back into him happy in this moment. The last few days have been such an adventure even if there has been scary moments.

"He may be large, but he eats mostly smaller fish," Lindon says, looking at us and then turning back to look over the side of the boat.

"Why is the water so clear here?" I ask them. "It wasn't farther back."

"Because we are getting closer to the water realm and the bed is more rock instead of dirt," Tate tells me, nipping at my ear.

"How many more days?" I ask, relaxing even more into him. It is a thrilling sensation, and I wonder when we will be able to do more.

"Two more," he says, rubbing his face against mine.

"Hey! How about we go for a swim?" Lindon says, smiling at us. "The water is fresh and nice, and I'm sure we could all use a good soaking."

"No, we keep moving," Brier scolds from behind the wheel.

"Come on, Brier," Tate says, looking at him. "half an hour will not kill us."

He exhales but finally says, "Fine, but then we are moving on. I want to get into the Water Realm within the next two days."

He cuts the boat's engine to the paddles and they slowly stop turning. They run off a charge of magic from a crystal spear hidden within the boat. One day, all its power will be gone but no telling how long before that happen. There were not many of these crystals in this world anymore, only the royal families have the few remaining. That is one way I know this is the royal boat.

"There should be a suit for me to wear below," I say, excited about going into the water. I rush down the steps, remembering that I'd seen some in one drawer. Once I get to my room, I reach inside a drawer and pull out a blue one, liking the color. Bathing suits are made to fit tight around the body and are a simple one piece. The bottoms are made short, coming up to mid-thigh, and the top has an entirely open back. The front covers well but is a little snug over my breasts. I don't remember swim suits fitting so tight before, but I am decent at least and rush back up on top.

"I like that even less than those stupid pants," Tate says, coming to stand in front of me but smiles. He wraps his arms around me, his hand grazing across my naked back. "Did you have to pick the sexiest one?"

"This was the least sexy," I tell him, placing my hands on his bare chest. He is just in his short pants from under his regular pants and damn, he looks good. "The other ones were not even a complete piece."

"Just get in the water before Lindon gets a good look at you." He pulls me over to the edge, and I look down. Lindon and Brier are already in. Lindon is dressed like Tate, but Brier has all his clothes on. I wonder why he didn't take them off, too.

"I haven't been swimming for a long time," I tell him, looking back at him. "I'm a little scared."

"Then jump with me," he says, taking my hand. "You're safe."

I step up to the edge with him; he counts to three, and we both jump in the water together. The coolness of it covers me, and I am in the heavens. I feel the connection of my element deep inside and it brings a sense of peace to me. I love the water and can't wait until I can feel the power of it in my hands.

I feel Tate pulling my hand, and we break the surface as he pulls me into his arms. I laugh as I wrap my arms around his shoulders. Our legs touch under the water as they slide around each other.

"That wasn't too bad," he tells me with a gigantic smile.

"Oh, this feels great," I say, leaning my head back in the water and putting my trust in him to hold me. "I haven't been swimming since when we were little."

"That long?" he asks me.

"I forgot how good the water feels," I say, looking back at him. "Thank you for talking Brier into this."

"It wasn't hard," he tells me. "He loves the water himself, you know."

If he loves it, why does he keep all his clothes on and not feel it wrap around his body? Even though I don't have my powers, I feel a connection to it. Brier should too.

"Come on, let's swim," Tate says, loosening his hold on me, and we begin to swim around in the water. Lindon joins us, but Brier stays away.

Lindon pulls me to him, and before I can even protest, he grabs me by the waist and pushes me up and out of the water. He throws me in the air and I am floating above them for a few seconds before falling back in.

"Why, you!" I splash him as Tate comes up behind me and does the same thing. I don't float in the air this time, but Tate throws me higher and I make a bigger splash coming down. I come up splashing at him as I shout, "Hey! Not you, too!"

Soon we are all splashing at each other, and I can't stop laughing.

"Wait, wait!" I shout at them. "I need to catch my breath."

Tate comes over and pulls me into his arms. He is smiling as he looks at me. "You look beautiful like this. Happy."

"You make me happy," I tell him softly as I place my hands on his shoulders.

"And what about me?" Lindon says, coming up behind me, pulling my hair off my shoulder and to one side. He is close but he doesn't touch me otherwise.

"You make me happy, too," I tell him, glancing over my shoulder. He looks over at Tate like he is asking his permission and I glance back at Tate seeing him nod as his eyes soften. He is trying with Lindon and it pleases me so much that he does.

Slowly, I lean forward and kiss the edge of his mouth. He groans softly and takes my lips entirely, pulling me closer to him. I gasp as his hands lift me by my backside. Willingly, I do as he directs me, feeling light in the water as I glide my legs around him.

I feel Lindon then, running his hands along my back and can't help but arch into Tate's arms at his touch. His hands run up and over my shoulders, not hiding it from Tate. Tate doesn't push him away as we kiss and I moan at intense pleasure of feeling them both so close and touching me.

Lindon's hand slowly runs over my shoulders and back, but he doesn't go further than that. One of Tate's hands travels up and cups one of my breasts. I gasp in his mouth at the sensation as he teases at the nipple, making it even harder and more sensitive.

His lips leave mine, trailing down my neck, kissing my ear, and I moan as his hand kneads my breast and his tender lips nip my ear. I kiss his neck, too, liking the taste of his skin and the water on him.

His hand slides away from my breast and up my neck, pulling my face back to his, kissing me again. It is wilder this time, and I can't help it as I feel my needs matching his. I wrap my arms tighter around his neck and shoulders.

Something about being in the water and with both of their hands on me has my pulse racing. Powers are moving inside me like I haven't felt before, churning faster and wanting out of their confinement.

"She is so passionate," Lindon says behind me as his hands glide up my sides. He comes more forward, kissing my shoulder lightly, surprising me with the sweet caress. I see specks of blue light all around us. I let my head fall back, and it lands on his shoulder as I feel him press against me, his desire clear. He gasps, his voice quivering. "Tate?"

"I know," Tate hisses and shocks me when he says, "Go ahead...kiss her."

Lindon turns my face to him, and as he kisses me, I feel myself tightening my legs around Tate as a flash of blue light in waves flows in my vision. We all moan at the same time as Lindon's hand comes under my arm and takes the breast Tate hasn't touched and kneads it now. His tongue slides deep into my mouth, claiming it as his as I lean back into him. My hand comes around his head, holding him to me, but I still keep my legs tightly around Tate. He slides his hardness against my center, driving me crazy with pleasure and need.

A rumbling pushes through me as my element hits the barrier inside me. It's a little painful in my stomach, but it shoots down into my core, and I gasp from the sensation as it hits me between my legs. With them both surrounding me, I felt my element hit a peak...

"All right! Playtime is over!" Brier yells at us, but I don't care. "Time to be on our way."

Lindon tastes so good, and I am so welcoming to his touch. He devours my lips with such a hunger that I can feel inside myself. I am just as in sync with him as our passion continues to grow.

"Lindon," Tate calls to him as he continues to kiss me. His tongue pushes farther into my mouth, and I suck on it, hopelessly out of control. I don't want Lindon to stop. Kissing Lindon is like a calling to my element. This is the second time he has kissed me, and I can't find it in myself once again to pull away from him, even in front of Tate.

"Lindon, stop," Tate says, pushing him and pulling me toward him at the same time. Finally, we break apart, and I gasp as I reach for Lindon even with Tate holding me.

Lindon growls at him, the wind picks up around us suddenly, and I can feel it coming between Tate and me, pulling me from his arms.

"Lindon, come with me!" Brier shouts from not far away, and I feel the resistance of the wind letting go of me. I look at Lindon, breathing hard as he slowly moves away from us.

"What was that, Celine?" Tate asks me as they are climbing the ladder.

"I'm sorry," I tell him, a little breathless as I look into his eyes. "I couldn't pull away from him."

"Have you kissed him before?" he asks me so directly that I know he already has the answer.

I can't lie to him. Yes, I had kissed Lindon before, but it had been an accident. We hadn't meant to kiss; it had just happened.

"Yes," I admit, and I see the anger come into his face.

Chapter Twenty-Eight

"You've kissed her before?" Tate shouts as we get back on the boat and he faces off with Lindon. "When did this happen? Were either of you going to tell me?"

"We didn't mean for it to happen," Lindon says in our defense as we are all dripping wet from just getting out of the water. "She was trying to bring out my powers and…"

"When?" Tate says, moving a step closer to him.

"Early in the trip," Lindon tells him. "I think on the second day."

He turns on me then, and I step back. "Why didn't you tell me?"

Brier spoke up then. "Lay off, Tate. I was watching them. She was trying to engage his powers, and it was working. They both were a little out of it at the time, and it just happened."

"How were you trying to engage his powers, Celine?" he growls at me. "By sticking your tongue down his throat?"

"No," I answer. "I…I was just trying to get him to breathe for me but something happen when he did. We lost control with the connection and…"

"How many times have you kissed him?" he asks me now.

"It was just the one time." I tell him. I knew this would upset him and had thought to just let it pass but when he asked me, I couldn't lie to him. "He was breathing for me and I didn't know if he realized he was, and so… I touched him. The next thing I know…we were kissing."

"Dammit! Why didn't you two tell me?" he asks me and turns to Lindon for an answer.

"Because we didn't mean for it to happen," Lindon says. "We had no control over it. Like just now when we couldn't pull away from each other."

"Then how did you pull away last time?" he asks Lindon.

"I pulled them away from each other," Brier answers him as he pulls the ladder up from the side of the boat. "Lindon had made a small tornado in the process and had beached the damn boat before I could get to them. That is how the cover got torn."

Tate seems to think about this for a minute. He is angry, and I am sorry for it, but kissing Lindon twice now, I realize the connection I want with him is building. It is profound that the pull for us to join is growing stronger for Lindon, just as it is for Tate.

"Tate, please understand, we didn't mean for it to happen," I tell him again. "We haven't been going behind your back or anything, but neither of us wanted to upset you. We just let it go."

"I think it has something to do with my powers," Lindon says. "I read that Wind has the ability of seduction. I don't have a handle on them, and I think when I kiss her, those powers flowed through to her."

"You keep your seduction to yourself and your hands off!" Tate yells at him, shoving him in the chest. "I told you I would try with you and her, but I will not allow you to go behind my back."

"Tate!" I shout at him, not wanting this to turn violent. "It wasn't his fault. It was mine!"

He lifts me and kisses me hard and forceful, like never before. His scent is so masculine and male to my senses; the urge to taste and mate with him sends a driving force through me. I don't understand this wild and animalistic side, but I don't try to pull away. It is like his nature somehow is claiming me and I let it.

Finally, he pulls away from me and looks directly into my eyes. I see animal heat in them filled not only with passion but with ever-consuming love. I melt into his gaze and in his arms, letting the rest fall away. Relishing that he is mine and I am his. "Don't go kissing Brier next."

"As if I would let her," Brier says with a scoff as he flicks the paddles on and we move down the river again. We are in the middle of it with nothing but forests all around.

Not that I see any of it. However, something is happening to me but it doesn't seem like it affects the men. The waves of color in my vision, the way I am feeling right now with Tate. It is time for us to take our bond and he has to know it too.

"I won't. Not until you're ready for me to," I tell Tate, ignoring Brier, hoping he will let it go. Tate is soft against me now, not as tense as before. He holds me to him and nuzzles the side of my face with his, breathing in my scent. I know he likes my smell as he grows more potent.

"Come with me," he whispers in my ear, pulling back slowly and running his hands down my arms. His eyes glow with an intense, animalistic look that wants something from me. It intrigues me so much that when he pulls me toward the steps, I follow without hesitation.

I look to Brier, who nods in approval and then to Lindon, but he quickly looks away from me. I find it hard to breathe for a moment and somehow know that it is hard for Lindon too. Tate pulls me down below, and it becomes easier to breathe once we walk into the small room.

He turns me around until my back is flush against his front and wraps his arms around me. He feels so good and right. I lean back into him.

"How much do you know of my powers?" he asks calmly as he grazes my ear with his lips.

"I know most of your Earth magic." I shiver as his lips travel downward to my shoulder. "That you give life to plants and animals."

"Yes, I do, but with an element, we take on the nature of them." His lips skim up to my ear again. "My instincts have always been protective of you but also very possessive. I can't help the way I am."

"I know, and I don't want you to," I say as we look into each other's eyes. "But sometimes, like now, your powers are affecting me. They sometimes overwhelm me, and it can be scary how powerful they are."

"I don't want you to be frightened of me." His fingers run through the strap of my swimsuit and pulls it down. "I could never hurt you. You have to believe that."

"I do, but I'm scared you might hurt someone else." I feel his other hand on my shoulder doing the same to it.

"I will not hurt Lindon because I know you care for him," he breathes as he rubs my upper arms. Just that firm caress has my pulse racing. He says, "But I am claiming you as mine as of now. I need you."

I gasp as he pulls the straps on my swimsuit down and it falls away from my chest, exposing my breasts. Instantly, I reach up and cover them with my arms. I shiver with fear and excitement, knowing what is to come.

"I smell the fear on you, but you know what else I smell?" he says, his hands falling to my hips. He pulls me closer against his hardness at my lower back. "I smell your arousal. It is much stronger than your fear."

I am breathing heavily now as his teeth graze over my shoulder. He is right. I am turned on by what he is doing. The slight fear I have is quickly being replaced by a need for him to touch me.

"Remember the pleasure I gave you before?" One of his hands slides into my swimsuit, down between my legs, and cups me there. "I want to give it to you now."

I almost fall, my legs becoming so weak as he presses into me and I uncover my breasts with my arms to keep from falling my grabbing his arms in front of me. *Yes, I remember.* I have thought about that ever since it happened.

"I couldn't even really touch you then," he tells me as his other arm comes around to hug me to him. His fingers move down my folds and push into me gently, and I moan as my body comes alive at his touch. He has me trapped in his arms, and if he didn't, I am sure I would have crumbled to the floor.

"How I wanted to suck off these perky little nipples, place little marks up and down this body of yours with my kisses." His words feel like a caress of their own, and I arch into him as he grazes his lips over my bare shoulder and neck.

"Are you willing to let me claim you now?" he asks as his fingers circle my bud and I feel my body quake in response. "Because my animal needs me to."

What does he mean by his animal? It is like he wants to scare me even as he is driving me crazy with need.

"What… what animal?" I ask curious more than fearful now.

"All of them," he tells me removing his hands and steps away. I turn to him then, and he looks at me with such a hunger and needs so overpowering to my senses. "If you want me, take off the suit."

Am I ready for this? To let him claim me as his? The other day I had asked him to, but that was then, and this is now. He is asking me this time.

"You first," I finally say, breathing a little hard. I am already half-naked in front of him, and I don't hide from him now. Will he be willing to take off his clothes as he is asking me to do? I get my answer when he reaches for the waist of his shorts and slowly pushes them down his massive legs.

I gasp when he stands back up and is bare for me to see. I close my eyes, seeing his arousal for the first time. It is the first time I have ever looked at a naked man and it is nothing like the statues I have seen. They had been so small, and Tate wasn't in any shape like them.

"You're not the only innocent here, Celine," he tells me, and I look back at him. "I have never been with a woman before."

"Really?" I ask, trying not to look down at his beautiful body. "But you're a man."

"I am, but I am only a year older than you," he says with a chuckle. "Since you, I have spent most of my time in the woods alone. I've never looked at another with desire as I do you."

It thrills me that he has never been with another woman before. I had never thought that he would be innocent like me in this. We were both of an age to explorer the physical side of pleasure and to know he hasn't makes this moment so much more special. "Have you ever seen a woman before?"

"Yes, but I have never been with one," he tells me. "I've never touched one as I have you."

Emboldened that we will be with each other first, I slip my fingers in my suit and push it down my legs, standing back up before him naked now. His eyes travel over me, and I finally allow myself to look at him again.

His shoulders are so broad, and muscles fill them in waves. All of them roll down his chest to his lean stomach, where a patch of hair lies in the middle of his chest. A line of it goes down his stomach into another patch of dark hair that has his powerful form standing out of it. His upper body is more tan than his lower half, but that doesn't take away from his beauty. The little curly hairs on his legs spring out over more thick muscles in his thighs and calves.

I take my time to look at the part that makes him a man again so curious of it the most. Just like the rest of him, it is thick and looks just as powerful.

"You're beautiful," he rasps as he steps closer to me, and I finally raise my eyes to his. I am glad that he likes what he sees in my body just as I am enjoying his.

"It's… bigger than I expected," I say, finding it hard to spit out the words. "I… I saw a statue and it didn't look like that."

He chuckles at me but doesn't touch me yet. "Statues are like little boys, not men."

"It wasn't of a little boy," I tell him. "Why make it look so small if it isn't true?"

"Well, maybe the statue wasn't turned on," he tells me. "They are only so big during mating."

"Oh," I say, looking down at it again.

He takes my arm and pulls me to the bed, sitting me down on it. Then he joins me.

"You can touch me if you like," he finally says, seeing my curiosity. I reach over and touch the tip with my fingers. I am surprised at how soft and warm it is. The skin is so smooth, and it jumps like it has a life of its own. Slowly, I slide my fingers down the side of it, seeing how hard it is underneath.

"It's soft yet hard," I say, looking back at him as I wrap my hand around it and gasped. "And it's getting bigger."

"I like your touch," he says as he places his hand over mine. "Touch it like this."

He strokes my hand up and down the length of it, and I feel it growing in size. A bead of moisture comes out of the top of it, and I touch it with my other hand, only to feel how slick it is. My finger glides over the tip of him.

He groans as he pulls my hands away from him then. "No more touching me there. I want to touch you."

"Are you going to make love to me now?" I ask him, needing to know if this is what we are about to do. I want him, and I am more than ready.

"No," he whispers, touching my cheek and rubbing his thumb across it. "We are going to make love to each other."

"I like the sound of that," I say, smiling at him as he pulls me closer and kisses me.

Chapter Twenty-Nine

His hands run through my hair as his lips travel from my mouth to my cheek and across my face. Finally, they take my lips once more. I take his wrist in my hands, bracing myself better for his kisses that make me dizzy with excitement and pleasure.

One of his hands slid down my back, lifting me up against him as he slowly moves us up and into the bed. He leans over me as his hand roams over my hips and backside. I place my hands on his chest, touching him.

His body feels so warm and hard compared to my soft one. His skin is smooth though, even the fine hairs on his chest, and I run my hands in the patch in the middle. It veers down narrower on his stomach, and I follow the line until it stops, feeling him shiver at my touch.

My touch can't feel as good to him as his fingers do to me as they lightly graze over my skin, causing goosebumps on my arms and legs. Or maybe it is the way he is kissing me with slow, even strokes of his tongue traveling in and around mine.

I can't believe we are finally doing this. After all these years, it is me and Tate, our first time, and we are together at last. Would it have been like this all those years ago? Would it have felt so beautiful and so right even as children? For some reason, I think the years in between have made it more meaningful. That the denial for us to explore each other at the first taste of love would have been right, but nothing like it feels now.

His hand comes up to cup my breast and he slides his lips from mine and down my neck. Slowly he lowers his head to my breast, taking a nipple into his mouth and kissing it as he had kissed my lips.

I moan and arch into him as my hand travels into his hair and pulls him closer to me. Gods, his lips feel even better than his hand as his tongue laps at it, making the tip even harder. He takes it fully into his mouth and sucks then, causing me to arch my body up and into his mouth.

"Oh, Tate," I moan as he takes the other breast in his mouth and does the same to it. A tingling sensation shoots through me all the way down into my core. His scent is more potent as I smell his wet hair as I run my hands through it. "That feels so good."

"Just wait," he growls at me as he takes my nipple in his mouth again and sucks a little harder. I gasp and jerk at his hair as the pleasure intensifies. He pulls my leg up and around his waist as he slides his hand back and around my backside.

His fingers travel down the valley there, following its path downwards until I feel his finger slide right into the folds at my opening once more

I groan and pull closer to him, about to cry out as he touches me so. I should have touched myself more often, so I would have been prepared for what it feels like. It is even better this time than the last with his hand rubbing against me. Before there had been some pain to it, and he had held back. He wasn't holding back now.

Finding my entrance, he presses one finger into me, and I gasp, feeling it entering my body. I raise my hips into his touch, wanting him deeper inside me.

"You're so wet, and you smell so good," he groans at my chest as he pulls his finger out and inserts two this time. I moan loudly at how full I feel and wonder for a minute how his member will fit. I had heard it hurts the first time, but I didn't know why. It has something to do with being a virgin.

I am so consumed with what his hand was doing that I don't even realize he is moving down my body until he pulls his hand away, kneels between my legs, and lifts them.

"What are you doing?" I gasp at him as I look down.

"I want to taste you," he rasps with a devilish smile.

"What?" I ask again, not sure what he is talking about. He just smiles bigger and lowers his head. When I realize he is about to put his face between my legs, I slide back. "No, no, no. Not there!"

I push his head away, and an animalistic growl comes from him. He crawls up my body, closer to my face, and sprinkles kisses on my lips as he presses into me. This is much better. I like it when he kisses me, and feeling him next to me again isn't bad at all. I want to feel his weight on top of me.

His kiss is way too short for my liking as I wrap my hands around his neck and bring him back to me, but he resists.

"I am going to kiss you down there. I have smelled you for way too long not to," he says, smiling at me. "You will like it, so just lie back and relax for me."

"But it's… such a private area for you to… put your head there," I say, not liking the idea. His hand feels so good there and I don't mind it in the least.

He chuckles and kisses my neck before asking, "Would you like to kiss me there first?"

"Are you serious?" I ask him, gripping his hair and pulling him up to look at me. "Is that what we are supposed to do?"

"Yes, it is," he tells me. "It's all about the foreplay from what I have been told."

Well, at least he seems to know about this even though I don't. I have no clue how this works. So far, I loved everything we have done, so there was no reason not to trust him.

"I'm sorry. I know nothing," I say, covering my face. "I've had no one to talk to about this stuff."

"I know you haven't, love," he says, taking my hands from my face. "Don't be ashamed; I like that I get to teach you. That we get to experience this for the first time together."

"But, I'm so stupid and ignorant." I am on the verge of tears and feel like a fool.

"You are not," he tells me with a soft smile. "This is all about instinct. You have that, yes? Your body naturally knows what it likes; you just have to trust it. Trust *me*."

"Okay," I finally nod, giving over all my trust to him. If he wanted to, then I would let him. I have no clue what I should do but I wanted this. I wanted to be with him and please him. "I trust you."

"Now, can I go first?" he asks me with a smile. "Because I am not sure I can handle your mouth on me right now."

I nod my head, and he kisses me again before raising back up on his knees right between my legs. His hands skim over my body from my chest, over my breasts, and down over my legs before coming back up again.

"Just relax," he says, his eyes never leaving mine as his hands roam. He bends forward, kissing each of my breasts again, and I like the sudden thrill that flows through me. His hands slowly move to the center of my body, touching around the area, and I can feel myself tightening at the anticipation of his touch.

His hands skim over me, and I groan with the vibrations of it. I want him to do that. I like it when he touches me there. I grasp the bed as his fingers rub at my bud and I feel my body giving over to his touch once more.

As one of his hands works softly at my flesh, his other moves lower and slide once again into my opening. I gasp and arch as the sensation takes over my body, my legs pressing around him, trying to bring him closer. Closing my eyes, I let the pleasure wash over me as it builds inside of me.

His fingers stroke the area so smoothly, and I vibrate all over as I moan and throw my head back. I feel him move, but I'm not paying any mind other than what his hands are doing. That is until he pulls them away and spreads my legs wider. I open my eyes to look at him, and at that moment, his tongue flicks over the bud, and I buck at the sensitive area being touched that way.

I can't move away now as he has me pinned down as he takes the bud into his mouth and sucks on it. I gasp, not believing this could feel so good. *How am I going to survive this?* His tongue flicks over my bud, still sucking softly, and I groan. I can't breathe, and I reach down, gripping him by the hair and pulling him away. "It's too much."

"Let go, Celine," he rasps at me as he slides one of his fingers into my opening. I grip his hair tighter, shaking my head. He pulls his finger out of me, and I sigh. "Let go, love, and I will continue to please you."

I'm breathing so hard, trying to get a few good draws in before I finally let go of his hair. He smiles up at me as he licks around the area and I can't stand it. I close my eyes once more. He grabs my backside and lifts my lower body into his face, filling it as he dives lower, and I feel his tongue at my opening now.

I groan at these new sensations and start to moan as he works my body like an instrument with his tongue. His mouth comes up and takes the bud once more in his mouth and sucks on it. I feel the brush of his beard on my sensitive flesh. With all of me being stimulated, he pushes my face around, hitting every nerve ending with his tongue.

My body is getting so tight; I don't know why I feel so tense and it is building so fast. My body vibrates as I can't control the spasms that start to release and my body convulses. I scream out in pleasure losing all control as I shudder, my head spinning, my legs shaking, my breathing ragged, and my heart about to burst from my chest. I can't help but weep from the fulfillment of it all.

Tate slowly settles me back on the bed as I feel like I am about to pass out from the pleasure I just felt. I don't recall it being like that last time he touched me. Yes, it had felt wonderful and I had found a release, but this was something else. This was…amazing.

He comes up and starts kissing my neck, bracing himself on both sides of me as I try to calm my breathing.

"I take it you liked that," he rasps in my ear as he sucks on the lobe.

"It was…wonderful," I tell him, still just trying to breathe. I run my hands down his sides as he presses his body against mine. "Now, I can do that for you?"

"Next time," he says with a chuckle. "I think you're ready for me now, and I'm not sure I can wait."

I feel his length pressing next to my opening then and realize that this is not over yet. We still haven't mated, and I can't see going through that again. Maybe it is better I had, now that the pain is supposed to come.

"Just relax for me," he says as he pushes forward a little.

"I am," I assure him as I raise my legs and wind them around his waist. I don't know what I am supposed to do, but if he wants me to do anything, I know he will tell me.

I feel him pressing into me again, and he slides easily against my wet skin. I'm not feeling any pain as he slides up and down my folds. The friction feels so good to my body. That is until he moves deeper inside me, and I wince at the sudden sharp pain.

"Hold on to me," he rasps as he pulls back. I grasp his shoulders as I feel him push one more time deep and another sharp pain tears at me on the inside. "Gods. You're so tight."

He pulls back again, and I feel the trembling in his own body. This seems to have hurt him more than me, and he looks hesitant for a second.

"I love you," I tell him needing to tell him as we are here in this moment that will be the beginning of our lives together. Forever.

He looks at me, his eyes already shining with love that makes me so happy. He whispers as his lips come down and brush mine, "I love you, too."

He kisses me, and in the next instant, he pushes forward hard, and I feel myself tear open as he presses into me.

We both gasp and break away from each other as I dig my hands into his shoulders and cry out from the pain. *Oh, fuck*! He is filling me so thoroughly and the pain is harsh. They didn't lie when they said the first time hurts.

Chapter Thirty

"Are you okay?" Tate breathes heavily as he brushes at the tears on my face and kisses me lightly along my jaw and neck. My body slowly releases the tension after the sudden pain of his intrusion.

"Yeah," I say now that the ache of him is leaving. "I didn't think it would hurt that much."

"I didn't think so either," he breathes. "We can stop if you like."

"There's more?" I ask him, knowing he is still inside me. I think we are both too scared to move.

"Yeah, there's more," he mumbles with a warm smile, and I let myself melt into his gaze.

"Well, that's good to know." I give a gleeful chuckle, wiping another tear away. I am so delighted at this moment. I feel so alive with him, and I want to explore more of that. "I am starting to like you inside me."

I feel his hand running from the back of my thigh to my knee and back down again as it climbs up my side. I let my hand roam down his side and along his back to his buttocks, where I feel the muscles flex.

"You feel so good wrapped around me," he says, chuckling as his hand roams along the side of my stomach and hip. A thrill runs down my side. I clench my legs around him, and he hisses. "Although you are squeezing the hell out of me right now."

"Is it painful?" I ask him, moving my legs up and down his as I cradle him between them. It drives him inside me a little and a new feeling of pleasure forms.

"Yes, it is," he draws back as he pushes into me, and I gasp at how full of him I am. "I feel ready to bust."

"Good," I groan, grasping his hips and holding him tight to me. "You feel so huge inside me."

"I am a little above average in that department. Do you want to stop?" he asks, becoming still again.

"No," I touch his face and looking into his eyes. "I want to finish this. I want you."

"I will move slowly." He braces himself above me before he shifts his hips. He groans just as I gasp and he pulls out of me completely. Awkwardly, he reaches between us and takes his male member and directs it back to my opening. I bite my lip as he pushes back in, grasping his shoulders as he slides in deep.

He is pulling back again, and I gasp as I realize this new motion and the pleasures that are coming with it. The friction of him moving in and out of me, filling me up and then pulling out has me gasping almost in time with his motions. I hold on to him one second, and then as he slides deep, I grip the bedsheets, trying to stabilize myself as waves of pleasure wash over me. I grip my legs around the back of his, discovering that he is the only anchor I need, and let go of the bed, letting my hands run across his chest.

I see him gripping the bed tightly as he moves and realizes that he is trying to find control like I am. He is as gentle as possible with me, and it is hurting him, but I'm not anymore.

I raise my head and kiss him, and he responds by kissing me back. He is so tense in my arms. I wonder if he likes this because I do. It is like every sense in my body is centered in one area, and he causes it.

"Relax, Tate," I say to him between kisses. "You feel so good... taste so good... I want all of you."

"And I need you," he says, kissing me, and I feel the trembles in his kiss, in his touch. "You're so beautiful... and this feels so right."

It feels so right. We are made for each other.

He relaxes and sinks deep into me, making us both gasp with a building spark of fire inside me. Now that he is relaxing, and his body melts into mine just as his kisses do, I slide my hands slowly down his back.

He moves faster in and out of me as his kisses fall to my neck, and I arch my entire body into him. So, this is what mating is? It is beautiful, the closeness, the connection with your man. He feels so good inside of me, and with each stroke, the heat between us gets more intense, and my blood is igniting my limbs, pulling him closer.

Rotating his hips, he changes the motions on me, moving slow then fast again. I raise my legs a little higher and gasp as I feel him moving deeper inside. Our kissing slows down as our movements become quicker and needier. Suddenly, he rolls over, gripping me around my waist and back as I feel myself being carried over on top of him.

"Move how you like," he tells me as he grasps my hips and raises me and sinks himself into me. I gasp at how deep he feels as I brace myself on his chest. Slowly, he helps me find a rhythm, and I take over, rotating my hips as I look down at him.

"Umm," I moan as the feel of him changes inside of me. More friction and fullness in this position, and it gives me control over our pleasures. I move my hips to the right and then to the left and gasp as heated pressure hits a new breaking point in me. I press down, taking him deeper inside me.

He growls as he takes my breasts in his hands and squeezes the mounds before rubbing his thumb over my nipples. Heat shoots into them, and I clench my legs as it slams down into my core.

I move faster, up and down on him, needing more. We are both reaching out to something as he pushes harder up into me. I feel tremors in my body and in his. Looking down at him, I see he is watching me, and I love the look in his eyes.

I raise my arms and arch my body as I run my hands in my hair, lifting it off my neck. His hands run down my breasts and stomach as he slides his thumb down and flicks it against my bud.

My body reacts instantly at his touch, and I buck against him, dropping my hands to him just to keep myself upright.

"Oh, Tate," I shout, starting to lose control and moving faster on him now. "I need you."

"I'm here," he rasps as he pulls me harder onto him with one hand as his other still flick at my clit. "Take all of me."

"Ah... please," I groan as my body vibrates and clench around him. I can't control my movements any longer, losing that part of myself a while ago. The sheer pleasure of this is taking over and suddenly, I spasm on top of him. I feel my body releasing wetness, making us both wet and slick as I slide along his body, the tremors still coming.

"Celine!" he shouts my name as he jerks inside me, and I feel his hot substance filling me. At that new heat flooding me, I explode again, my body tensing around him as I feel his pulsing manhood still alive inside of me.

The bond forms, tying our bodies and souls together. I see it as I open my eyes as hues of different colors swirl around us. I watch as they slowly disappear.

"Tate," I moan as I come down slowly and collapse on top of him. I am spent and not sure if I can ever move again. "That... amazing."

He chuckles under me, and his chest vibrates under my head. He is breathing hard, just as I am, but still says, "Yes, it was... I can't wait to do it again."

"Again?" I ask, tilting my head up to look at him. "When?"

"Hopefully... as soon as we recover... from this time," he tells me, still breathing hard.

"Okay," I agree.

I feel him slip out of me as we move around a bit. I finally slide off of him to the bed. We lie there, just looking at each other. He touches my face and kisses me lightly. This blissful moment after seems just as important as all the rest.

"You are wonderful," he says, lazily kissing my hand.

"You're not so bad yourself," I tell him, sliding his hand over to me and doing the same.

"Let me clean you up a bit," he finally says, ambling away from the bed to walk to the sink. He fixed it the other day as the pipes had just popped off. Most likely, when the others had put the boat back in the water.

I watch him, not sure if my legs will work as he cleans himself up and then comes back to bed with a wet cloth. I hold out my hand to take it, but he pulls it back from me. "Allow me."

"Tate," I say as he pushes my legs apart. I feel so sticky down there and must be a mess. "I can do this."

"I want to do this," he says firmly, kneeling between my legs. "Just this once, please."

"Oh, gods," I say, hiding my face as I let my legs open for him. Gently he cleans me, and I feel a tingling sensation build again as his hands stroke me. He then moves the wet cloth away from me, and I watch him as he wipes the bed. "Is that blood?"

"Virgins' blood," he says, smiling at me. "It is an honor for me, the husband, to clean it off his wife."

Virgins' blood? I didn't know I was to bleed, too. I feel like such an idiot for even asking. Would it be okay if we do it again? Would it hurt a second time? I'm not about to ask and look more like a fool.

He lies down beside me and takes me in his arms again. "We will change the bed later. For now, I just want to hold you."

I smile at him as we rest together. I lay my head on his chest, and he strokes my arm. As our legs tangle together, I feel content for one of the first times in my life.

"So that was mating?" I say, smiling as I look down at his soft member just laying on top of him. "I have to say, I kind of like it."

"It should get better," he tells me. "I think our first time might have been a little fast."

"Why do you say that?" I ask him.

"Because… I was… when I…" He seems to be having a hard time finding the words before finally saying, "Well, we didn't seem to last very long. I've heard others talk about going for hours."

"Hours?" I'm not able to help but look up at him in surprise. "You mean people can do that for hours?"

"That's what I have heard," he says, caressing my cheek. "Next time, hopefully, I will have better control of myself."

"I was… I mean, I couldn't control myself," I say, propping my head upon my hand. "I mean once we started moving, it was like… I craved the friction of our bodies."

"Um, yes," he agrees with a moan. "You held me so tight to you, and when you were riding me, you looked so beautiful."

"Do you find me beautiful?" I ask him. I remember people telling me that long ago, but nuns didn't praise each other like that. Tate has seen every part of me now, and I needed to know that he thought I was.

"So beautiful. I love you, Celine Clearwater," he tells me as he nuzzles my nose.

"I love you, Tate Forrester," I whisper as our lips meet and we kiss again. "I love everything about you."

"You're my life. My soulmate," he says as he deepens it more.

Soon our kisses turn hungrier once again, and I reach between us, taking his manhood into my hands. He groans as I feel it harden almost instantly.

"Do you want more already?" he asks me as he caresses one of my breasts.

"You said I could taste you here." I remind him of his promise. "I think it is my turn now."

"I said that." He groans as I raise onto my knees beside him. "But…"

"No, buts," I tell him as I slide both my hands down the length of his erection. "I just need you to show me how to get started."

"Well, you're doing a good job so far," he says with a chuckle. "I'm already getting hard again."

"Just tell me what to do," I exclaim, wanting to explore his body more.

"Okay, woman," he says, taking my hands in his around his shaft. "Slowly, you work your hands up and down me like you're doing."

He glides my hands over his erect member, a little harder than I would have thought, and I feel it getting harder with each stroke.

"And I do the same with my mouth?" I ask him as I bend down and kiss the top of it.

"Gods, yes," he moans, removing his hands from mine and letting me take over. "Just do whatever you want. I will enjoy it no matter what."

I smile as I gently kiss the head of his erection and let my hands glide over him as he showed me. I must do something right because after a few minutes, I take more of him in my mouth and he gives me a loud moan.

Slowly, I move him in and out of my mouth as he grows rock hard. He slips his hand under me and starts playing with my bud, and I groan at my pleasure, spreading my legs just a little more for him.

When I feel him slide a finger into me, I take him deeper into my mouth, imagining his member inside me again. He wrapped one hand in my hair, directing me just a little as he pushes his finger inside me.

I feel like I am about to come again after a little while and wait for it to take me as I move over his shaft harder and faster.

Suddenly, he pulls me back and lifts me, flipping me on my back. He brings my legs up high around him, and I feel him pressing between them once more.

"I want you," he rasps as he pushes forward already.

"Take me," I gasp as he slides into me. He moves slowly just as he did the last time, and I feel a slight discomfort as he presses inside.

"You're still so tight," he says, and then asks, "Am I hurting you?"

"No," I moan at him as I dig my heels into his ass. "Please, Tate, don't be so soft with me."

"You're going to hurt," he rasps as he moves slowly once more. "I can't."

"Yes, you can," I say. "Stop treating me like some little princess. I want my husband to fuck me."

"Watch your mouth, love." He tells me that even though he is moving faster and harder now. "I don't fuck my wife."

"Tate," I moan, surprised by how fast the sensation was building again. It hasn't been that long since our last time, and I think my body is still swollen from it. "More."

I raise my legs higher around him, taking him even more deeply, and he groans as my muscles tighten around him.

"Fuck!" he growls as he speeds up as I asked. My body is demanding more of him, and I feel the tightening around him. "You will make me come if you keep squeezing me like this."

"Watch your mouth," I warn him now.

Suddenly, he pulls me up into his arms, holding me in the air without breaking our bodies apart. I wrap my arms around his neck, holding on as he pushes me against the back wall. He thrusts hard into me, and I almost scream in rapture. I arch back into the wall, pressing my body harder down onto his. I brace my feet on the bed, and it gives me leverage to move against him as he grips my ass in his hands and pounds up into me.

"Oh, yes!" I shout as he hits every part of me that is screaming for attention. This isn't as gentle as the first time; this is way more than that. This is a drive built from pure hunger that has been penned up too long. Like an animal in sexual heat, calling out for something. "Yes, Tate. More!"

"Don't call to them, love," he growls at me as he follows my command. "You're not ready for my animal yet. Stop moving so."

"I can't help it," I say, arching into him and rotating my hips again. "I'm coming!"

He growls as he speeds up his movements more. "I… I can't let them loose."

I have no idea what he is talking about and I don't care. He feels so good inside me and his claiming of me is fierce and needy. Maybe even more so than mine.

"Yes! Yes!" I shout as I shudder. I buck hard against him as the wave that puts me over the edge hits, and I scream out one more time. "Yes!"

He rides me hard through it as I lose control and come all over him. In the next few seconds, I feel the vibration of him inside me go off, and I scream out again with one last wave.

This time, as we come down from our climax, I feel the warm coating of colors around us. It feels and smells like crisp leaves and water combined and the bond is still taking form. We finally have our genuine bond with one another.

Chapter Thirty-One

Tate is right. I am a little sore after that second time. My legs feel like jelly and the muscles between my legs I didn't know I had are aching. But it is a good pain, the right kind. He well loves me, and I feel it.

It is close to sunset now, and we have to get our clothes on to get off the boat. We help each other dress, not being able to keep our hands off of each other. Sneaking kisses every time we turn around. I am half-drunk on making love with him and feel almost like a silly girl with my infatuation.

"You ready to face the others?" he asks as he turns to me.

I stand up after putting my shoes on and take his hand. He kisses me lightly on the lips just once. He doesn't seem to mind so much when I put those pants back on. I'm not so sure he even sees what I am wearing as he is gazing into my eyes. "What do you think they will say?"

"Lindon will try to embarrass us. Brier will say nothing, I'm sure," he tells me as he backs me to the wall. "Don't let him get to you."

"I won't," I tell him. "You don't let him get to you, either."

"Oh, he will, I'm sure of it," he says, looking down at me. "But I promise not to behave."

"Well, I can live with that," I say as he pulls me toward the small door. He exits first.

"About time!" Lindon says with a sly smile. "Thought I was going to have to come down there and break you two up."

"If you did, you would be missing a head," Tate tells him as he pulls me into his arms. He looks around and then asks, "Where is Brier?"

"He jumped off as soon as we hit land," Lindon tells us. "We kind of pulled in a little early because we thought the boat was going to fall apart with all the rocking. You wouldn't have had anything to do with that, now would you?"

I smile at Lindon, biting my lip at his remark and how he is poking at Tate. I am so happy. I find it funny, and his grin widens at me.

Tate just looks at him hard. "Come on. We need to get off the boat."

I get a weird feeling and shiver as Tate slips away from me. It is like something is taking over my senses, and I look around at the forest is in front of me. The brush is thick here, but a narrow path runs through it a few feet away from the small beach by the river. It looks like a place that has been used often by boats throughout the years.

Tate jumps over the side, leaving me a moment alone with Lindon. He uses it, pulling me back against him. A sudden burst of heat hits me, and I feel angry at Lindon. I had just been with Tate and don't like Lindon's hands on me.

"Don't touch me!" I shout at him, pulling away. His touch doesn't feel like it usually does.

"I...I'm sorry." He is surprised and worried by my outburst. "What's up with you?"

"I don't care for your teasing right now is all," I tell him stepping back uncertain of him. "It's like you're judging me or something."

"I'm not judging you," he assures me. "I'm glad you and Tate finally popped your cherries."

"Cherries?" I ask his nickname for me started to take on a whole new meaning now. Is that how he sees me? Just some virgin that needed to get laid? His term of endearment takes an awkward turn in my head. "Was my innocence why you call me that? Because I was a virgin?"

"Woah, Celine," he says, backing up a step from me. "I like that innocence about you. It wasn't to put you down."

"I can't believe you!" I say, pushing him in the chest. "All this time, I thought it was some sweet endearment because you like cherries and it was just about sex to you."

"It was a sweet endearment!" he shouts. "I don't know what has your panties in a wad—hell, I don't even know if you have panties on right now—but you need to calm down."

"Celine, what's going on?" Tate calls from over the side of the boat. He is still waiting for me to get off the boat too.

I look at him and then to Lindon, not sure what I am feeling. As soon as Tate had let me go and Lindon put his hands on me, everything inside me turned upside down. I haven't been angry with Lindon before; in fact, I liked his teasing.

"I don't know," I tell them shaking my head. "I just feel angry and hot suddenly."

"At Lindon?" Tate asks with surprise in his voice.

"Looks like three is a crowd to me," Lindon says bitterly and walks past me. He then jumps off the boat. "I can see when I am not wanted."

"Lindon," Tate calls to him, but Lindon marches up the trail. I sigh, and he turns to me instead. Tate motions for me to come down, and I come to the edge and let him take me into his arms. He walks us to the bank before lowering me to my feet. Taking my face in his hands, he looked into my eyes. "Your skin feels hot, Celine. Do you feel okay?"

"I feel fine now that he is gone," I tell him. "I don't know why I reacted the way I did. I think I am just as surprised as he was."

"Come on. We can't stay here any longer," he tells me as he turns us to the side of the boat. "We will figure this out at camp."

My feet hit the ground, and as always, a few roars sound in the distance. I am glad this is almost over. Even though the ogres have thinned out in attacks, still one or two come every night. Tate takes my hand, leading me into the woods, not even bothering to acknowledge them.

Brier is at camp, but Lindon isn't anywhere in sight. I give Tate a concerned look, and he seems to get my thoughts. Everything feels heightened with Tate now. Every touch and emotion of one influences the other.

"Where is Lindon?" Tate asks Brier, who is cleaning some rabbits.

"He dropped his bags and just kept walking," Brier said, not stopping in his task. "Why?"

"I just need to talk to him," Tate says and then turns to me. "Stay here with Brier. I will look for Lindon."

"Will you please tell him I am sorry?" I beg him. "I didn't mean any of it."

"I will. I'm feeling different too. It's not just you," he says, caressing my cheek. "I think our bonding is still wrapping itself around us and Lindon was just too much for you right now."

"You think that's it?" I ask, relieved that I'm not the only one feeling off.

"Yes, I do," he breathes. "Bonding with me has you taking on some of my instincts. Mated females rarely care to be touched by others for a while."

I pull back from him and look at him hard. "Is that why we did that? Because you knew I wouldn't crave Lindon's touch?"

"No, it's not why we did that," he says, pulling me hard to him. "Trust me; I wasn't thinking about that at all."

I believe him and don't resist anymore as I place my head on his chest. "Please, just tell him I didn't mean to hurt him."

"I will help him understand," he says, kissing the top of my head. "Just stay here for now with Brier."

I nod and he then lets me go, turning to the woods and running off.

Brier is usually the one running off, so it is odd to be left alone with him. I wonder for a minute if I will feel the same feelings I felt with Lindon around him. It isn't like I am about to test it and find out. He won't let me touch him, anyway.

"Can I do anything?" I ask him instead.

"No. Camp is set. I was just about to leave when Lindon came storming through," he tells me as he forks a rabbit and sits it over the fire where two more are. "You have them fighting over you again?"

"They are not fighting over me," I tell him.

"Really?" he says, looking harshly at me. "What do you think that was earlier today?"

GINA MANIS

"A misunderstanding," I tell him, sitting down by the bags.

"Then why is Lindon so upset now?" he asks, taking the last rabbit and doing the same to it.

"Another misunderstanding," I tell him, playing with the strap of the bag. Yeah, that sounds reasonable.

"Seems like there are becoming plenty of those," he says, standing up, moving away from camp, throw the remaining pieces of the carcass into the woods.

"The only one I seem ever to be fighting with is you," I say, wishing he would just shut up about Tate and Lindon and tell me something about how he feels. "Why are you so grating all the time?"

"Because I don't care to be one of your boy toys," he says, looking hard at me as he sits down on the other side of the fire. "It will give you an incentive to stay out of my pants."

I gasp at his harsh words. They genuinely spark my anger, and it is real, not like it is from somewhere else.

"Oh, don't worry, Brier," I tell him, having enough of his attitude. "I have decided to take your advice and just find another Water element."

"Just do it after I leave," he tells me flatly. "Watching the two of them fall at your feet is bad enough. I don't want to have to watch a third."

"You wouldn't have a brother, would you?" I ask him, hoping it would hit something inside him and light a spark of jealousy. I don't want someone else. I want him, dammit!

"Why?" His shoulders tense and he stares back at me.

"Just thought I would try him if you didn't mind," I say casually. "I need a powerful Water element. A brother would be perfect for taking your place."

He says nothing, just stares at me before reaching forward and turning the rabbits on the fire. I don't think he will respond.

"My brother is dead for all I know," he grumbles as he sits back. "It's a good thing he is."

"Why is that?" I ask him curiously.

"Because like your sister, my brother is Fire," he tells me. "And you don't want any of that now, do you?"

He has a point there. I gave my offering to all the elements except for Fire.

"Well, I guess that idea is shit then," I admit, knowing full well that I have no interest in his brother or any other man. I have every intention of my Water element still being Brier. He just doesn't have to know that yet.

"I thought so," he says and sits back, letting the subject drop.

I have messed up with Lindon, and I don't even know why. Something isn't healthy about what just happened between us. It was like I was being led into a fight with him.

I hope Tate finds him and brings him back to me soon. I feel something is off in the woods waiting, but what? Tate and Lindon should be able to sense any danger, but they both seem calm.

I shouldn't be scared and worried, I tell myself, even as I get up and move closer to Brier. I look out into the woods, searching for the others, hoping they will soon return. Unsettledness crawls all over me like something is coming.

"What's wrong?" Brier asks after a few minutes, and I turn to him.

"Do you feel something… different this evening?" I ask him, looking back into the woods.

He says nothing. He scans the forest in front of us. After a bit, he asks me, "What are you feeling?"

"Like we are being watched," I tell him with a shiver. "Do you think it is Brown?"

"He is not far away. I am sure," he tells me, looking around. "Don't worry about him."

"Then what should I worry about? You all are not telling me something."

"There are always dangers, Celine." He is still scanning the woods for the sight of something. "A bear or cougars could come out of the woods at any moment. You don't have to know about all of them."

"You're messed up; you know that?" I say, getting up and moving away from him. "You put this knife on me, show me how to use it, and now you're telling me…"

He leaps up and grabs me suddenly, covering my mouth. I stop talking instantly, not resisting, knowing something is wrong. He never touches me unless it is necessary and is always so severe for me not to take this as a warning.

"There are men about fifty yards out," he whispers close to my ear. "Grab your bag and follow me. Quietly."

He lets me go as he walks to the fire. He throws dirt on it and chucks the rabbits into the woods. I grab my bag, taking Tate's also as Brier takes his and Lindon's. He ushers me back toward the water.

"What about the others?" I ask him.

"They will find us," he tells me. "We have to go."

I nod, and we take off.

Chapter Thirty-Two

They are after us and moving in quickly. Brier pulls me along, but it is like he knows they are close. He is searching the woods for what, I don't know, but I don't have time to ask him.

"They know we are here and they are too close," he finally says as he stops in a small clearing in the middle of low rising hills of the forest all around us. He pulls his sword and another long knife from his side as he looks around. "Call to Brown, Celine."

"What?" I say, taking a deep breath. "Why?"

"Because we need him," he says, continuing to look around in every direction.

I am surprised that he wants me to call to Brown when all this time he has been planning on killing him, but I am more concerned about my men. "Where are Tate and Lindon?"

"No time! Now call him!" he tells me. He tenses when the first warrior appears from the trees, followed by two more and then three to the right of us and even more on the left. Men surround us—warriors fully armed, just like Brier.

The warriors are dressed much like Brier, except their hair is lighter in shades of blond and red. The ones with red hair are large, like Brier.

"Brown!" I scream as loudly as I can, not wasting another second. I pull my knife, hoping I will help Brier. Our training has been one-on-one, not fighting a dozen men. "Brown, come to me!"

There is nowhere to run or hide as I look around. Eight men are advancing on us, and I can see even more coming over the hillsides. What do they all want with us?

Brier doesn't wait for anyone to speak but jumps straight into action, swinging his sword and knife at three of the men as they engage. He dodges their swords left and right and then jumps to the side as one of them tries to take out his legs.

"Brown!" I shout one more time as two men advance on me. I look to Brier, seeing him fighting off so many already. I know he isn't able to help me. They have swords but don't have them drawn, and I face them with only my knife. I am about to stab the closest one when suddenly brawny arms come around me and cover my mouth. I struggle against the warrior holding me as I watch the other two come at us, pulling ropes from their sides.

"Gods, she is hideous," one of them says as they surround me. I struggle against the one holding me, kicking out at the other two and hitting one of them in the stomach. The one holding me pushes me down to the ground as another bends over to tie my feet together.

"Just tie her up, Andre!" the guy behind me says as I struggle against his hold over my mouth. "She is stronger than she looks."

I kick the one in front of me in the head, and he rears back in a shout. "The bitch!"

"Bro…!" I get out before he covers my mouth again.

"Tie her!" he shouts at them. The third man sitting on my legs struggles to tie my hands and the other guy now works on tying my feet. "We have to get out of here!"

An earth-shattering roar rises a short distance away. I can't see, but I know it is Brown and almost sigh with relief. *He has come to me.*

"Shit!" the guy behind me yells, shoving the warrior off of me and picking me up off the ground. He turns me around with just my hands tied, and he throws me over his shoulder. "Let's move!"

"Brier!" I scream, trying to find him, but all I see is that he's surrounded by six men and more dead at his feet.

I look over and see Brown jump into the middle of the clearing, and one warrior throws a massive fireball at him and bursting Brown into flames. The warrior is a Fire element and I wonder how many of them are.

"Brown!" I scream, kicking at my capturer as I watch the fire consume Brown. He roars at me again, and I can only imagine his pain. "No!"

My two captors move off into the woods, and I can only see flames high in the air and smell pungent of smoke. If they can do that to Brown, Brier is sure to be next. I beat at the man holding me, but there is nothing I can do. I feel so helpless, knowing that Brier is fighting for his life, Brown is burning, and I have no power to help them, much less myself.

They continue to run in the woods with me, and four more men join them from nowhere. I am passed to a much larger man, and he throws me over his shoulder.

"We have taken care of the other two," someone says, and instantly I think of Tate and Lindon. "They will be no bother."

"No!" I cry at the thought of what has become of them. *Not Lindon! Not Tate!* Oh, gods, how can I survive if they are both dead? Why are they doing this? Why have they killed my loves?

"Good. You four make sure the other is dead. And that ogre as well," the man who handed me over says. He seems to be the one in charge, and they obey without another word.

They will kill Brier too if they haven't already. Brown is probably dead now. Nothing can stand up to being on fire like that. It had consumed him, and I felt the heat even from a distance. I can hear Brown's roars dying down into nothing as I am taken away.

I fight again, trying to get free, but I can't. I still have my knife, but they tie my hands in front of me, and I can't reach it. Not when I am slung over some man's shoulder.

"To camp!" the leader shouts, and they all run through the woods again. The leader has taken up the front position, and I can't see him as the biggest one has me in the middle, flanked by two more heavily armed warriors.

I don't know how long we run, and I don't care. All I can think about is my men, dead. What is there to live for anymore?

Suddenly, we stop in our tracks as two loud roars go off in front of us. I tense, knowing that sound well. I look over my shoulder and see two huge ogres standing in our path.

I don't care anymore if they have me. Let them kill these bastards and eat me for all I care. I will never see Lindon's smiling face again or feel Tate's arms around me.

"Fucking ogres!" the leader shouts as the ogres charge us. The two warriors behind us move in front with the leader now. I watch as they ignite their hands with fire and spin the flames until they grow two enormous globes. They then send them flying into the beasts.

The ogres dodge them, and the trees behind them explode in a wash of orange flames. One picks up a huge log and throws it in our direction. I gasp just before it hits the three men. The warriors fly backward into us, and the impact throws me to the ground.

The ogres take advantage of our predicament. One of them picks up one warrior, tears him in half with his bare hands, and drops the corpse to the ground.

I try to crawl away but the most prominent warrior, the one who I haven't heard speak, grabs my ankle, pulling me back and underneath him.

I scream as I see one ogre about to slam his fist down onto both of us. The warrior turns and sees him at the last moment. He throws his hands up in the air, and suddenly a haze of orange light surrounds us as the ogre's fist hits it. The ogre hits it again, trying to break through, but can't.

I look out of the orange haze and see the leader and another warrior battling with the other ogre. They gain the advantage on him as one plunges his sword into the ogre's neck like I have seen Tate and Lindon do so often.

I reach out to the shield, feeling the energy as my fingers grow closer until I touch it. My fingers slide over the bright orange glow turning into a yellow where I touch. The barrier doesn't give against my hand and I know I am trapped within it.

I kick at the man over me, grabbing a rock, and slam it down on his head. The blow stuns him for a second, and he drops the shield. I see the ogre rearing back to slam his fist down once more. The other two warriors come up on the beast from behind, thrusting their swords into his back.

Somehow, I am on my feet and running away from them all. I run back the way we had come, my thoughts only to get back to Brier. I need to know that he is okay.

I scream as someone jerks my hair and pulls me backward. Strong arms clasp around me.

"Where are you going?" It is the huge one, speaking now for the first time in a scratchy voice. His hair is redder than the others, and I notice his eyes are, too. He pulls my hair again, and I am immobile. My head won't go back any farther to relieve the pressure. "You broke my tooth, hag. You will pay."

"Edwin!" the leader shouts as several other ogres roar ring from not too far away. "More are coming. We need to hurry."

Red Eyes slings me around without another word and jerks me up over his shoulder with so much force that the world spins. My scalp is on fire, where he pulled my hair. It doesn't help matters much. The ache in my heart is even worse.

"But what about the ogres? They will follow," the youngest of the three of them asks as the big one brings us up with them. He looks kind of like Lindon with his long blond hair, but he doesn't have Lindon's gorgeous smile.

"It doesn't matter," the commander tells him as they all take off. "The beasts are not strong enough to break the shield around the camp."

Not long after, we come to a large clearing with a massive globe of orange surrounding a camp in the middle. The warriors take me up to it and stop as an opening pulls apart slowly, large enough for us to walk through.

"I want Brim and Coal war parties dressed and ready to go in one hour," the leader shouts at several men waiting inside. They are both young with red hair and salute the leader before leaving without a word. "Hand it to me, Edwin."

Edwin grabs me by the back of my shirt and drops me onto the ground in front of him. With my hands still tied, there is no bracing myself for the fall and my backside hits the ground hard, sending shocks of pain along my legs.

The leader grabs my arm and yanks me to my feet in front of him.

"I see you finally found the creature, Burns." Burns is a large, burly, red-headed man with a long beard that's the same color as his hair. With all the red and blond hair and the fireballs I have seen, I am coming to realize this is a band of Fire elements. But why are they looking for me, "the creature"?

"She's fucking evil," the leader Burns says. "Had ogres attacking my party and they've followed us in."

"Ogres, you say?" the burly man asks. "What is she, one of their females? Kind of small, don't you think?"

"That's none of your concern, Stan," Burns says to him. He has a strong drawl to his voice. "Has Petro's party come back?"

"No, they are still out."

"I have sent for two parties, and I want you to take them out within the next hour. We will leave soon, and I don't want the beasts to gather around the shields because of her."

"Yes, sir," Stan says, looking disdainfully at me. "Any orders for Petro when they return?"

"No new orders." Without another word, Burns pulls me through the camp. It looks like it has about fifty to a hundred men inside. Tents are around as if they had been there for some time; some clothing hangs from lines in various places. I see a few makeshift benches made by logs sitting around fires, and some of them have meat cooking over them.

It is night, but the orange glow of the shield around the camp gives it enough light so you can easily see throughout the field. When I look up at the sky, I see the moon and stars, and they are tinted orange from the shield.

Burns walks in long strides, and I have to hurry to keep up with him or be dragged behind. His hand on my arm is a death grip, but I prefer it around my neck. I feel like asking him to do just that, but I can't seem to speak. I can't seem to do much of anything. My mind is aware of everything going on around me, but I feel like I'm not even in my body. Like I have stepped away from myself for a time.

I am taken to a tent in the middle of the camp and Burns sits me in a chair at a table. I look across at a man who is sitting and eating a well-balanced dinner with corn on the cob, a steak platter with cooked onions and peppers, and a small bowl of beans. A pitcher of ale sits beside him. He picks up the pitcher and pours more inside a glass.

"Do you have to put her in front of me while I am eating?" the man says to Burns. This isn't just any man I realize after looking at him and his manners for a few minutes. I grew up in a royal house long enough to see the signs of nobility, and this man is precisely that. I can see by his clothes, his food, and even how he speaks. He has a robust frame so well structured even at his older age. If I had to guess, I would say this is the Fire King himself. But why would he be out here?

His hair is unlike so many others with a dark red and almost orange hue, just like the shield outside. His eyes are the same while he is using his power, but for now, they shine a burned brown.

"You wanted her as soon as possible, my king," Burns tells the man and sits in the chair next to him. "Would you have preferred I tried to have it cleaned up first? I don't think it would have made a difference."

"Watch how you speak of her," the king orders Burns as he pushes his half-empty plate away. "How she looks does not change who she is."

Do they know who I am? But how? At least I know the man is a king, and now I am sure I am sitting across from the Fire King.

"Did you see my son?" the royal asks, getting up and walking to a table behind him. He pours two glasses of a golden-brown liquid.

"No, I did not," Burns answers as he makes himself a plate with some leftover food. "Three warriors were with her, and she also had the ogres coming to her defense."

I may not know much about what is going on here, but they don't seem to know everything. These ogres are not coming to my rescue, but I'm not about to tell them that.

"She had a friendly ogre or two?" the king asks, looking down at me as he sips his drink. I don't bother picking up what he put in front of me. I sit there and wait for whatever is to happen.

"Appears so. But I took care of the beasts straight away," Burns says as he digs into the plate he fixed. "Two more attacked on our return, but we dealt with them too. Lost Charlie, though."

"Good," the king says, seeming like the doesn't even care what happened to the one called Charlie. I have a feeling it is the one who had been torn in half. "Have you looked inside her mind yet?"

"No, there wasn't time," Burns says from the table.

"So, you don't even know for sure it is the princess?" he says, looking at me. How does he know who I am?

"It is her. Why else would they be protecting her?" Burns tells him.

The king pulls a chair over and sits down in front of me.

"You are the princess, are you not? Don't lie to me, or I will just read your mind," he says, looking deep into my eyes.

I say nothing for the longest time, but then I feel an impulse inside me to speak and before I know it, I confirm for him who I am.

"Yes."

"And what is your name?" his voice invades my ears, making them ring.

"Celine Ariel Lafonte Clearwater." The ringing stops as soon as I answer his question. He is using some kind of power over me. "What do you want with me?"

"Information, my dear," he tells me with a smile. "Your sister, the queen, has done a great disservice to me. I don't trust her and what she has told me."

"I know nothing about my sister," I tell him. "I haven't seen her in over five years."

"I know." He sighs as he looks down for a second and then back into my eyes. "I have been looking for you for that long. It came as quite a surprise to me as word reached that you have been living in a convent all this time and cursed as you are. It almost makes me feel sad for you."

I say nothing, not knowing what to say to that. How does this man know so much about me? Most people don't even know I am alive.

"I am looking for my son," he says, leaning back in the chair. "He came to your castle a long time ago—oh say, five years. Nice timing, don't you think? I sent him there to meet with the queen and make an alliance, but he never returned. Your sister only sent word later that he ran away with her little sister, the princess, and next heir to the throne."

"I'm sorry. I don't know what you're talking about."

"My son's name is Damon Firestone."

"Damon."

The young man who had wanted to court me and before he left, I agreed. He had promised to come back. It was the same day Tate had later confessed his feelings for me, and I had promised to marry him. The day just before the night, my sister cursed me into a monster.

"So, you remember him."

Chapter Thirty-Three

"I remember him," I recall the young man, the Fire element who had come to my home long ago. He had spent most of his time with my sister and her officials, but there were a few times in the evenings when we would play a game of chess after dinner. But it was just a few days before he left that I pay attention to him.

Like that night at the carnival when Phillip had asked me to show him a good time. He had left us in the middle of it, and since it was my duty, I did as I was told. I wasn't resentful of it, though, and enjoyed being alone with him. Then Tate showed up, and things became tense between all of us.

Tate had been jealous of the way I was looking at Damon, but I couldn't seem to control myself. Damon was older than us by a few years. He was so tall and built like a man, so I was attracted to him. The night of the fair, as we played games and rode rides, I felt something for the first time with someone other than Tate.

"He must have made an impression if you remember him after all this time," he says, smiling a bit as he looks down like he remembers his son, too. "Just like his mother, his ability to bewitch someone."

Seeing this man in front of me, I know now that he is the king of the fire realm. Damon had been the prince and he has many of the same features as this man. The hair color, the eyes—but I never saw Damon glow as this man does.

"He was kind," I'm not sure what I should say, and figure honesty is the best way to go. Knowing Damon had been so long ago anyways. I don't know why he is speaking of him to me. "I liked him, but I don't know what happened to him. He left my home the day before my sister…"

"Cursed you?" he answers for me when I don't say it myself. "I am well aware of your story now, but I don't know what happened to my son at your home. You will help me figure it out."

I don't know how I can help, but he seems like he is a very determined and commanding figure. I'm not about to say anything against him just yet.

"I will untie you so you can eat but do not think of running from me," he says, looking directly in my eyes as he pulls a knife from his side and slashes at the ropes, cutting me free. "I will set you free only when you have fulfilled your purpose."

"What purpose is that?" I ask him, rubbing my red and bleeding wrists.

"Finding my son," he says, motioning to the food on the table as he gets up. "Eat. Burns will bring you to my personal quarters once you are done."

He exits the tent without another word, leaving me alone with Burns as he is finishing his meal.

I don't want to eat, but the second the king demanded me to, I can't help myself. My hunger feels intense, and I reach for a roll and a spread of cheese, biting into it as I go for one of the pork chops.

"My king has no wish to harm you. He is just looking for information." Burns wipes his mouth with a small towel. He rests his hand on my knife, which he brought in with us and hadn't let go of since he took it off me. "You're not here as a prisoner."

"You killed my men and took me by force. I say that makes me your prisoner."

"They were too powerful not to deal with harshly," he tells me like it is nothing. "They would not have let us take you otherwise, and my king demanded it."

"I don't know what happened to the king's son," I tell him, not feeling so hungry anymore and setting the half-eaten pork chop down. I finish the bread and cheese, though. "I watched him leave our home that morning with his royal guards. Why don't they know?"

"Your sister, the queen, said that you two ran away together." He doesn't answer my question. "I have searched all the worlds without a trace of him or you. Your sister hid you well. Then again, I didn't know you looked like this until recently."

Has he been searching for Damon and me for five years? It hits a nerve in me that something isn't right about this. No one has seen me because of the curse, but why hasn't anyone seen Damon? We went missing at the same time. Could my sister have been involved with both of our disappearances? Could he be Brown?

Brown had told me he wanted to take me to a man named Lee. Who is Lee? Would this man know?

"There is someone else who has been looking for me." I watch him closely as I say the next part. "A man by the name of Lee."

"Lee?" he says, looking confused and on alert. Am I wrong to tell him? "How do you know that name?"

"The ogre told me," I say. "But you saw to his death, didn't you? When you made him an enormous ball of fire?"

"The ogre?" he asks, sitting up straight. "You made sense out of an ogre's ramblings?"

"He spoke the name," I tell him. "Do you know who he is?"

The man looks at me before getting up and pacing back and forth. He seems to consider something, and I have the feeling he knows who Lee is.

He reaches for me suddenly, pulling me up and out of the tent. Hurriedly, we walk through the camp and into another tent where the king is writing at a desk. It is a large tent with just the desk at the back, several rows of chairs, and a small table with refreshments to one side.

The king looks up and frowns at us before returning his attention back to his papers. "I am not ready for her yet."

"She says a man by the name of Lee is looking for her," Burns says to the king, not caring that we were just dismissed. "Says an ogre told her this."

The king's head shoots up, and his eyes meet mine. "He is looking for her? Does the ogre know this? How? Where is the beast?"

"I killed him, remember?" Burns says to him. "Do you think the beast was working under him?"

"Dammit!" the king shouts as he slams his hand down on the desk, making me jump. "Does she know who Lee is?"

"I don't think so. She was asking me."

"But that fucking ogre knew." He points his finger at Burns. "And you killed him."

"He was a powerful beast, Devlin," Burns lets slip the king's given a name in front of me. I have already figured they are close friends, but this just confirms it. "There would have been no way to control him."

"Take her to my private tent as I told you before," the king says with a sigh and sits back down. The glow in his eyes and hair is a little dimmer now. "I will prepare and read her mind. She has to know something."

"Yes, sir," Burns says this time, and we leave the tent.

"Who is Lee?" I ask him now, not wanting to say anything in front of the king before. I didn't like the way he made me feel when his focus was on me. That he is preparing himself to read my mind doesn't sound like something I want to do, either.

"Shut up," he says, stopping and looking around. I do, too, and see all the men scrambling and shouting. It seems like they are preparing for battle. Burns grabs a man running by, stopping him in his tracks. "What's going on?"

"Ogres are surrounding the barrier shield," the man says breathlessly, looking at us with fear in his eyes. "Looks to be about forty or more, sir."

"Ogres?" He lets the man go and walks past some tents, and we come to face the barrier wall about fifty feet away.

I gasp as I see, circling all around, ogres lining up along the outside of the glowing orange shield. There are so many of them, but they do not dare touch it.

"What the fuck have you done?" he growls at me as he grabs my arms painfully.

"Nothing. I did nothing!" I stare back at him.

He says nothing else, but he turns and pulls me along behind him and I feel like my arm will snap off from the force of it. He calls several men over to him. "They cannot come in, but they look to be setting up for a standoff. Gather all the Fire elements."

"Sir, ogres are not known to work together in groups this size," one man says. "Something has to be leading them."

"Just get the Fire elements ready," he yells at him and then turns to me. "You seem to have some sway over the creatures. Can you call them off?"

"No, I can't. I have been running from them for over a week now. They want my blood, and apparently, they don't mind going through you to get it."

He pulls me around the rows of tents until, finally, he stops. I look to where he is and gasp as I see Brown on the other side of the barrier.

"I set him on fire," Burns says, more to himself than to me. "It can't be him."

"Brown," I say his name, knowing he is here for me. To protect me or to eat me, I'm not sure, but I don't care. If anyone can bring justice to what these men did to my loves, then I will gladly give myself up as a meal for revenge.

"He is leading them," he says, staring at Brown. "And I need him alive. Fuck!"

Brown sees me, and I step toward him, only to be jerked back hard by Burns. I see him roar, but I can't hear it. All sound is barred from entering the walls. I look to see the rest of them startup, and I can imagine what it must sound like on the outside of the barrier.

Suddenly, Brown raises his massive arms and strikes the barrier wall. A loud burst of cracking glass sounds and hits us, knocking everyone down to the ground. Before I can sit up to see what happened, a loud roar calls, followed by many more, and I cover my ears at the explosive volume of all the noise coming from every direction. As it dies down, I look up to see there is no longer a glowing orange barrier blocking the ogres as they all charge in.

"Fuck!" Burns yells as he pulls me to my feet. "Get to the king!"

I see men running all around as Burns takes off, pulling me roughly with him. I scream as pain shoots down my arm. I grind my feet into the ground, trying to get away from him, and he strikes me across the face.

I'm dizzy from the pain of the blow and would have fallen if he didn't pick me up and sling me over his shoulder. Everything blurs around me, and I hear screams as I see fireballs flying around.

I see an ogre running for us. He grabs two men by their arms and throws them sideways out of my view. He bursts into fire as several fireballs hit him and bellows in pain. Everything is moving so fast as a cart whizzes by my head, and I lose focus again. I hang loosely in Burns' arms until he is hit from the side. I hit the ground hard, and Burns loses his grip on me, and I try to steady myself from the dizziness.

I see Burns in front of me, fighting with the ogre, but my eyes focus on the shiny object lying on the ground just a few feet away. It is my knife. It must have fallen when Burns dropped me. I grab it and crawl slowly forward over some wood and under a turned-over wheel barrel.

"Brown," I say weakly, wondering where he is until he rips away the protection I crawled under, and I look up to see him. It is like he had heard me call him. "Brown."

He picks me up gently and cradles me in one of his massive arms like a child and roars. He takes off for what looks like the woods. Everything is still such a blur, so I'm not sure.

I feel a jerk in Brown's movements, and he stumbles and falls with me still in his arms. He rolls into a ball, protecting me just before we hit the ground. I see flames along the outline of his body, but none of them touch me. As we come to a stop, he leaves me on the ground, and I see smoke rolling off his back.

The fire can't hurt him. I know that a fireball had hit him square in the back just a moment ago. It had fired up around us, but hitting the ground must have helped put it out.

He charges the two Fire elements, leaving me to watch as I see him slam his fist into the massive balls right back at them. My vision is clearing, but I am unsteady as I try to stand up. I see more men running toward us and I know I have to get away. Brown can handle them and will find me, I know, so I run for the woods.

"Celine!" I hear my name and stop instantly. I see Tate fighting two men even as he is headed for me. I shake my head, not believing my eyes, and try to focus again. When I look back up and he is still there, my heart leaps with joy. He isn't dead, and neither is Lindon who is a short distance away. I see him sprinting over a broken cart, coming for me too.

"Tate! Lindon!" I scream and run toward them, letting everything around me go, knowing that they are alive. How I don't know or care. They are there with me, and we are together again.

Suddenly a wall of orange comes up in front of them, and I watch as Tate bounces off it. Lindon hits it with his fist and Tate joins him a second later. I reach the other side, already knowing I can't get to them.

"No!" They are so close, but I can't touch them. All I want to do is make contact with them. To make sure they are real. I see them shouting, but I can't hear their voices. I cry as I pound on the shield but know it is a lost cause.

Tate shouts at me and motions for me to go into the woods, and so does Lindon. I don't want to. The last thing I want to do is leave them.

I hear a roar to my left and turn to see an ogre standing a few feet from the shield. He is looking at me, and I watch as he turns his nose up in the air and inhales. I step backward as I see a haze come into his eyes. He huffs in and out in deep breaths but doesn't charge me.

The ogre's actions confuse me, but I turn back to Lindon, and our eyes connect for an instant. He is frantic, pointing toward the ogre and telling me to run. I know I should, but I can't help looking to Tate one last time.

He sees the ogre and urges me to run, too. I will, but I have to tell him first.

"I love you," I say to him, knowing he can't hear me. "I love you!"

The ogre roars again, but I don't take my eyes from Tate. I feel all the pain and love within him in that look. He mouths the words *I love you* to me and then one last time to go.

The ogre charges for me now, and I have no more time. I take off to the right, toward a group of warriors fighting another ogre along the shield wall. One warrior sees him barreling down on them and calls to the other three as he takes a position.

I run past them, not even taking the time to look back as I veer off and into the woods. I don't feel I am making much progress, but I keep running as fast as I can. Much of the dizziness has faded away now, but I feel weak.

I see a large stream of water and jump into it to get to the other side, but the current is more substantial than I realize, and it pulls me down, taking me farther away. I relax a bit, letting it keep pulling me, conserving my energy as much as possible.

It is only about two feet deep, and I hit rocks and sticks along the way, but I don't care. The pain keeps me alert and awake. As the current dies down, I reach for the bank once more and pull myself out.

I am covered in mud from the bank, and I feel heavy, but I pick myself up and run again. My head pounds and feels like it wants to explode.

"There she is!" I hear someone shouting. "Get her!"

Shit! I try to run faster, but my body will not allow it. I am covered in bruises and mud weighs me down, and before I know it, I am surrounded.

"Fuck, look at her!" one of them says, and I see none of them have their swords drawn. They plan to take me alive, but I'm not willing to go back.

I pull the knife from my side, daring one of them to attack me.

"Put down the knife, hag," the man from the entrance earlier says to me now. His name is Stan, I recall, and he is older than the others which flank him. "You know you can't fight us; you can barely stand."

"I'm not going back," I tell him, knowing he is right. "You better leave me before he comes for you."

"He's not coming. We have him now, and the others, except for the ones that got away."

He knows I am talking about Brown and knowing that they had captured him hurts me. Brown helped me, and after what I said to the king and his man, they will torture him for information.

"He might not be coming, but I'm here."

I turn around sharply at the sound to see Brier standing on a rock a few feet away. His arm is wrapped, and blood shows on the makeshift bandage, but he is alive, and I sigh in relief. *Thank the Gods; he is alive, too.*

"You have five seconds to drop your swords and clear out of here, or else you forfeit your lives," Brier warns them.

The men look at each other before drawing their swords and standing firm.

"You lose," Brier says as he jumps down and attacks them.

Swords swing in every direction, and I am right in the middle of it. I duck as the blade comes at my head and stab a leg with my knife as one of them comes near me. Suddenly, someone grabs me by my vest and slings me backward and out of the fight.

One man is dead on the ground, and the one I stabbed slides back as Brier circles around the last two. The older warrior named Stan smiles at Brier as he motions for the younger man to back up.

"You're just about as ugly as the hag," Stan says with a chuckle. "That the best you can get, Scar Face?"

Brier lunges, and their swords clash. Both are well-matched with a blade. I hear the whoosh from a few feet away as they dance around each other. Their swords clash once more than both are in a power play to throw the other off.

"What's the matter, Scar Face?" Stan grunts out as they face off. "You don't like me calling you ugly…or your woman?"

Brier rears his face back and slams his forehead into Stan's. The man stumbles back, blood pouring from his face, but brings his sword up before Brier can land a fatal blow to his chest.

"Don't think you will be so pretty anymore, either."

Stan charges Brier, and they meet head-on, their blades clanging as Brier slices sideways, his sword thrusting into Stan's side. Stan falls to his knees, looking up at Brier, his sword falling to the ground. I can't take my eyes off him as I watch the life drain from his body and he falls face forward on the ground.

Brier touches my shoulder, calling me out of the horrible haze I find myself in. I jump up into his arms. "Oh, Brier. I thought I lost you."

"You're a mess," he says lightly as he holds me close. "We need to move."

"Wait. What about Tate and Lindon?" I ask him, pulling back, but he doesn't let me go. "They are back at the camp. I tried to get to them, but someone threw up this barrier between us. An ogre came and…"

"They will find a way out," he tells me, reaching up and caressing my cheek. "We need to get you away from this area and fast."

"How did you survive?" I ask him, leaning into his caress. It is the first time he has ever touched me so gently. I want to linger in it for a moment, but he pulls his hand away. He moves me forward quickly and away from the area.

"That ogre Brown knocked me out once he saved me from those Fire elements. For what reason, I do not understand. When I came to, I heard all the noise in the distance and started toward it."

"The camp," I said, turning to look up at the night sky, at the glow among the trees. I can't see it from here, but it looks like the woods are on fire in the distance. "The Fire King was there."

"King Devlin was there?" Brier stops and turns to me. The color flickers in his eyes to a mixture of glowing red and blue, and he turns to look back at the camp. His face and body tense as he breathes heavily.

"Brier?" I touch his arm, and he jerks it away so fast it startles me.

"You sure it was him?" he asks again, looking at me with those flickering eyes. Something is off about them; they aren't right. Brier has told me numerous times his element is broken, but looking into them, I finally see it.

"It was him," I hiss, stepping back as it looks like he is about to go off. How I'm not sure, but I have a feeling it won't be good if he does.

"How did you escape him?" he asks, looking back toward the camp once more. I have a feeling he wants to go there and that it has something to do with the king.

"Brown showed up with an entire herd of ogres. He brought down the shields. Brier," I tell him. "They attacked the camp. Brown was taking me out when we were attacked, and then I saw Lindon and Tate. They told me to run into the woods."

"I wish that damn ogre could talk," Brier says as he leads us away. "We might find out who he is."

"He doesn't want to hurt me," I say as we hurry away again. I trip over a stick on the ground but don't fall as he still has my arm firmly. "I don't know why, but I think he needs me for something."

"Let's just get away from here for now. This place is swarming with warriors and ogres."

"What about the others?" I ask one more time.

"They will know we're heading for the border," he tells me. "We should meet up there."

Chapter Thirty-Four
CELINE

We finally stop several hours later to rest as the sun comes up. We don't make camp but stop by a small stream of water.

"Clean up while I look for something to eat," Brier tells me. "I won't be far. I see some berries over there we can snack on. Then we will rest."

I nod as I move to the creek and sit down, pulling my muddy boots off. I wash them up first, trying to keep the inside as dry as possible, but they have already gotten wet that it's futile to work. Still, I hope they can dry a bit before I need to put them back on.

Sliding out of my caked-on muddy pants and shirt, I wash them next, getting the dry mud out of them, and hang them on a branch to dry. In just my underwear, I step into the water and wash the rest of my clothing and myself. The freshwater feels good against my sore body, but I don't stay inside long. I clean up quickly and step out.

Brier is back. He comes to me, carrying an oversized shirt of his, and wraps it around me. I slip my arms in the sleeves and button a few of the buttons in front. Brier says nothing, walking away and sitting down on a pallet he has made.

"Come and eat, and then you should rest," he tells me, and I sit beside him, taking half of the berries he offers. "That bruise on your face doesn't look so good. I have something we should put on it."

"We should attend to your arm, too," I said, pointing to his bloody bandage. I can see the wound is still bleeding.

"I need stitches." He looks down at it as he pops some berries into his mouth. "Tate can heal it for me, though."

"Tate is not here, and you are still bleeding," I tell him. "I can do it."

"You sure?" he asks, raising his brow at me.

"Yeah, I've done it before," I tell him, setting my berries in a leaf. "I know the convent helped the sick and wounded, you know. I learned as all nuns but only treated them."

He pulls out a small pouch from his bag and hands it to me. "Everything you need should be in there."

I move back to the water and wash my hands in some soap I find inside the pouch. Then I kneel on the pallet beside him. Reaching up, I remove the bandage to see a nasty slice in the muscle of Brier's upper arm.

"This is terrible, Brier," I say, taking some alcohol out of another pouch and rubbing it on my hands. I set the other supplies out and dip some thread along with the needle. Then I clean the area as best I can.

He looks at it and then says, "I've had worse."

He doesn't even flinch as I work. I am wondering if it is just because he doesn't want me to see him in a vulnerable position or if it doesn't bother him. Taking my time sewing up the mess of his arm, making as tiny stitches as possible, so it doesn't leave a large scar. I know he has plenty of them already, and one more doesn't seem to matter to him, but it does to me. He is my hero, and one day I will bear one of his children. Even if he still denies it.

Once that is done, I bandage it back up for him. He reaches down, taking some cream I put on his arm and raises them to my face and I close my eyes.

"Your turn now," he mumbles as he strokes the cream on the side of my face. It is the second time he has touched me with a genuine tenderness. Unlike him, I flinch as I feel the cream slip inside the cut at my temple. "This will take a while to heal, but it doesn't need stitches."

"Then we can heal together," I say as his hand runs down closer to my jaw and the cold cream soothes the heated bruise. I open my eyes and see he is closer to me than I remember, and my breath hitches.

He looks into my eyes, and I see red and blue sparks inside them go off at being this close to me. "You're still beautiful."

He called me beautiful! He has never said something so kind to me. With his gentle touch, I want to melt into him.

"Only you can see that, though," I whisper to him. "The others back at the camp confirmed how they see me."

"Just because they can't see, doesn't mean you aren't beautiful." His hand caresses my cheek, and I lean closer to him. He stiffens and pulls his hand back. "Don't be getting any ideas just because I said you are beautiful. I'm still not going to be in your element."

The sparks of red and blue I saw in his eyes earlier come to mind. Is that his powers wanting to come out? If so, why are they such a mixture of colors?

"Brier?" I say his name softly. "Would you be my element if you could?"

"Celine," he whines, getting up and moving away from me. I just want to know if he feels anything for me because I do for him.

"I don't understand!" I stand, wanting to confront the issue once and for all. We are alone now and could have it out in the open. "I feel a pull to you. I can feel your powers, but you say you don't have any. How is that possible?"

"I have powers! They just are no longer Water!" he says, facing me. "They are powerful and bad, Celine. There is no good in them, and that is what you want. Something good for this world."

"What happened to them?" I hate this distance between us all this time, and still, he won't give in and let me get close to him. "Please, Brier, just tell me."

"They were burned out of me!" he shouts as he pounds his hands into his chest. "By my very own brother. He took them away from me and turned me into a monster just as your sister did to you."

The pain and fire in his eyes nearly break me and knowing his brother did that to him I can only gasp. Just as he says, my sister did the same to me with the curse. We have so much in common that I hadn't realized before. I don't know why he tries to hide so much of himself from me. Couldn't we not help each other?

"But why did the elements send you to me?" I ask him still not understanding why they would do such a thing if I wasn't meant to be with him. "Don't you think there is a chance that we can restore them?"

He rips his shirt open, baring his chest to me, and I see the scars for the first time. He is burned from the chest down with massive whip marks all over the old burns. Scars on top of more scars. I don't know how he could have survived such torture.

"They are all over me," he says, watching my reaction. "I'm not a man any woman wants or an element for this world any longer, Celine. You don't want this."

He is wrong. I do, but I don't know how to show him this. Tears come to my eyes, but I can't look away. It is hard to see, but if I look away now, he will never allow me in again.

Slowly, I step to him and reach up, touching his mutilated flesh. It is hard and rough, not feeling like skin at all. How could anyone do this to someone else?

"Get your feel in now, woman, because this is the last time you will ever see me," he says as if he can barely tolerate my touch. Like I am causing him pain.

I look up at him and see him straining to stay where he is. He is so strong and determined to push me away, but I am just as stubborn. I will find a way to fix this, and I will make him mine.

"No, it's not," I breathe to him. "they sent you to me for a reason, if not to be my element, then for something else. I am not giving up on you, Brier. I will never… turn my back on you."

His eyes soften. "You are a stubborn little thing."

"I can't help the way I feel about you," I tell him as I place another hand on his hard chest. "My instincts tell me… I belong to you."

"I can't be what you want." He reaches up and pulls my hands from his chest.

"Then I will take you as you are," I mumble, stepping closer to him and rubbing the front of my body against his.

"You… you say that now, but…" he says, but I cut him off.

"Kiss me," I tell him as I try to pull my hands away from his.

"What?" He grips them a little tighter and pulls them farther away. "No."

"Kiss me," I plead with him once more.

"No, you promised Tate you wouldn't," he says but doesn't move.

"This is more than a promise with someone who has jealousy issues." A small part of me feels like I am betraying Tate in this, but I can't stop now, not when Brier is opening up to me. He touched me with care. He told me I am beautiful. How can I not try now? If I don't, he might not never let me in again. "Do you not feel anything for me? Do you not want to kiss me?"

"I... I can't have feelings for you," he tells me, and I hear the pain in those words.

I step away from him, and he takes a step toward me. I feel like he is on the verge of giving in to me but isn't about to let himself cross that line. I need to do something that will push him over the edge. Something that could push *me* over the edge.

"All I ask for is one kiss, and you are bound and determined to not do that for me," I say with a soft smile. I reach up to my shirt and pop the top button loose. *Oh, gods, I can't believe I am about to do this!*

"What are you doing?" his low voice sounding almost dangerous. His gaze focuses on my hands as I move to the next button between my breasts.

"I am wondering if you can resist a naked woman asking you so easily," I say, popping the next button.

"You wouldn't dare." His eyes shoot up to mine.

"I am daring," I tell him as I undo the one at my stomach. Only one more to go, and I let it go. "I am daring you."

"Celine, no!" He shouts as I slowly open my shirt. I slide it over my shoulders and let it fall to the ground. I stand there in just my breast wrap on top. Not completely naked, but I feel exposed. "Put the shirt back on, Celine!"

"Not until you kiss me." I stand with my hands on my hips. I am putting myself on the line here. Going against what I promised Tate and myself, but I need Brier, too. This isn't about what just Tate or I want, but what we all need.

"No, dammit!" He stares hard into my eyes. He is so damn stubborn. Here I am, half-naked and asking him to kiss me, and still, he says no. Well, let him say no to this!

I reach for my breast wrapping, a little shy but I will not back down now.

"Stop!" he shouts again as I undo the hook and drop it. He looks away from me.

"You can turn away, but eventually, you will have to look," I tell him. "How else are you going to watch over me?"

"Fuck!" he says, not looking at me. "You're crazy; you know that?"

"Okay, then. Here goes the rest," I say, sliding my fingers into the top of my underthings.

He turns to me and in a flash, he has me in his arms, his mouth crashing down on mine in an unforgiving kiss. It is filled with anger and resentment but also a need and wanting unlike from the others.

I kiss him back as I wrap my arms around his neck. Our skin touches, his shirt still open. His rough skin brushes against my nipples, making them instantly sensitive to him.

He groans into my mouth as it slowly turns softer and gives me a chance actually to kiss him back. He drops to his knees with me in his arms, like his legs have become too weak to hold him. I use it to my advantage, surrounding him with my legs as he sits back on his heels.

Leisurely, he kisses me as his hands roam down my back and take my buttocks in his hands, massaging and kneading them. With me almost naked in his arms, I feel the heat of his body even through his clothes. He is so hard, and my body is reacting to him on instinct.

I push his shirt off his shoulders. It falls back over his arms, but I can't slide it off as he grips my body. I run my hands down his back, and he stiffens then, pulling his lips from mine.

"Are you happy now?" he asks me in a husky voice just inches from my lips.

"Yes." I moan more than say it as I lean closer to his lips. He slaps me hard on the backside, and I scream from the pain and shock as he lifts me off of him, standing me up as he stands and pulls his shirt back on.

"Then get dressed and go to sleep," he says as he walks away but stops and turns to me. His gaze travels over me one last time before he looks me in the eyes again. "Don't you ever do that to me again."

Then he walks away.

Hot tears push at my eyes at his rejection again. I had pushed him and lost. Would I ever win with him?

Chapter Thirty-Five

BRIER

I can't believe I fucking kissed her! What the hell was I thinking to let her get to me like that? I had succeeded at keeping away from her, and I lost all that in a moment in her arms.

I had done everything to keep her away from me. I even showed her my scars, something I haven't done with another woman in years. I am always so careful to keep them hidden even when I am bedding one of them. I never take my shirt off and make sure it is dark.

The woman had some nerve coming on to me and going as far as to take her clothes off. I felt like giving that gorgeous little ass of hers a real spanking, but dammit, I am sure that would have turned me on even more.

The idea of her touching me makes me moan aloud again. I couldn't feel it, but I so wanted to. I have no sensation in my chest or back anymore from the scars. Her touch made me angrier that I couldn't feel it.

She is right, though. I want her. I wanted her from the very first day, but that doesn't change the facts. She doesn't need me. What she needs is a Water element, and I have someone in mind.

I will bring him to her once she is safe. My cousin, Jacob, is a powerful Water element, and he could be what she needs. He is reliable and kind, more than able to protect her and give her what she wants. They will make a good match together. Hopefully, she will see that.

I glance back at her from my hiding spot. She is sleeping on the pallet by the stream. I would love nothing more than to lie down beside her, but I wouldn't dare.

From a distance, over several valleys and hills, I hear a roar in the afternoon sky. It must be Brown. The men say they had captured him, but it sounds like he is free. That can't be a good thing for us.

Where the hell are Tate and Lindon? They should catch up with us by now. Both have a sense of smell better than most. It shouldn't be that hard to track us. They should have picked up on our trail.

It is two days still to the border, and I don't see us making it there before Brown shows up. He wants her, and I'm not so sure I can protect her by myself. I have never encountered a beast like him before.

I saw the fire consume him when we were attacked. I knew he would come if Celine called to him. I was sure he wasn't far away from us. I was fighting several men at the time and paid him little attention but out of the corner of my eye, I saw the fire around him going out.

Five men were on me and I couldn't hold them back. Suddenly he was there swinging his massive fist taking two down. I thought for a moment he would help me with the others and I could get Celine back but he turned on me and before I realized it, his fist connected with my head, knocking me out. I woke sometime later seeing the other three warriors dead around me. There were even more men lying dead around me, than I recalled before. I knew Brown had killed them by the way their bodies were twisted and broken.

He may have protected me in that moment, but my concern still lies with his interest in Celine. I don't think he will hurt her, but he is on some mission of his own and whoever he is doing this for, could be a danger to her. She is the princess even with the curse and the next future queen. Many people would do just about anything to have her in their powers.

Now that I have her again, our only hope is the border, and hopefully, he will be trapped inside these walls like all ogres are supposed to be. If he can cross, then he will have her. I know it.

I get up. It is time to go. I will have to push Celine hard for the rest of today and into the night.

"Celine, I need you to get up and get dressed," I say as I reach down and shake her shoulder gently. She jolts awake and is alert instantly. She has been through too much these last few days and especially last night. "We need to move for the border now."

She moves quickly for her clothing, and I watch her as I bundle up the bed and pack away a few things.

"What about Lindon and Tate?" she asks me as she puts on her boots. "Shouldn't we wait for them?"

"I'm sure they are fine, but something is holding them up," I tell her, not wanting her to worry. We had all agreed that if we became separated, we would stay on course for the border. I don't know where Tate and Lindon are but I have to keep to our plan. Hopefully, they are okay and will catch up with us at nightfall. "We can't take the chance of waiting around for a hoard of ogres to attack us. We need to move."

"How will they find us?" she asks, getting to her feet.

"They will know we're headed for the border as I told you before," I say to her, standing and motioning for us to move. "Don't worry. They will follow us and most likely reach us before then. Come on."

We head off to the east, keeping a fast pace but not running as I don't want to tire her. It will be a long hard day and we are going to continue into the night. If Lindon and Tate do find us soon, that will be best, but I won't bet on it.

She says nothing but looks around. I can see the concern in her eyes for the others. I try to distract her by talking about the land and the views. This realm is beautiful as we are coming out of the woods now, into rolling hills and valleys in between. Trees are scattered over prairies full of purple flowers in sections, reds in others, and some are mixed. A few groups of boulders are scattered around the fields that add to its charm, too.

The sun is bright today in a blue sky with white clouds moving with us. When I look up to the sky, it always reminds me of sailing. There is nothing like being on a boat in the middle of the ocean.

As a young Water element, I spent most of my days fishing and exploring the oceans below. Jacob, who is just a year younger than me, came into his powers and joined me. We were more like brothers than I was with my real sibling.

One hour passes by, and then another, and still not one warrior comes for us. I am sure the ogres will be on us come nightfall. Considering how many Celine says are back at that camp, I hate to think of how many will come for her tonight.

As the day goes by and the sky darkens, I guide us to the woods for water in the springs. We stop as the last rays of the sun burn away, and we drink and eat some meat jerky. We don't rest long but continue, this time through the wooded area instead of out in the open.

Celine is leading the way when a single roar sounds in the distance. I stop to listen for others, wanting to know which way to best travel through, but there are none. *Why do I hear only one?*

I look to Celine, but she doesn't seem to notice this as she walks on. What the hell is going on with those damn beasts? I know they are out there. If Brown is, there has to be more.

We are leaving the woods now and entering a clearing on a small hillside. I hope it will give me some view of what is in the area all around. I have never been in these parts before, but I know the border is to the east, and we are heading in the right direction.

The wind stirs around us, and I hear Celine gasp. She is facing the wind with her eyes closed, smiling so sweetly that I want to kiss her again.

"I feel Lindon," she says, opening her eyes with excitement and points to the south. "He is that way. Brier, should we go to him?"

"It could be a trap," I tell her, shaking my head. "It's better if they come to us."

"Do you think the Fire elements have him?" she asks me. I am so tired that I am letting things slip. I need to rest, but I can't now. We need to get to that border.

"Let's just get to the border, Celine," I say, taking her arm, but she pulls herself from me.

"No!" she says. "What if Lindon and Tate are captured or hurt? We can't just leave them."

"We can and we will," I tell her. "They are big men. They can take care of themselves… unlike you. You're a moving target."

"Please, Brier. I'm worried about them." She looks from me and back toward where she senses Lindon. "Can't we just go…"

"I said, no!" I shout at her. I don't mean to, but still, I just snap. "A trap set by warriors or the ogres to lure you to them. You're out of your mind to think I would let you go to them."

"Then leave me here," she says, and I can't believe she suggested it. "I will stay put until you return."

"There is no way in hell I am leaving you alone," I tell her. "Trust me, Celine. We move on."

She looks down and finally nods her head, and we head back into the forest now. A roar shakes the ground from not far away. Again, it is only one, which gives me an uneasy feeling. One ogre is better than many, but maybe it depends on the ogre I will be facing.

He will be upon us soon, and I need a plan. It is getting hard to see, but the moonlight gives enough illumination on the hills ahead of us. I see one of them in the distance near a massive structure of boulders. Maybe I could make a stand there with Celine and give her some cover. We have to go through the thick woods in the valley below, but we have time if we hurry.

"We need to make it to that next rise," I tell Celine as I point to the boulders.

We take off hurriedly down the hill toward the wooded area. The boulders are about a mile away, and we should be there soon. With just a little more than a league left to go, I feel the rumble under my feet and know the ogre is not far away.

He comes into view on my right and runs straight for us. I push Celine to run faster. "Get to the boulders!"

The ogre roars a few feet from us just before he swings his massive fist at me. I bend forward, dodging the blow and stop fast, spinning and slashing at his side, his skin red and bleeding from a gash.

He stumbles backward, lunging for my shoulder. I fall to the ground, rolling away and jumping back to my feet. I look to Celine and see she has moved a distance away but is still near me.

The ogre leaps toward me, and I roll under his airborne body, coming up behind him. I jump to my feet, raise my sword high, and plunge it into his back between his shoulder blades. He groans, tenses in pain, and slowly goes to his knees.

He whimpers as he pulls me forward with my blade still impaled in his back. I try to yank my sword out, but it won't budge. I step over him as he crumples to the ground, blood dripping from his mouth.

He is dead.

I am stunned as I have never known an ogre to die without being stabbed in the heart. In all my training, you were to stun it first by stabbing it in the back of the neck and then plunge your sword into its heart.

I stabbed him between the shoulder blades. Not in the heart. It had been harder to do, and my sword had gotten stuck, but he died with one strike.

I have no more time to think as another runs out of the woods toward me. I yank on my sword, trying to get it out of the dead one, but it will not budge. I barely miss the ogre's blow as finally, the blade pulls free. I stumble away as he swings again, just barely missing me.

He lunges toward me, and I sidestep, leaping onto the dead one's back. I thrust my sword down and into his neck as I fall onto him. He collapses forward. I yank my blade out and plunge it into his heart.

I wipe my blade on the grass and then walk over to Celine. "I thought I told you to get to the boulders."

"I wasn't leaving you," she says defiantly as she tips her chin up at me.

A massive number of roars come from the south and that surprises me. Why am I hearing so many for the first time? Nothing is making sense with these creatures.

"Come on," I say, grabbing her hand. "We need to run."

I can't protect her from that many. We run fast through the woods, making for the clearing, and run uphill from there. They are closing in. I can hear tree branches and brush snap in the forest behind us. The ground shakes with such force it almost feels like an earthquake. Ahead, I see the massive boulders. I don't know if they will help us, but it is our only chance.

I pull her up the small hill, and as we reach them, we circle. I find a small opening that leads into the middle.

"Celine, listen to me!" I say, gently taking hold of her face and looking into her eyes. "I want you to climb inside these boulders and stay there until morning. Head due east and about midday, you will come to the border. There are warriors there, Water elements that can keep you safe. Tell them you must make it to the queen."

"What about you?" she says, holding onto my hands as she breathes hard.

"I'll be fine," I tell her, not having the heart to say more. "Just get inside, and no matter what, do not come out."

"Come with me," she begs me, and I can see she is scared, not for herself, but for me. She is smart enough to know what this is.

"There's no room." I look around before looking back at her. I can't resist caressing her face. This may be the last time I ever see her. "Celine… I'm sorry I have failed you. When this is over, head east like I say."

"No," she says as tears fall from her eyes. "Please, Brier, I need you with me."

"I can't," I tell her. She makes my heart ache for doing this to her. "Please, you have to get in now."

She throws her arms around my neck, and I can't help but wrap mine around her. I have denied my feelings for her, but now, in the end, I have no reason to. I am in love with her, but I will take those words with me—no reason to make her hurt anymore now.

Rain falls around us, but I am barely aware of it. I pull her tightly to me, hoping she will be okay. That the enormous boulders and the way they are arranged will make it impossible for the ogres to get to her. That they will seek shelter from the sun in the morning so she can escape and make it to the border. We are half a day away, and she can do it. But she will have to do it without me.

"I didn't mean all those cruel things I said," I tell her, needing to say that at least. "You just deserved so much more than this broken element."

She pulls back and looks at me sadly with so many emotions. "You may be broken, but you're mine… and I love you."

I can't help feeling the longing her words cause inside me. Bending down, I kiss her lightly on the lips before pulling back. I can't say those words to her, no matter that I feel them. She has Tate and Lindon, who can heal her broken heart, but if I tell her how I feel, it will make it harder for her to let me go.

"The others will come for you," I tell her, hoping that will ease any pain she has in losing me. The ground shakes; the massive beasts are just about on us. "Please, Celine, we are out of time."

She turns away and moves to the tiny opening and crawls inside.

I turn to look out into the darkness as the rain falls so thick that I can barely see in front of me. I see the outline of ogres all around. A dozen or more slowly walk toward me.

This is my fate. To die while protecting someone I love. It is a good death, and I welcome it. I should have died long ago, but maybe this is the reason why I hadn't.

Getting into a fighting stance, I prepare to die. And take as many of these bastards as I can with me, for Celine.

Chapter Thirty-Six
BROWN

I step out of the woods along with the other ogres as we advance on Brier. I give a mighty roar, letting him know I am there. All the ogres turn to me, but not Brier. He just stands there, his sword still raised, ready to battle with me now.

"Get back," I say in my head to the ogres, warning them away as I face Brier. It didn't do for them to be close to her also. The ones who haven't been able to resist have paid with their life by this man. They knew I would react just as strongly. *"Stay away from her and hold your temptations."*

"Yes, master," some of them say to me in my mind as they move back into the tree line. They are not the evil creatures man makes them out to be. Being one of them for so long, I have begun to understand their needs. Telepathy is one of the advantages of being an ogre. Words are hard to speak, but they are more intelligent creatures than man gives them credit for.

I weeded out the ones early on that could not resist her blood, letting them attack and be slaughtered by the other elements at her side. There are two dozen here now, and anyone of them could still break with her so close. I am sure their fear of my wrath will keep them in check for the most part.

I am ten times stronger than any of them and can break their necks with just a twist of my wrist. If that alone isn't enough to scare them, my powers to set their blood to boiling are enough to drive them mad.

It was the little trick I had played on Celine the other day. I was raising her anger at the Wind element, wanting him away first so I could get closer. Because she has ogre's blood running through her veins from the curse, I was able to do so. But my plan had gone to hell with the warriors showing up in the area not long after.

My father captured me. He was the only one powerful enough that could hold me for any amount of time. All I had to do was wait for his power to wane, and once it did, I was free again.

Her other two elements, Earth and Wind, had also been captured. I made sure they got out, but I also made sure they would be no problem for a while. My ogre friends I left behind were pushing them to the north, keeping them from following Celine's scent.

I didn't want them dead, as Celine needed them. Unlike them, I was there when she made the sacrifice. I had watched her give herself in offering and knew what it meant. Truthfully, I knew more than she did about it.

For years, I watched her and tried to get her to come to me, but her fear trapped her, and in return, it trapped me. I knew the elements she made the sacrifice to would come for her, and when they did, I needed to be ready.

Now it came down to just Brier and me, and Brier would not give her up willingly. Sure, there were all the ogres around, but they would not defy my orders. I have made my deal with the ogres who were strong enough to resist the curse for her blood. And if any of them went for her now, I would be the one to take their lives.

I have none of the fears a regular ogre had because I'm not one. I am a Fire element, one of the most powerful ever born. The Fire warrior party cannot hold me or take me out. Their powers cannot affect me because, at the end of the day, I am their true king. I will take my throne and rule my people my way! Not my father's.

I have hated the last five years of life. I am determined to get my real life back, and I need her to do so. Without her, I can never cross this stupid border that imprisons me inside, just like it has held her inside that convent.

She fears me, and I can understand why. I can't talk to her; my words are trapped inside my head. Just a few can be spoken at a time. I could never explain to her who I was or why I was there or anything. She only feared me, and I hated it.

Brier is the only person standing between us now. But I can't kill him, just like I can't kill the other two elements. I know what the three men mean to this world and what their purpose is. I am angry at her for what she did in that sacrifice—or I should say what she didn't do.

I walk up a few feet from him. The rain makes it hard to see.

"What the hell are you?" he asks, looking ready to kill me. I'm not sure what happened days ago at the convent when they all attacked me. I recall his sword sliding into my heart, and then suddenly, a blast of light shot me backward. The next thing I remember I was standing there and seeing the grizzly charging at me again. I turned knowing Brier was behind me and it was like he knew what happened too.

"Make easy," I struggle to say aloud to him, knowing I had to find a voice now. I have been practicing since that day, knowing we would meet like this again. Still, I can't say all that I want to. "Give her... go."

"Like hell, I will," he says back, and I know he won't. Brier is not a man who gives up easily. Our past is thick and bloody, and he does not understand who I truly am. It isn't like he wouldn't try to kill me if he did know.

"Need her... Curse," I tell him forcefully. "No hurt."

"Am I supposed to believe you?" he asks, and I am surprised he is listening.

"No hurt. Need her," I say again, straining for the words.

"Where are the other two men I was with?" he asks me instead. He must likely suspects they are not here because of me. He is right, but they should be catching up soon. It is why I had to do this now.

"Not dead," I say to him, knowing that is what he wants to know most of all. "Away."

"You lured them away. To face me? Why?" Brier asks. "I've already put my sword into you once. How many more times before you die?"

"We fight," I say, fighting the words. "But..."

He swings his sword at me, lunging into an attack. I jump back, dodging it. He brings it up again and thrusts down, and I raise my arm, parrying it, but it still slices into my thick skin. Minor damage done, but with the force of his blows, it cuts through.

My fist contacts his jaw, and he flies back against the rocks hard surface. I must end this quickly before I hurt him. Brier may hate me, but I can't kill him as he can't kill me.

I leap forward with a roar, knowing that the blade he holds out will cut deep. It slices into my side as I propel him backward and slam him against the boulders by his throat.

I yanked the sword from him and throw it to the ground. He kicks into my wounded side, and I growl, pinning him more laborious to the rock with my body. I have him trapped, and he stops struggling and looks into my eyes.

"Don't…hurt her," he pleads with me as he gasps with my large hand around his throat.

It is hard to provide him with an answer that makes much sense. I don't want any of them dead, but I have to take Celine with me now. I must show her things, make her see the truth, and it will be hard for her to believe.

"No, hurt her…ever," I try to tell him. "Soon, you, them… all join."

He looks at me with uncertainty and doubts in his eyes. Maybe not fully understanding. It is the best I can do for now to explain it to him.

"I will come for her," he promises to me, and that is just what I want.

"Yes…Brier…knows." I say his name as I lean down closer to his face. I have to leave him a clue so he can find us. That he knows me, and we have a past. It will give him the chance so they can come to her.

He looks at me, questioning how I know his name. I'm not about to tell him yet. He will find us too soon. He has to discover it on his own.

"Past… Fam…ly." I knock his head into the rock, and he falls to the ground, unconscious. I bend forward to check and make sure he is okay. Seeing that he is, I place my hand over his head and let myself wander into his mind. I find his unconsciousness that is screaming for him to wake up. I can't do this to him while he's awake, but with him out, I can give him some peace.

"Sleep and rest, for you need it. You're tired, and you have fought a good fight." I push the thoughts into his head, needing him to relax. "Celine is safe. Celine is protected. You will come to her soon when you are rested. The others are not far behind."

I don't like mind control, but being an ogre, I have to adapt to my powers, and it forces me to use the ones I don't like the most. I would have used it on Celine before if the nuns didn't shield her on the holy grounds of that convent. I had tried plenty of times to get inside her head but never could.

I repeat all that I have said before, and he finally gives in to my control and sleeps.

I stand and turn to the ogres as they walk toward me. They smell my blood, and it is in their nature, to want to take me out. The problem is, I might be hurt, but I am not weak.

I growl at them in a warning and let my powers flow in their veins, heating their blood. They like it when I do this, loving the warmth it gives them. I turn it up a notch, letting them feel more, and they stir and back off. It is becoming too much heat for them, and they know if they don't, I will destroy them all.

Ogres like blood because of the warmth of it from a fresh kill. It doesn't matter what animal, just blood, and the heat it gives. I can provide them with the warmth they crave and hunger for, but I can also punish them with it.

Over the years, I learned many things from fighting them away from the convent. I had helped them, and it calmed their beasts, and in return, it helped me.

"You did good, my friends." I praise them for their hard work and for helping me. I pull back my powers, and they stop backing away. *"I will reward you all soon. You may go."*

They all head back into the woods except for Con, the leader and alpha to them. It has been hard for him to bow to me these last few years. He will make sure I live up to the bargain for his kind.

"We wait for you where you say, Demon." He reminds me of the name they had given me long ago. "We join, and you take us home."

"I vow it," I assure him. "This prison will soon fall for you all. Make sure the other men cannot find our scent."

"Done," he growls and turns to leave, too.

A curse had locked almost all ogres in this realm long ago. There were so many of them going hungry because they couldn't leave and seek the warmth that they fed off of in the fire realm at night. Sensitive to the bright light of the sun, they returned during the daytime to the woods. Their lives depend on both domains, and when one was taken away, making them hungry, they became dangerous.

I have fed their hunger with my powers for years to keep them calm, and their numbers have grown. If I hadn't, the ogres would have eaten every animal and human in the earth realm and then would have turned on each other. I will be glad to be free of that burden.

Once they are all gone, I turn back to the boulders and Celine is there, hunched over Brier. She is crying as she caresses his face. She will fight me, and I know that, but we have to leave. The others will come soon, and we have to be away from them and hopefully over the border.

"You come now," I tell her, even though I know it will not be that easy.

"He is hurt," she says, standing and facing me. I am surprised she doesn't seem to fear me as she has for so long. "I don't know what you want with me. Why you attacked that camp, or why you have left Brier alive. But I am not leaving him like this."

So, she finally sees I mean her no harm. It makes me angry that she couldn't see it before. All this time I have been cursed because she wouldn't come to me.

"You…no come…he dies," I threaten her, knowing that there is no other way. I need her to fear me now, so she will come. She doesn't see me as anything more than an ogre anyway.

"Is what you said about the others true?" she asks me then. "That Tate and Lindon are alive and well, but just… away?"

She has been listening to Brier and me. I nod that it is accurate, and she sighs in relief as she looks at me. "Thank the gods."

She looks down, uncertain, at Brier once again before looking back at me. I give her time to decide for herself, but her decision doesn't matter. I will take her if need be. I just hate seeing the fear coming off her. I feel her emotions, and I see her thoughts now. The holy grounds no longer shield her from my powers.

She wants to believe that what I say is true, but she still doubts me. Her mind keeps thinking of each of them—Tate, Lindon, and Brier—a mixture of emotions and thoughts I can't make much sense about.

"Men safe… alive," I force myself to say. "No, come… they die."

That angers her, but her thoughts say she will give in to keep them safe. "I will go with you, but you harm any of my men, I will find a way to put you down."

I agree with her and point in a direction for her to walk. She takes up Brier's bag and walks, and I follow behind. I let her set the pace for a while, but we will have to pick it up soon.

When she had given me her blood, I didn't want to like it, but I did. It was the best thing I had tasted in years. It had been a precious warm liquid flowing over my tongue that tastes salty and sweet at the same time. Like the other ogres, I crave it too, but my will to deny it is stronger.

Her blood had sent waves of pleasure through my body with every sip. I had stood there in front of her with a hard-on as her excellence flowed inside me. She hadn't even been aware of it, and I couldn't blame her. An ogre wasn't well endowed, considering his size. I was unlike other ogres, who wore no cloth around their middle. You couldn't see their male parts because of the hunch over and big bellies they had. I, on the other hand, stood straight and tall and had no fat belly to hide anything.

Tasting Celine's blood, I think was the first time words seemed to come a little more naturally for me. It gave calmness to my speech, not much, but it was enough for me to feel a connection with her again. We had both felt it years ago when I was human, but I had lost it after I was cursed. The taste of her had brought back desires I hadn't felt in a long time.

I want her, and I want her to see me. To remember who I am. The border stretches on for a few more hours, but we can't go straight there. I hear that there are more warriors there, so we will have to stay in this realm for a few days until we are far enough away to cross safely.

When I cross the border, the other ogres will be free, too. Once one crosses, it should break both of our curses. They will join me at the Sun

Realm with their families, and I will lead them to a place they can feed off the heat in safety. They won't be a threat to humans anymore.

A place they will thrive. A place that can feed their hunger and give them no reason to seek blood again. All they need is peace because they are not just beasts. They are creatures of fire, and I need to protect them.

I can see that in them, and they can see what I am. Ogres see the fire in my eyes and the power I carry in this world. I am one of the most active Fire elements there is, and I know of none my equal.

Celine is the only one that can match me, and yet she doesn't even have her powers. They are still locked away. Her time is coming, and the only thing I can hope for is that she won't want to see me dead when she has them. Because I know I could never harm her.

Chapter Thirty-Seven
TATE

I've had enough of these damn ogres. They have pushed Lindon and me to the southwest back to the river. We had no choice but to board the boat once daylight hit. At least we were heading toward the border now and closer to Celine.

"I can smell her, I think," Lindon says at the front of the boat with his face in the wind. "About five leagues inland."

Lindon may smell her, but I feel her in the distance. It feels like a sharp, gut-wrenching pain being away from her. For every mile we travel down the river, it is lessening and I take that as a good sign.

"She is moving east," Lindon says, turning to look at me. "Toward the border still."

I feel she is okay. She is on the move. Lindon confirms what I think, and I am sure Brier has to be with her. If they keep traveling throughout the day and night, then they should reach the border sometime by tomorrow morning.

"The river bends east, and we are getting closer." Tonight, Lindon and I will take to the land again and find them. "Before sunset, we will move inland to them. Brier will need us tonight."

"I can't believe there were so many of them," Lindon says, sitting down on a bench. The ogres were on us for most of the night, about a dozen at least. To many for us to fight. Every time we tried to turn eastward, they circled and attacked, pushing us back. It was like they were herding us away. I didn't like it.

There were twice that many that attacked the Fire elements camp. Where are they now and why haven't they showed their numbers before? Somehow, I know it is Brown's doing as he is the one who had also helped us escape. Whatever he is planning, he wants us around for it. We must get to Brier and Celine tonight. It will be his last chance to take her. Tomorrow we could cross the border, and he would still be trapped in this one.

"Brown will make his move tonight," I tell Lindon. "I don't care if he got us out of the Fire elements' camp. We must bring him down before he can claim her."

"We will," Lindon says, looking me in the eye. "He will not take her from us."

"Lindon, you need to be aware of something about my power. If things go wrong, and he takes her, I will not be able to stop myself from changing. I don't always have control over the beast I become, especially when it is angered."

"What are you saying?" he asks me.

"My animal will go for Brown, and when it does, you take Celine and run," I tell him. "He will not hurt Celine as he will feel a connection with her, but I can't say the same with you and Brier."

"What kind of animal?" Lindon asks.

"A big one, most likely... the grizzly," I say, looking down. "He is the most dangerous in me. The one I have the least control over. If I change, it could be days before I turn back into a man. Get Celine safe, and I will come for her when I am in control again."

"How many animals can you become, anyway?" he asks me, his eyes twinkling in delight. This is my favorite part of being friends with Lindon. He is always interested and always makes hard topics bearable. I may be jealous of him and Celine, but in the end, I am glad it is him I will share her with.

"Most are predators and I can't always control their actions. The wolf, tiger, and fox, are the ones I most prefer, but none of them will take down Brown. Only the grizzly will have a chance."

"I understand, and I will do as you say," he tells me looking out over the water. "I am still learning my powers and wish I could help more."

"I saw that wicked tornado you made in the camp," I tell him, remembering before we were captured. He took out half the camp before that force field was thrown around us. "That looked pretty badass to me."

"Wind and air seem to be easier for me," Lindon says with a smile. "But there are so many more I haven't been able to do yet. Celine says I am a powerful element, but I don't feel like I am."

"I didn't start with all my powers," I say. "Turning into animals came later, and I don't have control over them all yet. I'm still learning, too."

"I wish I could do more," he admits getting up and walking toward me at the wheel. "I want Celine to be proud of me if I am to be her husband. Liza and I were friends growing up and we had a special bond. But I haven't done anything good with my life since her death. With

Celine and now these powers, I feel the urge to do something great but I don't know what."

I know I haven't helped him learn more of his powers, and I should be. We are a team, and he will be in my life too because of Celine. I regret trying to push him away from her now, but my instincts are still telling me she belongs to me. Maybe once we are all together again, I can work on that and give in to letting them explore their feelings more.

"I'm sorry for the way I have been with you." I haven't been fair to Lindon or Celine. "I can see my error now."

Even though I can see it, I don't want to share with him how extraordinary the bonding is. How my powers opened for Celine, but instead of me taking her in, somehow Celine enfolded me instead. I had been claimed, not her.

"Thanks, but I am okay with you two having some time," he says with a smile. "I think I need some time to figure out some things. Just know that when it is my turn, you will need to back off."

I can accept that. "Yeah, I'm sure you're not going to take it easy on me."

"Oh, no, I'm not," he says with a chuckle. "But don't worry. I will teach Cherry a few things you might like."

"I ought to kill you for that stupid nickname," I say, pointing at him. "If Celine tells me to... consider yourself warned."

Lindon laughs but doesn't push it any further. We fall silent then, and my thoughts turn to Celine again and what we had shared just a day ago.

Our first time had been fantastic. It had been so much more than just sex as the bond had sealed around us. I felt like she was a part of me now, and my powers have grown stronger since.

I noticed the change in them at the first signs of trouble when I had gone after Lindon. Celine had been upset with what she said and needed me to make sure he was okay. I was following his scent, and as I came upon a short ledge, I got the first scent of death.

My stomach turned in knots, thinking the worst as I followed the smell into a small grove. Lindon's scent was there, but Seth and Stan, the two warriors Brier had put in charge of tracking Brown, were dead. Brown didn't do this though. They had wounds made with swords, and looking around, and I could see that there was a battle.

My first instincts were to go back to Celine, but I knew she would hate me if I left Lindon in trouble. Going against them, I took off after him, hoping he wasn't too far ahead.

Two leagues north, I finally heard blades striking one another. Lindon was surrounded in a small clearing by five dead men at his feet, and he had his sword on the sixth. He glanced up and saw me before turning back to a man.

"You have ten seconds to tell me why a Fire war party is in the earth realm," Lindon said to the young man, who wasn't much younger than me. He wasn't an element, or else he would have tried to use his powers by now.

The man looked up at him and swallowed hard. "The king is looking for a creature. A female hag. I don't know why."

We found out there were two other parties in the woods, where the camp was located, and that the fire king was there too. We let the boy go, sending him in the other direction, swearing if we saw him again, he would die.

"If there are two more parties out patrolling the area, I'm sure one of them has rolled up on Brier, and he would have left the area with her. If not, she could be at that camp," Lindon had reasoned.

He was right, and I didn't want to think the worst. "The camp is closer, so let's check it out first."

We took off the way the boy directed, and half an hour later, as we came closer to camp, we both got the scent of ogres in the area. Not just one or two, but a lot of them in every direction.

We slowed down and picked our way through the bush. We heard the rumbles of their growls and started seeing them moving in the same direction as us. Something was different with them, and I held Lindon back, letting the ogres go in front of us as we stayed hidden.

I saw the orange dome glowing through the trees as we make our way closer to the large clearing it surrounds. The ogres stopped at the tree lines, and so did we. We were several yards back, hunching down behind some brush.

"What are they doing?" Lindon whispered.

I watched the ogres as they turned their heads back and forth to each other, nodding and shaking their heads. "I think they are talking to one another. It looks like the ogres will attack them."

"I'm sure that orange dome is some kind of shield," Lindon said.

"Whatever they are doing, it will happen soon. If they have Celine and the ogres attack, we have got to get her out of there."

Soon, a massive roar sounds and all the ogres join in. A loud boom goes off then and the orange force field sputters in light. Another loud crash against it and the shield breaks and splinters like glass. The ogres charge in roaring. Lindon and I made our move and followed them. Finding Celine in the middle of the camp made my heart stop. As we came together, another shield came up from the ground, keeping us apart.

Seeing her so close and not being able to help her was the worst feeling ever. The ground started to shake as I pounded my powers into the shield. It was only happening on our side of the shield, though. Lindon touched my arm, saying, "She needs to run, Tate. Tell her to go. We will find her soon."

I saw the ogre watching her, and I had to. Calmer than I felt, I told her to run. The tears and pain I saw in her eyes ripped at my heart as I told her I loved her. I watched her run into the woods and gave thanks to the gods for letting her get away.

Hours later, we were still trapped in the same shield with no way out. There were surrounding shields becoming not only a prison for Lindon and me but to many of the ogres around also. Including Brown but the shield holding him was red in hue. Two men stood outside of his shield, talking as they watched him. It wasn't until after they left that Brown stood up and broke the barrier around him.

That he broke it was a shock as I had watched him earlier pounding away at the orange one but the one on him now had held him for some time. I was even more amazed when he charged straight for our shield and smashed right through the middle of it. Lindon and I had to jump out of the way, barely dodging his large feet, as he ran through.

We didn't question it as we all took off for the woods. Then the ogres were on us and drove us away from where Celine had gone. I could smell her trail, but we couldn't follow it.

Finally, as daylight was breaking, we found ourselves close to the river. Lindon suggested we take the boat down so we could get to her faster, and here we are. Paddling down the river while Celine is somewhere without me to protect her.

As the day goes by, we jump off the boat, going overland before sunset. I don't have Celine's scent, but Lindon does, and I follow him as we run as fast as we can to get to her. All I can think about is all the ogres and how we will be fighting for our lives tonight.

We hear ogres in the distance just a league or so away. I finally pick up on Celine and Brier's scent with the ogres, too. It becomes stronger as we run, and I know we are close.

I lose her scent, though, as we come upon a massive structure of boulders. All I can smell is ogre urine as Lindon finds Brier lying on the ground, unconscious. He isn't dead, but he doesn't wake for us.

Celine is not here, but I know she is alive. I can still feel our bond and know that if something happens to her, I will know. But I don't have her scent anymore. All the tracks of ogres and their scent around are throwing it off.

"Where is she, Lindon?" I ask him, knowing his senses are different. Lindon smells deep in the air but shakes his head.

"I don't smell her," he tells me, looking around. "It's like the ogres have given off some scent and it is coming from every direction."

"I smell it, too." The stink is terrible, like rotting eggs. "Search for her tracks."

We spend an hour or more looking for her tracks and scent in every direction, but there is nothing. The ogres have destroyed any chance we have of tracking her.

"What are we doing, Tate?" Lindon asks as we meet back at the boulders where Brier is. "We have to find her and now."

Brown has her, I know it, and I must figure out his plan. The border is to the north, not too far away, but I don't see him taking her there. As I know it, he can't leave this realm, meaning he will stay within. But where would he go with her?

Brier stirs, and Lindon bends down to help him sit up. "Yes, you're alive, old man, but where is Celine?"

"Brown... he surrounded us with a pack of them," Brier says, rubbing the back of his head. "He took her."

"Did you see which way?" I ask him as I try to pick up her scent.

"No." He looks at me in regret. "He was too strong; he knocked me out. But he spoke to me before he did."

"He spoke to you?" Lindon asks.

"Yes... he wants us to follow him," Brier says.

"If he wanted us to follow, then why has he covered up every scent of her in the air and on land?" I shout at him, desperate to find her. I feel myself shake in anger as it builds up inside me.

"I don't know why, but he knew who I was. If he knows me, I know him. I just have to figure out who he is."

"But what about now?" I shout at him as the ground shakes around us. "He has her and to only the Gods know what the hell he is doing with her. I should never have left her with you!"

"Tate, you need to calm down," Lindon says, coming to stand in front of me. "You're getting angry, man. Brier didn't do this. Brown did."

I push him away from me, not able to deal with them any longer. I calm myself enough to stop the shaking as I turn and look out over the vast land of hills and prairies still dark in the night. She is out there alone with Brown. The ogre she has feared for years while I hid in the woods.

I gave up everything when I thought she was dead. I gave up my family, my city, myself, and surrendered to nature, letting it cover and shield me. While all the time, she was alive and needed my help. Years wasted when we could have been together.

I should never have trusted that she was dead. I knew how Elizabeth was with her, but I could say nothing against the queen. Still, I should have known it wasn't right the day I was told she was dead. I just closed myself off with pain, not even thinking that it could be a lie.

For the past few days, she has been with me, we shared so many things, and we made a bond. It wasn't gone, but stronger than ever.

I need to shift into an eagle so I can search for her. It is the only way. I call to my flying beast deep inside my heart, calling to him to help me. He leaps to life in my blood, sending tingles of electric sparks into my muscles as they begin to change.

I throw my head back, and the muscles build in my chest. My neck arches back into its form. My shoulders pop, changing the structure as bones grow where they weren't before. I fall to my knees, my thighs and upper legs exploding in strength and power as the magical light from my power changes me.

I raise my head, feeling my body completing itself into its new form. The discomfort and pain ebbs away as I look out at the valley and hills once more. My vision has changed, and everything looks as if it is daylight. I look down at the grass and can see the small details of each blade. That is when I discover I am not an eagle. I'm not an animal at all… but a beast.

Black scales now cover my stomach and feet, and large thick ones cover huge thighs. Holding my arms out, I see the bone structure in black flesh instead of feathers.

I hear my cry, and it is a loud, piercing roar that shakes the ground under me. I didn't change into an eagle like I have so many times before.

I changed into a dragon.

Chapter Thirty-Eight
CELINE

I can't believe I went willingly with this beast. Poor Brier. I hope he will be okay and that the others will find him soon. I keep telling myself that it is better this way. That if I hadn't gone, Brown would have fulfilled his threat and killed him and the others.

I look behind us for the hundredth time, hoping I would see them. *Tate, my love. Please come to me.*

My need for him is more substantial than it is for the others. I feel an ache deep in my stomach, and it is building with every step I take. It is the distance that is coming between us—most of all, Tate. Our bond is calling for me to turn back, to find him, but at what cost if I try?

It isn't only my body reacting, but my head, too. My mind is swimming with memories, current and long ago. As children, when he cut an apple for us to share, a moment where he picked a flower and put it in my hair, all treasured memories from our childhood. Then, at the convent, when we kissed and the ground shook. And the last day when he held me in his arms and made love to me. How wonderful the bond had felt as it settled over us.

Being away from Tate, I feel like I am starting to go through withdrawal the farther the distance comes between us. I hope he finds me soon. I don't think I can go on without him.

I try to think of Lindon and Brier after a while, but even that isn't helping. I care for them and am worried, but my mind is still focused on Tate.

We have been traveling for several hours and it is well into the night; the moon is already dropping for the sun to come out. I don't think I can do this any longer. The distance is becoming too much for me and I can't take another step. I stop, but before I can even turn around, Brown sweeps me up in his arms and carries me.

"Put me down!" I struggle against him, and when he doesn't give, I shout again. "Put me down, Brown!"

"You run," he growls as he continues walking, faster now. How does he know I was going to run?

"You're not really an ogre, are you?" I finally asked him.

He looks down at me and shakes his head. Well, that is something.

"Did I know you before?" I ask him since I can't get away.

He says nothing. I have a feeling of who he is, but if he doesn't respond, I'm not sure.

Still, I am feeling Tate's bond being pulled away. It feels like we are getting farther apart, but shouldn't he be coming for me? *Please, Tate.* I try to distract myself from the pain. See if I can find out something useful from Brown.

"The Fire King is looking for his son. He kept asking me questions about him," I tell Brown. "His name was Damon. Are you him?"

"Hate him," Brown says then. *Well, I guess that means he is not Damon.* The Fire prince had almost stolen my heart at one time.

"Are you Phillip?" I ask him that suspicion is still weighing on me. What if he is Phillip, my brother-in-law? Could I get him to let me go?

"No," he says, shaking his head.

"Would you tell me if I guess?" I'm flustered; I can't understand him, and the pain is getting worse.

"See you soon," he tells me, struggling. "No same."

"Fine." I see this isn't working, and it is hard to think anyway. "Can we stop? I am exhausted."

"No," he tells me and keeps moving. *Shit, I need to stop.*

"I can't keep going on, Brown!" I shout as I struggle against him, the pain is too much. Tears spill out of my eyes and fall down my cheeks. "Please stop, please!"

He stops, but he doesn't put me down. I stop struggling but can't stop the sobs. Losing Tate is too much; it is breaking me. "I need him, please. He is too far away."

Brown touches my head with one of his fingers, and I feel his chest as it starts to vibrate and purr as he hums in a low growl. My memories stop swimming around, and I can focus now on them.

I feel myself in the water, swimming with Tate. Lindon is there too and touches me. So is Brier this time. I look to each of them, reaching for their faces as they surround and calm me.

Lindon gently strokes my back, his smooth caresses leaving tingles where they touch. Brier's eyes are soft and inviting as he kisses me on the shoulder. And Tate. Tate gives me a loving smile as he reaches forward and pulls me into a breathless kiss.

The moment goes on and on with all of them, and I relax into their arms, feeling our love. I don't know how long I am in that world, but I wake and discover it is just a dream. But the pain is gone, and I don't feel like the wreck I was before.

Somehow, Brown had done this to me. He had given me that dream, those thoughts, and it had calmed down the need for Tate in me. I am relieved and yet upset that Brown took them away from me. I want to know why he did it, but I know I can't get answers from him.

"Brown, I need to relieve myself," I say to him, needing to get down.

He lowers me to the ground gently and turns away from me. I realize he is giving me a moment to do my business. "Um, I think I will just step over here for a moment."

"No," he says, turning to face me again. "Wolves."

"What?" I ask, looking around but not seeing anything. Are there wolves nearby?

"Stay here," he says and turns around again for me.

I look around again and see nothing, but I'm not about to chance it. Brown knows this land better than me; hell, he most likely can smell them. If he says there are wolves, I am going to trust him.

Embarrassing as it may be, I undo my pants, relieve myself, and tell Brown I am done. He turns and motions for me to start walking. My body is stiff from all the bruises. Resting on him for what looked like quite a few hours didn't help. I don't recall him moving me in my sleep, but shouldn't his arm be tired after so long? He doesn't seem to be affected by it.

He is so large compared to me. I felt like I was up in a tree in his arms. It feels good to be on land again.

"Where are we going, Brown?" I ask him after a little while, wanting to see if he would talk to me.

He looks at me through the trees as we keep walking. "Sea."

"The sea?" I ask, surprised he would take me there. I thought ogres didn't like water. "Is it nice in the sea?"

He huffs and struggles, and I got the sense he has never been there before. So why are we going?

"I saw the sea once," I tell him. "I loved it. So vast and it sparkled light and blue. I was maybe seven, and my parents had been there."

I would love to see the ocean again. How would my power would react to it. I wish more than anything to turn it loose. I made my peace that it would be a long time before I would be able to. Still, I cherish the feelings of it alive inside of me.

"Will there be others like you there?" I ask him, a little frightened at the idea.

"No one," he struggles to say. "Talk hard."

"I'm sorry. I know it is for you," I tell him. "But you're not dumb, are you, Brown? I can see how you have outsmarted us all."

"Years plan," he growls as he looks around the woods. We are in the thick of it again and not in the valleys or hills. "Wasted, trapped."

I fall silent for a minute, glancing over. "I feared you, and maybe I shouldn't have been. But I was alone and the one person I thought loved me the most cursed me to a life of misery. You just became another form of punishment to me."

"I know," he tells me. "Still mad."

"Okay, then," I say, glad to know where I stand. "Well, just so you know, I am mad at you for a lot of things too. Like the way you made me leave Brier back there."

He motions to my left and starts moving that way. The conversation dropped as he walks us toward the sound of running water. I gasp as we come upon a small waterfall with a pool below.

He bends down, taking a mouthful of water in his hand, and motions for me to drink, too. I look down at the pool, which is clear and has a rock bed that leads out into a spring.

I stick my hands in the water, and the flowing water calls to me. My powers want to connect to it as I gulp down the water in mouthfuls. Still, it does not soothe them, and I am left with a longing for my powers as well.

I look around at my surroundings seeing the trees are different, thicker, and with more branches here. Some trees look like they are weeping with the leaves hanging all the way to the ground.

The sun is rising in the sky behind the trees, and I wonder if he is going to stop and rest. I like the thought of that. Maybe I could slip away.

"Are we going to the border?" I ask him, considering the way we are traveling. "I mean, we do have to cross right to get to the sea?"

"Soon," he tells me, looking around sharply. He smells the air and then looks to the left over the spring. He pushes me behind him, saying, "Go. Tree, now."

I sense the danger and know he is telling me to run. I take off, not knowing why, but I am sure if he is nervous about whatever it is, I should be, too.

I hear Brown roar and turn and see him in full attack against a pack of wolves. There are six or more of them on him, but he is fighting them with all his strength.

Suddenly, I hear something in the woods beside me and see a massive black wolf. I can't outrun him and look around for a tree to climb. There is one a few feet away, and I run for it, climbing as fast as I can.

I feel teeth sinking in my calf through my boot and scream as I cling to the tree limb, trying not to fall. The wolf is strong and is pulling me down as I tighten my grip on the tree and let my other leg kick out. One lands on its face and the wolf lets go. I pull myself up even faster into the tree.

I look down to see a sizeable black wolf biting at me. He jumps up and circles the tree. A few seconds pass and another joins him, growling and know I am trapped. I turn toward Brown and see him still struggling with three wolves.

"Get them, Brown!" I shout, encouraging him, and it seems to help. With a burst of energy, he throws one into a tree, and it falls to the ground. I think it's dead.

The wolves are small compared to him, but there are so many. They are ripping at his arms, legs, and back. He grabs one by the long tail and slams him down onto the ground. He throws another off his back and through the woods, not to be seen again. The two below me see that they can't get to me and turn toward Brown now.

"Two more, Brown! They're coming!" I yell, and Brown spins in my direction and swings his fist at the two wolves before they reach him. They go flying in the air as well.

Brown roars again, and the other two wolves back off and move into the woods. They are defeated, and they know it. No telling how many ogres they have killed throughout the years, but Brown was too much for them.

He roars again, warning them to stay away before he returns to me. He is hurt. I can see blood all over him from bite marks and scratches, but he doesn't show any weakness or pain. Reaching up in the tree, he plucks me out of it and places me back on the ground.

"Come," he says, and we move quickly from the area. I feel terrible for him and wish I could help, but there was nothing I could do. I have no bandage or anything even remotely for his size. Several teeth marks bleed the most on his arms, and he has one large gash across his chest.

"Do you need to rest?" I ask after we are a reasonable distance from the area. He has slowed down from the wound of his chest and how much it is bleeding. "I could wash your wounds."

"No," he tells me and points to the top of a hill in front of us. "Come."

He reaches for me, pulling me into his arms, and I am startled by him carrying me. The blood from his chest soaks into the front of my clothing. He carries me loosely in his arms, but I wish he would put me back down.

"I can walk too, Brown," I tell him.

"Hold on," he says as we reach the top of the hill and the sun shines on us. Brown pulls me tighter to him as he steps fully into its light, and I wonder for a moment if the bright sun is hurting him. He stumbles, and I grab onto his right shoulder, looking to balance myself before falling. He growls, looking down at me as he takes several deep breaths.

Brown steps forward again, and when he does, his body tenses all around me, and he roars louder than I have ever heard before. A loud boom goes off around us, taking my own screams with it.

His arms loosen around me as he drops his head toward mine. Then he falls to his knees. I feel his body heating, and he becomes hot to the touch. I try pulling away from him, but he is falling forward, catching himself with his other arm before falling on me.

"Brown?" I question him as I hang in his arms, the heat of him almost unbearable. "You're hot."

He seems to hear me as his body shudders and arches in pain. He roars again, releasing me, and I slam into the ground, wrenching as I land on my already sore backside. His hands come down, and he plants them on both sides of me, pinning me under him. I try to move away, but I see something change in his face.

I look up, not bothering to move away as his color starts to flicker from brown to tan. He is becoming smaller, and it is drawing him closer to me. He looks down into my face, and I see the pain in him as he strains against it. "Ce..line!"

Suddenly, a burst of light comes from him, and I shield my eyes from it. He falls on top of me, but he is not as heavy as I expect him to be. I hesitantly look back up and am shocked to see that he is a man now. His head is buried at the side of my face, but I can see his bare shoulder and arm. I can't believe what I am seeing, and I touch his shoulder to feel that he is real.

"Brown?" I say softly, wondering if he is even awake or alive.

"Call me…" he whispers close to my ear as he is still breathing heavy. "Lee."

A shimmer of excitement runs through me at the sound of his voice. I can't see him, but I do feel the length of him all down my body. He is still hot, and I'm not even sure if he has clothing on. The top of his body is bare, I know that much.

"Who are you, Lee?" I ask, using his name. I need to know what just happened, but something about this moment is tender and soft.

He moans as he lifts his head and looked down at me. He is beautiful, with reddish-brown hair, long like Lindon's. Clean-shaven with warm, reddish eyes that gaze over my face as he brings a hand up to caress my ear.

"I am…your Fire," he says as his lips turn into a smile. "I am to be your fourth element."

"What?" I'm startled at the sheer fire in his eyes as they look at me. Consuming like they know every part of me. What he said falls away as I stare into them until I finally recall him claiming to be my fourth element. "No."

"You have much to learn, Celine," he says, still smiling down at me with those beautiful eyes, moving to gaze at my lips. His hand plays in my hair, his soft fingers that were moments ago as hard as rocks are stimulating. "But yes, I am yours."

"But I don't want a Fire element," I tell him, pushing at his chest, coming out of my fog, and struggling against him. "I didn't ask for one!"

"That was your mistake," he tells me, not moving an inch off me and pulling my hands above my head. "You were wrong to leave me out of your sacrifice, and you will have to fix that."

"Get off me!" I yell as I struggle against him. "I hate Fire!"

"You do now," he says, pulling back and letting me get up finally. "And I look forward to proving you wrong."

Message from Author

Thank you for reading my story of Claimed by Earth. This is the first book I published, and it will always hold a special place in my heart. I hope you enjoyed it as much as I did writing it.

Building a reverse harem can be difficult to keep that real and emotional connection. My thoughts on developing this series was to let each male character have his spotlight and slow things down in the romance, while keeping an adventure theme.

As you travel into the Elemental World everything is going to become more intense. I will not make it a secret that this harem is not going to turn out the way you may see at this point.

In book 2, Taken by Fire, I will introduce you to an new character. Two new characters in fact, so keep reading to meet the real man behind the ogre, Lee, the Fire Prince, and Jacob, a new Water Element.

Please give you thoughts on this book and how it made you feel after reading. As a new author, reviews are especially helpful to me.

About Author

GINA MANIS

I have lived in Alabama, US all my life and am a country girl though
and through. I have a small farm with my husband of twenty years and
our four kids, two sons and two daughters.

Growing up, I struggled to learn to read because of a learning disorder
call dyslexia. It is something that effects much of my family and my
father never learned to read at all. But I try not to look at dyslexia as a
learning disorder, instead as a different way to learn. It is hard to keep
that belief sometimes being a writer now and having to face the
handicap of sentence structures, but I have a great team of editors and
authors that help me. Because of them, I intend to write many more
novels in the future, and I am proud to say, with each one, I see myself
improving.

CURRENT BOOKS BY GINA MANIS

SERIES

The Elemental Chronicles Series

The Fifth Elemental Trilogy

The Wind Witch Series

The Fallen Starlight Series

STANDALONE NOVELS

Elemental Ruin (Prequel)

Arrow's Wind

Genie and the Shadow Kings

Genie and the Demon Slayers

Danica: Darkness of Winter

Made in the USA
Columbia, SC
04 October 2024

521e44e4-8c4d-4ecf-8dfc-633cc2b1808eR01